Nantucket Summer

{a collection}

BOOK ONE
Nantucket BLUE

BOOK TWO
Nantucket RED

LEILA HOWLAND

HYPERION
LOS ANGELES · NEW YORK

Nantucket Blue copyright © 2013 by Leila Howland
Nantucket Red copyright © 2014 by Leila Howland

All rights reserved. Published by Hyperion, an imprint of
Disney Book Group. No part of this book may be reproduced or
transmitted in any form or by any means, electronic or mechanical, including
photocopying, recording, or by any information storage and retrieval system,
without written permission from the publisher. For information address
Hyperion, 125 West End Avenue, New York, New York 10023.

10 9 8 7 6 5 4 3 2 1
FAC-025438-17069
Printed in the United States of America
This book is set in Adobe Caslon Pro/Monotype, Avant Garde/Monotype,
Blue Plaque/K-Type, Dawning of a New Day/Kimberly Geswein Fonts/
Fontspring, HT Gelateria/Schizotype Fonts, P22 Rodin/
P22 Type Foundry, Wingdings/Monotype
Designed by Marci Senders

Library of Congress Control Number for *Nantucket Blue* Hardcover:
2012035121
Library of Congress Control Number for *Nantucket Red* Hardcover:
2013049036
ISBN 978-1-368-00212-7

Visit www.hyperionteens.com

SUSTAINABLE
FORESTRY
INITIATIVE
Certified Chain of Custody
Promoting Sustainable Forestry
www.sfiprogram.org
SFI-01054
The SFI label applies to the text stock

Letter from the Author

WHEN I STARTED NANTUCKET BLUE IN 2011, I WAS TRYING to make sense of the loss of one the most important relationships in my life—the one between my best friend and me. I searched for a book, movie or TV show that would capture this singular kind of heartbreak, but couldn't find the solace I was looking for, and so I began to write.

In my desire to unpack, through writing, how awesome, complex, and important female friendships are, Cricket and Jules came to life. Of course, I also wanted to tell a good story! I knew nothing could test Cricket, or her friendship with Jules, more than falling in love with the one person who should be off limits. Far out at sea, with windswept beaches and a town that is almost too perfect to exist, Nantucket seemed the ideal place to set these books about friendship, love, and loss.

As all writers know, there comes a point in the process when the characters reveal their truths, and the author feels more like a witness than a creator. When Cricket did this, she taught me more about facing change than I expected. Because her journey still resonates so deeply, and because—let's face it—there is little better in life than a summer of lobster rolls, midnight swims, and first kisses, I am thrilled to have *Nantucket Blue* and *Nantucket Red* reissued for a new audience. Come aboard and enjoy the ride!

For my family

BOOK ONE

Nantucket BLUE

One

EVEN WITHOUT HOLLY HOWARD AND DORI ARCHER, WHO'D been suspended for drinking on campus, we were supposed to win that game. The sun was high and white, and the breeze carried the scent of sweaty, shampooed girls and a whiff of the fresh asphalt from the school's newly paved driveway. The sky was bright blue with three marshmallow clouds. It was such a perfect day for a lacrosse game in Rhode Island that it was hard to imagine anything else was happening anywhere in the world. I wiped my forehead with my arm, blinking my eyes against the sting of sunscreen. My cheeks were hot, my ponytail was tight, and my legs were aching to sprint.

We were playing Alden, our school's rival for the past hundred years. It used to be all girls, like us, but went coed fifty years ago. They'd been pretty weak all season because Hannah Higgins, Cat Whiting, Sarah McKinnon, and basically all of their strong seniors graduated last year, giving the Rosewood School for Girls a chance to break a ten-year losing streak. We'd kicked their ass when we played them at an away game; kicked everyone's asses all season long. Our girls' varsity lacrosse team was, for the first time in a decade, undefeated, and yet here we were, tied on our own turf with three minutes left on the clock, the ball in Alden's control as they tossed it around, calling out code words for plays: "Princeton," "Bates," "Hobart," "St. Lawrence"—probably where the seniors were headed in the fall. Some of them should've studied a little harder.

For a moment there, it was hard to care. It was kind of hard to care about anything the last week of school, with classes, APs, and exams behind us, and summer so close, I could almost taste it. (What does summer taste like? Iced lemonade and fried clams.) The only things left were Founder's Day, Prize Day, and watching the seniors graduate.

But all it took was a glance to the sidelines to begin to care, and care a lot. The silver bleachers, which usually glared as the sun hit the empty metallic seats, were filled with girls in variations of the school uniform. Siblings from the lower and middle school spilled onto the grass in front of them. Parents sat forward in their collapsible spectator chairs. As usual, mine were not among them. My mother was correcting papers in her fifth-grade classroom, and my father was at his office in the English department at the

Rhode Island School of Design, or maybe helping his new wife, Polly, and her adopted Ukrainian son, Alexi. Nina, my best friend Jules's mom, was usually there in jeans and one of her cashmere sweaters. They were gray or ivory or aqua—the colors changed, some had a belt or a ruffle; but this spring, Nina liked wraps, and she brought them back from New York in glossy shopping bags with ropey handles. That's where she was now, I remembered. New York.

The principal, former women's golf champion Edwina MacIntosh, was there in her favorite maroon suit, tortoise-shell glasses, and tightly permed hair. Teachers who don't come to games were there. Even Mrs. Hart, the ancient English teacher, was there in her panty hose and pumps, one hand on her hip, the other gripping the strap of her beat-up black pocketbook as she peered over her beak at the action.

More important, guys were there. The boys' lacrosse teams had finished their season last weekend. There was a whole group of Alden guys watching, including my future boyfriend, the delicious Jay Logan. Jules hated it when I used "delicious" to describe anything but food, but that day he was nothing if not a sugar cone of melting sea salt and caramel gelato. He was wearing worn-in jeans and a red T-shirt. His hand swept his chestnut-colored curls from in front of his eyes. I've had a serious crush on Jay Logan since the eighth grade. I have a Jay Logan playlist on my iPod with the fifteen songs that remind me of him. The Jay-Z song from when we fast-danced in a group at Dani Gold's bat mitzvah; the Elton John one that was playing in CVS when I saw him with his mother the summer after freshman year and he asked me what kind of shampoo I was buying; the Coldplay song I played over and over after that time we talked for almost ten minutes at a Brown ice hockey game, etc.

For the first time, Jay was starting to notice me. He'd paid me undeniable attention at Joey Rivera's post–Spring Dance party last weekend. He followed me onto the girl-dominated sunporch, where pink wine coolers matched pedicures and shades of glittering lip gloss. He didn't have to stay there with me, our legs touching on the sofa, for an hour and a half when the guys were drinking beer and playing video games in the basement, a mere staircase away. He didn't have to rest his arm behind me, making it impossible for me not to lean against his boy body, making it so easy to feel comfortable in the crook of his arm.

Now he threw his head back, laughing at something his buddy Chris said. I wondered if I could make him laugh like that, if he was the kind of guy who believed that girls could also be funny.

"Get in the game, Cricket," Miss Kang, our coach, called from the opposite sideline. I snapped out of my Jay Logan haze and turned to see my teammate Arti Rai, ambidextrous and MVP defensive player for two years running, hurtling downfield like an Acela Express.

"Out of the way, Joy," Miss Kang called. Joy Gunther, who always had a bud of snot in her left nostril and had only been promoted to varsity because Holly and Dori had been suspended, shrieked, covered her head, and backed out of the way.

I broke right, flying past three of the red-clad Alden girls, my stick in my right hand only. I'd practiced running one-handed catches in the park last summer. By September I was able to pluck the hard orange ball out of the air as effortlessly as catching an apple falling from a tree.

Arti issued one of her signature clean, powerful passes, and it landed with a satisfying weight in my crosse. I drew my stick close to my body, pivoted, and sprinted down the field so fast I could feel the flesh of my cheeks flattening. The bleachers erupted in applause. I heard cowbells, whistles, and cheers. I saw Jules out of my peripheral vision, wide open and angling for a pass. I tossed it to her, and of course she caught it. We always made the connection. The Alden defense flocked to her, freeing me, and she passed it back.

I was in the twelve-meter fan when I decided it was a good day for a bounce shot and propelled rapidly toward the eight-meter arc, then changed my mind, thinking I'd better make it an upper-left-corner drop down, when a metal stick slammed my jaw and a cleat perforated my shin. In two dark seconds, I was on the grass, eating dirt, my hands scraped and flat, my stick flung three feet away from me. I heard a collective gasp.

"Yellow flag," the ref called. *Red flag*, I thought. But before I had time to spit dirt, someone was next to me, smelling sweet and pink, like baby-powder deodorant or girlie body spray—the kind that comes in a can.

"Don't even think of going after Jay," a raspy voice said.

I lifted my face, holding my breath, afraid that if I inhaled, I'd start to cry, out of shock or pain or both. I turned to see Nora Malloy crouched in a posture that from a distance would suggest concern, but up close was that of a puma about to pounce. From the intensity of her glare, you'd think she was someone I not only knew well but had severely wronged. In reality, we'd probably spoken a total of four times in our lives, and one of those times was when I asked her where the bathrooms in the Alden Sports Center were.

Nora Malloy was a junior at Alden, and I guess she liked Jay so much that she was willing to disfigure the competition. Up close, her prettiness was magnified. I had seen Nora in a bikini last summer at First Beach. It's not every girl who can pull off boy shorts. You need a bubble butt and lady legs for that. While I had nothing to complain about in the body department, I was closer to a girl than a woman. I'm built like my mother, who even at forty-four is still more girl than woman.

I drew my shin to my chest. No skin had been broken, but I could feel a warm prune-colored bruise blooming on my bone.

"Hey, you got that?" she asked. "Stay away."

"Whatever," I said, removing my mouth guard and wiping my mouth. *Whatever?* Ugh. Why don't clever comebacks ever come to me in the moment? They only come later, when I'm in the shower or about to fall asleep, or stopped at a stop sign alone in my mom's Honda Civic, without a witness. Then the comebacks crackle in my brain like static electricity on freshly dried socks.

I touched my lip with my tongue. Please don't be a fat lip, I thought. Not tonight. Rumors were circulating about a party at Chris's house, a party where Jay would be. We'd so carefully laid the groundwork for a kiss at Joey Rivera's. I was determined to get one before Jay took off for Nantucket for the summer.

"You okay, Cricket?" Jules said from her position a few feet away. I nodded and stood, dusting off my knees, the crevices of which were packed with mashed grass. I tentatively put weight on my leg. It hurt, but I was going to be okay. The crowd clapped.

"Hey, Nora," Jules said in a stage whisper, "I heard you did some laundry at Joey's house. I'm curious, how many *loads* did he have?" Nora whipped around, speechless. I covered my swelling mouth with my hand.

"Damn," the goalie muttered under her breath.

Jules just raised her eyebrows, unblinking. Jules had so many comebacks on the tip of her tongue it was a wonder she could close her mouth. Where, I wondered, did she get the balls?

Miss Kang arrived with an ice pack and the first-aid kit.

"Are you all right?" she asked. I nodded, aware of the little granules of dirt in my teeth.

"I'm *really* sorry," Nora said in a syrupy voice.

"Four meters, sixteen," the ref said. Nora retreated to the twelve-meter mark.

Miss Kang tilted her head sympathetically. "You want to come out of the game, Thompson?"

"No way," I said, even though my lip and shin were both throbbing.

"That's the spirit." She looked at the clock. "Fifteen seconds. Okay, here's what's going to happen. You're going to go left, jag right like hell, and pop it in the lower pocket." She turned to the ref and nodded, then jogged backward off the field, smiling at me until she faced forward and strode to the sideline, her short black ponytail sticking straight out from the back of her head. I love Miss Kang.

"Yellow ball," the ref said. "Find your hash mark, number four." I did this, nodding at Jules as if to pass. The whistle blew. I cradled the ball, jogging calmly to the left before springing right, straight across the goal, snapping my stick so fast I heard the whoosh. It bounced high just as the goalie slid low, and the ball skimmed the upper-left corner of the net. It was downright elegant.

"Yes," I said, jumping in the air to high-five Jules. Arti Rai picked me up and swung me around. Miss Kang had dropped her clipboard and was running toward us with her hands raised in triumph. I'd scored my third goal of the game and won the first championship for Rosewood School for Girls in ten years.

"Good game, good game, good game." Our teams filed past each other in a single line. From ten bodies away, Nora bore holes in me with her eyes.

Nora. She'd been given all the raw materials for an enchanted high school existence: a pretty face, a body that just wouldn't quit, athletic ability, genuine confidence, her very own yellow Volkswagen bug with a bud vase on the dash. And that raspy voice that oozed sex, that was like a cherry on top, like finding a ten-dollar bill in jeans you haven't worn in a month. But she didn't know how to manage the attention that came with being popular. Obviously, in order to be popular, you need to be the kind of person to whom attention is naturally given. But then you have to manage it.

Nora's downhill journey started last summer when she'd had sex with Paul Duke, a real garbage can, as Jules said, but a popular one. He was known to hide in closets while his friends made out with girls, then jump out once the girl had her pants off. After he had sex with Nora, he'd told everyone the color of her pubic hair ("burnt sienna") and imitated the moans she'd supposedly made in a three-minute comical opera, whose crescendo was aped by underclassmen after they scored ice hockey goals.

In an effort to get back at Paul, she had sex with Matt Baldwin without him even being her boyfriend. Matt wouldn't talk to her the following Monday at school. Treated her like the plague. As if this weren't enough, she did it again with John Dwyer, a sophomore, on an overnight science trip. By September she was known as Nora the Whora. Even I knew she'd done it with a freshman on top of Joey Rivera's laundry machine last weekend at his party. For a junior girl to go after a freshman guy, that was bad. That was desperate.

It didn't have to be that way. There was another path.

A few years before, a shy but very big-boobed senior named Jenna Garbetti started to get a reputation. "Can't get any? Call Garbetti," the saying went. Instead of looking for validation in all the wrong places, she cut her raven locks into a flattering bob, quit going to parties for a couple of months, studied really hard, and took a silk-screening class at RISD. By April, she'd won some art award and been accepted to Yale. In other words, she turned the wrong kind of attention into the right kind of attention, and by the Spring Dance, she was back on top. Last year, when the senior girls asked me to hang out in their lounge with them and they actually listened to my stories, when I found out Greg Goldberg and Liam Hardiman had an argument over who would ask me to the Arden Spring Fling, when even teachers started telling me that I looked like the girl on the bicycle in the Maybelline commercials, I promised myself that if I started to attract the wrong kind of attention, I'd use the Jenna Garbetti method: lie low, look good, and learn.

"Good game, good game, good game." Nora and I were three bodies away, then two, then one. When it came time to shake, I put my hand out, but she turned away, leaving me hanging.

As usual, Arti Rai's mom had brought us mini bottles of Gatorade and made us chocolate cupcakes, this time with peanut butter frosting. As the team gathered around the bench, giddy and hungry, I hung back and made eye contact with Jay. He was standing with the Alden kids, but he was looking at me. He smiled and drew a line across his neck to suggest he couldn't possibly leave the Alden camp to congratulate the enemy without risking his life.

I laughed at his pantomime, which he dropped immediately when Chris caught on to his traitorous ways. He shrugged at Chris as if nothing had happened, then looked over his shoulder at me and winked. I was about to wink back when Edwina MacIntosh drew herself up to her full six feet and shook my hand. We called her Ed behind her back.

"You have star quality, Cricket Thompson," she said, nearly crushing my hand with hers. Sometimes she wasn't aware of her own strength.

"Thanks, Miss MacIntosh," I said. I've been going to this school since kindergarten, so Ed and I are not exactly strangers. Hell, I'd been here longer than she had. Both my mother and grandmother were Rosewood girls, too.

"Judy, wait one moment," Ed called with a finger in the air as the ref walked by.

"So you know how that party was supposed to be at Chris's house?" Jules said, handing me a cupcake and starting in on her second. Jules has her mom's brown ringlets, ski-jump nose, and strong, slim legs. She also has the metabolism of a cheetah.

"Yeah?"

"Well, there's been a change of plans," she said with a

full mouth. "I guess Chris's parents decided not to go to the Cape after all." She planted her stick in the ground and leaned against it, a makeshift chair. She crossed her ankles.

"So where is it?" I asked, peeling the cupcake wrapper and watching as the Alden crew filed onto their bus, painted the same red as their uniforms.

"Nora Malloy's," she said, and licked frosting from her fingers.

Two

"I'M KIND OF SCARED." I SAT UP ON THE TWIN BED CLOSEST to the window—the one that had pretty much become mine in the last few years, since my parents' official divorce—and pulled up the leg of my jeans to show my bruise. "Nora did this in public. Who knows what she's capable of on her own property."

"Oh, please. There's nothing she can do to us," Jules said, one arm folded over her bare stomach as she stood in front of her closet in her underwear and bra, considering what to wear. I heard her brother, Zack, come up the stairs and turn on the TV in the den. I loved being at Jules's house. It was big but not too big, buzzed with a mild, pleasant chaos, and smelled faintly like her mom's perfume. And Jules's room was my favorite. It had dark wooden floors and big windows with white, floaty curtains. It was painted a deep but calming blue. Jules called the color "Nantucket blue" because she said it was the color of the ocean on a clear day in Nantucket.

"Besides, it's so clear that Jay likes you," she said, rifling through her closet. I flopped back on the bed and grinned. I drummed my fingers on the pale-yellow coverlet as I smiled wildly.

"Do you think I'll lose my virginity to Jay?" I asked, biting my lip to hide my smile, not wanting to jinx anything. Jules and I were both virgins, although she'd come very close last summer with some boarding-school guy.

"It's possible," Jules said. "But don't do it right away."

"Oh my god, no. Six-month rule," I said. Jules and I decided that six months was the perfect amount of time to go out with a guy before sex. With that kind of time, you would know you weren't being used. I lay back on the bed and stared at the ceiling.

"I just thought of something bad," I said. "What if Jay turns out like his brother?" Jay has an older brother who was just like him in high school: gorgeous, popular, athletic, but he quit college, got arrested for drunk driving, and now lives at home and works at the bagel shop. And he can't drive, so I always see him walking places with big circles under his eyes. I could picture him so clearly. "He's such a loser."

"Cricket," Jules said. "That's mean." But she was smiling. This was the thing about Jules. I could always say what

I was really thinking to her and she wouldn't stop liking me. Actually, I got the feeling when I said stuff like this, stuff you can think but really shouldn't say, it made her like me more.

"Sorry, but it's true," I said. "He looks sad all the time. I feel bad going into the Bagel Place."

"I know what you mean. I hate it when he's working there. I can't just be myself when I order a bagel."

"I hope it doesn't run in the family, because I think Jay and I should get married someday. I mean, after we've both been to college."

"Can I be your maid of honor?"

"Of course." I sighed. "I can't believe I won't see him again for like, *months*!" He was leaving for Nantucket soon. So was Jules. Everyone was going somewhere for the summer. The Cape. Martha's Vineyard. Arti was going to an arts program in Innsbruck, Austria. Even Nora Malloy was going on an Outward Bound trip. She was going to scale Mount Rainier (and probably a few of her fellow mountaineers).

"You never know what can happen," Jules said, considering a pair of white jeans.

I wasn't looking forward to spending another summer in Providence babysitting Andrew King. I'd be setting up the baby pool in the King's driveway while everyone else was somewhere fabulous. But my family just didn't have enough money for a summer place or a European vacation. I could just see myself filling up that damn plastic pool with the hose in the heat of the midday and then stepping on its edge to let it drain when the streetlights came on.

The sound of a trumpet blasted into the room through the speaker in the ceiling.

"Guess my mom's home," Jules said. Nina had just discovered a South African jazz musician after she'd read about him in *The New Yorker*, and was listening to his new album on repeat like a teenager to the latest pop star, blasting it through the house's surround-sound system. We broke into the dance we'd made up to this now very familiar tune. Jules air-trumpeted and I twirled around her.

Jules and Zack made fun of Nina for her obsessions, but I loved how she'd focus on something—a poet or a film director or even a color, a particular shade of orange—then leave some corner of their house changed by her discovery: an oversized book of Mexican art in the front hall marked with neon Post-its, a William Carlos Williams quote stenciled in the downstairs bathroom, a vintage John Coltrane poster in the den, a yellow ceramic bowl filled with apricots on the dining room table.

Just last week she'd asked me to read aloud to her from a Jonathan Franzen book she couldn't put down while she cooked dinner. I was sitting cross-legged on their kitchen counter. "What would I do without you, Cricket?" Nina said when I finished a chapter. She was chopping onions. "No one else in this house will read to me."

Mr. Clayton was at work. Zack was studying for an exam. Jules was watching *Splash* in the den. She's obsessed with '80s movies.

"I love this guy," I said, flipping the book over to look at the author photo. "I love how he described the real estate lady in her jeans. And the way he talked about her haircut!"

Nina blinked away onion tears and looked at the author photo. "I bet he looks pretty excellent in jeans." She sipped her wine, then put the glass down and crushed some garlic. "Okay, keep going."

I smiled and turned the page.

I was pliéing around a barely dressed Jules to the flute solo in the South African jazz song when Zack opened the door. "Hey, Mom's in her dashiki." He strode in the room but stopped at the sight of Jules in her bra and underwear. "What the hell are you two doing? Jesus! Why didn't you warn me?"

He ran out.

"You should knock," Jules called after him, howling with laughter.

"I didn't know you were in your freaking lingerie. You've scarred me for life," he yelled from the hallway.

"At least she wasn't wearing a thong," I said, leaving Jules to get dressed, and shutting the door behind me.

"That doesn't make me feel better," he said, retreating into the den. I followed him. He sat on the sofa, his head in his hand. "In fact, great. Thanks for the image."

"What you saw was no different than a bathing suit."

"Oh, yes it is," he said. "I don't know how and I don't know why, but it is." The right corner of his mouth turned up. He put his feet on the coffee table. Crossed his ankles. "I have to make an appointment with the worry doctor now." The Claytons had moved here four years ago from New York. From what Jules had told me, Zack had been an anxious kid with thick glasses who'd seen a psychiatrist, his "worry doctor," during most of elementary school. Most people were embarrassed about therapy, but Zack owned his time in the chair—"It's not a couch," he said, "but a comfortable black leather chair and ottoman, very nineteen seventies"—and was happy to discuss it with anyone who asked. He'd stayed back a year when they had moved here, and now he was a funny, slightly under-the-radar freshman at Alden with plenty of friends and boldly framed glasses he wore with confidence.

"Nice game today, by the way, Cricket." I hadn't even noticed he was there. "And, yes, I'm aggressively changing the subject. You were awesome out there."

"Oh, thanks," I said, and plopped next to him on the sofa.

"You're so fast, like an animal running from whatever's above it on the food chain."

"Are you calling me an animal, Zack Clayton?" I smacked him with a needlepoint pillow of a crab.

"Hey, the crab is a lover, not a fighter," he said, taking the pillow from me and placing it behind his head. "I just meant that you looked like a prairie dog fleeing a jackal."

"I'm a prairie dog now?" He nodded. I looked around for another pillow, but by the time I'd spotted one, he'd grabbed it and was holding it in front of his face in self-defense.

He lowered it and said, "But who says being an animal is

bad? Personally, I think we should honor more of our animal instincts."

"If I ever catch you two following your animal instincts, I'll puke twice and die," Jules said, emerging from her room wearing jeans and a delicate cardigan over a loose, low-necked T-shirt.

"I wasn't flirting," I said.

"Who said anything about flirting?" Zack was smiling, eyebrows raised. I looked at him in shock.

"Busted," Jules said. Zack hugged the pillow and tilted his head back in a silent laugh.

"Don't be a cocky bastard, Zack," Jules said, and then turned to me. "Just so you know, he has a fungus on his back. There is literally a fungus among us."

"Hey, that cleared up," Zack said, adjusting the bill of his baseball cap. "And it was just on my shoulder."

"Hope you've been wearing flip-flops in the shower, Cricket," Jules said.

"Dinner's ready," Mr. Clayton called from downstairs.

Jules looped a long necklace over her head. "I wonder what Mom brought me from the city." I hopped off the sofa and followed her down the narrow back staircase.

Nina wasn't in a dashiki. She wasn't there. It was Mr. Clayton who'd put the South African jazz guy on the stereo. He was in his suit, phone cradled under his chin, as he unloaded some salads from a paper bag with the familiar Providence Pizza insignia. The pizzas were on the table.

Zack had opened the box and was pulling out a slice when Mr. Clayton handed him the phone. "Your mom wants to talk to you." Zack took the phone.

"Mom's not coming home?" Jules asked Mr. Clayton. Mr. Clayton said that no, Nina had a terrible headache and was so tired from a day of shopping with her friends that she'd ordered room service and was going to stay an extra night in the city, which I'd learned from hanging around the Claytons meant New York.

"But I thought we were going to . . . ?" Jules whispered something to Mr. Clayton, and he whispered back. Zack gave the phone to Jules, and she took it into the dining room to talk to Nina. Jules peeked around the corner, signaling for me to join her. She pulled the phone away from her mouth and said, "We want to know if you want to spend the summer with us on Nantucket?" I shrieked and wrapped my arms around Jules with such force we fell backward onto the cushioned window seat, and she dropped the phone. I felt her stomach tighten with laughter under my weight.

I'd heard a lot about Nantucket from Jules. I'd seen pictures of the Claytons suntanned, barefoot, and happy at their house with two benches out front facing each other, the big wraparound side porch, and the backyard that looked like an English garden, with bunny rabbits and butterflies. I'd heard the names of Nantucket places, which, together, sounded like a secret language: Shimmo, 'Sconset, Sankaty. Miacomet, Madaket, Madequecham. Cisco, Dionis, Wauwinet. I'd heard about moonlit, all-night parties on the beach, watching the sunrise with kids named Parker and Apple and Whit. I'd seen photos of a candy-striped lighthouse and a cobble-stoned town so safe that parents let their children wander free. I'd held Nina's jam jar of Nantucket sand as white and fine as sugar. I'd stared at the framed poster in Jules's bedroom of little sailboats with rainbow-colored sails so long that I could practically feel the salt wind on my cheeks.

"Is that a yes?" Nina's voice was tiny from the pinprick holes in the phone. I picked the cordless off the floor.

"Yes," I said. Then I remembered. "I guess I need to ask my mom."

"I already talked to her, sweetheart. She said it was up to you."

"Are you serious?" I squeezed Jules's hand. "Thank you, thank you," I said into the phone. No forced weekends with Dad and Polly and Alexi. No Saturday nights watching *Real Life Mysteries* with Mom, or worrying about why she was going to bed at eight thirty. Instead, Jules and I would get jobs and go to parties and stay out all night. I'd practically live in my bikini. I'd have sand in my shoes all summer, I'd go to bed with hair stiff from swimming in salt water, and I'd always be able to smell the ocean. I'd walk to town on cobblestoned streets. And Jay would be there. I felt pretty certain now that this would be the summer we'd fall in love.

Nina started to hang up, when out of nowhere I told her that I loved her. I blushed, cringing with embarrassment. Who says this to someone else's mom? I'd meant it, but I hadn't meant to say it. I was just so happy.

Nina didn't even pause. "Aw, I love you too, Cricket. And you're going to love the island. Once you spend a summer on Nantucket, a little piece of you will stay there forever. Now, tell everyone I'll call back later. I'm going to lie down. I'm not feeling so great." We hung up.

I had no idea that I'd chosen my words so well. I had no idea how important it was that I'd said what I did. Because by the time we'd pulled into Nora's driveway and marched past her pumping the keg, by the time Jules and I found Jay and all those guys reclining on the deck chairs around Nora's pool, by the time I'd told Jay I was going to Nantucket and he said that was "the best news," Nina was gone.

Three

HOTEL HOUSEKEEPING HAD FOUND NINA'S BODY. SHE'D HAD an aneurysm. (A freak thing; it can *just happen*.) She died not long after eight o'clock, about the time we'd hung up the phone. Mr. Clayton didn't tell me any of this that bright morning when I'd woken up earlier than Jules.

I'd been up for hours. While I was waiting for Jules to show signs of consciousness, for her eyes to blink open, her fists to uncurl, for that sudden intake of air that signaled her release from the depths of slumber, I made a list of the top five reasons I liked Jay. *First, he's beautiful.* He has big dreamy eyes and the best boy butt I've ever seen. *Second, he's such a talented athlete.* He looks like some kind of warrior on the lacrosse field. He's graceful and powerful at the same time. I think part of my attraction is some kind of primitive response to his potential ability to hunt food while I gather berries. *Third, I like the way he stands.* Okay, I know this is weird, but there's something about it I just love. I can't explain it. *Fourth, he has a cool family.* His mom is so pretty, with her long red hair that's always a little messy in a way that makes her seem young, and his dad has cool old cars. Even though his brother is having a rough time, I bet he still has greatness in him. You can kind of see it when he's walking around. His walk is still confident, even if some other part of him is shattered. *Fifth, Jay always sticks up for his brother, so I know he's a good guy with a real heart.* I know he'd be a great boyfriend.

At eleven o'clock, I finally kicked the covers off. I was hungry. I remembered dinner last night and grinned. The Nantucket invitation hadn't been a dream, had it? No, it was real. It was real, and it was all ahead of me, sparkling like a distant city.

I hesitated at the top of the stairs. Usually, I'd hear kitchen sounds: the fridge opening or closing, the cutlery drawer sliding on its rails, newspaper pages turning and snapping, bare feet padding the blond planks of the wood floor. Usually, I'd smell coffee, cinnamon swirl bread in the toaster, maybe bacon, and feel the warm currents of energy that Nina emanated in the cotton pajama bottoms and Brown University T-shirt she slept in. But on that morning, the house felt the way the world does after it's snowed all night: quiet, muffled, absent of sound. The air smelled like nothing. I went down anyway. Maybe they'd gone out?

I was so certain I was alone that I was talking to myself, replaying what Jay had said to me the night before. I was sitting on his lap in a lawn chair. "Do you even know how cute you are?" he'd asked, speaking into my neck, bouncing me slightly on his knee. "Do you?" I wouldn't be able to tell anyone this without sounding like I was bragging, without it sounding stupid and possibly sexist. Edwina MacIntosh dedicated a section of her yearly "Critical Eye" lecture on gender and the media to slides of women in magazines acting sexy in little-girl poses. Those pictures were really messed up. I'd felt a little guilty when I'd sat on Jay's lap like that, like I was disappointing Rosewood School for Girls. I couldn't tell anyone that it had made me feel shy and pretty and powerful all at once.

Also, I couldn't believe we hadn't kissed. He and his friends started playing some drinking game, and none of them were hanging out with girls. Still, I reminded myself with a grin, he'd asked for my phone number. I'd watched him enter it into his phone.

It wasn't until I'd pulled the bread out of the fridge that I'd turned and seen Mr. Clayton, a cup of to-go coffee in front of him, sitting as still and silent as the stone Abraham Lincoln in the memorial we'd visited on a class trip to Washington, D.C. He was fish-belly white. He was holding something. It was wrapped around his fist. A bandage? A pillowcase? He lowered his hand to his lap.

"You need to go," he said, and swallowed. His voice was low and serious and not the one he used to talk to his kids. Or to me.

I instinctively knew not to ask questions. I nodded and walked silently up the stairs two steps at a time, stuffed my feet into my tied sneakers, and walked out the front door with my half-packed overnight bag. I was confused, just following directions, aware that it was hot, almost the middle of the day, and I hadn't yet brushed my teeth or had a sip of water. I had a two-mile walk to my mom's house. Also, I'd left my cell phone plugged into Jules's wall.

When I got to the mailbox on the corner I realized that Mr. Clayton had been holding the T-shirt Nina slept in. He'd been pressing it to his face when I'd walked in the room. *Those red eyes. The strange, wobbly voice.* He'd been crying. And that's when, with no other evidence, I'd wondered if she'd died. I stopped, touched my fingers to my lips, and closed my eyes against the sunshine. A freezing darkness rushed through me, like I'd capsized, like I was attached to an anchor that was pulling me to the ocean floor. But it couldn't be true. It was horrible to even think it.

I let myself into the house. Mom's sad, solitary breakfast plate was in the sink, peppered with crumbs, next to her solitary coffee mug, the one that spelled out "teacher" in letters made by rulers and apples. Mostly we ate off of paper towels or from the plastic containers of the supermarket deli, using so few dishes that she only ran the dishwasher on Sundays.

It hadn't always been like this. There had been a time when I'd passed plates of cheese and crackers at the impromptu dinner parties she and Dad had. I would play waitress until my bedtime, when I'd fall asleep to the smell of roast chicken and the sounds of the party wafting through the heating vents. Mom would check on me before she went to bed, and said that sometimes she'd find me giggling in my sleep. I used to think it was because the last thing I'd hear before I drifted off was her laughter.

We always made a game of cleaning up in the morning in our pajamas. She'd make a big pot of coffee, Dad would buy a dozen doughnuts, and we'd see how many plates we could wash in the span of an '80s song. Barefoot, her toenails painted red, and high on coffee and sugar, Mom sang all the lyrics in perfect pitch. I remember watching her sing Bon Jovi with her hair down, and wondering why she wasn't famous.

But that was a long time ago, back when there was color in her cheeks, and her hair was long, and she got dressed up for school even though the other teachers wore jeans and sneakers. That was before the parties stopped and the fighting started. It was before I heard swearing through the vents instead of laughter. It was before Dad moved out and the house filled with silence: heavy, hovering, raincloud silence.

The phone rang, startling me out of my memory. I had a feeling it was Jules, but I couldn't find the phone. It wasn't on its base, and I had to follow the electronic beeps around the living room until I finally found it between the sofa cushions on the last ring. "Hello?"

"Hi, it's me," Jules said.

"Jules?" She didn't sound like herself.

"Hey," I said. "Are you okay?" There was a pause. My stomach dropped. I sat on the edge of the sofa. "Jules?"

"My mom died," she said. Her voice was flat and clipped. "She had an aneurysm in New York." She said the word like she'd known it her whole life.

"A what?" I asked, breathless.

"It's when the head bleeds, on the inside."

"Oh my god," I said, and lay down, shocked that Jules was defining the medical term. I closed my eyes. My throat cinched. My stomach hurt. "Jules, that's terrible. I'm so, so sorry. I can't believe it." I waited for her to cry or scream or say something, but I couldn't even hear her breathe.

"I love you," I said. "And if you need anything, anything at all, just call me, okay?"

"Thanks," Jules said. I gripped the phone, pressing it to my face. I didn't know what else to say. After a few more seconds of silence she said, "I need to go now," and hung up.

I ran up the stairs and crumbled into my mother's bed. I couldn't remember the last time I'd cried to her. I'd been stoic during the divorce—locked, lights off, like a school on Christmas. I'd been all politeness and competence. It was too dangerous to cry in front of her. It was what she wanted from me, to openly admit defeat, to hop aboard the sadness train, to check in with her at the broken-down Casa de

Divorce, and I wasn't going to do it. But this was different.

"I loved her," I said, breathing raggedly.

"I know you did," Mom said. I hung my chin over her shoulder, my whole body shaking, my breath ricocheting in my ribs. "Poor Jules," she said. "Poor, poor Jules."

My mom let me skip Founder's Day and Prize Day, even though I'd won the Anne Hutchinson Achievement in History Prize and the Chafee Citizenship Award. I could collect them later, Ed said. I went to graduation, where the seniors stood on the stage in tea-length white dresses. I sang "Simple Gifts" and "And Did Those Feet in Ancient Time" with the choir, as I had at every other school commencement. It actually made me feel a little better. Neither my mom nor my dad is religious; I guess those school songs, which I'd sung for eleven years now, were the closest things I had to prayers. Jules wasn't there.

I wanted to call her, to go over to the Claytons', climb into the twin bed, eat a box of Munchkins with her and Zack, and watch movies. I wanted to sit in the backyard on the striped cushions and listen to South African jazz. I wanted to drink a glass of Nina's red wine and cry with the rest of them. But my mother insisted that I stay put; said I needed to give them time alone to grieve as a family. She used her teacher voice. I knew she was right, but who else would understand? Who else was feeling like this? We sent a plant. I was jealous of the plant. It got to be with them.

On the third day, I made them lasagna. I found a healthy

recipe online (they need healthy food, I thought; they need vitamins), but the whole-wheat noodles were gooey in the middle and crunchy on the ends, and the thing didn't hold together. "We can't take this," my mom said, sticking a spatula into the congealed mess. Tomato-colored water leaked out the top. We picked them up some cookies and a loaf of Portuguese sweet bread. But Jules wasn't there when we dropped them off. Her grandmother had taken her to the movies. I slipped upstairs to get my phone. I don't know what I was expecting, but Jules's room looked the same as it always did. My phone was plugged into the wall. There were three texts from Jay in the last three days.

#1 Hi!

#2 Heard about Mrs. Clayton. I'm so sorry. (This was followed by a missed call, but no message.)

#3 Leaving for Nantucket tomorrow. See you there?

The memorial service was at the church near Brown University, the one Nina liked to go to every now and then because they had a good choir. It was an old New England–style church, pretty in a simple way, without pictures of Jesus or stained-glass windows. Nina had dragged Jules and me to a choral concert there once last spring, and the church had seemed almost spacious, but there had only been about twelve of us in the audience. Now it was packed with people, and it felt small and cramped, especially without any air-conditioning. Kids were using their programs to fan themselves. There were hardly any seats left when Mom and

I arrived. We found room in a pew a few rows back from the Claytons, on the opposite side of the aisle, next to some people I didn't know but who I guessed were from New York. I could see the sides of Zack's and Jules's faces as we all stood to sing "Morning Has Broken."

"And now I want to give her children a chance to speak," the minister said after delivering her eulogy. She had the gray hair of an old lady, but the smooth, tanned skin of a young one. "Jules?"

Jules walked to the front of the church and stood behind a plain wooden podium. She looked blank. Her lips were pressed together so tightly they were colorless. She seemed someplace else; I'd seen this expression when she checked out of math class. She scanned the crowd, gazing into some kind of middle distance for what felt like a hundred seconds too long.

"Um," Jules started. I watched her eyes dart to Zack, but his eyes were closed, his shoulders were shaking, and tears streamed down his face and dripped from his chin. I'd never seen a boy cry before. That's one of the things about going to an all-girls' school your whole life: it's hard to believe that boys are people too.

"Hi," Jules said, and waved a weird, stiff hand at the crowd. Her eyebrows rose. Oh my god, she was now biting her lip because she was trying not to *laugh*. It was happening. I'd heard about that happening to people at funerals, and now it was really happening to Jules. There was a long silence. A baby cooed. A few people whispered. One corner of Jules's mouth twitched upward. She looked like she was in physical pain. Breathe, I thought, as her face turned red. She needed oxygen or she was going to pass out.

I stood up.

"Cricket?" my mom whispered.

"She needs me," I whispered back and slid past her, out of the pew. Maybe my mom was the type to disappear into herself when things got rough, but I wasn't.

It couldn't have been more than ten paces from my pew to where Jules was standing, but it felt like it took forever to get there. I could feel everyone looking at me as I walked down the aisle. My ears were hot, and my feet were sweating inside my too-tight flats. I locked eyes with Jules. Her head tilted and her brow pinched as she watched me approach. For a second I wondered if I was doing the right thing, but leaving her standing there alone, suffocating in front of everyone, was not an option. Not for her best friend.

"It's okay," I whispered when I finally reached her. She looked at the ground and took a big gulp of air. I turned to face the crowd.

"The last time I saw Nina," I said, "I was over at Jules's studying for exams. I was really stressed out." I could hear myself speaking, like an echo on a cell phone. Then without meaning to, I started to focus on a pleasant-looking dad type with foppish hair and wire-rimmed glasses. There was something kind about him, like a beloved English teacher. His head tilted. "And she was in the backyard, painting a big fish, like applying paint to an actual trout or something." The man smiled, his eyes squinting behind his glasses.

"She was making these fish pictures. And she was bare- foot, one pant leg was rolled up, and her hair was doing that thing where it kind of stands up on one side." At least ten people laughed. Jules walked back to her seat. My mouth was dry, but I kept going. The story seemed to be telling itself. "And she had that look on her face. The one she got when she was really into something?" A horse-faced woman with a headband nodded. "That look that meant she was ready for anything, ready for action, ready for life." That last word hung in the air. My breath caught. "And before I knew it, I had a cold fish in my hand and she was teaching me how to use a trout to make a print, which was actually fun— gross and messy and fun. I forgot all about my exam. We made five and left them drying in the basement." I wiped my eyes with the back of my hand. "I don't remember what happened to the fish."

"So *that's* that smell," Mr. Clayton called from the front row. This time almost everyone laughed. Except Jules. She was slouched, her hands in the lap of her black crepe dress, her face as still as a doll's. I tried to make eye contact with her, but she was staring at the ground. Zack looked right at me, though. Something about the way he was smiling, cry- ing with his eyes open, urged me to keep going.

"And that was the thing about Nina. She looked at a dead fish and saw an art project; she'd look inside a refrigerator and find nothing but hot dogs and mayonnaise, and she'd throw them together and make you feel like you'd had the best meal of your life." I was gesturing wildly with my hands—they seemed to have a life of their own. "She looked at you," I choked, "at me, and saw someone to love." The man with the wire-rimmed glasses dabbed his eyes with a Kleenex. "She was the best, and I'm going to miss her so much," I said. I walked quickly back to my pew and slid in next to my mother. I looked at Jules, but she didn't turn around.

"You know, it's not healthy to be handling raw fish like that," Mom said, as she handed me a tissue. "You could've gotten sick."

I looked at her in disbelief. How could she have chosen this moment to criticize Nina? How could she have missed the whole point of that story? If I hadn't been crying, I would've screamed.

After, the church parlor was crowded. I knew a lot of the people—parents from school, people I'd seen around Providence. Practically our whole class was there, gathered in a corner, a cluster of navy and black dresses. Arti waved me over, but I didn't want to join them. They hardly knew Nina, and they certainly didn't love her. They wouldn't know how I was feeling. I didn't want to talk to anyone but the Claytons. While my mother talked to the woman with the yellow dogs from the yellow house on the corner, I studied a bulletin board of community announcements and ate a crustless egg salad sandwich and a handful of wet red grapes. I was hungrier than I'd been in days. In fact, I couldn't remember the last time I'd had an actual meal. I was reading a flyer advertising a playgroup for toddlers when someone tapped me on the shoulder.

"I know that you're drawn to the neon-pink paper, but you can't join that group," Zack said. He'd dripped Coke or coffee on his tie.

"Why not?" I asked.

"Too old." He shrugged. "And you have to be potty-trained, so there's that." His exhausted smile pained me.

"I'm working on it," I said. "Every day."

"Thanks for what you said about Mom," he said.

"Really? I was a little worried that maybe I shouldn't have," I said.

"No, it was good," he said. "It was funny. And sweet."

"Thanks," I said, taking in a sharp breath. "Where's Jules?" I asked. The reception was so packed that I'd lost sight of her. I'd figured we talk, finally, when it had thinned out a little.

"She just left," Zack said, and shrugged his shoulders. "She's on her way home. You might be able to catch her."

As soon as I stepped out of the church, I saw her down the street, three blocks away. I jogged in my flats, which were murdering my pinkie toes, and caught her as she was about to turn up her street.

"Hey," I said.

She gasped. "You scared me."

"Do you want to go and get some iced coffee or something?" I asked as I caught my breath. Little trickles of sweat ran down my back. "We could go to The Coffee Exchange."

"Um, no. Not right now."

"Later, maybe?" I licked my upper lip. Summer was here early.

"Sure," she said. I walked with her up her street. "Only thing is, my cousins are here, so I don't know what we'll be up to. Hey, I saw that Jay called you."

"Yes, but that's not important right now. You are." I put my hand on her shoulder, where it hung awkwardly as she walked fast and I tried to keep up. "Jules, are you okay?"

"Yeah," she said. We stopped in front of her house. I wanted to ask her if she'd been about to laugh up there, if she'd been sleeping okay, if she wanted to collapse in my arms the way I had in my mother's. I wanted to peel back the clear plastic curtain that seemed to be hanging between us so I could touch her. I wanted some proof that she was still herself. I wanted her to cry.

"Is it okay that I stood up there and said that stuff?" I asked.

"Yeah, it was great," she said. "I was freaking out. I'm just tired."

I sighed with relief. "Well, just so you know," I said, feeling a little shaky, "this summer, I'm there for you no matter what. We don't have to go to parties. We can stay in and watch '80s movies. We can go for walks on the beach every day. I'll do whatever. Just whatever makes you feel better. You're my best friend and I'm here for you one hundred percent." Anyone could come up with those words. Where were the right words?

"Thanks," she said, and crossed her arms. "I'm going to change out of this dress. I feel like a freakin' pilgrim."

"Okay," I said. She stood on the bottom step in front of the closed door. "I guess I'll head back to the church and find my mom. Call me, okay?"

I was standing in front of the mirror, brushing my teeth, when Jules called the next morning. I spat and picked up. "Hey!"

"Hey," she said, sounding like her old self again. "What's up?"

"Uh, not much," I answered. "How are you doing?"

"Oh my god, it's so crazy in this house," Jules said.

"I can't imagine," I said, and looked out the window. Frankie, the neighbors' beagle, was curled under the one patch of shade in their backyard. It was going to be another hot one.

"My little cousin is sleeping in my room, and she wet the bed last night, all the way down to the mattress. It stinks so bad in here. And my grandmother ironed all my jeans stiff as a board. With pleats. I'm not kidding."

"Well, that sucks," I said, surprised at how normal she sounded. "I was thinking maybe we could ride our bikes out to Bristol?" Bristol is a little seaside town with coffee shops and a cool antique store. Jules and I liked to look at the stacks of old photographs in back of the store.

"Not today," she said. "My whole family is here."

"Oh, right. I just thought, you know, it would be peaceful out there. Anyway, that reminds me, should I bring my bike to Nantucket?"

"Actually, that's what I was calling to tell you. You can't come with us anymore."

"Oh," I said, as I watched my face pale in the mirror. "Okay."

"It totally blows, but my dad said only family in the house this summer."

"Of course. I understand. Of course." I sat on the closed toilet seat and hung my head. How could I be thinking of myself? I burned with shame. "I totally get it."

She sighed and added, "But you can get your babysitting job back with the Kings, right?"

Four

THE FIRST TIME I THOUGHT OF GOING TO NANTUCKET BY myself, I was about to pick up the phone and call Deirdre King, mother of Andrew. I'd already typed in her number on my phone and was staring at it on the screen. My lip curled. Why, I wondered, was I doing it? I hated that job. Last summer, Andrew was obsessed with the word *boobies*. He'd say "boobies," then punch me in the boob. It really sucked. Especially when Mrs. King found it funny, which maybe it was if it wasn't *your* boob. I didn't want to play the straight man for Andrew King's comedy act again. I hung up the phone. I won't do it, I thought, falling back on my bed. *I won't.*

I started to think of other babysitting jobs, ones that

provided housing, ones that I heard paid twenty bucks an hour or more. Ones on Nantucket.

A little seed was planted.

The second time I thought of going to Nantucket by myself, I was sitting on the front porch, texting with Jay. It was supposed to have been my night at Dad's, but Alexi wasn't having a good night, so none of us was having a good night. Polly had adopted him from an orphanage in the Ukraine when he was three years old, and he'd had a pretty rough time there, which I guess is why he sometimes had these fits. Alexi loved the Beatles, and that night, after the fifth time of listening to "Yellow Submarine," I was going a little insane, so I changed the song. I put on James Taylor, one of Dad's favorites, but it set Alexi off. He started rocking on the floor, kicking his heels and wailing, even after I'd switched it back. Polly had to make him feel better, which meant that Dad had to make Polly feel better. I slipped out the back door without even touching my grilled steak. Dad was too swept up in the chaos to convince me to stay. He just waved good-bye and blew me a kiss.

At least it was peaceful at Mom's, I thought as I read a text from Jay. He'd gotten a job as a lifeguard out there on Nantucket, at a beach called Surfside. I started thinking about my almost-kiss with him and the moment when he'd pulled me onto his lap. I was thinking about sitting in a lifeguard chair with him in my new plum-colored J. Crew bikini with a ruffle. I was thinking about kissing him in the sand.

The seed burst from its husk and sprang green spindly roots.

The third time I thought about going to Nantucket alone, I was at the Brown University Bookstore. I was looking for my summer reading books when I saw a T-shirt just like Nina's. My heart cramped. I held my breath. I couldn't be away from Jules all summer. The Claytons might need alone time now, but in a week or so Jules would want me there, she'd need me. I wouldn't be in their house, so I wouldn't be a burden, and they'd still have their privacy. But I'd be close by. Ready to pitch in. Ready to load the dishwasher or run to the store for milk. I'd be ready to whip out a board game when that famous Nantucket fog rolled in. I'd make silver dollar pancakes for everyone. I'm good at that. I had an image of me setting the table.

But the vision was quickly replaced by one of Nina with the colorful place mats that she brought home from Mexico last spring. I could see her hands laying them on the table. I could see the wavy silver cuff bracelet around her wrist. I could see her eyes squinting in a laugh as Jules and I tied the matching napkins on our heads like bandannas. It made me miss her so much I felt like I'd been kicked. I held my breath until the sadness subsided.

I bought all my summer reading books except one (they didn't have the collection of Emily Dickinson poems for Mrs. Hart's class), and stopped to get a Del's from the cart on the corner. I handed over the dollar bills, soft and crinkled from a whole day in my back pocket, and took the cold little waxy dish of frozen lemonade. One lick woke up my mouth, chilled my sinuses. It would be *fun* to go alone. I was going to be eighteen in eight weeks, an official adult with the right to vote and join the armed services. I'd have my own paycheck and spend my money as I chose. I'd go to that café I'd heard Jules talking about, the Even Keel. I'd develop a croissant and coffee habit. I'd go running on the beach every morning and cool off in the ocean afterward. Maybe, in the evening, I'd carry a sketch pad. My whereabouts would not be known at all times, and this idea filled me with space: a pleasant, light-filled space.

I'll be like a college student, I thought as I stopped in front of a café popular with Brown students. The plastic bag of books strained and started to cut off the circulation in my hand. I switched my grip and peered in the window. A girl in a sundress with a purse slung over her chair was scribbling in an artist's notebook. I should wear dresses more. I need a notebook like that, I thought, when a cute guy walked in, kissed her, and sat down with a couple of drinks. As he touched her knee under the table and they clinked glasses, the idea of going to Nantucket by myself bloomed like a tropical flower.

I had to go.

Five

THE HORN SOUNDED, THE FERRY LAUNCHED, AND MY summer swung open like a saloon door. The engine hummed under my metal seat. I placed my duffel bag on the seat to save it—I had a good one, front row—and leaned on the cold, sticky railing. The breeze was soft, persistent, cool but not cold. I zipped up my hoodie and looked at the ocean. Farther out it was a deep blue, but right here, right under me, it was beer-bottle green and brown with flashes of gold. I lifted my face into the late afternoon sun and inhaled the salty Atlantic air.

The ferry was crowded with families. They seemed to own the place. Nearby, a little boy resisted the hugs of his mother, wrestling out of her arms to press his face against the grating. A girl in a hot-pink Lilly Pulitzer dress tried to climb up the viewfinder, begging her parents for a quarter. Kids in polo shirts darted around the seats, wanting to be chased. The parents were dressed in clothes as vivid as their children's. Grown men wore kelly-green pants stitched with yellow whales. The women were in an unofficial uniform: white jeans, bright-colored tops, and Jack Rogers sandals—I recognized the brand instantly because Jules had a pair in blue and another in pink. Six young moms talked in a circle; they looked like a fistful of lollipops.

"Uh-oh, here come the Range Rovers," said an old man with a weathered face and a light, sensible windbreaker, as a madras-clad couple walked past with monogrammed tote bags that looked freshly sprung from L.L. Bean. Their three blond kids wore T-shirts that said *Nantucket*.

"Why do they have to wear T-shirts that tell the world where they're going?" the old man's wife said, shaking her head. "I don't wear a shirt that says *New Hampshire* when I go there."

The old man saw me eavesdropping and leaned toward me. "To us, it's home; to them, it's *Nantucket*," he said with a tight jaw and an over-the-top snob accent.

I laughed and nodded as if I were a native, too. Then I made a mental note not to buy a T-shirt with *Nantucket* written on it. I didn't want to piss off the locals.

"Avery, come back here!" Here was the mother of the Lilly Pulitzer girl—in a skirt that matched her daughter's dress.

"No!" Avery stuck her tongue out at her.

"Avery, if you don't get back here right away," she stammered, "Theresa will get very mad at you." Disgust flashed across the face of a short, round Hispanic woman before she remembered herself and leaped to coax the girl off the viewfinder.

"Why would you want to be a servant?" Mom had asked when I'd accepted the live-in babysitting position it had taken me less than twenty-four hours to be offered.

All it took was a morning on the Web site for the local Nantucket newspaper, *The Inquirer and Mirror*, and a few e-mails before a woman named Mary Ellen called my cell asking if I'd be available to start on Monday. She was the house manager—basically a butler—to a wealthy family in Boston who was already on Nantucket. She'd heard of Rosewood. She actually knew Miss Kang from college. If I could hop on a bus and meet her that afternoon in Boston, and if my references checked out, I'd be on a ferry Sunday. I met her in a crowded Starbucks on Newbury Street.

"Oh, you're perfect," she said when we spotted each other. "Caroline is going to flip over you. And you can swim?"

I nodded. *Obviously.*

"And please tell me you drive. Do you drive?" I nodded. *What seventeen-year-old doesn't drive?*

She told me that it paid eight hundred dollars a week for eight weeks. Eight times eight was sixty-four! For a half a second I thought I was going to be making sixty thousand dollars (math is my worst subject), but when I got to six thousand four hundred dollars it was still an awesome amount of money.

"It's not easy, though. You're on from the minute the kids get up until they're dead asleep. If they wake up in the night, it's your problem."

I nodded, grinning. Eight hundred *a week*! It turned out the father was the famous national news anchor for CNN, Bradley Lucas. He seemed a little old to have kids who needed a nanny, but he was famous. Mom would definitely let me go now. There were three girls, and three nannies rotating shifts around the clock. She told me that one nanny, a local Nantucket girl, hadn't worked out and they were "in a pickle." Then she bought me an iced tea, took a map of Nantucket out of her purse, and drew a path in blue pen from where the ferry would drop me to the house on 25 Cliff Road. At the bottom she wrote her phone number.

"Should I have the Lucases' number as well?" I asked.

"No," she said, chuckling to herself. "You need anything, call me. My cell is on all the time." She gave me money for the ferry ticket and an extra fifty for "my time," and told me that she'd be out there in a week.

I was thrilled when I told my mom. But she wasn't.

"Babysitting again?" Mom asked as she ate the last bite of moo shu pork from the carton. "I thought you hated babysitting."

"I don't hate it," I said. "I just don't *love* it." Mom leveled me with a look as she sipped her wine. "I want to go to Nantucket, and there's no other way. Besides, I'd be a servant here, to Andrew King."

"That's different," she said. "You wouldn't live with the Kings. You don't want to live in anyone's home. It's beneath you. They'll think they own you." She finished her glass of white wine and poured herself another. "And what if that news anchor is creepy? He's too smooth, and he has that hairpiece."

"If he tries anything, I'll call the Law Offices of Snell and Garabedian," I said, using the name of a criminal law firm whose ad, which featured two meaty guys holding up a golden set of scales in front of a wall of law books, was on every bus stop bench. Mom laughed. I could count the number of times she'd laughed this year on one hand. "Besides, Mom, you did it."

My mom had spent one summer on Nantucket when she was my age. She'd worked at a hotel on the beach. I found a picture of her on a little sailboat in a blue bikini, grinning, a pointed foot dangling over the edge. The wind is sweeping her blond hair across her freckled cheek, and she's laughing at whoever took the picture.

It's pretty crazy how alike we look. For a minute I'd thought it was me. How could I have forgotten that day? It looked like the best day of my life. It only took a second to register that the picture was small and square with a matte finish; it was taken a long time ago. On the back it said *Nantucket, 1984.*

"I wasn't by myself. I was staying with family, with my

aunt Betty," my mother said. "It can be really snotty out there, honey."

"Can I stay with Aunt Betty?" I cracked open my fortune cookie: *Surprise doubles happiness.*

"She died in 1993." Mom sat up a little and tucked her hair behind her ear. "And she also read my diary, which infuriated me. But you'll be all alone. I don't want you to go. You're only seventeen. What if something happened to you?"

"I'll be eighteen in August. And what could be safer than Nantucket?" I asked. "It's not exactly the Gaza Strip. And I won't be alone. I'll have the Claytons and the other nannies."

"The Claytons," Mom said. "What is so fascinating to you about those people? From the way you follow them around you'd think they were the Kennedys." She took another sip from her glass. "Some people thought Nina was a little weird, you know. Last month I saw her in a turban on Thayer Street. I was like, really? A turban?"

"Mom!" I said, feeling my face get hot. "How can you say that right now?"

"You're right," she said. "Sorry." She didn't sound sorry, and she was speaking in a near whisper, a trick she used with her students when they got rowdy. When she lowered her voice, they lowered theirs. But it only made me louder.

"She was a bohemian," I said, my hands curled into tight fists. "That turban was for yoga."

"People don't wear turbans to yoga, Cricket," she said. I could tell that the second glass of wine had worked its way through her system.

"Yes, they do," I said, my voice shaking. "For a special kind of yoga in New York. And Nina wasn't weird, she was just . . . herself." I choked on the last word. Tears filled my eyes.

"Okay, okay." Mom looked me in the eye and took a deep breath. "I'm sorry. I shouldn't have said it." She meant it this time.

"And I don't follow them around," I said quietly. "They're like family."

"I'm going to go take a shower," she said, then sighed and headed up the back stairs.

"Wait, so can I go to Nantucket?" I shut my eyes and crossed my fingers as I awaited her reply.

She paused on the creaky stairs. "I'll think about it."

While she was taking one of her half-hour showers, I packed my bag. I was going to get her to say yes if it killed me. As I put the summer reading books in my suitcase, I decided to check the bookcase in the hallway, where Mom kept her old school books. I was looking for the Emily Dickinson collection. She had had Mrs. Hart, too. Sure enough, there it was. Had the summer reading really not changed in all these years? I plucked it by its spine. It was a little dusty, and the font on the cover was different, but it was the right book.

A little later, when I thought we'd both cooled off, I went into her room. Mom was lying in bed reading her mystery novel.

"Well?"

"I'm still thinking," she said, and turned the page.

I took the novel from her hands, marked her page, and placed it carefully on the nightstand. I sat on the edge of her bed and looked in her eyes.

"Mom, it's very lonely for me here," I said.

"Oh, but we have each other," she said, and took my face in her soft, light hands. She turned out her lower lip.

"I want more than that," I said, pulling back sharply. Anger crept up my throat like a poisonous spider.

"Cricket," Mom said quietly, and shrank back into her pillow. "I love you too, you know. I love you more than the Claytons do."

"I know, Mom. And I love you. I love you so much." Her eyes brightened. "It's just that—" *It's just that you shouldn't take me down with you. It's just that I want a life, even if you don't. It's just that you're like a ghost, a strong ghost, barely here but holding on to me too tightly.* I drew a deep, calming breath. "All of my friends are away for the summer on an adventure, and I want an adventure, too. It's been a hard year for me, Mom, with Dad and Polly getting married." Mom leaned closer. I was talking about it. I was *going there.* "I need to get away from it, so that I can move on from this—" *Say it,* her eyes begged. "Divorce." There. "I need to move on. We both need to. I don't know if I can do that in Providence. And I don't know if you can, either."

She took a long breath, relaxing a little more deeply into her pillow. She folded her hands in front of her and looked out the window. "Okay," she said.

"Really?"

"You can go."

"Thank you," I said, and hugged her. "Thank you."

Nantucket emerged between the sea and the lavender sky like a make-believe village. White church spires peeked above lush treetops. Sailboats dotted the harbor. On a sandy point, a lighthouse flashed green. When the boat docked, people on land waved to friends and family on the ferry. I didn't mind that no one was waiting for me. I had it all planned out. I hadn't told Jules. I was going to surprise her. *Surprise doubles happiness.* As I stepped onto the busy dock, the lowering sun left a path on the water. It had followed me here like a spotlight.

Six

I IMMEDIATELY WANTED TO CHANGE OUT OF MY SCRUFFY jeans and hoodie and into one of two nice outfits I'd brought to Nantucket. Maybe I should've told Jules I was coming. She might've warned me that a different league of people existed here. No wonder she read those beauty magazines all year. Everyone was pretty here. And I could see them all. It wasn't like walking around Providence, where I didn't notice much because I was busy doing my own thing. There was something about being alone in a new place that pushed the world a little closer, like when I put on the huge reading glasses from the kiosk in CVS to make Jules laugh.

Even the old lady in the powder-blue sweater carrying one of those basket purses was the prettiest old lady I'd ever seen. She had white-gold hair and eyes the color of a

Tiffany box. Nina had given Jules a necklace from there for her sixteenth birthday, and Jules returned it to its original box every night when she took it off. It was a bean-shaped pendant. It was delicate and grown-up, and I liked to try it on when Jules was in the shower.

Nina, I thought, and for a second I swore I smelled her perfume.

I walked passed an ice cream store with a line around the corner, a bookstore, the Whaling Museum, and an inn with three rocking chairs on the porch. Everything was quaint, preserved, one of a kind, looking like it wouldn't ever change and couldn't exist anywhere but here. The sidewalks were brick. The fire hydrants were tennis-ball yellow. With my duffel bag slung over my shoulder, I walked past a row of fancy restaurants bustling with a spiffy dinner crowd, and a quiet art gallery where a woman stood ballerina-like in the doorway, smoking a cigarette.

I turned up Cliff Road, which was exactly where the map said it would be. The street sign looked hand-painted. Maybe that's what they make the prisoners in the Nantucket jail do, I thought. Instead of making license plates, they had to hand paint the street signs. Instead of orange jumpsuits, they were issued fisherman sweaters.

Three guys rode by on bicycles, calling after each other in an undecipherable boy language. None of them wore a helmet, and two were barefoot. The smaller one stood on his peddles, coasted, and gave me a double take. I smiled. The bicycle ticked. Where were they going?

I reached a mailbox with the Lucases' address on it. Tall hedges surrounded the house, so I couldn't see it until I lifted the latch of the wooden gate and turned to walk down the driveway. The house was huge. It was definitely bigger than Sophie Toscano's house, and she was the richest girl in our class. She got dropped off at school in a Rolls-Royce. This place seemed to exceed the boundaries of a house; it was an *estate*, closer in size to the mansions my parents and I used to see in Newport. We sometimes drove around town on a rainy day. We'd go to Sue's Clam Shack for bowls of clam chowder and then visit Ocean Avenue, pretending to pick out the house we were going to buy.

"Welcome home," my dad would say as we slowed down in front of a glorious shingled place with a wraparound porch and a stunning view.

"Honey, why didn't you tell me? I would've brought our suitcases!" my mom would say. I'd laugh from the backseat and point out my bedroom window—always in a turret, if there was one.

This house, this mansion, was alive with the sounds of a party. I heard peels of laughter and music. Jazz—was it live? In the driveway was a Nantucket Catering Company van and a line of SUVs, most of them Range Rovers, just like the old man on the ferry had said, and a few older-looking Jeeps, the bumpers plastered with beach permit stickers. As I made my way up the stone path lined with lanterns, I heard the murmur of adult conversation, the exclamations of dressed-up ladies, the clinks of silverware and glass. I could feel the ocean in the air.

I rang the doorbell. After a few minutes, no one answered. I opened the door and walked inside.

"Hello?" I called into the entryway. All the lights were on. And there was no sign of people living here. There were no family photographs, no kid drawings on the fridge, no tiny stray socks. It was a house-hotel. "Hello?"

A girl in frog pajamas popped up from behind a sofa, clutching a blanket.

"Hi," I said, and dropped my bags. "I'm Cricket."

"I'm Lucy," she said, hiding behind her blanket.

"I'm the new babysitter," I said.

"Another one?" she asked, peering at me from behind her blanket. I nodded, smiling. She held the blanket over her nose and mouth and narrowed her eyes at me.

"Are you a robber?" I asked.

"Yes!" she said, her eyes widening. "I'm going to rob you!"

"Uh-oh," I said, and cowered dramatically. She giggled. "Robber, I think we should find your mom so that I can introduce myself."

"Okay," she said. "Come on." She led me through a palatial kitchen and out to a large, crowded patio with a bar and a live jazz band playing "Moondance." Nearby, a college-age girl in a Nantucket Catering Company apron grilled shrimp kabobs. A waiter passed a tray of fizzing cocktails, each glass topped with an impaled twist of lime. The ocean sparkled darkly in the distance. The sun was gone now, and a band of deep pink glowed on the horizon. The breeze carried the sweet smell of honeysuckle and beach grass.

There was a small rectangular pool bordered by eight trim recliners. A group of women sat on them, looking adoringly at a broad-shouldered blond man. His bold hand gestures seemed to be conducting their laughter like an orchestra. Bradley Lucas! I thought. Telling funny stories! Twenty feet away!

If I'd felt a little messy and underdressed when I stepped off the ferry, I was now officially in Oliver Twist territory. The men wore Nantucket Reds—I recognized the salmon-colored pants because Jules had teased Zack when he wore his to the Spring Dance, even though I think she was secretly proud of him—and the women swished like tropical fish in silky, brightly colored summer dresses.

"Which one is your mom?" I asked Lucy. The only woman with any mom pudge was the one crooning into the microphone in a fringed vest and scuffed flats. Lucy pointed to a tall woman who stood on coltish legs in a short white dress and very high heels, conversing with a man in seersucker pants and a fedora.

"Mommy!" Lucy called. Mrs. Lucas's head turned. Her ponytail, which looked like it had been gathered and fastened by a professional, brushed the air. Her brow furrowed.

"Lucy, why aren't you in bed?" Her eyes widened as she

took me in and strode toward us. "Caroline Lucas," she said, and extended a narrow, bejeweled hand. She blinked.

"Cricket Thompson," I said, and shook her hand.

"She's the new babysitter," Lucy said. "Another one!" She smacked her head with an open hand like a cartoon character.

Mrs. Lucas put a hand over her mouth. The band transitioned into "Killing Me Softly." Usually, I love that song, but for some reason my stomach sank.

"Let's go inside, shall we?" She gestured to the sliding glass doors I'd left open. "Come on, Lucy. You need to be in bed."

"But it's not even dark out," Lucy said, and hopped inside.

"Who's your grown-up tonight?" Mrs. Lucas asked.

"Sharon."

"Go find her."

"She's asleep," Lucy said. "Snoring!"

"Well, wake her up," Mrs. Lucas said.

"I'm so frustrated, Mommy," Lucy said as she traipsed upstairs, dragging her blanket behind her.

"I've made a terrible mistake," Mrs. Lucas said to me. I could smell the cocktail on her breath as she exhaled and placed one tan hand on a boney hip and the other on her temple. "I'm completely overstaffed. Mary Ellen was hiring in Boston and I was hiring out here and we didn't communicate very well and now I've got babysitters up to my eyeballs. They're packed to the rafters in the cottage," she said, laughing. "I've got one on an air mattress above the garage." Her laughter trailed off as she took in my expression. "Mary Ellen didn't call you, huh?"

"No."

"Well, I apologize. I'll talk to her about that. But I can't keep you. I just don't need another babysitter. I have backups for the backups." She tilted her head. "But you can still catch the last ferry back. Those things run until ten o'clock, at least." She checked her watch and tapped it with her perfect red fingernail. "Oh yeah, you've got plenty of time."

"But I'd still need to catch a bus back to Providence," I said. "There won't be another bus by the time I get back to Hyannis." As if this were my biggest problem, as if disappointment weren't hovering over my heart like a bee over a slice of watermelon, as if my dream weren't fading into nothingness, a Polaroid picture in reverse—there goes Jay in the lifeguard chair, there go my rainy afternoons watching movies with Jules, my morning runs on the beach, my eight hundred dollars a week.

"Right, how stupid of me," she said, shaking her head. "You'll need a taxi." She walked to the kitchen island and opened a drawer. She swayed a little as she counted out some cash. She handed me three stiff hundred-dollar bills. "That ought to get you home with a little extra." She hiccupped. "Now, do you want me to have someone drop you at the ferry, or can you walk from here?"

Seven

I CONSIDERED MY OPTIONS AS I LEFT THE LUCASES'.

Option one: catch the ten o'clock ferry. I didn't want to go back home. If I did, Mom would pretend like we were having a great girls' weekend all summer even though we were both miserable; she because she missed Dad, and I because I wanted to be with other kids. She promised we would go on trips to Newport and Block Island but would always come down with a headache when it came time to get in the car. She would get that look in her eye like I was betraying her every time I went to Dad's house. It was a soft, pleading look that made me want to wrap my arms around her and comfort her and, at the same time, sprint away from her as fast as I could. I nixed the thought before I'd even reached the end of the driveway. I couldn't give up yet.

Option two: go to Jules's house. "It's right in town," she'd told me. "A five-minute walk to the Hub." The Hub, Jules told me, was a little store where she bought all her magazines. "They also sell postcards, little things, Tic Tacs, gum, Nantucket key chains, crap like that. Oh, and also, there's no CVS on Nantucket, no Target, no Costco, nothing even close."

She went on to tell me that no one locked their doors at night, people left their keys dangling in the ignitions of their Jeeps, and everyone bought their bread from a bakery and their vegetables from a farm, not the supermarket. She'd made Nantucket sound like a foreign land whose customs I might have difficulty comprehending. It bugged me. It was only one state away. My mother had spent a summer here. I'd been to Cape Cod a bunch of times. And there was a farm stand in Tiverton that Mom, Dad, and I used to go to in the summer for blueberries, tomatoes, and Silver Queen corn. I wasn't a total ignoramus. Still, I'd packed two big boxes of tampons just in case they were scarce out here, or really expensive, like in Russia.

I had her address memorized, 4 Darling Street, and could picture the house perfectly. The Claytons' Christmas card every year was of the family standing in front of the blue door with the scallop-shell knocker. A gold "4" hung above them, as if counting the perfect family: mom, dad, sister, brother. In last year's card, Nina is looking up and laughing. What would the picture be like this year? Would they still stand in front of the door? I felt another kick of sadness, right in the stomach. I was realizing that loss has a kind of violence to it.

When I got closer to town I took out my map and, straining my eyes in the darkness, found the Claytons' address. Insects thrummed in the nearby yards as I traced my finger over the route.

I passed back through town and crossed the busy, cobblestoned Main Street. Jeez, was there a beautiful-people factory out here? A breeding ground for J. Crew models? The older ones walked in close teams of two and four, the younger ones in looser packs of six or eight. The uneven sidewalk was illuminated by glowing, old-fashioned street-lamps. The shop windows were decorated with sea-motif jewelry. Gold starfish earrings lay in pools of green silk, and diamond-crusted anchors hung on velvet necks.

The windows of the interior-design stores were so warm and inviting I wanted to crawl inside and curl up in one of their nautical tableaus, bury my toes in the knotty rugs, and fall backward into the plump pillows. How funny would that be, I thought, if Jules walked by in the morning and I was sleeping in the bed of a shop window?

I turned onto Fair Street, about to head toward Jules's, when I heard my mother's teacher voice in my head telling me that Jules said I couldn't stay with her, and I needed to respect that. I couldn't just drop in unless I had a place to stay for certain. A church bell rang, and I counted the low gongs. It was ten o'clock. I paused, dropped my duffel, and looked at the map. I was four blocks shy of Darling Street, standing in front of an inn. It was white with dark red shutters and a front porch, and had a carved, gold-lettered sign.

Option three: the Cranberry Inn.

The door was unlocked. The lobby, with the bookcases, worn oriental rugs, and clusters of sofas and armchairs around a fireplace, looked like a living room. A man with a ponytail and goatee sat behind an antique desk, reading a paperback with one of those dark, manly-man covers. A pair of drugstore glasses sat on the end of his nose. He was sitting cross-legged in an armchair in what looked like pajama bottoms or maybe karate pants. The string of a tea bag hung over his mug. He sipped his tea and turned the page quickly, his eyes darting to the top of the next page.

"Excuse me, are there any rooms available at the inn?" I asked. Oh god, I was actually saying a line from our fifth-grade Christmas pageant when I played Mary!

The man jerked his head up, eyes wide, startled for a second, then laughed a little.

"I didn't even hear you come in," he said as if he knew me. He held up the book. "People leave these mysteries behind, and I can't put them down. They get me every time." He shook his head, disappointed with himself, and waved me over. "Come on in. I'm Gavin." He glanced through the open door behind me. "Are you with your parents?"

I shook my head.

"A solo traveler," he said. "Nothing like traveling alone to get to know yourself. Sit down. Have a cookie." He gestured to a table with a pitcher of water and a plate of chocolate chip cookies. I took one. He tilted his head and consulted his reservation book. "We have one room. It's the Admiral's Suite."

The kitchen door swung open, and a girl walked through with a tray of fresh glasses. She stacked them next to the pitcher of water.

"Oh, great," I said, covering my mouth as I swallowed. I was hungrier than I'd realized. "I'll take it."

"It's three ninety-nine." He sighed and added, "Plus tax."

"Oh," I said. "I can't do that. I'm not exactly on vacation, I'm looking for a job." I needed my three hundred dollars to last at least two or three nights. I sank a little lower in the chair. I was tired for the first time since I'd woken up at five a.m., wired with anticipation.

"Give her Rebecca's room," the girl said in a thick accent. Was she Irish? "Can't charge more than a hundred for that, can you?" Was she his daughter? She was a little chubby, with pink cheeks and a sunburned nose. She pushed a black curl back behind her ear and gestured to me. "Poor thing looks knackered."

"Rebecca won't mind?" I asked, wondering who Rebecca was.

"She's halfway to England by now," Gavin said.

"I got my cousin a job on Nantucket, and she quit after a week 'cause she missed her lug of a boyfriend." I wasn't sure if this was funny because of her accent, or even if it was meant to be a joke, but I laughed. "And he's a right wanker."

"I'm looking for a job," I said, sitting up and tapping

the table with my palms. "And I need one that comes with housing."

"Well, this works out perfectly, then, doesn't it?" the girl said, a hand on her sturdy hip. "You get a job, Gavin doesn't have to go on the great chambermaid search, and I don't have to share a bathroom with a freak of nature. You're not a freak of nature, are you?"

"Nope." I shook my head. Chambermaid? It sounded like a job from another century, like a charwoman or a scullery maid. Would I be churning butter, cleaning chimneys, beating rugs with a broom? Who cared? I'd have a job and a place to stay for free on Nantucket.

"We don't even know her name," he said to the girl, then put a hand to his chest and turned to me. "Excuse us, what's your name?"

"Cricket," I said. "Cricket Thompson."

"Amazing," Gavin said. "I was noticing, really *noticing* the crickets earlier. I thought to myself, Ah, the song of the cricket, the song of summer."

"See, it's a sign," Liz said. "I'm Liz, by the way. Not Liza, not Lizzy, and"—she shot Gavin a look—"definitely not Lizard."

"Nice to meet you, Liz."

"What do you say, Gavin?" she asked.

"I'm interviewing someone tomorrow," he said. "But I don't see why I couldn't interview Cricket as well. Come back in the afternoon, say around three?"

"Okay," I said, and shook his hand. "Sounds great."

"Wait, who are you interviewing?" Liz asked.

"Svetlana," he said.

"Svetlana . . . *the cow*?" Liz asked with a look of horror. She sounded dead serious, so I tried not to laugh.

"She has good references," Gavin said.

"She flirted with Shane in front of my face at The Chicken Box," Liz said.

"It's not your decision, Liz," Gavin said, now sounding officially annoyed. "See you tomorrow, Cricket?"

"Yes," I said, and smiled. I felt too awkward to ask about Rebecca's room again. "I'll see you then."

I gave him my cell phone number, picked up my duffel bag, and walked out the front door. As soon as I hit Main Street I sat on a bench in front of one of the beautiful shops, wondering where I was going to spend the night now. My phone rang. I prayed it was Jules and that she'd invite me over right away. But it was my mom.

A part of me didn't want to pick up. I'd have to tell her that the job didn't work out and I was considering sleeping on a park bench. It would show that she had been right and Nantucket was a bad idea. It would be evidence that I wasn't the independent girl I worked so hard to be. But the other part of me, the tired part of me, with a blister forming on my left foot, a growling stomach, and no idea where I was going to sleep tonight, wanted to talk to her.

"Mom?"

"Honey? What happened?" She had always been able to tell by the way I said even one word if something was wrong. If Mom had a superpower, it was her hearing. When it came to me, her ears were as keen as a wolf's. It was no use lying to her.

"Well, the babysitting job didn't work out," I said.

"Oh, I'm sorry," she said. "You must be really disappointed."

"Yeah," I said.

"But do you remember when Andrew pooped in the minivan and you had to clean it up? Or when he insisted you play Transformers . . . for a week?"

"Yes. That minivan was disgusting."

"So, you hate babysitting, remember?"

"I guess I do."

"So, this is a good thing. That family's letting you spend the night there, at least?"

"Not exactly," I said.

Her voice dropped an octave. "What do you mean? Where are you?"

"Before you freak out, here's the good news. I have a job interview at an inn tomorrow. And I have a fifty percent chance of getting it. Maybe even like sixty percent."

"To be what?" she asked.

"A chambermaid."

"A maid? No, no, no. And where are you staying tonight? It's late!"

"I don't know," I said.

"Well, where are you *right now*?"

"I'm in town," I said, taking in the cobblestones, the

misty evening air, the books nestled in the display of the bookstore across the street, the elegant well-dressed couples holding hands, "and it's perfect."

"Here's what I'm going to do," she said as if she hadn't even heard me. "You're going to sit tight. I'm going to call around, find a place for you to stay, and pay for a room with my credit card. I wonder if the Jared Coffin House is still there."

"Thanks, Mom." I felt cool relief wash through me. With a good night's sleep and at least another day out here, I knew I could make something work.

"Then tomorrow morning, first thing, you'll get on a ferry back to Hyannis. I'll pick you up, and you'll spend the summer with me. Just us girls."

Now I had wolf ears. I could hear her smile. Her relief laced through my disappointment with delicate, painful stitches. Just as I was about to protest, I got another call. It was a Nantucket number.

"Mom, hold on one sec," I said, and switched lines. "Hello?"

"Cricket, it's Liz. Where are you, you daft girl? You fled."

"I'm in town," I said. This was good news. I could feel it.

"Well, come on back! I convinced Gavin to give you a try tomorrow. I told him if you were a disaster, he could hire Svetlana and I wouldn't say a word about it."

"That's great," I said, smiling. "That's so great. Thank you!"

"So, don't be a disaster!"

"I won't," I said. "I promise. See you in a sec."

I switched back to Mom. "Mom, I just got the chamber-maiding job!"

"What? Just now?"

"Yes! I can stay on Nantucket!"

"As a maid?"

"Yeah, but so what? It's better than babysitting, right? And this place is really cute. It's called the Cranberry Inn." I picked up my duffel bag for the zillionth time that day and headed back toward Fair Street. "If you saw this place, I swear you'd love it. It's cozy and old-fashioned and they make cookies every afternoon. Google it." I waited for her to find the Web site. "You could even come and visit."

"It looks like a really nice place," she said. I had to give her credit. She was trying. "Okay, now, if you change your mind, I'm right here—"

"I'll call you when I get settled—okay, Mom?"

"All right," she said, and hung up.

I turned up Fair Street, picturing Mom turning in for the night with a mystery novel, a glass of tepid tap water by her bed, and the picture of my father she still kept in the drawer of her bedside table. I knew she had nothing to do tonight or tomorrow night or the night after that. As Liz opened the door for me and led me to a tiny room with rose wallpaper, a window with peeling paint, a twin bed, a sink, a dresser, and a slanted ceiling, I tried to tell myself that it wasn't my fault my mother was alone.

"We start tomorrow at six a.m. sharp," Liz said.

"Got it," I said, and dropped my duffel bag on the floor of my new room. I'd wait until tomorrow to ask what exactly being a chambermaid involved and how much I was going to be paid. Now that I had it, the job seemed like a small deal compared to the real purpose of my Nantucket adventure: to be there for Jules, and maybe, just maybe, fall in love with Jay Logan. I splashed some cold water on my face, slipped out the front door, which Liz promised was always unlocked, and walked to Darling Street. It was 10:43. Hopefully, Jules was awake.

Eight

AS I WALKED TO THE HOUSE, I IMAGINED LIFTING THE scallop-shell knocker—Jules's eyes huge at the happy surprise—how she might do that little jump-flutter-kick thing, then link her arm in mine and pull me to the two-seater swing on the porch, another spot well documented in the Clayton family photos.

I got there in no time at all. The house was exactly as I'd imagined it. Rose-covered trellis, soft inviting lawn with a garden, bushes with big flowers lining the front of the house, a wraparound porch with beach towels hung over the railing to dry, two bicycles leaning against the garage, a wood-paneled Wagoneer parked in the driveway (the land yacht, Zack called it).

I knocked. Jules answered the door right away. Her hair was up and she had on makeup.

"Ta-da," I said, and stretched out my arms.

"What?" She blinked. She wore new earrings. Dangly ones.

"It's me, Cricket," I said. I wondered if in her grief she'd forgotten who I was.

"I know," she said. "What are you doing here?"

"I'm living here. I got a job and a place to stay and everything!" I said, holding my arms open like Jules might jump into them. But she just stood there in the doorway with a blank face. I put my hands in my pockets. "I'm a chambermaid." God, it sounded so weird.

"Oh." She stepped outside and shut the door behind her, switching on a light that hung above the door. "Where?"

"The Cranberry Inn?" Jules shook her head, didn't know it. "It's so close. It's practically around the corner."

"Wow." She smiled, but it looked like it hurt.

"So this is the famous Nantucket house," I said, taking a few steps backward. The damp grass brushed my ankles. The light bulb buzzed inside its glass walls. Dark moths fluttered around it. The sky above was filled with stars. I breathed in the night air. "It's beautiful."

She nodded and sat on one of the benches. I sat across from her, tucking my hands under my thighs. She was quiet, so I just started talking. I told her about the bus ride to Boston and the Lucas kid. I told her about Gavin in his hippie pants, and Liz's accent. I told her about my room at the Cranberry Inn, the slanted ceiling, the tiny dresser and the little window, the front door that was never locked. I told her that it took me less than five minutes to get to her house from there. I talked so much my mouth was dry; she didn't say anything back.

"I completely understand why you can't have any house-guests this summer," I said. "I mean, of course. But I figured this way I could be here for you. If you need me at any time, you just call out my name, that kind of thing."

"Thanks," she said, staring past me. She crossed her legs and pulled out a cigarette. I tried not to act surprised. We'd only smoked once before. It was in her basement. It felt terrible, like breathing exhaust from an old school bus, and it made me nauseous and lightheaded. Nina smelled the smoke from the garage, where she'd been doing one of her projects—something with a sawhorse. She ran into the basement saying *no, no, no,* and waving a broom in a way that was unintentionally hilarious.

Later, she'd sat us down for a serious chat, showing us pictures on the Internet of black, shriveled lungs and faces so wrinkled they looked like they were made of corduroy. I hadn't had a cigarette since then, but Jules was smoking like she knew how, tapping her finger on the end so that ash fell like snow into a Coke can. The beach towels on the porch rail stirred in the breeze.

"Want one?" she asked. I shook my head.

"Where's your dad?" I asked.

"At the Club Car." I nodded as if I knew what this meant. I heard someone laughing inside the house—a girl.

"Who's here?" I asked.

"Zack and this girl."

"Who is it?" As far as I knew, Zack hadn't ever really had a girlfriend. There was Valerie, a French girl he'd met on a ski trip to Vail, but after a few weeks of video chatting, she'd sent Zack a dramatic e-mail and moved on. He wouldn't eat french fries for a month, and all French words were banned from the house, including *omelet*, *perfume*, and *champagne*.

"This girl out here," Jules said. She dropped her cigarette into the Coke can. It hissed.

"Cool. Hey, have you seen Jay?" I asked. "He said he was a lifeguard at Surfer's Beach."

"Surfside," Jules said. "And, yeah, I saw him last night."

"How'd he look?" *Was he with anyone? Did he ask about me?*

"Hot," she said with a quickness and certainty that made me want to remind her how much I liked him.

"I can't believe how close we came to kissing at Nora's. It was amazing."

"Must be something about a whore's house."

"I can't wait to see him. I don't know if I should text him, or if it's better for me to just run into him."

"I'd wait to run into him," she said.

"You think?"

She nodded. "Anyway, I'm really tired. I think I'm going to hit the sack."

"Well, all right," I said, standing up. I hadn't had a puff of the cigarette, but I had that lightheadedness anyway. I turned to head down the path that led back out to the street. "So I guess I'll see you tomorrow?"

"Sure," Jules said. I opened the gate to leave.

"Are you hacking butts again, Jules?" I turned around. Zack was leaning out a first-floor window. He squinted in my direction. "Hey, who's that?"

"It's Cricket," I said, and waved. Seconds later, the screen door was snapping shut behind him. He was barefoot and his hair was sticking up, like he hadn't taken a shower since he'd come home from the beach. Jules stepped out of the way as he walked toward me in a half jog. Had he grown an inch in the last week?

"What are you doing here?" He gave me a quick, hard hug. He smelled like sunscreen and salt water. "I thought you weren't coming. I thought you had a babysitting job in Providence. When did you get here? Are you staying with us?"

"No, remember what Dad said?" Jules said, standing several feet behind us. Zack looked confused.

"I got here tonight. I got a job at the Cranberry Inn, and I'm staying there."

"Oh, I've seen that place. Don't they have famous muffins?"

"I don't know," I said, smiling at the thought of Zack keeping up with the Nantucket muffin gossip.

"What?" he asked.

"Nothing."

"Are you coming to the party in 'Sconset tomorrow?"

"What party?"

"It's not a party," Jules said. She was now silhouetted in the doorway, and I could see Nina in her shape so well that I felt a light pressure on my chest. "Just a few kids who come every summer, getting together." I wondered if this meant that Jay would be there. I had a feeling it did.

"Fine. We'll call it a mixer," Zack said to Jules. "I didn't know you had such a penchant for precision."

"Don't be a dick," she said.

"Penchant?" I asked with raised eyebrows.

"I'm a Word Warrior," he said. That was the SAT vocabulary-building program everyone had. Zack took a pen from his pocket. Then he took my hand, uncurled it, smoothed it, and wrote on my palm: *15 Sand Dollar Lane.*

"I don't know where that is," I said.

"Just take Milestone Road."

"Can I walk?"

"No. I'm getting a ride from work. But text Jules. She'll take you." We turned to her, but she was gone.

Nine

"EVERYONE EATS BREAKFAST IN THE GARDEN, EXCEPT when it rains," Liz said as she expertly pulled silverware from the dishwasher and wiped it with a checkered dishrag. "Then we put them in the dining room."

"Got it," I said, and sipped my coffee, the first cup from the percolator I'd just been shown how to set up and get started (fill with water, twenty scoops in the filter, plug it in, flip the switch). I sipped some more, hoping I'd start to feel more alert soon. Liz pulled a stack of little bowls from the dishwasher and handed them to me. "There's some jam in the fridge. Put it in these ramekins."

"Okay, no problem," I said, noting the new word *ramekins*, which sounded like a species of rambunctious munchkins, and took another gulp of coffee.

Gavin took a fresh batch of blueberry corn muffins out of the oven, and their scent made my cheeks pucker with desire and my stomach growl so loud that he and Liz laughed. Gavin gingerly plied a muffin from the tin, placed it on a saucer, and slid it down the counter with just enough force that it landed right in front of me. "You might want to let it cool," he said. But I couldn't wait. I tore off the crusty top, smeared it with butter, and stuffed it in my mouth. I hadn't finished the last bite before I took another.

"Come on, piglet," Liz said, "we have to wipe down the chairs in the garden."

I ate another bite, grabbed a clean rag from the stack under the sink, and followed Liz outside. Eight wrought-iron tables with matching chairs sat nestled in dewy green grass, awaiting sweethearts. They were surrounded by hedges, roses, and bushes that looked like they had blue pom-poms on them. A gray rabbit hopped across the lawn and into a bush with pink berries, right next to the window I'd propped open with the Emily Dickinson book.

"You didn't have any visitors last night, did you?" Liz asked as she wiped off the tables.

"No," I said. Gavin emerged with some clippers from the back door and was headed down the brick path, past the gurgling fountain, to the rosebushes, no doubt to make an arrangement for the buffet table. "What do you mean?"

"Don't scare her," Gavin said as he passed, smelling faintly of patchouli oil.

"It's only fair that I warn her about Mr. Whiskers," she said.

"Do you have a cat here?" I asked.

"Better. A ghost," Liz said. "An old sea captain with a great, bushy beard." She stuck out her chin and gestured as to the bigness of the beard.

"I've worked here eight years and I've never seen him," Gavin said as he inspected a rose for clipping. *Huh. I thought Gavin owned this place.*

"I don't believe in ghosts," I said. I never have. It always seemed like there was too much in real life I was supposed to be afraid of: drunk drivers, rapists, unwanted pregnancy, HPV, undercooked chicken, toxic shock syndrome, and a bad reputation. I just couldn't add the unseen and paranormal to my list. Besides, there was always someone with one eye open sliding the thing across the Ouija board, someone's brother outside the tent making the footsteps or wagging the flashlight under his pimply chin.

"But he's heard the ghost," Liz said. "Heard the door latch opening and closing."

"Could've been the wind," Gavin said, moving on to the pom-pom flowers.

Liz looked up from the chair she was drying. "Opening a latch?"

"Liz, if you scare away Cricket like you did Rebecca, I won't hire anyone else. You'll be stuck doing this alone."

"Twice the tips for me, then," she muttered.

"Have you actually seen this ghost?" I asked Liz.

"No, but one of the guests saw him. Standing by the stairs in an old-fashioned mac, he was."

"That's a raincoat to you and me," Gavin said.

"He looked in her direction," Liz continued, "but it was more like he was looking *through* her, and then he turned around very slowly, and as he walked up the stairs she saw he was floating, for"—she slowed down her speech—"he had no feet."

"Ew," I said, a little creeped out. "But wait, was she high?"

"Good question," Gavin said. "Yes, probably. Also, Liz didn't hear this story directly. It was told to us by the woman's friend, who was stoned out of her gourd at breakfast."

Liz waved him away. "Anyway, I was in a gallery on Main Street, and they were doing a portrait show about old Nantucket."

"Don't tell me," I said, wiping the heart-shaped chair backs. "There was a picture of a bushy-bearded captain."

"Don't worry about the backs," Liz said. "You just need to do the seats. Anyway, yes. And under it was a grim account of how he'd fallen overboard, his legs tangled in ropes. He thought he'd seen a mermaid and was calling out to her. I'll spare you the details, but I will tell you this." She folded her arms, pausing for dramatic effect. "Lost his feet at sea."

I laughed aloud.

"Fine, don't believe me," she said, and inhaled sharply, her nose in the air. "But don't come crying to me when you bump into a gimpy, transparent sea captain on your way to the loo."

Gavin turned to Liz, a bouquet in his hand. "It's almost seven, we have two couples trying to make the seven-thirty boat, and you still need to set up the creamers and the napkins. Could you *try* to focus?"

Liz plucked a rose from the bouquet and stuck it behind her ear, turned on her heel, and sashayed inside.

"Don't listen to her," Gavin said. "Nantucket is full of people who know someone who's seen a ghost, but I have yet to meet anyone who actually has."

"I'm not worried," I said, checking to make sure the address Zack had written was still on my hand after handling the damp rag, and thought, At least not about ghosts.

Ten

BY THREE O'CLOCK, I WAS READY TO THROW IN THE cleaning rag. Vacuuming was no big deal—kind of satisfying to push the heavy thing (it was mustard yellow and dated back to the 1900s) across the floor and leave those stripes on the carpets. And dusting was a piece of cake. Changing the beds wasn't so bad, either; people had been sleeping in them for two days at the most. But I hated cleaning the bathrooms. There were certain smells, certain unmistakable dribbles and marks that inevitably evoked mental pictures of what had left them. The more I tried to block the pictures, the faster and stronger they came on. A few times, I thought I was actually going to barf.

And on the seats, in the bathtub, on the floor, and in the sink was hair. Hair, hair, hair! It was everywhere, and nine times out of ten, it was not the kind that grows on the head. I couldn't help but wonder what people did to shed so much in this region. Were they combing it daily, letting the hair just fall where it may? Did everyone do this but me?

The best part was checking the little tip envelopes on the dressers. Liz had drawn cartoon pictures of whales on them, with smiles and water spouting out their blowholes. Usually there were just a few dollars inside, but sometimes there was a five or a ten. We'd made nineteen bucks apiece in tips, and on top of my twelve dollars an hour, I'd made almost a hundred bucks in one day. It was no eight hundred a week, but it wasn't so bad, either. Liz warned me that the tips today were especially good; we'd had a lot of turnovers.

"Don't get too used to it," she said. "Usually we're lucky to get ten apiece."

We locked the last door at three o'clock, and flipped a nickel we'd found in the hallway for the first shower. Liz snatched the nickel in midair and slapped it against the back of her hand. "Heads, I win," she said. After her shower she was going to see her boyfriend, Shane, who worked at a bar on Jetties Beach. "He's twenty-three. An older man," she said as I followed her down the back steps to where our rooms were. "A tall, dashing Irishman who gives me free whiskey sours, calls me 'sexy delicious,' and reads Yeats in his free time."

Liz had a definite swagger. She was not a skinny girl; her boobs were big and unwieldy, and she had mom thighs with cellulite. She was wearing short shorts and a baby T anyway. She sauntered down the steps like a perfect hottie even though her pudge was poking out the top and bottom of her shorts. I felt a little rush of admiration for her confidence. I hated to admit it, but I couldn't imagine not caring what people thought about how I looked. It almost scared me to contemplate it.

"Shane sounds rad," I said, using a classic Jules word. We passed through the hallway where the supposed ghost liked to hang out, pausing in front of our bedroom doors.

"He's an absolute dream," Liz said, and went into her room.

I wondered what Jay read in his free time. I didn't know much about Yeats, but I knew it was impressive that Shane read him. If Shane called Liz sexy delicious, I bet they were having sex. It was too ridiculous a thing to say to someone if you weren't. I wondered if Jay and I would be having lots of sex by the end of the summer. I wondered what he'd call me. Was I sexy delicious? I worried I wasn't. Partially it was the word *sexy*, which just seemed funny, not real, not connected to an actual way of feeling.

"You want to meet me at the beach later tonight?" Liz asked, poking her head into my room without knocking. "It's really fun."

"Thanks," I said. "But I'm going to a party."

"Suit yourself," she said. "But Shane has friends." I doubted I'd be interested in anyone over eighteen.

When Liz was done, I took a long shower, using so

much soap that it was a mere sliver at the end of twenty minutes. Then I took a two-hour nap.

I texted Jules twice and she didn't respond. She's busy, I thought for the first hour, wondering if she'd gotten her job back at Needle and Thread, one of the high-end boutiques on Main Street. She's definitely mad at me, I thought around seven o'clock, when she didn't respond to my second text. I walked to the pizza place near the ferry because I wasn't sure what else to do for dinner. After I finished my pizza, I called her. I felt desperate, a feeling I hated. Jules didn't pick up. "Can I get a ride to the party with you?" I said to the dead air of her voicemail.

It was almost nine by the time she texted me back.

There's no room in the Jeep.

I felt a flash of anger, could almost hear it, like a sizzling pat of butter on a skillet. What the hell, I thought. She's blowing me off so hard that I'm getting windburn. There was another text:

Sorry ☹.

I gave the phone the finger, then took a deep breath. You're thinking like a desperate person, I said to myself. You're thinking like a Nora. Maybe there really is no room in the Jeep.

Besides, I didn't do anything wrong, I told myself as I clasped a necklace around my neck and squeezed into my nice jeans. I unpacked a green tank top that had once made a random guy stop me on the street to tell me my eyes looked like emeralds. I pinched my ears with delicate gold hoops.

I blew out my hair and swiped on shimmery lip gloss. I dusted my cheeks with some blush.

No room in the Jeep, no problem. Gavin had said it would be fine for me to borrow one of the inn's bikes as long as a guest wasn't using it, and 'Sconset was only six miles away by Milestone Road. It would probably only take me a half hour at the most. I chose a blue bike with a big basket. It looked kind of old, but it was the only one with a low-enough seat. As I rode the bike out of the garden, Gavin waved to me from the kitchen window, where he was cooking ratatouille for his chiropractor girlfriend, Melissa, a glass of red wine in his hand.

The moon was so bright, I had a shadow. There was something freeing about the whole thing, about getting myself there without waiting for someone to take me, about the air, which felt soft and smelled like hay, and listening to the invisible insects. Jeeps and mopeds sped past me, some of them blasting music, but there were long stretches of road that were quiet, just me, my breath, my shadow, and the sound of the wheels whirring on the pavement. The best part was that I wasn't afraid of being alone at night. This is why people come to Nantucket, I thought. So they don't have to be afraid at night.

I coasted around a rotary; 'Sconset was its own little town with a coffee shop, market, and the smallest post office I'd ever seen. I was in front of some kind of country club, the flags out front snapping in the wind. I remembered that I needed to bear right to get to Sand Dollar Lane. It wasn't long before I found it. It was pretty obvious where the party was, from the sounds of kids talking. The conversations were clear even a few houses away.

I hopped off of my bike and walked it down a driveway. My legs were wobbly and I was thirsty. My heart was beating fast, snapping like that country club flag, and my pretty green tank top was sticking to my back. I wished I'd brought a sweater. I wanted to cover up. As I was looking for a good place to put the bike (against the house? Inside the half-open garage?) I stumbled, my ankles suddenly soft as custard, and dropped the bike. It bounced off of a rock. Shit. I picked it up and placed it gingerly against the house. Pull it together, I thought, and applied more lip gloss. You're fine.

I heard Jules's laugh, her unmistakable "ha," and a chill went through me. I should've gotten back on the bike and turned around, because I actually did know then, the way you just know sometimes, what was about to happen. You didn't need a worry doctor to know that's what jelly legs are all about. But for some reason, even though it was blasting as loudly as a mattress commercial, I just couldn't hear the truth. So I straightened up and walked right into that party, practically begging for it.

Eleven

A LOUD TEXTURED BELCH CAME FROM THE FRONT PORCH.
It was so specifically disgusting, I could practically taste it.

"So, you're trying to say that there's a truth with a capital
T," the guy on the porch said to his friend as he watched me
approach. He was overweight, with a flat, smooched face,
but he wasn't acting like it. He was sitting there like some
kind of million-dollar man. It's not fair. Guys can embrace
their fatness as a unique personality trait, but we girls have
to sit on the very edge of chairs in our shorts so as not to
reveal the back-of-the-leg cellulite we feel bad for having
even though everyone does. Well, everyone but Jules.

"Absolutely, dude," Fitzy said, as cool and lean as a race-
horse. He was wearing '80s-style sunglasses even though
it was ten o'clock at night. "How else do you explain the

commonality of instincts for good and bad across wildly divergent cultures?"

I climbed the three stairs onto the porch. There was a bottle of Jim Beam between them, a pair of empty shot glasses, and plates with sandwich remains.

"I'm Oliver," the fat one in the Deerfield Academy shirt said with a little chin nod. Okay, so I guess this was his house.

"Uh, hi," I said. I stuck my sweaty hands in my pockets. "I'm Cricket."

His eyes widened, full of thoughts. "I've heard about you. You know a friend of mine, Jay Logan."

"Yeah," I said, shifting my weight, glad I'd worn my good jeans. "Is he here?"

"I know he's anxious to see you." Oliver laughed. "He should be here any minute. In the meantime, have at it." He opened the door and I stepped through.

Some sort of rap music was playing. . . . But wait, it wasn't rap. It was more mellow and sophisticated. And I heard un–raplike instruments. I wanted to find out who it was so that I could download it. This could be part of my summer sound track. I could add it to the Jay playlist.

Jules was right. This wasn't a big party. There were maybe twenty people here, and from the way they were lounging, leaning in door frames, draped on the furniture, on one another, I could tell they were all friends. I felt just a little foreign, like I was from Canada, or California.

Jules was sitting on the sofa holding a beer. She was wearing a little dress, and a Jack Rogers sandal dangled from her foot. She was tan, like she'd been at the beach all day. She also looked skinny—not anorexic or anything, just a tiny bit too thin. Actually, it was kind of the perfect amount. The pounds Jules had unnecessarily dropped made her features clearer, her cheekbones elegant. She looked older, that's what it was. Why hadn't I noticed last night?

Her Tiffany necklace dropped over the ridge of her clavicle and sparkled off center. She tried to cross her legs, but her crossing leg fell short. She swung her head back in a laugh. It took that extra effort for her to pull it back up, like the three pounds she'd lost had gathered in the ponytail spot. She was already drunk.

"Hey, Jules," I said as I took a seat on the sofa between her and another girl, who I recognized almost immediately as Parker Carmichael. She had long, shampoo-commercial hair. I'd seen pictures of her at Jules's house, and Jules talked about her sometimes. She was one of those horse girls who won jumping contests and had rock-hard thighs. Also, she was one of *the* Carmichaels, the big political family. The sofa felt a little snug for three people, but it was the only place to sit.

"Hey," Jules said, and took another sip of beer. She made eye contact with Parker, then flapped her hand around to introduce us. "Parker, Cricket; Cricket, Parker."

"Hi," we said at the same time with zero enthusiasm.

"So, is Zack here?" I asked, filling the awkward silence.

"Still working," Jules said, and wrinkled her brow. "How'd you get here?"

"I rode my bike," I said, and shrugged, sensing that I was the only one who'd arrived on two wheels. I'd worn sneakers because I always wore sneakers when I rode a bike. It was the safe thing to do. But all the other girls had delicate shoes and pedicured feet. My dirty white Converses didn't match the rest of me, which was kind of dressed up. And I was still a little sweaty. My bangs were sticking to my forehead. I felt the opposite of drunk. "So, where can I get a beer?"

"Kitchen," Jules said, not even looking at me. She stood up, put a hand on her hip. "Hey, where's Ginny? Is she on the trampoline?" she asked no one in particular.

"I think she's with Fitzy," Parker said. "Showing him those bodacious ta-tas." Parker and Jules burst into laughter.

"Seriously, they got so big this year," Jules said. "I've got to go get another look at them." She staggered forward, but her foot caught on the carpet. I leaped to catch her, but not fast enough. She fell backward and landed on the floor with her dress around her waist. Parker was nearly dry-heaving with laughter. Jules was laughing so hard she couldn't even sit up. She pounded the floor with her fists. I yanked her dress down over her freckled thighs.

"Nice thong," Parker said. "Leopard print." Now a couple of guys leaned in from the kitchen. Since when did Jules wear animal-print underwear? Or thongs? We'd read an article in one of those magazines about thongs and fecal matter, which had scared, well, the shit out of us.

"My bodacious cha-cha," Jules said, laughing so hard she was drooling.

"Jules, you need some water," I whispered. "You're really wasted."

"That's some good police work, Captain Cricket," Jules said, slapping me on the knee, then using her grip on my leg to hoist herself up. Parker rode a fresh wave of laughter and wiped tears from her eyes.

"Whatever," I said, stinging, and made my way to the kitchen to find a beer. This was an old house. It had wooden walls, low ceilings, and small, old furniture. There was a group of guys at the table. They had men's voices and men's hands. They were concentrating on a card game. Poker, I think.

"Do you have a bottle opener?" I asked, a cold beer in my hand.

"It's a twist-off," one of them said without even looking at me.

"Oh. Thanks." I twisted the top off and wondered what my next move would be now that I had the beer. I was about to make my way back out to the front porch when I saw that Jay had arrived. He looked gorgeous, with a new haircut and a tan that had a little bit of sunburn in it. He had such a nice body. He didn't have a girl butt or anything, but unlike a lot of guys, he actually had one, and you could totally see it in his jeans. And he wasn't too tall, just the most perfect height for kissing on my tiptoes.

Also, he had muscles. I bet when he was in his lifeguard bathing suit, he had those diagonal lines that go from his hips down to his you know what. I almost called out to him, but I thought it would be better if he noticed me first, so I pretended to read the calendar that was hanging on the wall, figuring he'd definitely be coming this way for a beer. I was so excited to see Jay walking toward me, but when he saw me, he looked away with disgust, and moved past me to get a beer.

"Hi, Jay," I said, biting my lip to try to restrain a smile. He didn't seem to hear me. "Jay?"

"Don't talk to me, bitch," he said.

I was so stunned I couldn't move. I had never been called "bitch" before. With anger behind it, that word has knuckles. It has nails. Jay grabbed two beers and stepped past me, careful that not even our shirts brushed.

"Wait," I said, finding my voice and following him down the hallway toward the back door. "What is this about?"

He turned around so fast that I jumped a little. "You think my brother's a loser?" His face was red. His eyes were hard. He was squeezing the beers so tightly I thought the bottles might break.

"No," I said. My heart was pounding. My cheeks burned. Jules had told him that I'd said his brother was a loser for having a DUI and working at the bagel shop. He was looking at me with such intensity I couldn't lie. "I mean, I'm sorry. I didn't mean it."

"Who says shit like that?" He glared at me like I was

lower than dirt. I looked at the floor, grabbed my stomach. I felt dizzy and sick. I opened my mouth to speak, but nothing came out. He took a step backward and shook his head. "You know what? Forget it. I don't care what you think. I don't even want to bother getting angry at someone like you. It's not worth my time." He turned around and kicked open the back door with his foot. It slammed shut behind him.

Twelve

"CAN WE TALK?" I ASKED JULES. "OUTSIDE."

"Whoa. Sure." She stood, straightened her dress, and followed me out the door.

"Someone's in trouble," Parker sang, slapping her knees.

Jules turned to face her. "If I get killed out there, her name is Cricket Thompson and she's like, a really fast runner. So you may need to hop into the Jeep if you want to catch her. They call her 'Wheels' back in Provy."

I led us to the top of the driveway, where I thought we'd be out of earshot.

"You told Jay what I said about his brother?" I asked.

"It just kind of came out," she said.

"But I didn't actually mean it. You know I was joking. I like him, Jules. I really like him. You know that."

"You have to admit, it was a really mean thing to say," Jules said.

"But I was saying it to *you*. In private. I wasn't trying to be mean. You say mean things all the time. How could you tell him something like that?"

"Sorry," she said, not meaning it *at all*, and threw her hands in the air.

"And why are you acting like this?" I asked. "Saying that thing about police work? I was trying to help you. All I've tried to do is help you."

"I don't need your help," she said.

"You were making a fool out of yourself," I whispered.

"No. Those are my friends. I've known them forever. I've known them longer than I've known you." She crossed her arms and looked up at the sky, eyelids fluttering in frustration.

"She was just having a little fun." It was Parker. How long had she been standing there? "Don't you want her to have fun? Don't you think she deserves that?"

"Of course," I said, my voice rising. I clapped my hand to my chest. "I'm her best friend. Of course I want her to have fun."

"Are you a lesbian?" Parker asked, her head cocked, her magazine hair shining in the moonlight.

"Oh. My. God," I said, looking at Jules. "Jules? What the hell?"

"I want you to leave me alone, Cricket. I want you to stop bothering me." *I was bothering her?* The worst part was that she said it in this really calm, steady, grown-up voice. "You need to get your own life."

"Fine," I said, shaking. "Fine. I'll stop *bothering* you."

"I didn't want to have to say it. But you're like, making me, Cricket." Jules screwed her hands over her eyes. "I didn't want you to come here. I told you not to come."

It took all my strength to walk, not sprint, back down the driveway to get my bike. I felt hot, neon with pain, all lit up for everyone to see. My hands were trembling; I dropped the bike and it clanked against the drainpipe. Fitzy stood up.

"Is that chick okay?" he asked Oliver. Then called to me, "Hey, you okay?"

I waved awkwardly, not daring to speak, not risking public tears. My foot slipped twice on the pedal before I was able to push off, turn the wheels, and ride back into the night, alone.

I had wanted to be best friends with Jules since she'd come to Rosewood in the eighth grade. I'd been with the same group of girls for ten years already. I knew their handwriting, whether they chewed with their mouth open, and how they sneezed. So when on the first day of eighth grade, the social studies teacher asked us to find a partner with whom we'd be working for the next six weeks, I immediately turned to Jules, the new girl from New York.

From the moment we drew our time line, to the rap we wrote about Roger Williams, the founder of Rhode

Island, I liked the way I felt around Jules—like I was tipping backward in a chair, on the edge of falling. We thought that this was the best thing about an all-girls school. You could write a rap about Rhode Island history and not worry about what guys would say or if they thought it was lame. We decided it was funny, so it was funny.

It was Jules who made me cool. I'd been just a middle-of-the-pack girl before Jules. It was she who told me I was pretty, who convinced me to grow out my hair and cut my bangs and taught me about plucking my eyebrows and what a big difference the right pair of jeans could make. It was she who laughed hardest at my stories so that the other girls started laughing, too. It was Jules who told me to try out for varsity lacrosse as a freshman. "You're the only one in our class who's good enough," she'd said. And she was right. After a year of her looking at me like I was the prettiest, funniest, coolest girl in our class, I started to believe it, too.

As long as she was near me.

Thirteen

"AND THIS IS WHY MOST AMERICANS WON'T DO THIS JOB," Liz said as I turned in disgust from the dirty toilet in the honeymoon suite. "Or Brits, for that matter."

"But here we are," I said. "Confronted with skid marks."

"I can't believe these people are on their honeymoon." Liz shook her head and we promised each other we would never allow such things in our future marriages. "Once you let them see you pee, it's all downhill," she added. I nodded in agreement. I couldn't imagine letting a guy see me pee. Disgusting. Friends, yes. Boys, never.

I used a clean rag to wipe down the sink and thought of the young couple who had been smooching all through breakfast. The man had muscles you could see through his T-shirt, and the woman had perfect white teeth. "You'd think they'd have at least closed the seat," I said.

"Must be true love," Liz said, and snapped on the extra-long, yellow latex gloves. "Go tackle the bedroom. I've got this loo, but you have to get the next."

"Deal," I said, and went to plug in the vacuum cleaner.

For the past week, I'd been consumed by what had happened with Jules. While I was emptying the dishwasher, vacuuming the rugs, or tucking crisp sheets under the corner of a mattress, I was reviewing the scene, obsessing over each word, slowing the fight down, trying to get a grip on it, hoping to figure out exactly where it all went wrong. I'd expected her to call me with an apology, but there hadn't been a word.

The biggest question in my mind was . . . why? Why had Jules told Jay what I'd said about his brother? If she didn't want to hang out with me for some crime too great to be named, if I was *bothering* her, fine, okay. But to go and ruin my chance with Jay?

I tried to picture the moment she'd done it. Had she exaggerated my comment for a crowd, or had she said it to him with a sisterly pat on the arm, her voice low and dripping with concern, like, *Oh, Jay, this is something you should know?* I put the blanket the couple had left in a tangled heap on the floor back on the bed, but decided to vacuum around the clothes that were strewn everywhere. Was true love really this messy? Wait a second, I thought as I picked up a still-damp towel with my thumb and forefinger and dropped it in the laundry bag. Had Jules been flirting with

Jay? Oh my god, why hadn't I thought of that earlier?

This wave of anger, just like every other, was dragged back out to sea when I remembered that her mother had died. Her *mother*. *Died*. Even though she drove me crazy sometimes, the thought of losing my own mother made me feel like I had a dry cleaning bag over my head. But still. What the hell had I done except try to be good, except offer to help, except try to be there for my best friend at the worst moment of her life?

I switched on the TV to give my mind a break. Liz said it was fine as long as Gavin was out and we kept the volume way down. I thought I'd stumbled onto some local Nantucket channel when I saw Bradley Lucas standing in front of a big Nantucket house. Isn't that nice of Mr. Lucas, lending his talent to the local station, I thought as I bent to find the switch on the vacuum. But after a few seconds I realized this was no local TV station, but CNN. This was national news. As the shot widened, I saw other news vans in the background and a small crowd of people.

A banner ran at the bottom announcing the death of William "Boaty" Carmichael, the Massachusetts senator whose family vacationed here. He was famous for his boyish good looks and his weird nickname. He was also Parker's uncle. He was around my parents' age, with a baby face and blond curly hair. I remembered during one election season when my mother was driving me home from an away lacrosse game, somewhere near Boston. We passed a sign with Boaty Carmichael's picture on it.

"I'd vote for him," I said, prying some dirt from my cleats. "He's so handsome."

"That's no reason to elect a person," my mother said, a look of horror on her face. She saw a clump of dirt that had fallen from my cleat and added, "Stop that. This is my car, not a stable."

"I still think he's cute," I said, releasing my foot to the floor and tossing the hunk of dirt out the window.

"Really, Cricket? I'm sending you to an all-girls' school and you think it's a good idea to vote for a man *based on looks*? Do you know anything about him? About his policies?" She stepped on the accelerator.

"Mom!" I said, gripping the door as the driver of a silver minivan slammed on her brakes to avoid hitting us. "That was a stop sign."

Now I looked at the clip of him on the TV, shaking hands with the less handsome people of the world. He looked like such a great guy the way he made eye contact, smiling so vigorously his curls shook. As he leaned in to listen to a liver-spotted old lady, his blues eyes crinkled with friendliness.

"Liz, come here," I said.

"What happened?" Liz looked around the room to see if I'd broken or spilled something.

"On the TV. Senator Carmichael died. Heart attack."

"You're kidding," she said, and grabbed the remote off the quilt. She turned up the volume. "They're out by the family compound. Poor Boaty."

"You knew him?" With her swagger and that accent, Liz seemed capable of knowing senators, of knowing anyone she wanted to.

"He came here at least once a summer. Big muffin fan. Rhubarb was his favorite." She shook her head. "What a shame. He has those two small children." As if on cue, an old clip of the young family flashed on the screen, probably from the night he'd been elected. They were all dressed up and waving on a stage. I could see bits of Parker in them. I could see her toothy smile, the high cheekbones, and the big round eyes, all of which made the family seem part of a Disney movie. The Carmichael family possessed features that should have added up to beauty but somehow fell short. All except Boaty.

Now Parker and Jules would be more bonded than ever. I felt like curling up in the bed, pulling the sheets over my head, and taking a nap. And then I remembered that this was probably where the honeymooners were having sex all night long, so I leaned forward and put my head in my hands.

"Don't take it so hard," Liz said, patting my back. "His brother will surely take his place."

Fourteen

LATER, I RODE THE BLUE BIKE THAT BY NOW HAD SORT OF become mine into town, where faces were downcast, heads were bowed, and hands were shoved into brightly colored pockets. All the children tucked closer into the sides of their parents. My mother's dislike of Boaty Carmichael was a buffer against all the solemn, complimentary chatter, making me feel like less of a Nantucket person than ever. "A loss for the whole country." "On his way to the White House." "Nantucket's son, *America's* son." I was afraid if anyone looked at me for a second too long they'd be able to tell that my mother hated the guy.

I saw a short dress in the window of a boutique. It was a slim, silk, one-shouldered number with a thin gold belt around the waist. It filled me with hope, and I decided to try it on to cheer myself up. I went into the store, which was empty except for the saleslady, who looked pale despite her tan. She held a tissue to her lips as she watched the TV, the same loop I'd seen earlier, reviewing the same news.

"Can I try this on?" I asked. She nodded vaguely in my direction, her eyes glued to the TV, then dabbed her reddened nose with the shredded tissue. I felt like a criminal for smiling.

Once in the dressing room with the canvas curtain closed, I slipped the dress over my head. The cool silk kissed my skin and skimmed my body. It hit my mid-thigh, flirting with being too short but staying, somehow, classy beyond a doubt. I peeled off my sweaty socks and slid my feet into a pair of strappy gold heels that were under the bench, waiting for me. The high waist made my legs look longer, and the deep emerald green brought out the blond streaks in my hair, which I took out of my ponytail and shook to my shoulders. The one bare shoulder was the secret, the reveal. I look like I could be on TV, I thought, turning to see the back. I look like I could be famous. If I wore this dress it would be impossible for anyone to make me feel bad. Powers would shift.

I checked out the price tag dangling beneath my armpit. Four hundred and ninety-five dollars! That was more than a week's pay. I thought about how difficult my first week had been. My elbows were sore from scrubbing, my hands felt rougher from the various cleaning chemicals. My summer earnings were the only money I had all year for trips to the movies, clothes that weren't uniforms, and my cell phone bill. But I wanted this so badly that my wanting began to grow a life of its own. I unzipped carefully, leaning forward and rounding my back to pull the dress over my head, trying not to touch the silk too much, afraid to matte its gloss. I sat on the bench to think.

The bell that hung over the front door rang faintly.

"Hi, doll," said the saleslady. Her voice was surprisingly rough: a smoker, a drinker, or maybe a yeller.

"Hey, Nan." That voice I knew. It was Jules. It was her *talking to a grown-up she didn't like but had to be nice to* voice. I went pale, stuck my hands in my armpits, felt lightheaded. I lifted my bare feet from the ground onto the little bench, my toes as cold as frozen peas. As much as I wanted to run into her, as much as I wanted to force her to face me, as much as I wanted to ask her why she'd done what she'd done and said what she'd said; as much as I wanted to scream and cry and really have it out with her, I couldn't seem to move from this shell shape. I felt stupid for being here all by myself and trying on a dress without an occasion. What would I say I was shopping for? Next year's Spring Dance? I could smell my deodorant. I could smell Formula 409 in my fingernails.

"I just came in for my check," Jules said. "Anyone come in today?"

Of course: this was where she worked! I glanced at the price tag on the dress where the name of the store was printed in pink: Needle and Thread. How had I not noticed? How had I not put it together?

"There's someone in the dressing room, with the Chloé dress, I think."

"Great dress," Jules said, under her breath. They whispered something to each other that I couldn't make out. Then Jules sighed, and I imagined one hand was on her hip, because that's usually how she stands when she sighs like that. From the silence, it seemed like they were watching the TV.

"Can you believe this?" Nan asked, and blew her nose.

"It's so sad. You know Parker Carmichael is my best friend." My stomach twisted. I clutched my knees. Parker wasn't her best friend! Parker didn't know how worried she got about her skin, that she went to the dermatologist sometimes once a week for treatments to prevent a relapse of the acne that had plagued her for a semester our freshman year. Parker didn't know that even though Jules had the quickest comebacks, trying to conjugate French verbs could make her cry with frustration. She didn't know that she had a team of tutors and even then couldn't get above a B in pretty much anything; that she had failed her driver's-ed test three times. Parker didn't know that she actually had hooked up with Jeremy Stein sophomore year at the Winter Ball, even though she denied it so much and so often that by now even she believed it hadn't happened. No one knew that stuff but me.

"Oh, poor girl," said Nan.

"Are you going to close the shop this week?" Jules asked. I could hear the hope in her voice. Jules liked having a job but hated the working part.

"In July? Are you kidding me?" Sadness vanished from the woman's voice. "I'll see you tomorrow."

Jules thanked her for the check, and I heard the bells jingle softly.

I waited a few minutes, soundlessly got dressed, left the dress on the hanger in the dressing room, and fled.

I hopped on my bike and cruised out of town, in the opposite direction of Jules's house. It was hot—the air thick with future rain—and sweat prickled my upper lip. I followed one of those hand-painted-looking signs to Jetties Beach, where I thought maybe I'd find Liz. But when I got there, there was a group of kids my age, the girls with their arms slung around each other. Was Jules among them? I couldn't risk it. I turned around and headed up a cobblestone hill bordered by a wall of golden moss.

It didn't matter how good my grades were or that I'd made varsity as a freshman; it didn't matter how carefully, how perfectly, I'd managed my popularity; it didn't matter that I'd measured and doled out my flirtations like teaspoons of sugar—never too much to be a tease, always enough to be sweet. Jules was able to take my happiness away from me with one swift betrayal. My social life had slid from good to bad like a hockey puck across a rink. It wasn't fair. I wanted to take her to friend court. I wanted to sue her. But I could see the faces of the jury when it was revealed that her mother had just died. *Died.*

I coasted on a quiet little cul-de-sac, peering over

hedges, looking at the huge estates, all of them with their flags at half mast. I was wishing I were that kind of rich, the kind where people have to respect you, because that's what money does. It makes people shut up. It means you live in the big house, throw the cool birthday parties, belong to the country club that has its own jokes, its own dances; take awesome vacations, go skiing enough to get really good at it, own the best clothes, get the green dress.

I was thinking about how being rich was protection, armor, authority, a cushion, a parachute, something to fall back on when the rest of your life sucked. I was pedaling slowly and looking at the biggest house on the street, gazing upward into its turret, pretending I lived there with a three-hundred-and-sixty-five-degree ocean view, a telescope, and a Jacuzzi, when a huge black Navigator peeled out of nowhere, swerved to avoid me, and screeched to a halt an inch from my body. I froze, wincing, shutting my eyes against the spray of gravel and the heat from the car's engine. A big mean man with fat baby cheeks and a white baseball hat leaned on his horn. The sound moved through my muscles, pulsing the marrow in my bones.

"Get out of the street," he said, shaking a fist at me, his complexion ruddy with anger.

I got off my bike and jogged it to the sidewalk. I let the bike fall on the grass and sat, my head in my hands, waiting for the man to drive away. I wouldn't look at him, but I could feel him looking at me, his anger like a scorching ray of sun.

"Fuckin' idiot," he said. My legs were shaking. My throat was dry. I was past crying. "You tryin' to get yourself killed? Stay on the sidewalk."

"You slow down, Mr. Big Shot!" shouted an old woman in tennis whites walking an even older-looking standard poodle, one hand cupped around her mouth like a megaphone. She had wobbly knees on legs so tanned they looked like they'd stepped on the tennis court in 1975 and never stepped off. "New Yorkers," she said, eyes narrowed, catching his license plate as the car turned down the hill. Her mouth was pinched, like she'd just chewed a lemon. And I wasn't sure if she was talking to the poodle or me. "Well, you're okay," she said. I nodded quickly. "He was completely out of order. You're not *supposed* to ride your bicycle on the sidewalk."

As she walked past me on her long, old, freckled legs, her proud standard poodle strutting beside her, I wondered how it was that on this tiny island off Massachusetts, with its candy-cane lighthouse, church bells on the hour, daffodils, and ice-cream cones, nowhere felt safe.

Fifteen

I COULDN'T SLEEP THAT NIGHT. MY NERVES WERE JANGLING from almost being hit by that Navigator. There was a fluttery, unsettling lightness in my body that made me want to hug myself just to feel my own weight. The pillow was too squishy and the sheets were scratchy against my skin. I tried counting the roses on the wallpaper, but I couldn't get past ten without my mind wandering back to Jules or Jay.

Earlier that day, I'd bought a chutney-and-cheddar sandwich from Something Natural, a place Gavin said was the best on the island. The thing was so huge it was like two sandwiches, and I'd only been able to eat a quarter of it, saving the rest for later. That sandwich seemed like the best thing in the world around 2 a.m., when my stomach remembered about lunch and dinner and was demanding both. I walked quietly into the dark kitchen and opened the refrigerator, which Gavin kept gleaming and clean. Where was my sandwich? My perfect, delicious sandwich, full of such odd flavors I almost couldn't believe I liked it. I'd put it right here, I thought, touching the empty shelf as if the sandwich were only momentarily invisible. I opened the crisper and the meats-and-cheeses drawer, mystified in the cold breath of the refrigerator.

Behind me, the floor creaked, though softer than when Liz was marching around the kitchen—almost as if it were bending under the weight of cat or a child. It creaked again, even more softly, as if it weren't really being stepped on but moved over. Oh my god. I heard breathing. I froze, my feet nailed to the floor. A cool, silvery sweat lined my body. *I don't believe in ghosts*, I told myself as I stared ahead. But the chords of my neck were as stiff as cables. My heart was thwacking. I let go of the fridge door and told my feet to *move*. My eyes shifted to the kitchen door, which had swung shut behind me on my way in, and I wondered if my lead arms would be able to push it open as I took my first giant step toward it.

"Hey, didn't mean to scare you," said a voice.

I flung my hand on the light switch, an act of bravery worthy of getting my picture in the paper. My other hand rested on my jumping heart. I turned to see a guy with messy brown hair, a crooked smile, and a wrinkled shirt sitting at the kitchen table. His back was to me, and he was twisted around in his seat, chewing. A pair of crutches leaned against the table.

"I'm George Gust," he said, wiping his mouth with a napkin. He looked too old for college but too young to be a dad. "Are you staying here, too?"

"I work here." I leaned against the wall and took deep breaths. "Sorry, I thought you were a ghost."

"Is this place haunted?" he asked, completely serious.

"Supposedly. I don't believe it, though."

He raised an eyebrow, like, *Sure you don't.* "Well, I apologize again. I thought at first you were sleepwalking, and you know how they say you should never wake up a sleepwalker? Anyway, my bad." He wiped his hand on his jeans and extended it. "I didn't catch your name."

"I'm Cricket Thompson," I said, taking his hand and catching a full view of his plate. "And you're eating my sandwich."

Sixteen

"I HAVE A WHOLE MONTH TO MAKE THIS UP TO YOU,"
George Gust said as he swallowed the last bite, explaining
that he was staying in the annex, a little studio cottage in
the backyard, for all of July and probably August, too. We
sat there talking for at least a half hour. He seemed to have
a lot of talking in him, and I wasn't exactly dying to get back
to my rose-covered chamber. He was writing a biography of
Senator William "Boaty" Carmichael. He'd sold his idea to
a big publishing house over a year ago and had been taking
his sweet time. But with the latest news, his editors were
pushing for a draft by the end of August. He was staying at
the inn to do research and to write his ass off.

"I don't know how I'm going to do it," he said, his forehead crimping. "Especially with a broken leg."

"But you don't write with your leg." I grabbed one of Liz's beloved key-lime-pie-flavored yogurts (or, as she said, "yah-gurts") from the fridge. She loved this stuff. I thought it tasted like whipped soap, but it was pretty much my only option tonight. Luckily, it was her day off tomorrow and she was at Shane's, so I'd have time to replace it before she noticed.

"But everything takes me twice as long," the man said. "Buying a cup of coffee is like a half-hour adventure. And I need to interview people. I can't drive. It sucks." He shook his head. "Are you a night owl, too?" He crumpled the butcher paper the sandwich had been wrapped in into a ball.

"Not usually. Can't sleep."

George aimed the paper ball toward the garbage. It landed next to the dishwasher. "I've never been good at that," he said. "I've never been the guy who makes the basket with my trash unless I'm right next to it."

"And this bothers you?" I polished off the yogurt and washed the spoon.

"You know, it kinda does. I'd really like to be one of those guys. Everyone would say, 'he shoots, he scores,' and I'd feel like a big deal just for throwing something out."

I took five steps backward, assumed a basketball pose, and tossed the empty yogurt container directly into the bin.

"You're one of those guys," he said.

"One of those girls." I picked up his paper ball and handed it back to him. "You need a loose wrist." He rolled his wrist around. "Now, you've got to look where you want it to land." George narrowed his eyes at the trash can. "Just kind of put yourself in that place."

"In the trash?"

I laughed. "Yup."

"I'm there," he said. "It's not pretty, but I'm there." He lifted his arm to throw.

"Okay, now keep your eyes on the can and trust. Trust that your arm knows when to release." I was pretty much quoting Miss Kang directly. He reared back his arm, took a breath, and shot.

"He shoots, he scores," I said as the butcher paper landed in the trash.

"Look at that." He clapped once, smiling broadly. "Thanks!"

"You just needed a coach," I said, and shrugged. He stood up, balancing on one leg as he grabbed his crutches.

"What I really need," he said, as he hobbled toward the stairs and used the butt of his crutch to push the door, "is an intern."

Seventeen

"SHE LISTENS TO THE JESUS STATION SO LOUDLY THAT YOU might find yourself converted by the end of the day," Liz said. We were standing at the window, watching Bernadette walk around the inn to the kitchen door. Bernadette was the chambermaid who worked when Liz or I had the day off. She wore a little radio fastened around her waist. It had old-fashioned headphones that covered her ears entirely, lobes included. Today was Liz's day off, and my first time working without her. I already missed her.

I didn't know where Bernadette lived, but she arrived at the inn via an old van with tinted windows. It dropped her off, then rattled away. "She thinks we're lazy, and she's not afraid to tell us."

"I'm not lazy," I said. I had straight A's, excluding math but including physics.

"Well, she thinks so. Oh, and there's one more thing." Liz poured herself coffee in one of the to-go cups we gave to guests who were headed to the ferry. "She doesn't take a lunch break and she'll yell at you if you do. So eat up while you can."

"She can't yell at us for taking a lunch break," I said. "That's like, illegal, I think. Does Gavin know about that?"

"He loves her." She laughed. "It's a love that springs from fear, but he says Bernadette is the only one who gets this place truly clean."

"So why doesn't she work here full-time if he loves her so much?" I asked.

"She refuses to work anywhere more than twice a week. Considers herself freelance. That way she maintains her autonomy." She patted my hand. "Just remember, it's better to work straight through to the end or eat something quick when she's on her cigarette break."

"No lunch break for us, but she takes a cigarette break?" I said with a full mouth of muffin.

"Look on the bright side. You'll be done early. Ta-ta," Liz said, and flounced out the door, twirling her bikini around her finger. I took another slug of coffee as Bernadette walked through the door, took me in, sighed disappointedly, and headed for the laundry room. We had a big day ahead;

almost all the rooms were turnovers. I stuck the rest of the scone in the pocket of my apron.

Bernadette emerged from the laundry room with an armload of clean rags. "Put down your coffee. It's time to work, girl."

I took one last gulp and chucked the rest down the sink.

Okay, fine, I'm lazy, I thought, three hours later, shaking with hunger, covered in a fine mélange of sweat, filth, and Lysol, and on the verge of tears. Bernadette cleaned so hard it was like she saw the devil's face in the toilet bowl and his asshole in the shower drains. She could snap sheets onto beds with one jerk of her long arms—her quick, cracked hands folding hospital corners too fast for me to understand how she did it.

She appeared to be ignoring me, but at the same time I felt like I was being watched by the FBI. I'd leave a room, thinking I was done, and she'd go back in and check over my work. Inevitably, she'd come out of what I thought was a perfectly clean room shaking her head and sucking air through her teeth. I'd missed some scum in the caulking around the tub, grime in the corner of bathroom floors, perhaps a bit of dust along the baseboard.

"You girls are so lazy," she said, checking under a bed I'd just made. "Look under there." I got on my hands and knees to peer under the dust ruffle. A man-eating dust bunny stared back at me. The worst part was that I *had* actually swept under there. "Go on, get it."

"With what?" I asked. I had stopped trying to be nice. "Broom won't work at this angle."

"With the hands the Good Lord gave you."

As I crept on my elbows like an alligator in a swamp, my head brushing the bottom of the box spring, I wondered what the hell I was doing on Nantucket. This job sucked. My best friend and the guy I liked both hated me. I reached for the dust ball, and feeling my own soft arm against my cheek, lay my head on it for a moment. This small, protected part of me still smelled sweet, still felt pretty. I held my breath to keep from crying. I missed Jules, who I wasn't going to be able to tell this story to. Without a best friend to tell stories to, it almost didn't matter if they even happened.

"Get your head out of the clouds," Bernadette said to me, grabbed my ankle, and yanked on it. My elbows burned on the wooden floor. I pursed my lips and twisted my head to keep from literally mopping the floor with my lips. I pushed myself all the way out.

"I'm taking a cigarette break. Here." I handed her the dust monster. I stormed down the stairs, not making eye contact with a sunburned couple, back early from the beach, their eyes full of concern as I stomped past them.

I sat in the shade of the bike shed, on a stone that faced away from the backyard to the hedges, wanting to quit so badly. I shut my eyes. I could do it. But if I did, I'd just be back at home, back with Mom and her white wine, her phone that didn't ring, her furrowed brow, and eight-thirty bedtimes. I'd be back to Dad's new life, to his new house, where the floors were made of eggshells, and Alexi's temper bombs ticked in every corner. In his new family I had to be polite all the time, like he was someone else's dad, which he was now.

It was better to stay here. It was better to try to make things work. I just needed to turn things around. I remembered Jenna Garbetti, the shy, big-boobed senior from a few years ago who had turned around her bad reputation by disappearing from the social scene, getting a new look, and focusing on her studies. If there was ever a time to use the Jenna Garbetti method, it was now.

Lie low, look good, and learn, I said to myself. I was already lying low, I thought. I lifted the twig in the air, pretending to smoke it like a cigarette in case Bernadette was watching. I couldn't lie much lower than this. I just needed to figure out how to achieve the other two. I stood up and moved around the shed so that I could stand in the sun. I saw George coming around the corner on his crutches, a bag from Something Natural in his hand. I dropped the twig.

"Just the person I was looking for," he said. "Your sandwich."

"Mmm, lunch," I said, and took the bag. "I really needed this today."

"Well, good. There's a cookie in there, too." He smiled in a way that made me feel like my old confident self again. "I don't know how you feel about chocolate chip. Bought it on spec."

"Yum. Um, hey listen, so I was thinking"—this took some courage—"that I could be your intern. I have straight A's, except in math, and English is my best subject."

He smiled. "Don't you already have a job?"

"I get off at three o'clock. You said last night that you're not even functional until one."

"That's true. But I can't exactly pay you," he said, his forehead crinkling.

"I just want my name somewhere in the book. Like the thank-you section?"

"That wouldn't be a problem at all."

"We could try it out and see if it works." I shrugged.

"This is called marketing," he said. "You've just sold me." We shook hands.

"I have to go; my cigarette break is almost over."

"You smoke?" he asked.

"No, but don't tell." George looked confused. "Long story."

"Got it. We'll talk later today, then? Iron out the details?"

I nodded. *Lie low, look good, and learn.* I was two-thirds of the way there.

After I finished with Bernadette, who wouldn't even look at me, I went back to Needle and Thread. I peeked in the window of the tiny shop to make sure that Jules wasn't there, and then I bought the dress. It was a whole paycheck, but if I was going to make the Jenna Garbetti method work, I had to go all the way. I carried the bag back to the inn, peeking into the tissue paper a few times to make sure it hadn't disappeared on me. It was twilight, the crickets were chirping, and the air smelled like flowers. Thank you, Jenna Garbetti, I thought. I hoped she'd grown her hair long again, that she was in love with a guy who loved her back, and that her life at Yale was nothing less than beautiful.

Eighteen

THE NEXT DAY WAS MY DAY OFF—MY TURN TO WALK OUT the door in my bikini, with a big Saturday smile on my lips on a Tuesday morning. George, having probably finally crashed when the sun rose, was going to be asleep until at least noon, so I had the whole morning to myself. It's better to have the morning to yourself than the evening. You don't have to feel lonely when you're alone in the morning.

I wanted to go to the beach. I'd already been on Nantucket for ten days and still hadn't gone in the actual ocean. On a run the other night, I'd found myself back on the street where I'd had my brush with the Navigator. I hadn't meant to, but I'd somehow just wound up there. That's when I discovered the path to Steps Beach. I noticed a few people with beach chairs emerging from what looked like someone's backyard. I jogged over. "Welcome to Steps Beach" was engraved on a rock. I followed a leafy path where a few people had left their bikes leaning unlocked against an old twisty-wood fence, and others had shed their flip-flops mid-walk, one in front of the other, staggered like footprints. There was a set of steep stairs that went down to the sand. Then there was one little dune to climb, a mound of low green bushes, tangled roses, sun-bleached, hay-colored grass, and red berries. The path split in two around it and opened up to a field of warm sand and a calm slice of ocean.

Today there were about fifteen people there, all spread out: a few pretty moms playing with their naked babies, a group of old ladies under the shade of umbrellas in their skirted suits, a fully dressed couple, pants rolled up, lying on their stomachs, sifting sand between their fingers. A few people walked in the distance. I lifted my beach towel to the breeze and spread it on the perfect spot, off to the side but not too close to the little fence, and about halfway to the water. I watched a single sailboat glide on the horizon's rim.

That's when I noticed the color of the water. It was a million different shades at once, changing with the few clouds that floated above, darkening with depth, reflecting the deep canyons and sandbar stripes below the surface; but in the distance, in a wide, sparkling, uniform band, was a color peeled from the hot summer sky and chilled by the sea. It was cool and bright, brand new, and yet so familiar. It was the exact color of Jules's bedroom. Nantucket blue.

Would I ever get to sit in her bedroom again? I didn't know. But if I did, it would never be the same, not after our fight, not without Nina.

I sat on my towel, let the sun drip into my bones, and combed the sand with my toes. This was my day off, I reminded myself, my Saturday on a Tuesday. I leafed though the *Us Weekly* I'd bought at the Hub on my way over here, but then decided that I might as well take a crack at Emily Dickinson. Since fifth grade, we'd had to read at least one poem of hers a year. I'd never really understood what made her so famous. What did she really have to write about, hiding alone in her Amherst attic all the time? I unfolded the paper with the list of poems we were supposed to read and opened the book.

It was filled with my mother's familiar loopy handwriting in what appeared to be letters to Emily Dickinson. Mrs. Hart had wanted us to get this special edition because there was only one poem per page, leaving lots of white space for our "thoughts, reflections, and in-depth analysis of this American genius." At first I thought that Mom had just had a lot to say about Emily Dickinson, that she was not only a secret fan of the poet, but some kind of Emily fanatic. But when I looked closer, I saw dates, dashes, *fucks*, *shits*, exclamation points, Aerosmith lyrics—this wasn't poetry analysis. This was her diary. I flipped on my stomach and turned to the title page.

6.30.84

Dear Emily D.,

Since Aunt Betty reads my diary, since she basically admitted it over her third gin and tonic on the porch last night, I've decided to write here, in your book, where Aunt Betty will never look. She told me she always hated your work. Don't take it personally—she's sexist! So, all my secrets will go right here. This will be like putting my pearls in the freezer to hide them from thieves. I feel better already! I need to write down my thoughts because I'm completely busting at the seams, bursting with the best news. After years of loneliness and desperation, I am here to report that I, Kate Campbell, am in the process of falling in LOVE. I can't write his name in case this document is discovered, but I met him today, so I will call him Lover Boy. He is THE ONE. I can feel it. I need to record this, as this is, without a doubt, going to be the best summer of my life. He's not a preppy guy. He's actually kind of a guido. But you know what? I like it! Aunt Betty, if you are reading this, put it down or risk being totally scandalized! Hee, hee, hee.

I closed the book. Took a breath. Opened it again randomly.

I ran into him at the A&P. We smiled at each other and pretended to be chatting casually, but he was totally undressing me with his eyes again. I took off those jean shorts of his with my baby blues. I'll take them off for real soon!

OMG. I flipped again. And this time the book opened to a photo of a guy sleeping on his stomach naked. I put a hand over my mouth. My mother was a slut! And kind of a funny one.

"Hey, what are you reading?" I flinched and looked up to see Zack, dripping wet, a beach towel slung low around his hips.

"Poetry," I said, and slammed the book shut. If Zack was here, then maybe Jules was, too. I squinted and looked across the beach. Was she on her way down? My chest contracted, pulled tight as if by an invisible corset.

"Are you okay?" he asked.

"Yeah," I said, shoving the book into my bag and grabbing a bottle of water. It took a couple of tries for my nervous fingers to unscrew the cap. "Who are you with?"

"No one," he said, smiling at me with bemusement.

"You're alone?"

"Yup," he said. I exhaled and guzzled some water. "That must have been some poetry." He ran his hand over his face, flicked away some water. "You were pretty into it. And now you're . . . kind of a mess."

"Well, Emily Dickinson is an American genius," I said.

"Guess so," he said, and laughed. I laughed, too. Partially out of relief that Jules wasn't here, and partially because I knew I'd sounded so serious about Emily Dickinson.

"I'm going to have to see if they have another copy at the library," he said. Then he took off his towel and wiped down the rest of his body, which I had to admit, was really nice. Soccer player nice. "Are you looking at my nipples?"

"What? Zack. No. So, what are you doing here?"

He opened his arms in a gesture like, *What does it look like I'm doing?*

"I just felt like going for a dip. I like this beach. It's quiet and I know I won't run into anyone."

"Except me," I said.

"I don't mind that," he said, and smiled. "That's a good thing." I jammed my heels in the sand, biting my smile. "What are you doing on Saturday?"

"What's Saturday?"

"Fourth of July?"

"Oh, I don't know," I said. Shit. I kept trying to forget about it. It loomed. A national holiday I was going to have to spend alone. I'd overheard Liz saying something about a party. Maybe I could tag along. "I might be going to a party on a beach. Nober . . . Nobersomething."

"Nobadeer?" His eyebrows rose. I nodded. "Careful. Those things can be kind of crazy. And the police are going to be everywhere this year."

"Police? Well, I'm not sure yet." I buried my feet, patted the sand over them. "What are you doing?"

"Did you meet Fitzy?" he asked. I nodded, shading my eyes with my hand as I looked up at him. "He's having a little party on his dad's boat. That's where Jules and Parker and everyone is going."

"That's cool," I said, trying to sound neutral. I wondered what Jules had told him about the fight, but didn't want to ask. It would've been almost worse if she hadn't said anything at all. It occurred to me that Jules had erased me from her life, that she wasn't thinking of me, that she had so much going on with Parker that she hadn't noticed my absence. That she hadn't actually been affected by it.

"Seems boring to me. I don't know if it's my scene." He looked out at the ocean. "Are you going to go in?"

"I don't know," I said, and stood up. I dusted some sand off my butt, then lifted my arms out to the side, feeling the air. "I'm not quite hot enough."

"Oh, you're hot enough." It took a second for it to sink in. He was smiling in this goofy, adorable way. I opened my mouth, but he spoke first. "I'll race you to that rock out there." I followed his gaze to the top of a rock not too far out.

"Okay." Zack drew a line in the sand with his toe and we struck runner's poses. "On your mark, get set, go!"

We were both grinning like idiots as we took off, though it was clear by the time we hit the water that Zack was going to win. Bikinis aren't exactly made for racing.

Nineteen

"SHANE AND I GOT IN A MASSIVE FIGHT LAST NIGHT ABOUT the Fourth of July," Liz said the next day as we made the beds. "He wants to go do a little backyard barbecue with just a couple of mates, and I want to go to the party on Nobadeer." I'd been asking her about Fourth of July all morning, hoping for an invitation, and she hadn't seemed to pick up on it. "But I really don't mind the fighting all that much because the makeup sex is fabulous."

"That's awesome," I said, as if I had a clue. The truth was that I wasn't exactly experienced. I'd only been to third base once with Greg Goldberg last fall, after we'd dated for three whole months. I hated to admit it, but I hadn't actually felt anything that great. I thought that when a boy touched you it would feel amazing, but instead it was like he was programming his DVR with my vagina. I wondered if something was wrong with me. I could do this to myself, I'd thought, and not in *that* kind of a way, not in a *touching myself* kind of way. I just wasn't into that, either, even though we'd been told in seventh grade by Mrs. Levander, the school's sixty-nine-year-old nurse and self-declared earth mama, that there was *nothing wrong with that.* That we wouldn't go cross-eyed or blind if we touched our "area," no matter what anyone told us.

That's what they told me," she'd said, shaking her head. "And I have twenty-twenty vision. Believe you me, I should be blind as a bat!" She threw her head back in a laugh. All of us were biting our cheeks or doodling in our notebooks with a kind of glazed-over madness.

"Ooookay," she'd said after realizing she was having a moment entirely separate from the rest of us. "Let's see what difficult questions we have today." She drew a question from the "difficult questions" box. It was a shoe box covered with shiny green wrapping paper where we were supposed to put anonymous, sex-related questions.

Mrs. Levander's eyebrows rose and she made an O with her lips. "Here's an interesting one. 'What does horny mean?' Anyone want to share?" We couldn't take it, we all laughed. I laughed hardest, of course, because it was my question.

I was beginning to think that Liz and Mrs. Levander would really get along by the way Liz was going on and on in graphic detail.

"This is the best sex of my life," Liz said as she unfolded

a fresh duvet cover. We had to work as a team to fit the duvet back inside it. Because I was smaller, I was deemed the intrepid explorer, sent inside the cover with the corners of the duvet in hand. "It's cinematic. It's Technicolor. Do you know what I mean?" I thought that British people were all stuck up and only liked to talk about tea and crumpets and the queen.

"Well, I wouldn't exactly know," I said from inside the duvet.

"Wait a second," Liz said. "Are you a virgin?" I froze, sensing this wasn't cool in her book. Liz burst out laughing. "You are! You're a virgin." I felt her grab the corners of the duvet, and I crawled out, my cheeks on fire.

"There's got to be an easier way to do this," I said, patting down my staticky hair. Liz stood on the bed and shook out the duvet in place. I smoothed it out and zipped the bottom.

"Cricket's a virgin," she sang as she jumped on the bed. "I knew it. That explains everything."

"Oh my god, Gavin is like, wandering the halls!" I said.

"You're getting a bit old. How old are you?"

"I'll be eighteen in August."

"Eighteen!"

"That's normal," I said. "It's like, perfect, for a girl."

"Americans." She stepped off the bed with narrowed eyes. "People think British people are prudes, but the truth is that Americans are. And why should it be any different for girls?"

I didn't know why it was different for girls. It shouldn't be, but it was. I hated it when people pretended otherwise.

"We're going to have to fix this by your birthday," Liz said. "I'm going to make it my mission."

"That's okay," I said. Liz ignored me, stuffing a pillow into its case.

"Fourth of July, you'll come with me." At least I'd gotten an invitation out of this whole ordeal. "I'll tell Shane, and we'll get his friends in a lineup. You choose."

"No, no, no, no."

"I'm thinking Colin. His willy is just the right size. Not too big and not too small. It's perfect for Goldilocks!"

"No, no, no, no." God, I regretted this conversation. What I wouldn't give to take it back. "The thing is, and this is actually really important to me, I want to be in love."

"Don't be ridiculous," Liz said, laughing. "You can't expect to fall in love by August."

"Well, I want to at least really like him."

"Do you have any candidates?"

"There was one guy, but"—I shook my head—"that's over."

"Oh! What about that writer fellow?" She wiggled her eyebrows. "An older man knows how to please a woman."

"Gross!" I said, shaking a pillow into its case. "He's married with a pregnant wife."

"You girls almost done in here?" Gavin stepped into the room with a pile of fresh towels. "Sometimes I think Bernadette is right about you two."

"You aren't going to believe what I just learned," Liz said, all lit up.

"Liz." My voice was low. "Don't you dare!"

"Cricket is an eighteen-year-old—" I smooshed the pillow in her face.

"I don't want to know," Gavin said, dropping the towels on the bed and leaving. "And change that pillowcase."

Twenty

"YOU'RE THE BEST," GEORGE SAID, LOWERING THE NOISE-canceling headphones from his ears as I put a six-pack of Coke Zero, peanut butter pretzels, and turkey jerky on his desk—the three items he claimed gave him special writing powers. He was sitting in an old office chair that Gavin had found in the basement, behind his makeshift desk, which was really a card table, on which sat his digital voice recorder, laptop, a few files, four notebooks, and the laser printer his wife had shipped and I'd set up yesterday. The windows were all the way up, the door was propped open, and his good foot was in a bowl of ice water. But it was sweating weather inside the annex. George had started calling it the hot box.

"Crack me open one of those sweet, sweet man-sodas," he said, rubbing his hands together. I laughed, opened a

Coke Zero, and handed it to him. He tipped his head back, guzzled half the can, and then held it up with a big smile like he was in a commercial. "Like a refreshing mountain stream."

"Wait, there's more," I said, and unveiled my big prize: a fan I'd found at the Nantucket Hospital Thrift Shop. It only had one speed, and the blade tips were covered with a layer of dust, but it would take the edge off.

"What? What? Am I hallucinating?" George said as I propped it on his dresser and plugged it in. "I was told there wasn't a single fan or air conditioner for sale on this god-forsaken island. The guy at the hardware store laughed in my face when I asked if he had any."

"I found it at the thrift store," I said, getting on my knees to plug it into the circuit breaker. "It was way in the back, behind a framed poster of a whale they were trying to sell for four hundred dollars."

"You're resourceful and intrepid, and I like it," George said, pulling out his wallet and handing me a twenty-dollar bill.

"It was only five dollars," I said, dusting my hands off on my shorts.

"Keep the change," he said.

"Are you sure?" I said, holding the crisp bill. "It doesn't oscillate."

"I like my warm stale air blowing in a steady stream right on my face."

"Okay." I folded the twenty and tucked it in my back

pocket, then handed him a manila envelope from my bag. "And here are the pictures." I'd gone to the Nantucket Yacht Club to pick up some old photographs of Boaty from when he was in his twenties and just married. There was one of him at a clambake, shaking hands and smiling thoughtfully, a golden afternoon glow on his serious face. The people around him gazed at him adoringly. One guy had his hand on his shoulder and was looking at him like he was his favorite son. Boaty definitely had what Edwina MacIntosh would call "star quality."

"He was so popular," I said.

"With most people, yes. But not everyone was a fan. Some people hated him."

"Like who?" I asked. "I mean, besides Republicans." And my mother, I thought.

He pointed to the guy with his hand on his shoulder. "That guy. Tom Frost. Boaty met him out here on Nantucket. Frost was the first person to hire him. He took him under his wing in the state Senate, showed him the ropes, treated him like a son. Tom Frost was gearing up to make a run for Congress. Boaty decided he wanted to do the same. And after five years of friendship, Boaty planted a story about him in the press."

"Oh my god," I said. "What was it?"

"An affair with the nanny."

"Sounds like a soap opera."

"It ruined Tom Frost, and Boaty got elected."

"That's terrible," I said.

"Well, technically, Boaty didn't plant the story. 'His people' did, but one of those 'people' told me Boaty signed off on it," George said. "Some of that is just par for the course in politics, but not generally with people you know and love. Boaty had spent Christmases with the guy."

"Why'd he do it?" I said.

"To win."

I thought that the feeling of wanting to be popular went away after high school. Our parents and teachers were always telling us that "winning" and "being cool" didn't matter. What mattered, they said, was being a good, happy person who did the right thing. Edwina McIntosh gave the same speech every year, in which she took a poem about a man in the mirror and changed the words to be about a girl in the mirror. "The only person who needs to think you're cool," Edwina MacIntosh said, "is the girl in the mirror. The approval you need is your own." So, were they all lying, not telling the truth about what it was really like to be an adult?

"On the other hand," George said as he cracked open another Coke Zero, "Boaty made huge strides in health care reform, and Tom Frost was an old fart. It's all very complicated, which is why it will make a good book, which is why I need to get writing."

"Well, do you need anything else?" I asked.

"I think that's it for today. I'm good to go," George said. "I just need to crank out another, oh, twenty pages, and I'll be right on schedule."

"Good luck with that, and don't forget to drink some water in between your man sodas."

"You're a good influence, Thompson," he said, and I was out the door—where it was a whole five degrees cooler—thinking of the beach, a yellow butterfly of anticipation circling my chest, half hoping, half dreading, that I'd see Zack again.

As I walked back to the beach, I thought about the other day when I'd run into Zack. We stayed in the water for what felt like hours, just talking and swimming around, following the warm patches, until our fingers and toes were puckering. I knew Jules wouldn't like me hanging out with him. And I know it had only been a week of feeling so alone in the world, but a week is actually a long time to feel like that.

I honestly tried to walk away from the Zack situation twice, but the first time he'd made me laugh, pretending to rescue me when a tiny wave pathetically knocked me on my ass, and the second time, right when I'd gotten too cold and come to my senses, he promised me half of his Something Natural sandwich if I stayed. It was turkey with cranberry and avocado. "On sourdough," he added. My teeth were chattering, partially because of the cold and also out of fear of what Jules would say when she found out we'd spent a whole day together.

He looked up. "If the sun comes out in the next five seconds, you have to stay." For some reason, I acted like this was a real rule.

"Five, four, three." We started counting, and by "two" I was squinting into bright sunshine, floating on my back, once again under its spell. We stayed until he had to go to work at Gigi's, the restaurant where he was a busboy. We shared my towel because his was sandy. And then we shared his sandwich.

When I arrived at Steps, I scanned the beach looking for him. He wasn't there. I reminded myself that that was a good thing.

Twenty-one

Zack: Happy 4th!

Me: You too.

Zack: Where r u?

Me: I don't know!!! Not Nobadeer. Some other beach. Cops at Nobadeer.

Zack: 40th Pole?

Me: Let me ask.

Me: Tom Nevers.

Zack: K. Want me to come get u?

Me: OMG. Yes pls.

Zack: See you in 20. Meet me at shuttle stop.

"I think I'm going to leave," I said to Liz, who was downing her fourth beer in less than an hour. My first beer was still almost full and had grown warm in my hand. We hadn't even tried to go to Nobadeer, because the cops had found out about that one. This was supposedly the secret, small, underground one. And yet, it was the biggest party I'd ever been to, even though Shane said it was lame compared to 2010, where there were almost three thousand partiers.

I couldn't tell how many were here now, but there were at least a hundred Jeeps parked on the beach, all of them filled with people in their bathing suits, all of the people getting shitfaced, blasting loud music, and peeing in plain sight. *Shit*, I thought when I accidentally turned my head and saw a gross, chinless guy whip it out to take a leak in the dunes.

"But you can't leave yet," Liz said. "I haven't introduced you to Colin! Where is that wanker? He said he'd be here by now." She checked her phone for messages. "You shouldn't go yet. You should stay and experience this bacchanalia. This is just the type of atmosphere you need to loosen you up—literally!" She laughed.

"Ha-ha," I said. Nearby, a guy in stars-and-stripes swimming trunks threw up in the dunes, and he looked like a real adult, with a bald spot and everything. He wiped strings of vomit from his mouth with the back of his hand. "I really have to go, Liz."

"Suit yourself," she said under her breath. "But you need to relax if you ever want to—" She made a circle with one hand and drove her index finger through it with the other.

"That's gross," I said.

"Wimp," she said as I walked away.

"Tart," I called back, laughing.

"I take that as a compliment!"

I hadn't seen Zack since our meeting at Steps. I closed my eyes as I waited for him at the shuttle stop, remembering how good it had felt to float around with him in the shallow water, how funny it was when he pretended to be the lifeguard, how strong he was when he picked me up and then flipped me in the deeper water, how it had finally, finally started to feel like summer.

When I saw Zack coming toward me in the land yacht, I felt a happy relief at feeling known, recognized, understood, familiar, the same feeling I used to get at the sight of Jules in the cafeteria when we hadn't seen each other all morning. He pulled up next to me, pretended that he didn't know me, and asked me if I needed a ride. He wasn't wearing a shirt. The feeling changed. It transitioned, spinning into a warm glow that spread up to my cheeks and to the last knob of my spine. I tipped back on my heels. Maybe the quarter of a beer I'd had in the sun had been too much. My heart picked up, but my pulse slowed down. Then the feeling changed again, into something brighter, something alive and jumping, like a sparkler in my chest, when I slid into the front seat next to him and our thighs touched.

What is wrong with me? I wondered as the engine hummed under the hot vinyl seat. I flipped down the sun visor to see if my cheeks were as red as they felt. They were. And my eyes and lips were shining. Was I coming down with something? It didn't feel like it. This was different. What was this feeling anyway? This need to move? This need to get a little more air, cross my legs, squeeze something? Had someone put something in my beer?

"You okay?" Zack asked, touching my knee. I jumped a little.

"Yeah," I said, shifting in my seat as we took off. "I'm just a little . . ." I was searching for the right word when an image came to me. Mrs. Levander holding the folded-up piece of paper that I'd dropped in the Difficult Questions box. My eyes went wide. Here, years later in the Claytons' land yacht, was the answer to my question. I reached for a bottle of water in the cup holder, opened it, and downed the three swallows that were left. "Thirsty," I said. "I'm really thirsty."

"I guess so. What's wrong?" he asked.

"Nothing," I said, sliding away from him. I wasn't supposed to be feeling this way about Zack. "Um, can we stop somewhere for water?"

"Sure," he said, and turned up the radio.

A few miles down the road, we spotted a water fountain along the bike path, and Zack pulled over. I hopped out and filled the water bottle up, trying to remember if Mrs. Levander had given us any information on how long this feeling lasted and what might make it pass. Besides the obvious.

"Hey, do you feel anything?" Zack asked.

"What do you mean?" I asked.

"There are a bunch of kids who say that there's a ghost here." I noticed a white cross, the kind they put up when someone gets killed on the road. "And they say if you drive by at night, you suddenly get cold when you hit this spot. I guess there was a girl who was killed out here in the '70s or something."

"What is it with Nantucket and ghosts?" I asked.

"There's just a lot of ghosts here," he said. I gave him a look of doubt. "You don't believe in ghosts?"

"Do you?"

"I think there's something out there, I guess."

"Do you think that your mom's a ghost?" Zack took a deep breath, and for a second I wondered if I'd just asked the worst question in the world.

"You mean, do I think she's hanging around, lifting up the chair in that hotel room? Or juggling candlesticks in our dining room?" I laughed. I couldn't help it. He smiled, and I could tell he was imagining something. "Like, when the lights go out at Bloomingdale's, she's thumbing through the racks, making herself a cappuccino in the home goods department?"

"Or lifting almond croissants off the trays at Seven Stars Bakery?" I asked.

"Taking the Mini Cooper for a spin?"

"So it looks like it's driving itself?"

"Really fast, right in the middle of the street?" We both laughed. Nina was a terrible driver. She thought stop signs were suggestions, but would stop in the intersection, surrendering her right of way, confusing everyone involved. Zack crossed his arms and shook his head. "No, Mom's not a ghost." His smile faded and he was quiet, staring at a patch of grass, his eyes still and brimming, like a water glass filled to the very top.

"But she's here," I said, focusing on my own patch of grass. "I feel it."

"Me too," he said, and took several deep breaths. The sun was low. A few distant fireworks went off. The insects were singing. Zack took my hand, weaving his fingers with mine. "Come on, I want to show you something."

Twenty-two

ZACK HELD THE LITTLE ROWBOAT CLOSE TO THE DOCK, AND I stepped in. He handed me the canvas bag with the champagne and plastic cups he'd taken from 4 Darling Street. "Dad hates champagne, and Jules forgot all about it. So that whole case of Dom Perignon in the pantry is for me."

"What's Dom Perignon?" I asked, lowering the bag into the stern.

"The good stuff," he said, untying the line.

"Won't your dad notice it's gone?"

"I don't think he'd notice if the fridge was gone and a white tiger sat in its place," he said, and stepped in. I couldn't help but picture the bizarre image. He slipped the oarlocks into place, slid in the oars, and rowed us into the harbor with long, even strokes.

"Hey, you said *champagne*. Does this mean you've gotten over the French girl?"

"Maybe," he said, smiling. I leaned back, elbows on the edge, and looked up. The sun had set, but it wasn't dark yet. The sky was purple. Above us, a half-moon tipped. We rowed past the homes that lined the harbor; past the squares of lighted interiors; past people sitting on verandas, drinking and laughing. Voices floated out to us on waves, turned to wisps, drifted away. The oars slapped the dark water, slid under and emerged, tilted and weeping as they skimmed the surface. I dropped an arm, let my fingers trace the water. I felt like I could've stayed in the back of that boat all summer and been happy.

"So, you see that McMansion with all the lights on?" Zack asked, taking both oars in one hand as he turned and pointed to a house on a distant cliff.

"Yeah." It was a huge place with a hundred windows.

"Okay, now, you see the one next to it, with only one light on? That's where we're headed. It's the best spot to see the fireworks." He turned to face me again, rowing with effortless strength and confidence. Maybe this was where he got his soccer-player body. The thought made me shiver.

"Here," he said, taking off his sweatshirt and tossing it to me.

"I thought you had a fungus," I teased.

"I told you, it cleared up," he said, splashing me a little with the oar. I wiped up the drops on my leg with the sweatshirt and put it on. It smelled like the beach.

Farther out were some yachts. On one of them, there were at least thirty people, all dressed up like they were set to sail to the Academy Awards. A tall, thin woman with long red hair in a short, sparkling gold dress talked to two men in tuxedos. I wondered if that was Jay's mom. It was hard to tell, but she had the same model-like silhouette. Zack waved. One of the tuxedoed men waved back.

"Looking for Bella Figura?" the man asked.

"Excuse me?" asked Zack.

"Bella Figura!" the man said.

"Bella what?" Zack asked, rowing us closer to the yacht. Now the woman in gold was looking at us. I felt certain she was Jay's mother. Oh god. Had Jay told her what I'd said about his brother?

"Aren't you the one we sent to bring us more wine?"

"No," Zack said. He handed me the oars and stood up, hands on his hips.

"Oh my god," I said under my breath. I hid my face in his sweatshirt.

"On my yacht"—he unfurled his arm, his forehead crinkling as he named the little boat—"*La Principessa*, we only drink Dom Perignon!" Zack said. "Isn't that right, Principessa?"

"Uh . . . yes?" I said quietly. I was afraid to look at the reactions of the fancy party people. Especially Mrs. Logan.

Zack sat down, took the oars, and rowed on. "Hey, why were you hiding?"

"Wasn't that Mrs. Logan?"

"Was it?" He shrugged. "So?"

"So? We know her. And who knows who those people are. Maybe they're important."

"You care too much what other people think."

"Well, it matters."

"No it doesn't," he said, maintaining eye contact. "Anyway, she was laughing."

"Hey, can I row?" I asked, anxious to change the subject and get back the mood of five minutes ago.

"Sure." The boat rocked as we switched spots. "Keep your eye on that buoy." My strokes were choppy and uneven. "So, you don't need to go so deep in the water. Just go right beneath the surface. And you want to keep the oar pretty flat." I did what he said. "Okay, that's better. The tide's coming in. It will be easier on the way back." He lay back, put his feet up. "I kind of like this whole girl-in-charge thing."

"We're not going to get lost at sea, are we?" I asked.

"Not unless you want to." Zack smiled. There was the feeling again. The warmth. The fluttering. The heart buzz. I focused on rowing. A few fireworks shot off from a distant beach. Little gold ones.

"So, where's your family?" he asked.

"Providence. What do you mean?"

"Most people spend holidays with their family."

"Fourth of July isn't exactly Christmas."

"You're a little heavy on that left oar; we're veering." I looked over my shoulder and then used the right oar to get us back on track. "You were at our house on Christmas, too."

"Christmas night, not Christmas morning."

"You were there by two o'clock."

"Whatever." Neither of us spoke for a minute. I was doing the choppy thing with the oars again. I took a deep breath, tried to get them at that perfect angle. "Well, your family is so fun. And my mom, it's like she *wants* to be sad all the time. I'm like, 'Go out, Mom. Please, make some friends. You're not eighty years old,' you know? It's like she's forgotten how to be happy."

"Did she ever know how?" he asked.

"Yes," I said, thinking about when we used to go to Newport together, about sitting on her bed when I was little and watching her put on her makeup. I paused. My hands were starting to hurt. And where had these words come from? I'd never said them aloud before. It was like I was stirring them up from the ocean.

"Want to switch?" Zack asked.

"Not yet."

"Where's your dad? Did he move?"

"He's still in Providence," I said. "He's just really busy. With his new family." Zack raised an eyebrow. There was a weird lump in my throat. I pushed it down, rowed on, my eyes fixed on the buoy. "Well, his wife has this son. She adopted him from an orphanage in the Ukraine when he was three years old. She basically rescued him, which was a pretty incredible thing. She didn't have a husband or anything when she went over there and got him. And he's actually a really cute little boy.

"But I guess he wasn't held as a baby, and he didn't get the proper nutrition, so he has all these problems. Like, every night, he wakes up screaming. He has these nightmares and wets the bed and stays up all night just rocking, and Dad and Polly stay up with him, and then everyone's exhausted the next day. I know he can't help it, and I know Polly and my dad are basically heroes, but sometimes I don't know." I shook my head. "Never mind. Anyway, it doesn't matter, because I'm almost eighteen."

"So?" Zack asked. The lump rose. I swallowed, sending it back to my gut.

"So, I'll be in college soon. Gone." The sky was blacker now, the moon whiter. Silver fireworks shot into the sky. "Look, they're starting," I said.

"Nice," Zack said, looking up for a second before turning his attention back to me. "But he's still your dad, and it sounds like these people make it impossible for you to spend time with him. That must be hard."

"No, I'm glad he has a life. I wish my mom would get one. Once, like, three years ago, when I started to realize that she wasn't getting out at all, I actually signed her up for an online dating site for divorced people. It was called Second Glances." I hadn't told anyone about this, not even Jules.

Zack laughed. "How'd that turn out?"

"It started out good," I said. "I made her a great profile, and I put up this old video I had of her singing 'My

Girl' to me on my birthday. You know that song by the Temptations? She looked so pretty in that video, and she has such a good voice. I knew if guys saw it they'd want to meet her."

"Did it work?"

"Oh my god, yes. So many guys were 'glancing' at her—that's what they call it on the site when someone checks out your profile. And I was 'glancing' back as her, just to keep them interested until I could get her into it. But every time I brought up online dating she was like, 'No way.' And then we were at Whole Foods and we ran into one of the guys. And he started to talk to her and she was like, 'I don't know you.' And he was like, 'Yes, you do. We've been glancing for two weeks now.' He pulled up her profile and played the video right there by the bananas."

"Oh shit," Zack said, laughing. "She must've been so pissed."

"She was. I got in so much trouble. And it was really expensive. It turned out I'd signed her up for a two-year nonrefundable membership. She made me pay for it with my babysitting money." Zack laughed harder. So did I. "Twenty bucks a month."

"When did you finally stop paying for it?" he asked.

"Actually, I renewed the membership last year," I said. "But I didn't tell her."

"What? Why?"

"Well, there's this one music teacher in Newton. He's not the best-looking guy in the world—he's kinda bald and he has a big nose—but he plays the guitar and the piano, and he just seems nice. I keep thinking that if she'd just give him a chance . . ."

"Or a glance," Zack said.

"Yeah," I said, laughing. "Exactly. If she just gave him a glance, she might actually be happy." But when I thought of her telling me over and over again that she wasn't interested in dating, my smile got swallowed up by the sea.

"Let's switch places," Zack said. "You've been rowing a while." The boat rocked again as we switched places. The fireworks were picking up. An umbrella of red light opened above us. There was the faint smell of something burning. A blue umbrella followed with a boom, turning to silver rain. "Oh my god, it's so beautiful."

"And we're almost there," Zack said.

I looked at the house. It was so close now. I hadn't realized how far I'd rowed. It looked spooky, leaning to the left, like one strong wind would blow it over. There was a steep hill that went from the back door to a perfect little horseshoe-shaped beach, a rickety staircase between them. I felt the boat scratch against the pebbly bottom.

"Come on." Zack took the bag with the champagne and jumped out of the boat and pulled it almost all the way to shore.

"Is this public?" I asked as I took off my flats and hopped out. The water was ankle-deep and surprisingly warm.

"No," he said, dragging the boat up onto the beach. "But

I've always thought this little beach would be the best spot to see the fireworks."

"So, this is someone's private land?"

"Yeah, but she won't bother us. She's just some super old lady who barely comes out of her house. She's a famous miser and she has the best view on the island. She should want to share it."

"So, are we like, trespassing?"

"Yes, but whose land really is it?"

"Ah, hers?"

Zack spread out a blanket, secured it with four rocks. "Wrong. It belongs to the children of tomorrow. And they don't mind that we're here. Now, let's open that bub!"

"Who's down there?" said an old voice.

"Oh shit," Zack said, our eyes locking.

"Who's on my property?" said the voice.

"Uh, just a couple of friendly youths," Zack said, shoving the blanket into the bag. I took off my shoes again and stuck them in as well.

"We're really sorry," I said. We ran to the shore and pushed the boat into the water. Above us the sky was in gold and silver hysterics. The old lady searched for us with a high-powered flashlight.

"You're trespassing and it's against the law!" She made it halfway down the stairs, shining the light right on us. For a super old lady, she sure was quick. The boat scraped the sand until it was deep enough to float. The bottom of my shorts were now soaked. Zack hoisted me by the waist and I hopped in. He followed, the boat wobbling. I scrambled to the seat in the stern, pulling my wet shorts away from my body. Zack bit his lip as he fumbled with the oarlocks. He lifted an oar while I guided it into place. Zack rowed us quickly away, out to sea, both of us cracking up.

"Youths?" I asked.

"It's what we are," he said, and then shouted, "Happy Fourth of July!" The old lady said something in response, but we couldn't understand. Above us the fireworks were in a riot. Little rockets of light shot upward and popped open, full of sequins.

"Look," I said as the explosions quick-fired, getting bigger and more dramatic. "The grand finale."

"The Fourth of July, aboard *La Principessa*!" Zack added in an Italian accent.

"Oh! Champagne!" I said, and clapped my hands.

"Yeah, get it."

I unwrapped the gold paper and tried to pull off the wire cage over the top of the bottle, but couldn't figure it out.

"Here," Zack handed me the oars. His knees were outside mine. Our legs touched, his knees squeezing mine. He untwisted the wire and popped the bottle. The cork flew into the water, and champagne spilled over the top of his fingers and all over my lap.

"Sorry," he said, and tried to wipe it off with the bottom of his T-shirt. We were both laughing. The bubbles were cool and tingly on my thighs.

"I'm totally soaked!" I looked up; he was so close. Our cheeks touched.

"You are just. . . ." he said into my ear. My eyes closed, eyelashes like matches striking my cheeks, setting them on fire. He kissed me, long and sweet, on the mouth.

"Just what?" I asked when I came up for air, stunned, heart stomping like a parade, wrists aching from holding the oars.

He seemed unable to finish his sentence with words. He pulled the wet oars inside the boat, wrapped his arms around me, and kissed me again. He gripped my waist. His fingers slipped down the back of my shorts.

"She'll kill me," I said, pulling away. "Literally."

"She'll kill me twice," he said, and pulled me closer.

"That's impossible," I said.

"Not if I turned into a zombie."

"Zack." I removed his hands and placed them on his own knees. I put my hands behind my back and took three deep breaths. "It can't happen again."

"Okay," he said. A warm wind twisted my hair. The boat drifted, and his hands did too, back to my legs, up my arms and neck. We kissed. We drifted and kissed and drifted and kissed as the sky flashed and clapped and bloomed and broke.

Twenty-three

"AW, BLESS, SOMEONE'S BEEN SNOGGING," LIZ SAID THE next morning when I walked into the kitchen, which was warm and fragrant from the baking muffins. Gingerbread, I guessed. Liz leaned against the counter, one blue-nail-polished hand on her mama-sized hip, and the other wrapped around her coffee cup. Her curls looked wild, backlit by the rising sun that shone through the sliding glass door.

"What are you talking about?" I asked innocently, and tied one of the new Cranberry Inn aprons that Gavin's chiropractor girlfriend had stenciled for us and were now part of our breakfast uniform. It was no use. There was a permanent blush on my face. I could feel it.

"Oh, it doesn't exactly take a detective, now, does it? Your lips are practically bruised—" I put a hand to my mouth. "Fess up, Goldilocks!" She pointed a croissant at me like a pistol.

"No," I said, pouring myself coffee. I tried to stop smiling, but the corners of my mouth would not be deterred, even with only four hours of sleep. I was a smiling fool. "I've got nothing to say." I added cream and sugar, and stirred.

"There's no use denying it. You look like you've just lifted the crown jewels. Besides, I saw you on the porch last night." My eyes popped wide. She smiled at me defiantly, rubbing her hands together. "But I could only make out that it was you. I couldn't see the guy. So, was it the writer? Did he lure you to the annex with sweets?"

"No!"

"Well, don't be so coy. Who is he? And more importantly, is he a contender for the big bang?"

"No," I said. "Definitely not." Zack and I had sworn that these kissing attacks wouldn't happen again, that it was probably best if we didn't see each other for at least a week in hopes that our newfound, red-hot attraction would fade. Also, making out with Zack was one thing, but sleeping with him? Forget it. Jules wouldn't ever speak to me again. Not to mention that it was understood that she would lose her virginity first, since she'd come so close last year. It was an unspoken pact.

"Why? What's the secret?" Liz's voice dropped low, her eyebrows arching. "Was it . . . Gavin?"

"Oh my god, Liz. Don't be disgusting!"

"Well, you're acting like it's so scandalous. What am I to think?"

"Okay," I said, folding under the charm of her accent. "It's this guy I know from home. But it's kind of . . . bad."

"All the better, my dear," Liz said, taking the industrial block of butter from the fridge and pulling the special butter knife from the drawer—the one that sliced the butter into pats with a wavy design.

"He's my friend's younger brother." I couldn't believe I was telling her this after the way she'd reacted when I'd confessed my virginity. But I wanted to tell someone so badly, and Liz was pretty much my only option.

"How young?"

"Sixteen."

"Oh, well, what's wrong with that?"

I looked at the timer on the microwave. Gavin would be here in three minutes to take the muffins out of the oven. He was kind of a control freak about his muffins.

"Are you kidding? A *younger* brother? It's like the worst thing a friend can do."

"Don't be ridiculous. People get together with friends' brothers all the time. It's totally natural. Unless your friend has some kind of sick fascination with him. In which case, I suggest you stay far away, lest they try to pull you into their web of perversion."

"It's nothing like that," I said. "I just know she's going to hate me for it. We had this fight." I took the chilled ramekins from the fridge, and Liz placed a fat, wavy pat of butter in each one.

"There's nothing worse than fighting with a friend," she said, her voice soft. "You can be awful to your mum or sister, but they're stuck with you, aren't they? But a friend . . . a friend can disappear. Have you talked since your fight?"

"She won't talk to me," I said. "And I came to Nantucket to spend the summer with her. She told me I was bothering her."

"Well, she doesn't sound like a very good friend," Liz said, putting down the knife and facing me. "That's a terrible thing to say." The protective tone of her voice and the sympathetic tilt of her head felt like a cool balm on the place inside where Jules's words had landed and burned.

"Well, the thing is that her mom—"

"I won't hear it." Liz cut me off. "I don't like the sounds of her, and I say what she doesn't know can't hurt her. I like seeing you all aglow. Suits you, actually."

The oven timer went off, Gavin breezed into the kitchen in his 2004 IYENGAR YOGA RETREAT T-shirt, lifted the muffins from the oven, switched on the singer-songwriter breakfast playlist, and put on the kettle for his second cup of green tea. And despite the tectonic plates that had shifted last night, my morning began just like any other.

Twenty-four

IT WAS ALREADY A ROUGH DAY AT TEN O'CLOCK, AND IT WAS only going to get rougher. Except for the older Australian couple, all the visitors who were here for the Fourth of July weekend were headed home today; all the rooms were turnovers and required bathroom scrubbings, vacuuming, fresh towels and sheets, and, of course, the dreaded duvet covers.

And they'd all decided to eat breakfast at the same time. The backyard, the porch, and even the big wooden table in the kitchen were packed. Liz and I were sweating as we cleared dishes, refreshed coffees, and refilled butters and jams. Gavin was washing the glasses by hand in the sink—no time to run the dishwasher.

"Excuse me," said a sunburned woman, holding a writhing toddler. "How do I get a cab to the airport?"

"We've got cards on the reception desk," Gavin said. "Pat's Cabs. Pat's the best. Normally I'd call for you, but I'm . . . in up to my elbows." He laughed because he literally had suds up his arms. Not amused, the woman disappeared into the living room.

I was about to show her where the cards were before I headed outside with the coffees when someone tapped me on the shoulder. I turned, expecting Liz, but instead found a tall middle-aged guy in Nantucket Reds grinning at me like I was his favorite movie star.

"If you aren't Kate Campbell's daughter, then my name is mud," he said, leaning forward, anticipating my reaction.

"I am her daughter," I said.

"Paul Morgan," he said, putting out his hand to shake mine. But I just shrugged, nodding toward my full hands. He squeezed my shoulder instead. "I knew it, I knew it." He rocked back and forth on his boat shoes, shaking his head. "We worked at the Nantucket Beach Club together years ago. I saw you standing across the room and I felt like it was twenty-five years ago. You look just like her."

"Are you staying here?" I asked.

"No, I just stopped by for one of Gavin's muffins."

"Hate to interrupt, but I need these," Liz said, taking the coffees from my hands and glaring at me. "We're very busy, in case you didn't notice."

Liz was invisible to Paul Morgan. He kept talking. "Is she still a firecracker? She is, isn't she?"

"She's a teacher." I didn't want to lie, and I also didn't

163

want to tell him that she more closely resembled a wet sock.

"I bet she's a great one," he said. "She was the prettiest, most vivacious girl on the island that summer. Now, don't look so shocked; us old people were young once, too." I studied his face. I was having a crazy urge to go check the diary and look at that picture again.

"Cricket," Liz called. I turned to see her gesturing at a table full of dirty plates and a family hovering nearby, wanting to sit down.

"It was nice to meet you," I said. "I've got to get back to work."

"Give your mother my best, won't you?" He reached into his pocket, pulled out his wallet, wrote something on a business card and handed it to me: *Paul T. Morgan, Esquire.* "That's my cell phone number. If you need anything while you're on Nantucket, let me know."

"Thanks." I slipped his card into the back pocket of my shorts and walked outside, where I made an absentminded, totally unhelpful loop around the yard, imagining my mother's firecracker self captured and held hostage somewhere on Nantucket, waiting to be shot into the sky.

As soon as we were done cleaning, I flopped on my bed and opened the Emily Dickinson diary. I studied the picture, but it was pointless. You couldn't see the guy's face.

I read the next entry, written around a poem about the

"majesty of death." Obviously, Mom wasn't too influenced by Emily Dickinson.

> Dear Emily,
> Alarm! Alarm! Call 9-1-1. It's a LOVE EMERGENCY! On second thought, call the fire department because I am hot to trot! Lover Boy and I talked for almost a half hour today. He stopped to chat with me at the reception desk for his whole break.

Hot to trot? Love emergency? Who was this person?

> Emily, from his ice-blue eyes to his cute butt, he's a head-to-tail fox. If you lived now and you saw him strolling under your window, you might even come out of your house. The attraction is undeniable. Right before a guest arrived and asked him to help with his bags, he leaned over the desk and told me I was making it hard for him to concentrate! I nearly had to wring out my underwear.

Oh, Mom. Disgusting!

> He has this smile that made talking to him so easy, like the most natural thing in the world. Oh, I found out that he's twenty-two and just

graduated from college. He was a little shocked when he found out I was seventeen, but I have a feeling it's not going to stop our love OR our lust.

Love, K. No longer the owner of a lonely heart.

I tried to visualize Paul T. Morgan, Esquire. I could see his big smile with the deep lines on either side of his mouth, the perfect top teeth and crooked bottom ones, the distinguished nose and thick head of graying hair. I don't know if it was just my imagination fueled by hope, but when I closed my eyes and let the image of his face fill my mind, his eyes were glacial blue. Maybe it was time to close Mom's Second Glances account after all.

Twenty-five

"DON'T TOUCH ANYTHING," GEORGE SAID WHEN I WALKED into the annex later that week with his cheddar and chutney sandwich in one hand and a cold lemonade for myself in the other. The sandwich was his reward for finishing three chapters in one week. One look at his dishevelment and you'd have hoped he'd done something significant. There were big circles under his eyes, his T-shirt was rumpled like it'd been slept in, and I could see the plaque on his teeth. He needed a hot shower with some powerful deodorant soap and a vegetable brush. And I'm no neat freak, but it was gamey in the annex. Liz and I had been instructed not to clean in there, for fear we'd mess something up, but now the smell was a little too human. I took a step toward the window. George put a hand up to stop me. "Seriously, don't touch. I have a system. Each pile is a zone. The zones cannot be messed with."

"George, it's a toxic zone," I said, and opened the window.

It was true that while there wasn't one patch of clear space in the whole annex, there did appear to be a strange order to the room. The index cards I'd brought him yesterday covered the floor in a rainbow. The bed was blanketed with documents on which I could see George's now-familiar chicken scrawl. His dresser was stacked with papers, and by the bathroom door was a pile of magazines that were marked with Post-it notes. The one on top was a *Vanity Fair* opened to a picture of Boaty and his wife, Lilly, sitting in what I now recognized as a classic Nantucket garden, with a weathered wooden bench and a trellis climbing with roses.

"And where should I put this?" I held up the sandwich.

"Oh yeah. Um"—he put a finger to his lips and scanned the room—"there." He pointed to a chair covered with clothes.

"Really? Like *on* the clothes?" George nodded as if this were perfectly normal. "Oookay." I cleared a little spot on the chair for the sandwich. He spun around in his chair and focused on the computer like it was about to tell him the secret of life.

"Come on, Bernie, you said four o'clock; it's four eighteen. I love you, buddy, but don't make promises that you can't keep." George tugged at his hair with one hand and refreshed his e-mail with the other. He studied the screen with intense concentration, refreshed again, and then hooted with glee. "Yes," he said, pointing to the computer screen. "You the MAN!"

"Who's Bernie?" I asked.

"The guy who does my transcribing." He hit a button and the printer sprung to life, spitting out pages. "And I need these interviews now, because I've got some momentum, Cricket, and I'll be goddamned if I lose it. I'm actually on schedule."

"Who are those interviews with?" I asked as he collected the papers from the printer and scanned them quickly with his eyes.

"Lilly Carmichael," he said, stacking the papers on his desk. "We talked about their courtship and his proposal. Gotta have romance. The ladies will love it, and let's face it, they're going to be the ones buying my book."

"She looks kind of . . ."

"Uptight?" George asked.

"Yes," I said, picking up the *Vanity Fair* with the picture of Boaty and Lilly. She was pretty, but in an overly delicate way. Boaty was leaning forward, animated, like he was in the middle of a story, and she was sitting back, looking to the side. I couldn't help but think that the photographer was making a statement with this picture.

"Yeah, well. She's not exactly the life of the party," George said, tilting his head and raising his eyebrows

"That's kind of weird. You would've thought he could get any girl he wanted."

"What can I tell you? Love is strange."

"Where did he propose?"

"Nantucket, of course. Her family's been coming here forever. He washed ashore for a summer job and they fell in love. It was a quick engagement. People thought she was knocked up, but she wasn't. Not for another ten years." He slapped a Post-it note on the transcription, scribbled something on it, and then looked up with big happy eyes. "Oh, guess what? I got an interview with Robert next week."

"Awesome." We high-fived. I knew he'd wanted to interview Robert Carmichael, Boaty's brother and Parker's father, for a long time, and that Robert had been hard to nail down. He was going to run for Boaty's seat in the Senate in the special election next month and was crazy busy.

"I'm going to need you to drive me to their home and pick me up. I'm finally going to use that damn car." Before he'd broken his ankle, George had arranged to rent a car, but of course he couldn't drive it and he couldn't get a refund. So it sat in the inn's driveway, swallowing money. George claimed he could hear it make a *ka-ching!* cash register sound effect each evening. "You might have to hang out there and wait for me. We'll get a sense for what the scene is."

"Right," I said. Where would I "hang out"? I was picturing some sort of maids' quarters. Possibly a pantry area stocked with gourmet canned goods. Would Parker be there? Would Jules? I'd stay in the car, I told myself. I'd park in the shade, bring a book.

"And please, please, please remind me to use both my phone and digital voice recorder," he said, his hands pressed together in a prayer. "If I lost that file, I'd be screwed. In the next few weeks I may need your help a little more than usual. We're in the thick of it, Cricket. We're right in the thick of it."

Twenty-six

HURRICANE KAYLA HAD A DATE WITH NANTUCKET ON
Friday. Everyone awaited her arrival like she was a gorgeous, petulant diva. Whether I was serving coffee at the
inn, buying sunscreen at the pharmacy, or picking up a
ham-and-cheese croissant for George at the Even Keel Café,
Kayla's name was uttered again and again under the gray
restless sky.

The shops on the harbor boarded up their windows in
preparation for the destructive winds. Surfers, who I could
pick out by their wet-suit tans and *I'm not a preppy or tour-
ist* snarls, looked more purposeful and had a gleeful spark
in their eyes. Many guests canceled their trips or went
home early, hurrying to get tickets on the last ferries and
planes, leaving the inn less than half full in the height of

the season. Those who stayed played the board games that'd been around for decades and read books by the fire in the library. They ate slices of Gavin's blueberry and peach pie and sipped tea or red wine, feet curled under them, peeking out the windows, analyzing clouds, reveling in coziness and anticipation. They wanted a hurricane story. I did too.

But Kayla stood us up, swirled her windy skirts, moved out to sea, and cooled her temper over the deep impartial ocean, leaving us with three days of rain. Fat, ceaseless drops filled the sidewalk cracks, overflowed puddles, and sent little streams twisting down Main Street. The grass in the backyard was rain drunk, so green it was practically humming.

The deluge gave George new drive and power. He was like the water wheel in the Industrial Revolution–era mill we'd toured for social studies in the seventh grade, cranking out chapters ahead of schedule, appearing in the kitchen for pie and dances of glee, and then disappearing back into the annex for another round of Coke Zero–fueled productivity.

With so few guests and such a light cleaning schedule, Liz and I finished early and went to the one movie theater on Nantucket. It doesn't look like a theater from the outside. It's just a regular-sized gray-shingled Nantucket building that's also a restaurant and bar. I'm not sure if it's because people were in a hurricane mindset where normal rules didn't apply, but the ticket taker didn't card us and he let us bring drinks into the theater.

We drank Irish coffees with whipped cream as we watched a romantic comedy. It was about this girl who works in a New York City flower shop and falls in love with a corporate lawyer who wants to build a megamall next door. It was dumb, but I still loved it, because in the dark, in the glow of someone else's story, I was free to think about Zack—how he tasted like mint and salt, how his hands left little swirls of energy where he'd touched me.

It had been over a week, and Zack and I hadn't texted, talked, or seen each other. My guilt had started to subside, heading out to sea with Kayla. I watched the lawyer kiss the florist girl, the city sparkling behind them. As a spare, sweet folk song filled the theater and the girl on screen gave in to the lawyer's lips, loosened his tie, and staggered to pull off her funky cowboy boots, my cell vibrated with a text. It was Zack:

I'm breaking our rule. Join me?

Twenty-seven

THAT NIGHT, I PICKED UP MOM'S DIARY AGAIN, SKIPPING over her make-out sessions with "Lover Boy," which she described in way too much detail for me to handle. There are certain words one just doesn't ever want to associate with one's mom and her activities. Words like "hard-on." It was especially gross now that I had a picture of Paul Morgan, Esquire, in my head. Instead, I started looking for romantic clues, places, and things I could mention that might dust off some shiny magnetic piece of her and pull her back out to this island. Once she was here, I'd arrange a meeting with Paul in one of their favorite places, and their old love would bring Mom fully back to life. I'd have to be subtle. I'd have to make it seem like it was her idea. I found an entry that looked relatively innocent and, pencil in hand, searched for key words.

> Dear Emily D.,
>
> Lover Boy and I dared to meet in public today. It was hard to get away. Aunt Betty took me to the yacht club for tennis (Aunt Betty's athletic, for a seventy-three-year-old biddy) and she insisted on us having lunch with her friends afterward. But finally (after Aunt Betty's second martini), I was able to sneak off. I met Lover Boy at Cisco and we spent the whole afternoon kissing in the surf like the cover of the Against All Odds album. Then we went back to his place, where we ate lobsters and drank beer and made out some more. Aunt Betty would kill me if she knew, but this is what being seventeen is all about. What is life, if not for living?

Cisco Beach, I wrote in my notebook. *Lobsters and beer.*

> I know I write a lot about how hot he gets me, but the truth is that I could spend all day with him every day. He's a cocky bastard, but he makes me laugh. There's this weird part of me that's like, <u>Be careful</u>. I can practically see the red flag warnings each time I close my eyes and we kiss. But I honestly don't give a shit. He's like a drug! And I'm addicted! Sometimes, I feel like we're that

Air Supply song, and that we're making love out of nothing at all.

I had to laugh. Oh my god! That song is so cheesy!

There was a tap on my window, and I sat up quickly, my body contracting in a flash of tension. But I smiled when I saw it was Zack. He laughed at my scared reaction, and my heart raced for a different reason. I opened the window. It had finally stopped raining, but the air was misty, full of secrets.

"I couldn't wait anymore," he said.

"Shh," I said, putting the book and notebook on the dresser and gesturing for him to come inside. Zack crawled in the window. He looked around.

"Nice room." He reached up and touched the slanted ceiling. "I like these old places."

"This one is haunted," I said, gathering the sheet around me. I was only wearing a T-shirt and underwear. "By a sea captain."

"Doesn't surprise me. Oh, hey. Fitzy saw that ghost again. The seventies girl."

"How does he know she's from the seventies?" I asked.

"Her clothes."

"Is she wearing bell-bottoms?"

"I don't know. But ghosts wear clothes. I mean, when people see ghosts they're always dressed, which is really weird when you think about it. Whatever you die in is the outfit you're stuck with for eternity."

"I guess it'd be creepy if they were all naked," I said.

"Good point. You love poetry, huh?" Zack asked.

"Not really," I said.

"I saw you. Your eyes were glued to that book." He sat on the edge of the bed.

"You were watching me?"

"For like a second." He reached for the book on my dresser.

"Don't touch that!"

"Whoa," he said, searching my eyes. "What's in that book?"

"Nothing," I said.

"I want to see," he said, picking it up.

"It's private." I leaped up, letting the sheet fall in order to grab the book from him. He smiled, staring at me, as I shoved it under the bed.

"Underwear is just like a bathing suit," I said as I climbed back under the sheet, blushing like a fever.

"No," he said. "It's different. We've been through this before. Remember?"

"Oh, yeah," I said, recalling the conversation we'd had at the Claytons' house when he'd seen Jules in her bra.

"What's wrong?"

"Nothing," I said. I was thinking about that night. It was the night Nina died, but Zack hadn't put it together, and I didn't want to remind him.

"Jules misses you, you know. I saw her looking at one of

those books you guys make, with all the letters and magazine clippings. What do you guys do with those things anyway? Are they like scrapbooks?"

"No. They're collage books. Jules brought one of our books with her?" Zack nodded. Jules and I bought hardcover sketch pads from the RISD art store and made collages in them. We saved all the notes we passed to each other in class and used rubber cement to glue them into the book. Then we made collages based on the notes. The collages and notes could be on any subject, from Jay Logan, to a book, to a certain style of jeans, to the way a movie made us feel. The fact that she even brought one to Nantucket was a good sign. We traded it back and forth every week, each of us adding a new entry. That was *our* book, *our* thing. She couldn't just add to it without thinking of me. "Maybe I should call her."

"I don't know," Zack said as he leaned against the wall. We held each other's gaze. Part of the reason he was climbing in my window was because Jules and I weren't talking. "It's like there's this wall around her right now. And no one is allowed in. No one."

"Parker is," I said.

"Parker can't even see the wall. That's the whole point."

"Oooh," I said. I hadn't thought about it like that before. It made me feel stupid and better at the same time. Zack put his hand on my sheet-covered foot and started to massage it.

I inhaled sharply. "Zack, we promised. No touching."

"It's just a foot," he said. "A foot under a sheet."

"Have you done this before?" His hands were strong, seemed to know what they were doing.

"Rubbed a girl's feet? No," he said. He looked older than sixteen. It was something about the way his jaw flexed. "This is pure instinct."

"You might have a future in it." I wiggled my other foot out from under the sheet. He covered it with his hands, went to work, barely touching my toes.

"Stop," I said, laughing. But he was grazing my toes even more lightly now, and I tried to kick my feet free. "Stop." I twisted free, sat up, and grabbed his hands. "Stop." Our eyes locked, and we sat there staring at each other. He slid the sheet up to my knees, drew little circles on my kneecaps, maintaining eye contact. I watched him register the smile I was fighting. He leaned in and kissed me.

"Zack," I said, trying to be calm. "We can't do this. We promised."

"Just one more time," he said, smiling. "We won't tell anyone."

"But this is it," I said.

"This is it," he said, his hand sliding up my thigh.

"And no one can know. Ever."

"Would you be embarrassed to go out with me?" he asked.

"No," I said. "Of course not." But I knew a part of me was lying. I was going to be a senior, and Zack was only going to be a sophomore. "It's just Jules. She'd be mad."

"Okay, no one will know," he said, lying back on the bed.

"We'll be secret lovers," I said. I wasn't thinking.

He grinned. "I didn't know we were going that far."

I shook my head, realizing that lovers meant sex. "We're not. That's not what I meant."

"Are you sure?" he asked as he pulled me down next to him.

"I'm sure," I said as he took off his glasses and his lips found mine. I closed my eyes and saw flecks of red.

Were they the little warning flags Mom had written about?

Twenty-eight

"BEEP-BEEP," I CALLED OUT THE WINDOW OF GEORGE'S rented Jeep. I didn't think Gavin or the old lady in the muu-muu who was snoozing in the hammock would appreciate it if I leaned on the car horn. Today was the big interview with Robert Carmichael. I drummed my fingers on the steering wheel, which was hot from the sun. "Beep-beep," I said again. George told me that we needed to be ready at three o'clock, and it was already 3:10. What was he doing, curling his hair? He waved from his window, giving me the one-minute signal.

I tilted the rearview mirror in my direction. Even though George had assured me I wouldn't have to hang out at the house, that this was purely a drop-off/pick-up situation, I was still nervous about running into Parker. I wanted to look good. Composed. Liz trimmed my bangs last night, and I had on just a teeny bit of lip gloss and blush. I was already sweating a little through my white blouse with the tiny blue flowers on it. I fiddled with the air conditioner and smoothed my linen skirt over my knees.

I wondered if part of my desire to look so wholesome and put together was to cover up for what I was doing at night. Zack had been sneaking into my room for make-out sessions that were becoming more and more intense. I had two rules: One, underwear stayed on. This prevented sex and other irrevocable acts. Two, no sleeping over. If he didn't spend the night at home, Jules or Mr. Clayton would definitely start to notice. Each night we said was "the last time," but the phrase had become a joke. Night after night he appeared at my window with a big grin, even though I'd told him the front door worked just fine.

"I like the window," he'd said. "I mean, since we're '*secret lovers*,'" he added in a breathy voice.

"Shut up," I'd said, and helped him tumble inside.

Last night had felt a little dangerous. We'd fallen asleep for a few hours, our limbs entangled. Luckily, I'd awakened before the sun came up, and he'd climbed on top of me, stealing one more hip-to-hip kiss before he slipped back out the window, into the dark pre-dawn air. I heated up like an August afternoon at the thought of it, and dabbed some cool foundation under my eyes. At least I knew he wouldn't be there. He works on Tuesdays.

"George?" I called out the window.

"Give me five minutes," he called back.

I opened the diary. Maybe I could find a clue as to how Mom and Paul broke up.

> Dear Emily,
> This girl from Miss Driscoll's, that boarding school where I spent one miserable semester, was at Cisco today.

Oh, yeah. I'd forgotten that Mom had spent a semester at a boarding school. She told me that she hated it. She described living in a dorm called Tittsworth Hall, where at least half the girls were anorexic. At night, they would ball up slices of Wonder Bread and eat "bread balls" and red-hot candies and play truth or truth because no one wanted to dare. It sounded creepy.

> She always acted so much cooler and better than me. Her dad is some kind of megamillionaire. She started talking to us and she was ALL OVER Lover Boy, batting her eyelashes and smooshing her boobs together. She invited me to some party, but I could tell it was just to get to Lover Boy. In front of my face! Gag me with a spoon. Get your own boyfriend. After she left, Lover Boy called her pig nose. Ha, ha, ha.
> Anyway, his parents are visiting this weekend. I wanted to meet them. I know they would like me

if they met me, but he says he wants to wait. He says they won't understand him dating a girl who's in high school.

I wrote in my notebook: *Possible reason for breakup = age difference.* This made me feel better. They were so old now. No one cared if a forty-nine-year-old and a forty-four-year-old got together.

Anyway, last night we did it in the dunes under a full moon.

Dunes, I wrote in my notebook and underlined it, and did my best to block out the "doing it" part.

And after, he told me that he loved me! I guess I knew this all along, but to hear him actually say it, Emily, I swear there's nothing better in this whole world. If you only knew, you wouldn't have stayed inside your house in Amherst. Although, I have to say . . . some of these poems make me think maybe you had a lover. "Wild Nights" isn't about the weather!

I flipped to the index, found the poem, and read it. Mom was right. This poem was definitely about sex. I earmarked the page, certain it was going to be one of the ones Mrs. Hart would focus on. I learned from our ninth-grade discussions of *The Canterbury Tales* that Mrs. Hart might be ancient but she was also raunchy. It was no wonder she and Mrs. Levander were such good friends. They probably got together on the weekends for wine and Bonnie Raitt and sex talk.

"Let's blow this pop stand," George said, startling me as he shoved his crutches in the backseat and hopped into the Jeep. I shut the diary and my notebook and buried them in my bag. George was all cleaned up for the interview. He'd shaved, showered, and was wearing clothes that were either brand new or that had actually been ironed. Somehow, it seemed more likely to me he'd bought them. He had a leather satchel in one hand and a Coke Zero in the other.

"I see you have your man-soda," I said.

"You know it," he said as I started the engine and backed out of the inn's driveway. Sometimes I wondered if George had Coke Zero pulsing through his veins instead of blood. "And I see you're wearing your business casuals. Very nice." Noticing my confusion, he added, "You're dressed for work in an office. It's a good thing. Very appropriate, very professional."

"Well, I'm going to a future senator's house. So, how long are interviews?" I asked.

"Well," he said, "that's kind of like asking how long a conversation is. It all depends."

"How long should I hang around 'Sconset?" I asked.

"Shouldn't be more than an hour. I'll text you when I need to be picked up. Just don't go too far. I don't want to be hanging around on their front lawn, waiting to get picked up. That could get awkward."

"Got it."

He glanced at the Emily Dickinson book in my bag. "I see you brought a little light reading."

"For school," I said, slowing as I passed a helmeted family on bikes. "So how do you get these people to tell you anything good?"

"Here's the thing. Everyone has a story to tell." Out of the corner of my eye I saw George fan out his fingers, the way he does when he's explaining something he's passionate about. "Everyone's life has love and death and drama and hope and fear. And if you make them comfortable, if they feel they can trust you, they'll tell you. They actually *want* to tell someone." I always know when George is done making a point because he folds his hands together and rests them on his big belly.

"What are you looking for from Boaty's brother?" I asked. "What do you want him to tell you?"

"Family stories. The humanizing details. Anecdotes that reveal character. Boaty wasn't born into this world. He scrambled to get to where he was. I want stories that show that incredible determination, drive, and intelligence. I also wonder when he started stepping on people. Who was that first rung on his ladder to the top? People think his career started at the state house, but I think it also started when he figured out how to charm the right people into leaning over so he could step on their backs."

"You think his brother's going to tell you *that?*"

"He might tell me without telling me, if you know what I mean."

George shifted in his seat. I slowed down to take a look at the cross that Zack had pointed out to me, the one where the ghost likes to hang out. As I looked out the window, I noticed that George shuddered. I screamed, which made George scream and grab at his chest.

"You just got the chills! You just got the chills!" I said, slapping the steering wheel and accidentally slamming the horn.

"You scared the living shit out of me!"

"Holy, holy shit, you just got the chills."

"Eyes on the road, Thompson," George said, putting his hand on the wheel and steering us more solidly to the right side of the road. "Eyes. On. The. Road. Jesus, how long have you been driving?"

"Almost two years, but holy, holy shit." I shook my head and pointed at him. "I can't believe it, you got the chills."

"Yes, I've been coming down with something since, like, May."

"The ghost," I said. "There's a ghost girl at that cross back there. And they say that's why people get chills when they pass it. And that's why I was watching you, and oh my god. Oooh, should we drive by and see if it happens again?" I couldn't wait to tell Zack. How come it never happened to me? Was I not spiritual enough for ghosts to contact?

"No, no, no. Let's just focus on getting there alive."

"All the kids are talking about it," I said, knowing George liked to know what "the kids were talking about." As a journalist, he felt it was his duty, but he was too focused today and he didn't bite.

"Oh, okay, slow down. It's up here." I braked, looking for the correct address. "And turn left," George said as we turned into a wide driveway. "Secret service," he said to me, and rolled down the window to talk to two guys in dark suits wearing wires. I felt bad for them. They looked so hot. One guy said something into a walkie-talkie-type thing and waved us in so that I could drop off George by the front door.

"You okay?" George asked as he reached for his crutches in the back. "You look like you just saw that ghost."

"Yeah." The house was huge; it looked like it could hold at least four of my mom's house. But that's not what was making me sweat through my white blouse. Next to a Mercedes, a silver Porsche Cayenne, and a red Volvo with a Hotchkiss sticker (Parker's boarding school) was the Claytons' land yacht. Jules was here. My heart pounded.

"Hey, this is just money," George said. "Don't let it intimidate you, okay?" Then he opened the door and stepped out, balancing as he gathered his satchel and notebook. I could hear kids' voices coming from the backyard. There was obviously a pool, because I heard cannonball splashes and girls laughing. It sounded like fun, like what I'd had in mind for myself when I came here. Shit, shit, shit.

George closed the car door with the butt of his crutch

and headed up the front steps. He had just reached the front door and was about to knock when I noticed his phone on the seat.

"George, wait," I said, hopping out of the car and jogging to him with the phone.

"You're the best," he said as I pressed it into his hand.

"I'll be waiting for your text," I said, and walked quickly back to the car I'd left running.

I heard Jules's unmistakable laugh: the confident, contagious one that always made me feel we were at the center of the world. I felt sad in a bottomless way—like a plane dropping in turbulence, an elevator plummeting to the basement. I hurried into the car and drove away, my palms sticky and my breath sharp and shallow.

Twenty-nine

WHEN I PULLED INTO THE CARMICHAELS' DRIVEWAY AFTER an hour of driving around Nantucket with the radio blaring as I tried to get my head together, I saw Jules following Parker into the house. She was barefoot, wearing a yellow bikini, with a short white towel fastened around her hips. She was hopping on one foot and pounding the side of her head as she tried to get water out of her ear. I winced as I drove up. She looked up, squinting. Our eyes met. We both froze. I was going to have to get out of the car now. I couldn't just sit there. I parked, trembling. I took a deep breath and stepped out of the car.

"What are you doing here?" she asked as I approached her. I saw her eyes darting over my body, taking in my business casuals.

"I have an internship," I said. "With a journalist. And he's here."

"The guy who's interviewing my dad?" Parker asked. She was dripping with pool water. She dabbed her face and stuck a towel-covered finger into her ear, grimacing as she screwed it in. Parker was so confident about her place in the world she could do that kind of thing in public. I looked at those rock-hard thighs. Parker looked like she could kick her Volvo over to Martha's Vineyard.

"How'd you get an internship?" Jules asked.

"It's a long story," I said.

"The book is about the whole American royalty thing, right?" Parker asked. I nodded, smiling. "What do you do for him?"

"Basically, I just help keep him organized; I get him whatever he needs. Sometimes I give him feedback," I said. "You know, on the writing." I figured on some level this was true. Just the other day he'd asked my opinion about an interview.

Jules was staring at a rock. With one pointed foot she traced an arc in the Carmichaels' spongy green grass. It was bright, uniform grass, the kind that's bought and then unfurled on the ground like bolts of fabric. "It's your birthday in a few weeks," she said, shielding the sun from her eyes, squinting at me.

I nodded. "My eighteenth."

"Whoa, you're old," Parker said. "No wonder you have an internship. I feel better." She snorted. "For a second there

I was like, should I have an internship?" She picked at a bud on the branch of a tree and decimated it with her short fingernails. "But I'm only sixteen."

"You'll be seventeen in September," Jules said, not even looking at her. Was she standing up for me?

"Bitch," Parker said, like this was her little pet name for Jules. "C'mon, let's get ready. I don't want to be late meeting Jay."

Jules and I had eighteen conversations with our eyes.

"There you guys are," said Zack, who emerged from the backyard in his bathing suit. He must've seen me before I saw him, because he didn't look surprised. He smiled as he jogged over. Now it was my turn to study rocks. Ever since Zack and I had started making out, my body had taken on a life of its own. My breath was unpredictable, my skin capable of burning up in an instant and searing my hairline, and there was this lightness that occasionally took me over, making me feel like I was made of balloons. He shook out his hair, spraying us all with little beads of water. Jules pushed him absentmindedly and he pushed her back. Why did he have to be her brother?

"Hello, Cricket. How are you?" he asked. He sounded stiff and formal.

"I'm fine," I said. *I thought you worked on Tuesdays.* I could feel myself making a weird expression. He looked good in his trunks. God, did he look good. He was pale but strong. The sun was glistening off of his wet skin. I knew that body now. My heart was like a dog, hopping and pulling on the leash, like it wanted to jump up and lick his face.

"Is that your journalist?" Jules asked. I turned, relieved to see George come out of the front door, his satchel swinging awkwardly at his side.

"I gotta go," I said, turning on my heels and jogging to meet George.

"Do you know those kids?" George asked as we climbed into the Jeep and I started the engine.

"Yeah," I said. "Kinda." I looked in the rearview mirror, expecting Zack to be the one watching us go. But he and Parker were gone. It was Jules who was watching me drive away. She looked frozen, standing on the edge of that perfect lawn in front of that perfect house. Her eyes were wide, mouth half open, like she was stopping herself from running after me.

Thirty

"THAT WAS SO WEIRD TODAY," ZACK SAID THAT NIGHT when he crawled in my window. "You were so nervous. You were sweating."

"But you don't think she caught on, do you?" I asked. I was sitting on my bed in a tank top and the girlie boxers I wore as pajamas.

"No way," he said. "She has no idea." I sighed and closed my eyes. Inside I tuned to the relief channel, but quickly switched to the guilt channel and back to relief and then guilt again. I hadn't been able to get Jules out of my head. The worst part was how badly I wanted to share with her what was happening to me. I wanted to tell her how I wasn't doing that thing that I do with guys, making mental notes of who had called or texted whom last, always keeping score and trying to stay on top. I wasn't planning out what I would say to Zack in advance or practicing lines that I thought might make him like me more. I was just being me. I wanted to tell her how I was actually enjoying making out, not just because it reassured me that a guy liked and wanted me, but because it felt good. And I wanted to know how she was. I wanted to hear her stories. The guilt channel was on full blast now, hissing its fuzzy reception. How to make it stop? I promised her, silently, to stop this with Zack.

"I'm too old for you," I said, sliding down the bed, away from him.

"I know. A whole eighteen months or something. You're corrupting me." He slid closer. "Have you ever had sex?"

"No." I pulled back, examining his face. "You have?" He nodded, laughing at my shocked expression. "Valerie?"

"She *is* French," he said.

"Were you in eighth grade?" He nodded. *"Eighth grade?"*

He snaked his hand around my waist, but I pushed it away.

"Does Jules know?"

"No."

"Did your mom know?"

"No." He put a hand on my knee.

"We shouldn't be doing this. We really shouldn't." I stood up and walked to the other side of the tiny room.

"Don't say that," he said, following me. He kissed me. I pulled away.

"But we can't keep doing this. I was thinking about what

you said about the wall around Jules. And I feel like I looked over the wall today for like a second, and I saw how sad she really is. And if we keep doing what we're doing, I'm just going to be heaping more sadness on her."

"Okay, well . . ." He let go of my hand. "Let's get away from the bed. Let's go somewhere," he said. "Let's get out of here."

"Where?"

"I don't know," he said. "But I need you to put on as many clothes as possible."

"Oh, I know," I said, remembering George and the shiver. I grabbed a sweatshirt. "Let's go see the ghost."

I told him about George getting the chills, as we headed out to the white cross in the land yacht. We drove by a few times, seeing if one of us would get the chills, but nothing happened. So we just parked in front of it. We sat and waited for something to happen, for the temperature to drop or a ghostly pair of bell-bottoms to strut past the headlights.

"Where does Jules think you go at night?" I asked as we waited. The air was soft and still and full of summer. The crickets were loud.

"She doesn't know I'm gone. No one knows I'm gone." He slapped a mosquito on his arm.

"What about your dad?"

"Jules is so out of it right now, and with my dad, it's like an actor is playing him. A bad actor. They won't even say her name. It's like living with people who are only half here."

"I know what that's like," I said, thinking of Mom and the way I could look into her eyes and see she was somewhere else, somewhere very far away that I didn't know about. It made me want to scream at her. Life was happening here in front of her, not in that faraway world. "I know exactly what that's like."

I pushed the seat back and dangled my feet out the window. We sat there in silence for a bit, each of us in our own world. The image of Jay's face came to my mind. I could hear him telling me off. I could hear myself telling Jules I thought his brother was a loser. My whole body tensed as I remembered it. I wish I'd never told Jules anything. What about my other secrets, the other things I shouldn't have said but did because I'd trusted her? Forget girls who died decades ago; words were ghosts. They were what haunted me.

"I don't think the ghost girl is going to show," I said.

"Yeah," he said. "Ghost girl's not into us. Let's go someplace better."

We went to Steps. The moon was three-quarters full—bright, glowing, shining on the black ocean. The waves were low and calm. We rolled up our jeans and walked in up to our ankles. The water was warm, holding the memory of the sun.

"That's it, I'm going in. I have to," Zack said. I watched as he lifted his sweatshirt and T-shirt off his head in one move. He was so lean and strong.

"In your underwear?" I asked.

"Hell, no," Zack said, and unbuttoned his jeans. I covered my mouth with my hands. He met my gaze and pulled them down, with his boxers, over his hips. There it was! I'd felt it, but I hadn't seen it. "Oh my god," I said, not realizing I was thinking aloud.

"Feast your eyes." He laughed. Then he beat his chest and let out a war cry.

"Zack!" I laughed, intoxicated.

He turned around, faced the ocean. Boy butts are so different, so compact. "Woo-hoo!" He whooped, ran into the waves, and dove under. "It's perfect," he said when his head popped up. "You have to come in. It's beautiful."

"I can't," I said, remembering my promise to myself about Jules.

"Your loss," Zack said. "It's amazing in here." It looked amazing. He looked amazing bobbing up and down in the silvery black water. I thought of Mom's words to Emily Dickinson: *What is life, if not for living?* I took a deep breath, then stripped off my clothes and ran in, covering myself with my hands until I was in the water. I slipped under a gentle wave, and when I came up, Zack was in front of me. He was smiling but serious, and I felt my cheeks brighten. He took my hands and pulled me close to him.

"Come to me, mermaid," he said.

"La le loo-loo la lee loo." I floated my legs up, dipped my head back, and sang an off-key mermaid song. I felt like the moon itself, all lit up. Then I noticed little lights around us in the water.

"Oh my god, what is this?" I asked. The water was sparking, glowing, like there were fireflies underwater.

"Phosphorescence," he said, splashing the water to make it glow.

"It's crazy." I ran my hands through the water, trying to catch it, then kicked my legs up and floated around on my back. I wasn't made of bones anymore. I was made of starfish and moonlight and phosphorescence. I started laughing for no reason at all.

"What?" Zack asked, treading water, his hands leaving trails of light.

I put my feet back on the bottom and laughed again. I'd never felt so full, so bright, so completely alive. "I think," I started, but then ducked back under, finishing the thought underwater so that I'd get to say it, but he wouldn't hear. *I think I'm in love.*

Thirty-one

"HONEY, I DON'T SEE THE NEED FOR ME TO COME TO Nantucket. You're doing just fine, and it's only a few more weeks until the summer's over." Even through the phone, I could tell Mom was distracted. She was probably playing computer hearts. I sat on the back steps of the porch, sipping lemonade from a fresh batch Gavin had just made. I used Mom's distraction as an opportunity to skim my notebook for key words and phrases I'd copied from the diary.

"But, Mom?" I said into the phone.

"Yeah?"

"*What is life, if not for living?*" I was hoping she would recognize her own quote.

"Is that from that Weight Watchers commercial?"

"No. It's from something else."

"Well, I don't see what it has to do with me coming to Nantucket, especially since I get seasick on boats." Yeah right, I thought. In the diary, she and Lover Boy had been on numerous boat trips. There was a ferry ride to Cape Cod for a stolen night in a motel, into which they checked in as "Mr. and Mrs. Donald Duck." There was also a zippy cruise in a Boston Whaler out to Tuckernuck Island, not to mention a secret sunrise sail. Mom's computer zinged with a hearts victory.

"Mom, are you sure you have seasickness? Are you sure that you're not inventing that?"

"Excuse me, but I think I know whether or not I get sick on boats."

"Then take a pill!" I said.

"Watch your tone, please," she said.

Gavin knocked on the sliding glass door and made a "keep it down" gesture. I gave him the okay signal. I hadn't realized I'd yelled.

"Sorry, Mom. I just want you to picture this." I glanced at the notebook, skipping over any boat-related notes. "Dunes. Sunsets. Lobster. Cisco Beach. Beer."

"Beer? I don't drink beer," she said. "What's this about? Oh no. Have you signed me up for some singles' thing? I told you—"

"No, Mom. I just want you to come out here for my birthday," I said. "It's only a week away."

"You were nine the last time you wanted me around on your birthday."

"Yeah, well, I'm going to college next year so maybe I'm feeling sentimental."

"Well, that's very sweet. But I'm afraid I'd come all the way out there and you'd just want to be with your friends, not boring old Mom." Boring old Mom? I was staring at the words "nude beach" in her diary. "How about when you get back, we go out to Sue's Clam Shack? Are you sure there's no one that you want to see out here?"

"The only person on Nantucket I want to see is you, and I'm going to see you in just a few short weeks." *Zing!* A hearts success.

"I just want you to think about it. Promise me you'll think about it."

I hung up and opened the book, wishing I could find the right words, the ones that would lure her back out to this island, this unlikely rock of love. The problem was that in the diary she was more specific about what she and Lover Boy had done to each other's bodies than where exactly they'd been. I wasn't about to recite those passages to her. I could barely read them without wanting to barf. A page caught my attention—she'd written in a circle around a poem.

Dear Emily,
    Right now I'm sitting in front of the library,
where I've come to escape Aunt Betty, who was
lecturing me on the importance of knowing how to

properly set a table. She thinks my parents haven't taught me any feminine charms. All I want to do is think about last night with Lover Boy. On one hand, I'm confused because he canceled our last date. He said he needed to work on law school applications and it gave me a weird feeling. It's still only summer and he's barely mentioned law school this whole time! On the other hand, I wonder if I'm being paranoid. He cares so much about his future. He has big dreams. I want him to follow his dreams! And it was just last week when he told me that he loves me, and I knew it was true when he said it, the way you just know. He loves me!

I'm listening to the crickets as I write this. And I just realized that I'm writing here on your poem about the cricket. I love that crickets are here in this magical time, when it's not night or day but some in-between time. I'm deciding right now that when I want to think of a day with magic in it, I'll think of this day. I will say to myself: Cricket. It will be my secret code word for magic or love or both.

Love, K.

My name. Mom had always said that I got my name because I used to chirp in my crib. But that wasn't the whole truth. I read the poem.

The cricket sang
And set the sun,
And workmen finished, one by one,
Their seam the day upon.

The low grass loaded with the dew,
The twilight stood as strangers do
With hat in hand, polite and new,
To stay as if, or go.

A vastness, as a neighbor, came,—
A wisdom without face or name,
A peace, as hemispheres at home,—
And so the night became.

I wasn't just Mom's daughter. I was her word for magic.

"What's up with you?" I looked up. It was George, taking a fresh-air break, something I'd encouraged him to do. I'd told him it didn't matter that he was on crutches, he needed to hobble around the block every six hours or so. His skin had started to look yellow.

"I think I finally get Emily Dickinson," I said.

"That makes one of us," he said. "Hey, will you come listen to this? I need your young ears to decipher part of Lilly Carmichael's interview. I've been to too many White Stripes concerts or something."

"Sure." I closed the diary and followed George into the

annex, which was officially on the verge of spontaneous combustion.

He played the digital recording on the computer. Mrs. Carmichael's voice was smooth, like one of Mom's books on tape: *"Boaty's proposal was very romantic. It came as a great surprise. I'd had a mad crush on him all summer. But that hardly made me unique; so did all the girls."*

"Yada yada yada," George said, skipping ahead. "She goes on about this for a while. Tell me something I don't know." He pressed PLAY. "Okay, now listen."

"Boaty and I went for a sunset sail. I didn't even want to go! Can you imagine? I kept telling him that there was a big clambake I'd been looking forward to and we could always go sailing tomorrow night, but he insisted that the sunset that evening was going to be the best of the summer. And it was. It was glorious. As I was admiring it, he pulled from his pocket a ring made out of seaweed. He had no money then." Lilly's voice softened. I could hear her smiling. *"It was such a surprise! The only thing on my mind the whole day was getting to Paul Morgan's clambake, always the party of the season."* On the recording, George asked who Paul Morgan was. Lilly answered. *"Paul was the boy my parents wanted me to marry. He was from an old Nantucket family, had all the money in the world, all the right credentials. My mother always thought he was the one for me because—"* Here the voice became indecipherable.

"Oh, Paul Morgan!" I said as the familiarity of the name landed.

"You know him?" George asked, pausing the interview.

"Yeah, I do." This wasn't true; I just felt like I did. "Well, not really. I've just met him and I've heard a lot about him."

"From whom?"

"My mom. They dated at one time."

"Oh." George tilted his head. "Interesting. Okay, so listen hard; this is the part I can't understand. It sounds like she's saying her mother always thought Boaty was interested in Lilly's 'local vision.' But that makes no sense," George said. What the hell is 'local vision'? And why would that be a bad thing for him to be interested in?"

"Play it again." I said. He did. "One more time." He watched me as if I were a medium. I clapped my hand on his shoulder. "Social position. She's saying social position." My eyes widened. "Her mom thought that Boaty was a social climber!"

"I think you're right." George played it again, his face frozen in concentration. He sighed with relief. "That's it." He scratched his neck. "No wonder she mumbled."

He was waiting for me to respond, but my mind wasn't on the recording. It was on Paul Morgan.

I hadn't realized that Paul Morgan was such a prominent, wealthy man. I wondered if that would scare Mom away. She said she didn't trust rich people. I'd have to make sure they met someplace low-key. How was I ever going to make it seem like this was all her idea?

Thirty-two

"WHAT'S THIS?" I ASKED, THE NEXT AFTERNOON. LIZ AND I were in the kitchen. I was staring at a neat little package wrapped up sweetly in pink tissue paper. It was tied with a strand of lace. Liz and I were relaxing after a long morning. All the beds were made, all the toilets had been wiped clean, and all the wicker wastebaskets emptied.

"Early birthday present," Liz said. "Go on, now. Open it."

"Liz, you didn't have to," I said. "My birthday isn't until Tuesday."

"Open the damn present," she said, a mischievous grin plastered on her face. Gavin wandered into the kitchen with a stack of mail.

"Something came for you, Cricket," he said, handing me

a fat manila envelope with my name and the inn's address written in my father's familiar chicken scrawl.

"Thanks," I said.

"Gavin, did you know that it's Cricket's birthday next week?" Liz said. "She's going to be eighteen years old."

"Is that so?" Gavin said. "I'll have to make a cake. Chocolate with a raspberry filling okay?"

"Yum. Thanks, Gavin," I said as I worked at the knot of lace that was binding my gift. Gavin turned on the teakettle and sorted through his bills, not knowing how relieved I was that I was going to have a birthday cake—a chocolate one, with raspberry filling! I needed something to replace the tradition Jules and I had started five years ago.

Ever since Jules came to Rosewood, we did pajama birthdays. On our birthdays, Jules and I always brought each other waffles with strawberries and whipped cream in bed. And the breakfast tray was always adorned with Lulu, a stuffed pig we'd bought when Nina took us to FAO Schwarz in New York.

We were way past the age of stuffed animals, and neither of us was a stuffed animal kind of girl, but we both loved this pig. There was only one left in the store, and we'd fought over who would get to buy her, or "adopt" her, as Jules insisted. Nina suggested we split the cost and have joint custody. So every birthday we traded her back and forth. Whoever had Lulu in her possession had to take care of her and give the other "mother" monthly reports on her well-being. *Lulu has thrived this spring,* Jules had written in one note. *She continues to be fuzzy and friendly and has developed a passion for Bruce Springsteen.*

Lulu has experienced her first crush, I wrote to Jules the next year. *On a stuffed giraffe in our attic. He's a little old for her, I think, but these sorts of urges are natural in a young pig.*

The teakettle whistled. Gavin poured the water and dunked the teabag.

"Oh, for Christ's sake," Liz said, using kitchen sheers to cut the ribbon.

"I love watching people receive gifts," Gavin said as he blew on his tea. It was some weird medicinal tea, and its bitter aroma filled the room. "Go on, open it."

Very slowly, I unwrapped the tissue paper, which smelled faintly like perfume, and lifted up a delicate, minuscule black lace thong.

I crumpled it in my hand, hiding it from Gavin. Liz squealed with glee.

"You set me up, Liz," Gavin said, shielding his eyes and walking back into the living room. "That's not nice."

"Didn't want to rob an old man of a thrill," she said, wiping tears of laughter from her eyes.

"Liz!" My face was burning up. "What am I supposed to do with this?"

"Do I have to explain?" she asked, cackling. "Don't act like such an innocent. We share a wall. A very thin wall. I know what you're up to at night, and I can't stand the thought of you shagging in your cotton knickers."

"How do you know I wear cotton underwear?"

"Oh, I'm sorry, what do you wear, then?" Liz asked. I stared at the table. The only underwear I owned were cotton. Mrs. Levander told us other materials led to yeast infections. "Just as I thought. Well, not anymore. Cotton knickers are for little girls, and you, my dear, are about to become a woman."

Thirty-three

ZACK AND I WERE AT THE BEACH WHEN I FINALLY OPENED the manila envelope from Dad. I couldn't wait until next week, but there was something about opening a birthday present alone that was just sad. Half the fun is someone watching.

"Let's see what you got," Zack said. Inside was a birthday card with a sparkly fairy on it, something more appropriate for an eight-year-old. But I didn't mind that. Dad still thought I loved girlie-girl stuff, and I smiled thinking of him searching the card aisle in CVS for something he thought was glittery enough for me. It was signed Dad and Polly, each in their own handwriting. There was also a note that said Alexi was having a sixth birthday party at their house, and if I wanted to come home for the party, they'd pay my way.

"'Alexi wants to spend more time with his new big sister,'" I read aloud to Zack. "Yeah right. That kid doesn't like me." It was true. Whenever I sat at the kitchen table for dinner, he turned his chair to face the other way.

"What's the gift?" Zack asked.

I unwrapped the present: a pair of jeans. Not just any pair. Clover, the new brand I'd seen in *InStyle* magazine that all the celebrities were wearing. I squealed with happiness. "Check it out," I said, and held them up. "Oh my god, they're awesome. I actually like them."

"You sound so surprised," Zack said as I slipped them over my bathing suit and spun around. They fit perfectly.

"This is a first," I said. "My Dad met the Great Birthday Challenge."

"What's that?" Zack asked.

"Every year since I was twelve, Dad has bought me an outfit that he picked out himself," I explained as I pulled the jeans off and folded them back up into the envelope. It was way too hot for jeans. "He said it was one of the great challenges of a father's life to buy his teenage daughter clothes that she actually liked and wore. The true test would be if I didn't exchange it."

"What was the worst gift?" Zack asked.

"My fourteenth," I said, and lay back in the sand. "It was a sparkly pink jean jacket." I looked up at the clouds, remembering some of the other "fashions." "And another time, he bought me one of those knitted dresses, but it looked like it'd been made by someone's drunk grandma." Zack laughed and started pouring sand over my legs in loose fistfuls. Zack was definitely a guy who thought girls were funny.

"But last year he actually came really close with this T-shirt dress thing." I shut my eyes and pictured it. It was the absolute best version of the scoop neck, cap-sleeve, empire waist style that everyone was wearing last summer. It looked so good but also had that "I'm not even trying" look.

"So what was wrong with that one?" Zack asked, patting sand around my legs.

"It was the color of mustard."

"Dijon or French's?"

"Grey Poupon." I ran the warm sand through my fingers. "I told him I loved it when I unwrapped it."

"Why?" Zack asked. He was covering my knees now.

"It was my first birthday since the divorce, and we were eating lobster at a nice restaurant and he was looking happy again. I didn't want to ruin it." I realized now that Dad had probably just started dating Polly around that time. I remembered noticing how cheerful Dad had been, that the color had returned to his face. Zack scooped sand around my thighs. I continued the story. "Dad was like, 'You really love it? You're not going to take it back?' and I was like, 'Yup, I love it.' But he didn't believe me." I could picture him narrowing his eyes and studying my face. The more I tried to convince him, the more obvious it was I didn't actually love it. "I finally fessed up after the chocolate mousse."

"Was he sad?" Zack asked, patting the sand over my legs.

"No," I said. I remembered Dad laughing and slapping the table with his hand. "God, I came so close!" he'd said. "So close and yet so far. I've failed the Great Birthday Challenge again, and I don't have that many more years left. I have to get it right while you're a teenager."

"It just made him more determined," I told Zack. "He said, 'Next year, on your eighteenth, I'm going to nail it. Mark my words. Next year I'll have a victory, even if I have to get a subscription to *Vogue*.'"

"He did it," Zack said. He was now carving a design into the sand that covered my legs. "He met the Great Birthday Challenge."

"Yup," I said.

"Why do you sound disappointed?" Zack asked.

"I don't know." Even though I loved the jeans and I wouldn't have traded them for anything, I kind of missed the sparkly jean jacket, the floral overalls, the purple jumper. I was too old for them now. For the first time on a birthday, I actually did feel older. Zack pulled my arms so that I was sitting upright. He'd transformed my legs into a fishtail, with scales and fins.

"I'm a mermaid," I said.

"A mer-chamber-maid," Zack said. "A very rare species. One hasn't washed up on these shores in a hundred years, and you need to get back in the water before the evil scientists spot you and take you to their lab for experiments."

"Oh," I said as he stood and opened his arms. I looked up at his eyes crinkling at the corners with a smile that was meant just for me. Warmth flooded my chest. I broke out of my sand encasement, put my arms around his neck, and hopped up. He caught my legs. "Hurry," I said. "Get me to the sea! We don't have much time!"

As we charged toward the water, a family of shorebirds scattered. I screamed as he dropped me in the cold salty water.

Thirty-four

THE NEXT DAY, I WAS CLEANING OFF THE TABLES ON THE patio after the breakfast rush when my phone buzzed in my back pocket. A text. I thought it was going to be Zack, who'd sometimes send me a quick message when he woke up; or maybe Liz, who sent me ridiculous sex tips throughout the day with suggestions for various positions. But it was Jules.

Meet me for lunch at the Even Keel?

I texted back immediately. My hand was shaking.

Yes! When?

Noon.

I work until 3 ☹.

We usually finished by two thirty, but I'd need some time to get my head together.

3:30?

OK C U then.

"Put that phone down," Bernadette said as she wiped down the tables, piling dirty cloth napkins in the laundry basket. "This isn't break time." I was too stunned to let Bernadette's tone bother me. I slipped my phone back in my pocket and carried an armload of dirty dishes into the kitchen, where Gavin was mixing something up in a ceramic bowl.

"Try this," he said, handing the batter-covered rubber spatula for me to sample. He was expanding his afternoon cookie repertoire lately, experimenting with new flavors. I ran my finger along the spatula's edge and tasted the sweet batter.

"Lime?" I asked.

"New recipe," Gavin said. "What do you think?"

"It's sweet and tart. It's kinda . . . complicated," I said.

"Complicated, huh? That's not exactly what I'm going for with my cookies."

"I mean complex," I said. I was mixing up my own recipe inside as I thought about seeing Jules. There was a half a cup of guilt over the fact that I was secretly dating her brother, a tablespoon of ice-cold fear that she'd found out about Zack and me, two pinches of boiling anger when I remembered how she'd acted at that party, a teaspoon of whipped hope that she missed me as much as I missed her, and a sprinkling of giddiness that I might get my best friend back.

Gavin sighed. "Well, I guess 'complex' could be good."

He used a tablespoon to drop the batter on a cookie sheet.

"Lime cookies will taste so good with your sweet peach sun tea."

"Now, that's a good idea, Cricket." Gavin's face brightened, his big smile deepening the lines around his mouth and revealing his slightly tea-stained teeth. "I knew I hired you for a reason." If I thought sweet peach sun tea would make this conversation with Jules easier, I'd have downed a gallon.

I was shaking when I entered the busy café. It was noisy with fifty conversations. It was 3:28 and the place was still slamming. I scanned the room for Jules, hoping that I'd arrived first. She wasn't inside, so I walked to the back patio. Jules was sitting at a shady table, a cup of coffee in hand. My ears started to hum. She looked up and waved, a half smile on her face.

"Hey. How's it going?" she asked.

"Fine," I said. I was so relieved when the waitress approached almost immediately. I ordered a chicken Caesar salad and an iced tea.

"I'm all set with coffee," Jules said to the waitress.

"Oh," I said, feeling dumb that I was going to be the only one eating. She had said lunch in her text, right? Shit. I wasn't even hungry.

"I already ate," she said with a shrug. "So, what's going on with you?"

I'm wearing a thong! I want to tell her. *I went swimming with a boy! Buck-ass naked! I think I'm in love. With your brother!*

"Not much," I said, folding my hands in front of me on the table. We were like those people we would see at The Coffee Exchange in Providence on Internet dates. While we were doing homework we listened to people on coffee dates have the world's most awkward conversations. We'd pass notes back and forth with our commentary. *He just wants to squeeze her big boobs,* Jules once wrote on my social studies folder as a girl went on and on about feminist theory and her bearded date made noises of pretend interest. *She's refusing to mention his vampire fangs!* I scribbled to Jules on the corner of her math homework another time when a guy at the next table polished his fake fangs with his index finger while his date talked about her dance class. *And he's dying to discuss!*

We sat there for another thirty seconds in awkward silence, each of us taking in the café surroundings as if we were foreigners observing American island culture. Finally, I just came out with it. "Let me just start by saying that I'm really glad you texted me. I've been so, so worried about you."

"You don't have to worry about me, Cricket."

"But, Jules. I care about you. I'm your . . . friend." I'd stopped myself from saying best friend.

"My mom died," she said. "You can't expect me to act normal."

"No," I said. "I know."

"You have to let me act how I want to," she said. The tips of her ears reddened.

"But even if you want to act mean? Like telling Jay what I said about his brother. Do you like him?"

"No," she said, shaking her head.

"Why did you do that?" The waitress dropped off my iced tea. I looked her in the eye and smiled. "Thank you so much," I said. If she overheard any of this, I wanted her to be on my side. I pounded the straw out of its paper case and took a long drink.

"I was drunk, and it just came out."

"Yeah, well, thanks. He'll never go out with me now. And that night, at the party, you were acting like a different person."

"I am different," she said, as if I were proving her point.

"But you're still you," I said. "You're still Jules Clayton."

"I'm not," she said.

"But *I* didn't do anything wrong."

"My family is mine. You've been acting like it's yours."

"We were all acting like that," I said, my voice trembling with hurt. I crossed my arms. "You invited me to spend the night all the time. Nina always set a place for me at the table. Even on school nights. I didn't do anything wrong." Jules raised her eyebrows at me. "What? What did I do?"

"The memorial service?" She said this like it was the most obvious thing in the world. I looked at her blankly. The Caesar salad landed in front of me.

"Fresh pepper?" the waitress asked.

"No, thank you." I turned back to Jules. "What did I do?"

221

"You weren't supposed to talk," Jules said. She sat back and folded her arms.

"But I asked you afterward, remember? And you said it was fine. You said it was great."

"Mom had just died," she whispered. "I didn't know what I was saying."

I stared at the salad I knew I wasn't going to be able to eat. "I thought . . . I mean, when you were up there you looked like you were about to laugh or die. You even said yourself that you were freaking out."

"It wasn't your place. She wasn't your mom. She was mine."

"I thought I was helping," I said.

"Well, you were wrong."

"Your dad didn't mind. Zack didn't mind."

"I did," Jules said. I sat back, inhaling the coffee-scented café air. I didn't want to be wrong and I didn't want her to be right, but as I watched her shoulders rising and falling with deep, shaky breaths, it was so clear.

"I'm sorry," I said. "I'm really, really sorry." I wanted to fling myself over the table and hug her. I wanted to reach out and touch her hands. She put her hands in her lap in such a way that made me feel like I might never be able to touch her again. I balled up my hands. My eyes filled.

"Sometimes I think I smell her perfume," I said, wiping the tears away with a stiff napkin. "It happened once when I got off the ferry, and again when I was walking past The

White Elephant. Does that ever happen to you? Do you ever smell her perfume?"

"Marc Jacobs perfume is really popular." Jules shook her head and stirred her coffee. I sensed I was annoying her. I willed my tears to stop. "Look, I can't explain how I'm feeling, but that's the thing. I don't want to explain how I'm feeling, and I shouldn't have to. No one else is asking me to."

"Okay," I said. "I understand." I pushed the salad around on my plate. "What made you text me?"

"Zack," she said. "Freak boy."

"Oh." My shoulders caved as guilt flooded my chest.

"He said I owed it to you to at least tell you why I was mad. He believes in discussing feelings." She rolled her eyes.

"Oh," I said, and slid the pepper toward her, wondering if she'd build a leaning pepper tower like she always did at school.

"So what are you doing for your birthday? It's on Tuesday, right?" she asked, ignoring the pepper.

"Yeah. I think the people at the inn are going to have a little party maybe."

"That sounds nice," she said. I met her eyes. "I better go. I'm working tonight." She picked up her bag like it weighed a hundred pounds. "Look, I feel bad, okay? I know you didn't mean it."

"It's okay."

"And I know I've been a total bitch." She closed her

eyes, defeated, and then swung her bag over her shoulder and sighed.

"It's okay."

"Happy birthday, Cricket." She smiled. It wasn't a real smile. But it was close.

Thirty-five

"I'D KILL FOR YOUR FLAXEN TRESSES," LIZ SAID OVER THE noise of the hair dryer. I was sitting in front of the vanity in her room in my bathrobe. She had put hot curlers in my hair a half hour ago, and now she was taking them out, revealing wavy perfection. My hair had never looked so good. I'd thought curlers were for grandmas, but now I was thinking I needed to ask for a set of these for Christmas.

"You're giving me magazine hair!" I clapped.

"Tonight is the night," Liz said.

"I don't know about that," I said.

"Oh, who are you kidding?" Liz said, laughing.

"Seriously, I can't do it with this guy, but I still want to look hot."

"You're going to torture this poor bloke," Liz said.

Zack was taking me out on a real date for my birthday, which was technically at 12:31 a.m. He wanted to be with me the moment I turned eighteen, so we were celebrating Monday night. We were going out to dinner at Gigi's, the place where he worked as a busboy and one of the nicest, most expensive restaurants on Nantucket. It was not a place for children. It was a place for women in high heels and expensive dresses and men in ties and loafers. I'd peeked in the windows once and seen a grown couple making out.

"Are you sure you want to take me there?" I'd asked Zack when he told me the plan. The cheapest thing on the menu was the bleu cheese hamburger, and it was thirty-three dollars. But he'd said yes. He and the chef, Anne-Marie, had become friends this summer.

"Anne-Marie promised me an unforgettable meal, on the house. And Jeff, the manager, said he'd turn a blind eye if I happened to bring in a bottle of champagne, which you know I have."

"Are you sure your dad won't miss that champagne?"

"Uh, yeah," Zack said. "I'm sure."

"Okay, then," I said. "I'll meet you there."

"Eight o'clock?"

"Eight o'clock."

I was a little worried about people seeing us together. Every day felt like an extension on a paper, one more day of putting off something we had to do—break it off. But every day also tasted like ice cream. And I always wanted another bite.

I'd been thinking about this date all day while I cleaned. After Liz and I finished the rooms, I checked in with George, who was now communicating only with hand signals. The particular one he was giving me meant go away.

So I took a long shower, using the Bumble and bumble shampoo a guest had left behind. I'd waited a week for the guest to call and reclaim it, but there hadn't been a word. The shampoo was mine. I sat down in the shower to shave my legs. I toweled off, put on some nice lotion, and once I was completely dry, I slipped the green dress over my head. I looked in the mirror. Perfection. Liz insisted I put a robe over my dress as she did my hair and makeup.

"Ouch," I said, when one of her curlers snagged, pulling my hair.

"Well, do you want to be beautiful or do you want to be comfortable?" Liz asked as she untangled it.

"Can't I be both?" I asked.

"No," she said, slapping some product on her hands and twisting the ends of my hair. "You must choose. Beauty or comfort."

"Fine," I said. "Beauty."

"Good girl."

Thirty-six

WHEN I HEARD THE WHISTLE ACROSS THE STREET, I KNEW
it was meant for me. Since I'd stepped out of the inn, I'd felt
eyes on me. Liz had worked wonders with my hair, making it appear thicker and bouncier than ever before, and
she'd applied little fake eyelashes one by one with a pair of
tweezers to "open up" my eyes. At first I told her there was
no way I was going to let her put fake eyelashes on me, but
she assured me they'd look great. She was right.

But it was the dress that was turning heads. This dress
was a beautiful-girl costume. Another whistle. I thought
maybe it was Zack, but when I turned my head, it was Jay.
He was across the street, flanked by Fitzy and Oliver. They
had fishing poles over their shoulders. Jay was holding a
tackle box, and Fitzy was barefoot, smoking a cigar.

"C.T.," Jay said.

"Hi," I said, and waved.

They watched me cross the street. Fitzy narrowed his eyes and puffed on his cigar. Before I'd arrived, I had this idea that Nantucket was so small that it would be impossible not to run into the people you knew. But it wasn't like that. I hadn't seen these guys since that night at the party in 'Sconset. A few times, I'd actually tried to will Jay to appear so I could explain to him, in my own words, how sorry I was about what I said about his brother. Maybe there'd been a delayed reaction to my prayers, because there he was, looking happy to see me. I wondered for a second if I should be nervous, if this was a trick, if Jay was going to make me think everything was cool and then tell me off, but I didn't think so. He was drinking me in like a cold glass of lemonade.

"I don't believe we've met," Fitzy said.

"Yes, we have," I said.

"I think I'd remember," he said. "What's your name?"

"Cricket," I said. I watched him listen. This was the power of looking good. It made boys pay attention. It popped their little independence bubble.

"I'm Andrew Fitzpatrick," he said, and planted a cool kiss on my hand.

"Cricket Thompson"—Jay glared at him—"is a friend of mine from Providence." A friend? I met his gaze. Jay's bright blue eyes shone against his tanned caramel skin. There was no doubt about it: Jay was probably one of the best-looking guys in the world, and summer had given him a glowing confidence. He's going to be important someday, I thought.

"Where are you off to looking so beautiful?" he asked.

"Dinner," I said, feeling myself flush.

"What I wouldn't do to be dinner," Fitzy said, shaking his head and biting his cigar.

"You sound like someone's gross uncle," Oliver said, laughing.

"How about you guys go ahead," Jay said, nodding his head at Fitzy and Oliver. "I'll catch up with you later."

"How come you get a private audience with this gorgeous woman?" Fitzy asked him.

"Because she's my friend," Jay said. There was that word again. *Friend.*

"We'll just pop into the pharmacy for a hot dog," Oliver said, slapping Fitzy on the back. "Would you like a dog, Jay?"

"I could eat a dog," said Jay. Fitzy snuffed his cigar, and the two of them went inside the pharmacy.

"Listen," I said, "I need to apologize. I'm so sorry for what I said. It was horrible and judgmental and I'm just so sorry."

"Apology accepted," he said.

"Really?" This seemed too easy.

"Jules told me she'd taken the comment out of context."

"She did? Really?" He nodded. "Oh my god, that's great."
I breathed in deeply. Air filled a spot in my lungs that had been puckering since the fight. Jules had made things right. She had forgiven me.

"She also showed me this." Jay pulled out of his pocket the list I'd made the morning after the party at Nora's, my top five reasons for liking Jay Logan.

There was tape along the edges, and I could tell that Jules had saved it in our notebook and removed it to give to Jay. "I especially liked number five," he said, and I reread it. *Jay always sticks up for his brother so I know he's a good guy with a real heart.* "I guess I also like number one." *He has big, dreamy eyes and the best boy butt I've ever seen.*

"I'm so embarrassed," I said.

"Don't be," he said. "It's nice."

"Oh," I said. "Well, I'm just so glad this is cleared up. . . ." I trailed off. He was gazing at me the way I'd wanted him to since the eighth grade. His smile was so bright and winning, I was in a spotlight. The people passing by all seemed to notice us. They were looking at us the way I'd looked at the glossy, dressed-up Nantucketers when I'd stepped off the ferry. My throat was dry.

"Me too. 'Cause I was hoping you'd be my girl next year." His girl? So old-fashioned. And yet . . . like something Jay-Z might say to Beyoncé. It was the invitation I'd been waiting for for three years. Was he asking me out? He was, right? Being Jay Logan's girlfriend would be like winning a prize. I'd be untouchable. Golden. Chosen for a better life. It would be like getting into Princeton, early admission, with a full ride for specialness. I smiled.

"Is that a yes?" Jay asked, and stepped closer to me.

He was standing so close, glimmering like some kind of

American hero in his faded Whale's Tale beer T-shirt. We would be the couple of the year. I drank in the possibility. There had been times when I'd imagined this moment at lacrosse practice, and it always made me run faster.

"I've thought about that night at Nora's," he said. "I really wanted to kiss you."

"Me too," I said. It was true. I'd obsessed about that moment at the beginning of the summer. But not recently. Now that I thought about it, I hadn't fantasized about kissing him, or played the Jay playlist for weeks. It struck me that I didn't want to go any further with him than this. Right here. This was enough. This was the fantasy. Maybe this whole time, the possibility of Jay was all I'd wanted. But before I could tease this thought apart from all the others that were going through my mind, he placed a gentle hand on my back, leaned in, and pressed his lips to mine. Jay Logan was actually kissing me!

I pressed back. I did. I kissed him back because I had to know if it was the idea of Jay or Jay himself that I liked so much. I tingled with a feeling that I was doing something wrong, which was confusing because tingling is tingling.

"Nice move, Logan," said Fitzy. "Way to break your buddy's heart." We pulled apart. There were Fitzy and Oliver, hands full of hot dogs. The church bells chimed eight o'clock.

"I'm having a party on Friday," Fitzy said. "Eighty-two Cliff Road. Bring your sister."

"I don't have a sister," I said.

"Damn," he said.

"I have to go," I said.

I spotted Zack as soon as I pushed open the bright red door of Gigi's. He was sitting at a table by a window with a bouquet of wildflowers and a bottle of champagne, looking at his watch. He was wearing a button-down shirt and his Nantucket Reds.

"Hi," I said. He looked at me and stood up. He was only six feet away, but I couldn't get to him fast enough. Any confusion I'd experienced on the walk over vanished like a drop of water in direct sunlight. He put his arms around me and I kissed him. And when I did: phosphorescence.

"I'm in love with you, Zack Clayton," I said.

"I'm in love with you, too," he said, and kissed me again. "I'm in love with my secret lover."

Thirty-seven

IT HAPPENED IN MY LITTLE ROOM WITH THE SLANTED ceiling right before the sun came up and all the champagne was gone. It wasn't what I thought it would be at all. It wasn't as easy as they make it look in the movies. It took kind of a while to get everything all lined up and protected and ready to go. The actual sex part was pretty short, and I was relieved it was short. I know I'm supposed to want it to last, but I didn't. I've heard that's kind of normal for a first time. I kept my eyes open, when I always thought I'd be the type to keep them shut. Oh, and the kissing was still my favorite part, which isn't what I thought, that the first thing you do with a boy could be the best. And I did feel different afterward; I felt all shaky and energized. Maybe that's because it's good exercise. I think that's what they say, anyway. And my face was really hot, and that made me feel pretty. I didn't think I would feel pretty. Or if I did, I thought it would be in a flowing-white-nightgown kind of way, not a cheeks-full-of-embers way.

I wanted to call someone. And not because I wanted to spill every little detail, but because I wanted it to be known that something had happened to me. I wanted to stay awake, even as Zack seemed to be drifting off. I touched his muscular back. He was the most beautiful thing I had ever seen. I picked his button-down shirt off the floor and put it on to sleep in. It smelled like him. I promised myself I would always remember the moment of putting on his shirt.

"Are you sure you wouldn't be embarrassed to go out with me?" he asked, his arm around me as we spooned.

"Yes," I said. "I'm sure." This time, I meant it.

He kissed my hair and I heard his breath deepen as he fell asleep.

I thought I was awake all night, because I remember the sky whitening and the birdsong and smiling at the ceiling. But I must've drifted off, because when I heard the knock at the door, I was dreaming I was back in Providence, sitting in front of a roaring fire on the big sofa in the living room. In my dream it was winter. Outside, a snowstorm howled. The sky was purple-gray, snow was flying sideways, and the wind was knocking against the windows, but I was under the cream-colored blanket. I was warm, warm, warm.

But the knocking was too persistent for a dream. It was real.

"Cricket?" a voice said. I knew that voice. I missed that voice. I loved that voice. The sound of it lured me out of the warm bath of sleep. My eyes fluttered open. There was Jules with Lulu the pig in one hand and a waffle topped with whipped cream in the other. For a second, I smiled. She'd brought Lulu to Nantucket! She'd found my room! She'd remembered my birthday! She'd made a waffle and carried it all the way from Darling Street! And oh, there was something I needed to tell her. As I held my breath trying to remember what it was that was so important, so wonderfully important, I watched her face register disgust.

"Zack?" she asked.

Thirty-eight

I SAT ON THE PATIO, WEARING THE CONSTRUCTION PAPER birthday crown Liz had made me, taking deep breaths, trying to focus on the bouquet of yellow and white flowers in a vase in front of me, which had arrived just an hour ago. I'd read somewhere that flowers absorb negative energy, making the space around them more positive; this was why flowers made sick or angry people feel better. I was hoping it worked for worried people, too. It was almost four o'clock and I hadn't heard from Jules or Zack since they'd left this morning at seven, even though I'd been calling both of them obsessively. As soon as Jules saw Zack sleeping shirtless beside me, she'd put Lulu and the waffle on the floor and left without another word. She slammed the door on her way out, which woke up Zack. When I told him what had just happened, he kissed me once and left to find her.

When the delivery boy dropped the flowers at the front desk and Gavin called out, "Flowers for the birthday girl!" I thought they were from Zack, and my heart pushed against my ribs as I stripped off my pink latex gloves and dove for the card. For a second I thought that maybe he hadn't been able to return my four phone calls and six texts because Jules had been nearby, but somehow he'd found time to send me flowers. Or maybe, I thought, he felt that because we'd had sex for the first time last night, some higher form of communication was necessary—communication by flowers. But I opened the little white envelope and my eyes landed on the word *Mom* with a thud.

"They're from my mom," I said to Gavin.

"That was lovely of her!" Gavin admonished me gently. "Don't sound so disappointed."

It had been Liz's day off. (I was surprised when she didn't switch with me for my birthday, but she and Shane had both orchestrated Tuesdays as their day off and they were sacred to her. They refused to spend a single Tuesday apart. She was bringing him to my little birthday party.) She'd spent the night at Shane's, so I hadn't even been able to tell her what happened. I wondered if Bernadette had been able to sense my anxiety, because she'd been nicer to me than usual, meaning that she left me alone and didn't make me crawl under beds to hunt the dust bunnies.

The first time I'd seen Liz today was fifteen minutes ago when she placed the crown on my head and disappeared into the kitchen, leaving Shane and me to make awkward conversation on the patio. Thankfully, he'd gone inside after a minute, leaving me alone with my thoughts. My head was too busy and too tangled to make small talk. On the one hand, I was thrilled. I'd had sex! I was in love! I was different and my cheeks had been blushing for eight hours straight to prove it. I'd catch glimpses of myself in mirrors and place a hand on my new face. I was warm and glowing. At the same time, guilt and shame washed over me in waves, sending acid to my stomach. All I wanted to do was steal Liz away so that I could tell her everything, and she could both celebrate with me and reassure me that I wasn't a terrible person, that what I'd done was understandable and okay, that Jules would come around and be happy for me.

I could feel the late afternoon sun burning my arms as I listened to Gavin and Liz gather plates, forks, and glasses for the iced tea for my mini birthday party.

"You look like one conflicted birthday girl," George said as he walked up the porch steps. He was finally off of his crutches and was carrying something in his hand. It was wrapped in newspaper.

"I have a lot on my mind," I said, forcing a smile.

"I can see that." He put the newspaper-wrapped item in front of me. "Here. This is for you. Open it."

"Wow, thanks, George." I hadn't expected a gift from him. I smiled when I saw the Apple logo on the box. "Oh my god, George, is this the new iPad?" It was the one that just came out. "Wow! Are you sure?"

"Yes." George put his elbow on the table and rested his hand in his palm. He smiled. "Do you like it?"

"I love it! This is so nice."

"You've been a great intern. I couldn't have done it without you. It's the least I can do." He tapped out a beat on the table.

"It's so cool." I took it out of its box. "Thank you so much."

"And check this out," he said, motioning for me to hand it to him. He showed me a voice-recording app. "I don't know if working with me this summer will have any influence on you, but just in case, I figure you should be prepared. You never know when you might find yourself in the middle of a great story. They're happening all the time, and now you can record them." He nodded at someone inside and put an arm on my shoulder. "Now, cover your ears, Thompson, I don't want to hurt you with my singing voice."

"Happy birthday to you. . . ." George started as Gavin carried a dark chocolate cake decorated with a wreath of sugary violets and topped with eighteen sparkling candles out to the patio. Liz followed with a pitcher of iced tea topped with lemon slices, and Shane carried a tray of glasses, forks, and the nice, gold-rimmed china plates.

"Happy birthday to Cricket," they all sang. "Happy birthday to you!"

As I was blowing out the candles, I wished for two things at once.

Liz shrieked. She was looking at the newspaper the iPad

was wrapped in that I'd left on the table. It was *The Inquirer and Mirror*, the local Nantucket paper. "Cricket, it's you!" she said, pointing at the cover photograph. "It's you in your green dress with your secret boyfriend." It was a big picture of Jay and me, kissing on Main Street. The headline read: "Young Love Blooms in the Perfect Summer Weather." She laughed. "I guess he's not your secret boyfriend anymore!"

Thirty-nine

ZACK HAD TO HAVE SEEN THE PAPER. IT WAS EVERYWHERE on this island. *The Inquirer and Mirror*, with Jay's and my picture on the front page, would not go unnoticed, not in a million years.

After the birthday party, after I'd forced myself to eat a piece of cake and smile and thank everybody for celebrating with me, I decided to go for a run. Liz had made pointed eye contact with me throughout the party. She kept pinching my thigh and asking me if I felt different. I'd managed to nod and give her a thumbs-up and even laugh a little, but it had taken all of my strength.

I didn't want to talk to her about what had happened anymore. I didn't even want to try to get her on my side. I wasn't even on my side. Why would she be? What I had done to Jules, losing my virginity to her little brother only a few months after her mom died, was terrible. And kissing Jay, while it had seemed innocent at the time, even *productive* in some way, had been a huge betrayal of Zack's trust. How would I have felt if I saw a picture of Zack kissing another girl on the very same night we'd had sex? Horrible. Miserable. Pissed. I clutched my stomach as though I were swallowing poison, not buttercream frosting. Thankfully, Shane wanted to take Liz surfing, and she never said no to surfing with Shane. So when the party ended, I could just drop the charade and remove the happy mask.

I was too anxious to stay inside. I was too anxious to merely walk. I needed to run. I needed to sprint. I needed to work up a salty sweat and hear my feet pound the pavement and feel the sun searing the back of my neck. I needed to feel my heart pump blood and my breath get ragged and scratchy in my lungs. I needed to jump into the depths of the cold Atlantic Ocean. I needed to plunge my head under the water, open my mouth, and scream so loud the ferries rocked.

I put on my sports bra and bikini bottoms under shorts and a T-shirt and laced up my sneakers tight. I slipped my ponytail through a Red Sox hat that had been lingering in the lost and found for three weeks, and pulled the brim low over my eyebrows. I jogged out of town on Centre Street to Cliff Road.

I was halfway to the beach when I saw the red Volvo coming toward me. That was Parker's car! Quills of panic pierced my stomach. I bet Parker knew everything. I bet Jules had told her. Parker was confident, fearless, and mean. And she was driving fast. I stopped and turned away from the road, wishing I had a shell to hide under. Was Jules in the car? Was Zack? I tried to make it look like I was tying my shoe. I was shaking, practically hyperventilating.

What had happened back in Providence was an accident. I thought I was doing the right thing by speaking at Nina's memorial service. I had stood up and spoken with the best of intentions. And no matter what Jules thought, I'd followed her out to Nantucket out of love for her. But what had happened last night was no accident. And kissing Jay wasn't a mistake, either. I'd kissed him back.

I heard the Volvo slow and I squeezed my eyes shut, covering my face in some primal pose of protection. I heard a window roll down. My heart was knocking desperately against my ribs. "Are you okay?" someone asked. It wasn't Parker and Jules in the Volvo, but a grandma and grandpa. "Do you need some help, sweetheart?"

"Just a runner's cramp," I said, catching my breath. "I'm okay." I stood up.

"You're positively crimson. And probably dehydrated." The woman handed me an Evian. "It's too hot for running. Do you want a ride somewhere?"

"No. No, thank you," I said, taking the chilled bottle. They drove off.

It wasn't Parker, but I couldn't seem to transmit this

message from my brain to the rest of my body. I was shaking. My legs felt like jelly. I couldn't seem to fill my lungs with the air they needed. I wanted to get back to the inn, turn off the lights, and hide under the covers in my little room with the rose wallpaper and the slanted ceiling. How was I going to get there if I couldn't walk, if I couldn't even breathe?

"I'm taking a few days off," I said to Gavin the next morning. He was sitting at the reception desk, penciling something into the giant reservation book. "I think Bernadette can cover for me."

"What?" he said with a furrowed brow. He sounded annoyed for the first time since I'd met him. "You know, usually you try to arrange someone to cover for you *before* you announce that you're taking time off."

"I'm really sorry, but it's a family emergency." This wasn't a lie. This did feel like an emergency. Hot tears pricked my eyes.

"Is everything okay?" he asked. I nodded, unable to speak. "When are you leaving?"

"Tomorrow," I said. I'd called Dad last night and he was still willing to fly me back to Providence for Alexi's birthday party. He booked me on a flight that would land in Providence at three thirty. I'd be at his house by four o'clock. I wanted to get off this island as soon as possible. They call Nantucket the faraway island. It's so self-contained that it really can make you feel like you're in an enchanted, distant world, that some magical mist separates you from reality. But it can also make you feel trapped and isolated. I wanted to get out of there.

"Cricket," Gavin called as I walked down the hall. "You are coming back, aren't you?"

"Yes," I said, without looking at him. "I'll only be gone for two days." I'd already hurt and pissed off so many people, what was one more lie?

"You look like hell," George said when I went to tell him that I'd be gone for a few days. George's leg was healed, he was off his crutches, and he was almost done with the book. He really didn't need me anymore.

"It's a family emergency," I said. That phrase had stopped Gavin from asking more questions, and it had the same effect on George.

"I'm really sorry to hear that," George said. "Is there anything I can do?" I shook my head. "Okay. Well, you'll be back by the weekend, right?"

"I think," I said, looking at the carpet.

"Because I was hoping you'd do an interview for me."

"For the book?" He nodded. For one quick second I wasn't thinking about Zack or Jules. "Like, a real live journalist interview?"

"Yes." He smiled. "A real live journalist interview."

"Who would I interview?"

"Paul Morgan. He's a friend of your mom's, right?"

"Yeah."

"I've been going through my notes, and his name comes up more than once. I think he and Boaty were pretty good friends at one point. He might have some unexpected treasure for me."

"How will I know what to ask?" I wanted to get out of there, but it would have been a shame to miss out on this. It was my chance to really be a part of the book.

"I'll help you," he said. "That is, if you think you'll have time to do it."

Forty

"FIRST OF ALL, THANK YOU SO MUCH FOR MEETING ME,"
I said to Paul Morgan. I'd called him right from the annex,
and he'd agreed to meet with me the next morning before
my flight. We were sitting in the living room of his house
on Union Street. It had wooden floors and a mix of antique
furniture and modern things. There were some paintings
of boats on the walls, framed nautical charts, and also the
kind of unexpected things that Nina would've picked out.
A bright red rocking chair. A poster from a theater festival
in France. The guy had style. Mom would like this place,
I thought. I scanned the mantelpiece for pictures of a wife
and family, but only saw people who looked like friends. I
think it was safe to say that Paul Morgan was single.

"Oh, I'm happy to do it," Paul said. "My schedule on Nantucket is very open."

"Well, I really appreciate it. I know your time is valuable." I was remembering what George said about being polite. He told me how important it was to make the interviewees comfortable so that they'll reveal their own stories, hand them over like the keys to their house. George said that a lot of journalists were jerks in the way that they tried to get information. They tried to catch people off guard and make them uncomfortable, but George's philosophy was the opposite.

"If you don't mind, I'm going to record this," I said, and pressed the screen of my iPad. The chair I sat in was so big that I needed to sit on the very edge of it for my feet to touch the ground.

"I don't mind a bit," he said, laughing a little. "I've got nothing to hide. So, you're writing a book about Boaty Carmichael?"

"No, *I'm* not," I said. My brow furrowed. He thought that this was some kind of school project. "George Gust the journalist is."

"George Gust the journalist?"

"He writes for *The New York Times* and *The New Yorker*," I said. George had only been published once in *The New Yorker*, but it sounded so impressive to me. "The book is being published by Random House. It will be out in the spring." Paul Morgan nodded, making the "I'm impressed" frown. "I'm his intern," I continued, "and he thought since you were a *special friend* of my mother's that it would be okay if I interviewed you." I watched his face closely as I said "special friend." Sure enough, his eyes twinkled. More on this later, I thought. Even if I didn't come back to Nantucket, it didn't mean I couldn't arrange a meeting with Paul and Mom somewhere else. In Boston, maybe.

"Well, what would you like to know?" he asked, and clapped his hands once.

"I guess I'd like to know about any particularly fond memories of Boaty."

"Well, let's see. I met Boaty the summer after college. I've been coming here all my life, but it was Boaty's first summer on the island. After a month, he knew everyone. He was very charming. My own mother had a crush on him. I remember him bringing her a birthday present, and forget it, it's like he was already building his campaign. He had her vote for life."

"What was the present?"

"A bottle of Oil of Olay!" he said, as if he were realizing for the first time how funny that was. We both laughed. "He was kind of a hick when I first met him, but, boy, he got savvy fast."

And we were off. Paul settled back in his chair and spoke of a sailing trip they went on, and how Boaty made the best ham-and-pickle sandwich in the world by slipping potato chips under white bread slathered with yellow mustard, and the bonfire beach parties that lasted until dawn. George was right. People liked to talk. I looked at the grandfather clock. An hour had gone by, and with the exception of a few questions asking Paul to elaborate or "tell me more about that," I'd hardly been able to get a word in. It was almost time for me to go. I wasn't sure I'd gotten anything out of him that we'd be able to use, but my plane was leaving in a few hours and I needed to wrap it up.

"Thank you so much," I said at the first awkward silence. "This was very helpful." I closed my notebook and shut off my iPad.

"So," Paul said, gripping the edges of his armchair, "your mother and father must be so proud of you, an intern for a journalist and you're not even out of high school. Are they planning on visiting you?"

"I'm trying to convince my mother," I said. "But they won't come together. They're divorced."

"I'm so sorry to hear that," he said.

"It happens, I guess."

"If your mother visits, I'd love to take you two out to dinner."

"I'll pass along the message."

He smiled at me warmly as he stood from his chair and walked me to the door. I trailed him through the kitchen with the speckled floor and the old-fashioned-looking sink. Blue and white dishes were stacked on open shelves. Lemon-yellow curtains billowed in the breeze. I could definitely see Mom in this kitchen, if she would only give it a chance.

"Oh, here's a detail you might like," he said. "Everyone thought Boaty got his nickname because he loved boats so much."

"Yeah, there's a story that as a toddler he made a boat out of a laundry basket and insisted on sleeping in it," I said. Paul opened the front door and we stepped onto the porch into the perfect Nantucket morning—warm, breezy, sweet-smelling.

"That may be true," Paul Morgan said, "but that's not how he got his name."

"Oh. How'd he get it?"

"His little brother gave it to him. He had a big birthmark in the shape of a boat, on his lower back." I smiled and made a note in my notebook. This was exactly the kind of detail that George was after. I'd succeeded after all!

"You look just like your mother when you smile," he said. "I bet you're a real heartbreaker."

You have no idea, I thought as I shook his hand and thanked him one last time. *You have no idea.*

Forty-one

DAD PLANTED A KISS ON MY FOREHEAD WHEN I STEPPED out of the cab. He handed the driver some money and took my duffel bag. There were bunches of balloons tied to the porch railing. In front of the house hung a big colorful banner that spelled out HAPPY BIRTHDAY, ALEXI! in primary colors.

"Hi, Dad." I leaned into his shirt. He wrapped his arms around me and gave me a squeeze. This is what I'd needed. A Dad hug. I couldn't exactly tell him what had happened (who wants to tell their dad the details of their love life?), but I was hoping he might be able to sense my wound and apply his special Dad Band-Aid. When I was little and I'd fallen down and scraped my knee, he would sweep me into his arms so fast that I'd actually forget to cry. The tears were coming now, so I squeezed him back, hard, hoping to make them stop.

I hadn't told Mom I was coming home yet. I couldn't take her sadness. It was so dark and deep, I was afraid, now more than ever, that it'd pull me in and I wouldn't be able to get out. What if I was like her? What if I became permanently sad? What if the same cloud was destined to hover over my head?

Dad ended our hug with three pats on the back and guided me up the walkway. "Come on, the party is in full swing."

"Okay," I said.

"Your Aunt Phyllis is here," he said. "And so is Uncle Rob." I was about to ask why Aunt Phyllis, who lived in Maine and only visited at Christmas, was here in Providence, when Dad opened the gate to the backyard. There were llamas in my father's backyard. Llamas! There were other animals, too. There was a sheep, a goat, and a pig—an entire petting zoo. There was one of those jumpy castles. There was a guy in overalls sitting on a bale of hay playing songs for kids. There was a popcorn maker, like the kind they have in movie theaters. And who were all these people? Was that a waitress serving the punch? The only thing that had come close to this was Mom's fortieth birthday party, and even that hadn't included a waitress.

"Oh my god, Dad. This is amazing. What's all this for?"

"Alexi's birthday," he said. "He's six!"

"It's so cool that you did all this."

"Well, it made Polly happy for me to make a big to-do," Dad said, beaming. "And if Polly's happy, I'm happy." There was Polly in a sundress. She did look happy. Her hands were on Alexi's shoulder. He was watching the guitar guy, riveted. Polly waved to me and I waved back.

"So, Dad, do you notice anything?" I asked, and twirled around in my new jeans.

"A haircut?" Dad asked.

"No! I'm wearing the jeans you got me. My Clovers!"

"Oh, do you like them?"

"I love them!"

"Good. Polly picked them out," he said. I kept smiling, even as my thoughts were suddenly treading dark pathways. He hadn't met the Great Birthday Challenge after all. Polly had chosen my present. He had given up on the very last year.

A woman I didn't know approached us. She and Dad started talking about the special school Alexi was going to in the fall.

"Your father is an absolute saint," the woman said to me. "An angel!"

"I know," I said, my cheeks hurting from smiling. One of the goats bleated. Dad didn't even like zoos. He was allergic to all animals.

"Go put your bag inside, honey, so you can enjoy the party," he said, and gave my shoulder a squeeze.

"Okay." I headed into the house. I put my bag in the kitchen and looked for a glass to fill with water. I couldn't find the glasses. I didn't know where they were kept. So

I grabbed a mug and held it under the tap. As it filled, I looked out the kitchen window at Polly and Alexi.

I watched as Dad brought Polly a drink and put his arm around her. He tussled Alexi's hair. Polly called Dad her "knight in shining armor," her "dream guy." And I got it now. He would do anything for them. He would turn his yard into a zoo. He *loves* them, I thought as I watched Polly lean on him. He *really loves* them.

I took a sip of water and found my hand shaking. Dad had traded Mom and me in for Polly and Alexi. We were out and they were in, and it was just our tough luck. It wasn't fair. It wasn't fair at all. Those people, those *strangers*, stole my family. I drank the water. Then I spotted an open bottle of wine. With a shaky hand, I filled the mug to the top and downed it in just a few swallows. My empty stomach seemed to curl around it. A scream sat at the bottom of my lungs, waiting, like a crocodile.

"Hey, honey, you find what you needed?" Dad asked as the screen door slammed behind him.

I turned around and crossed my arms, glaring at him.

"You okay?" Dad asked.

"Eighteen is a much bigger birthday than six," I said. I hated how bratty I sounded, but the wine had gone straight to my head. I was dizzy and warm and certain I was right.

"Don't tell me that you wanted a petting zoo, Cricket." He was smiling, but he looked kind of scared. His eyes searched mine as if to ask, *"Are you joking?"*

"You couldn't pick something out for me, but you got

Alexi a . . . a . . . farm festival?" My voice was shrill, loud. I could hear it, but I couldn't stop it, like it was coming from a different person.

"I thought you liked the jeans." He put a hand on my back. I recoiled from it like it was a hot iron.

"That's not the point," I said.

"Well, what *is* the point?" he asked.

"I wanted *you* to pick them out. Only you."

"Well, Polly and I are a team now."

A team? Barf. "You know, maybe if you'd done something like *this* for Mom she wouldn't have gotten so depressed. But you never even tried."

"Yes, I did," he whispered.

"Not like this," I said, pointing to the party outside. Tears sprang to my eyes. "You never tried *this* hard!"

"Oh, honey." He opened his arms, but I took a quick step backward.

"Why didn't you fight for her? Why didn't you fight for us?" I pressed my fingertips to my chest so hard I left a red mark. Tears poured down my cheeks. I couldn't catch my breath. Dad tried to hug me, but I sidestepped him, turned away, and gripped the counter. "I don't even know why you love them. Polly's not that great and Alexi isn't even your kid. Who knows whose kid he really is."

"Cricket, that's enough," Dad said. His voice was low and angry.

I turned around. Polly was standing there, covering her mouth.

"You need to leave," Polly said. Dad wrapped his arms around her as if she were a little girl, as if she were his one and only daughter, as if she needed protection from some awful stranger who'd barged into their home.

"I didn't mean it like that," I said to Dad, pleading. My ears were ringing. "It's not fair. I didn't know she was there."

"Go to your mom's," Dad said, shaking his head at me. "Just get your things and go to your mom's."

I grabbed my duffel bag and ran out the back door.

I was at the Claytons' house in twenty minutes. Not the Nantucket house, but the real house. The Providence one. I knew where the key was hidden, under the stone mermaid in the backyard, and I knew the alarm code. I let myself in to the peacock-blue vestibule with the rustic coat rack and the dark wood table with the curvy silver bowl on it and the portrait of the woman with the green scarf.

I climbed the stairs, two at a time, and opened the door to Jules's room, which was stuffy and hot, familiar and safe. I kicked off my shoes, threw off the quilted coverlet, and crawled under the sheets—the cool, beautiful sheets that Nina had brought back from Italy. Nina, I thought. Nina would've known what to say and how to make me feel better. She would've given me words to hold on to as the world swung around. "Nina," I said aloud. "Please be a ghost, please be a ghost." I kicked my legs against the mattress and waited for the lights to flash. I listened for the house to creek, for footsteps to land, or a window to fly open, for the stereo to blare. I waited for a chill to pass over me, for her presence to be made known, but there was nothing but silence. Dead, empty silence.

I'm eighteen, I told myself. This divorce stuff wasn't supposed to bother me anymore. I was leaving for college next year. I'd even found a really nice guy for Mom. So why was I such a wreck? And why was this just sinking in? Why didn't this happen right after the divorce? Or when Dad got remarried?

Zack. It was sinking in because I had fallen in love. This was the thing about feelings. They find each other. You let one in and others follow. I pulled the sheet over my head, curled myself into a cocoon, and let the tears fall until I was tired and ragged and my eyes were raw and my stomach muscles hurt. An hour passed, and then another, and then I fell asleep.

It was dusk when I woke up. The light switched on. Mom stood in the doorway.

"Cricket," she said. She ran to the bed and opened her arms. "Oh, my sweetheart, I was so worried. Oh, my dear girl, here you are." She wrapped her arms around me.

"Mom," I said, and wept into her sweater. "Mom, I'm so alone."

"No, you're not. I'm right here." And for the first time in I don't know how long, I let her hold me. Really hold me. She smelled like Paul Mitchell shampoo and almond soap and a little bit like Cheerios. She smelled like home.

Forty-two

"DAD SAID YOU SAID SOMETHING TERRIBLE ABOUT THAT child, drank a mug of pinot grigio, and took off through the backyard like a bat out of hell. I didn't even know you'd left Nantucket. What happened? What's wrong?"

"You wouldn't understand."

"Try me."

I started at the beginning, at the memorial service. I told her about the party and Parker and the mean thing I'd said about Jay and his brother. I told her that Zack and I had started dating secretly, that I hadn't meant for it to happen, but that our relationship seemed to have a life of its own. I told her that it'd become serious.

"How serious?" she asked.

"Serious," I said.

"Serious serious?" She closed her eyes.

"Yes."

"I'm not ready for this," she said, now covering her entire face with her hands. "Were you safe?"

"Mom! I don't want to talk about that right now."

"As your mother, I have to ask. It's my job. Were you safe?"

"Fine. Yes."

"Good. Are you planning on getting serious again soon? We need to make you a doctor's appointment."

"Mom, not now."

"Okay, okay. We can talk about it later." She cleared her throat. "Are you and Zack still together?"

I told her about Jay and the picture in *The Inquirer and Mirror*, and how everyone on Nantucket hated me and I couldn't go back. I told her that we needed to look into boarding schools for the fall. Boarding schools that were at least two states away.

"You're not going to boarding school," Mom said.

"Why not?"

"Because you have to face this."

"Why?"

"Because you can't just run away. Do you love him?"

"Yes."

Mom smiled. "No hesitation there."

"I know I love him. But I don't know what to do."

"First we need to get out of here."

"Why?"

"Because we've broken into the Claytons' house, that's why," she said, a little amused that I couldn't see this for myself.

"How did you know where I was?"

"I had a feeling. You love this house."

"How did you get in?"

"You left the door wide open, and all the lights were on, leading right to this room. You may as well have left a trail of bread crumbs. Come on, now. I think we should get some dinner and talk it over." I shook my head. "I'm craving fried clams." I moaned. She knows how much I love fried clams. She took my hand and looked me in the eye. "You can handle this."

"I can't go back to Nantucket," I said.

"Right now I'm just asking you to get out of bed and splash water on your face. That's it." Okay, I thought. Okay. I can do that. "One leg on the ground," she said. I put one leg on the floor. "Now the other." Both feet were on the floor. Once I'd done that, it wasn't as hard to climb out of those soft Italian sheets. I opened the door to Jules's little bathroom and ran the cold tap. It'd been a long time since I'd heard that take-charge tone in Mom's voice. It'd been years.

"I do have *some* good news," I said as I brought a handful of water to my face.

"What's that?" she asked.

"Paul Morgan is still in love with you." I patted my face dry with a hand towel monogrammed with Jules's loopy initials.

"What? Who's Paul Morgan?"

"Your first love?"

"I have no idea who you're talking about." In the bathroom mirror, I watched her make up the bed. It didn't look like she was lying. She didn't seem to be having any emotional reaction at all. She was focused on tucking in the sheets.

"The name Paul Morgan doesn't ring a single bell?" I asked.

"Not one," Mom said. She fluffed the pillows.

"Maybe this will help." I dried my hands and pulled the Emily Dickinson book out of my bag. I fanned the pages until I saw the picture of Mom and the guy. I plucked it out. That's when I saw the boat-shaped birthmark on Lover Boy's lower back.

"Oh my god, Paul Morgan wasn't your first love. Boaty Carmichael was."

Forty-three

WE WENT TO SUE'S CLAM SHACK IN NEWPORT. WE ORDERED fried clams, coleslaw, and lemonade, the kind that's neon yellow and tastes wonderfully fake. We sat on the same side of the picnic bench so that we were both facing the ocean. I told Mom about working for George, and she told me about Boaty.

She said that they'd been in love. The relationship had only lasted six weeks, but at that time, it was the most exciting, romantic six weeks of her life. She felt like she was the star of her own movie. "He could light up a room with his smile. By our second day together we were making out in the broom closet and pledging our love under the moonlight. We were so happy, but our relationship was a secret."

This was because of their jobs. The employees at the

Nantucket Beach Club weren't allowed to date each other. The beach club had two locations. One in 'Sconset and one near town. Mom worked at both. She worked at the one in 'Sconset with Boaty during the week, and the one near town with Paul Morgan on the weekends. Even though Mom didn't recognize Paul yet, I knew this was true because Paul had talked about working at the club in town and so distinctly remembered her. I guess Mom had just been too gaga for Boaty to notice anyone else. The manager thought that employee dating, even between the two hotels, caused drama and distracted them from their jobs. "I was still in high school, but Boaty needed that money." Also, what they were doing was technically illegal. Boaty was twenty-two. Mom was seventeen. "But," she added, "I think the secrecy made it more exciting." I knew exactly what she meant.

"So what happened?"

"Lilly Francis," Mom said. "I knew her from my one semester at that awful boarding school. She was from one of the wealthiest, most powerful and well-connected families in the country. What Lilly wanted, Lilly got. And she had her eye on Boaty from the minute she saw him."

"Did he like her too?"

"Not at first. He used to call her pig nose because she looked like this." Mom used her index finger to push her nose up.

"That's mean," I said, laughing.

Mom shrugged. "But she was persistent, and as he came to understand who she was and the amount of wealth and connections she had . . ." Mom paused, ate a clam, and shook her head. She wiped her fingers on one of our stack of paper napkins. "Well, he stopped calling her pig nose and started calling her Lilly."

"But he was in love with you," I said.

"Yes, he was. I cut off his mullet and turned up his collar so that someone like Lilly would notice him in the first place. And I introduced them. I realized later he was dating us at the same time. But I guess the reasons I was so unbelievably attracted to him was the reason he left me: his ambition. When he met Lilly Francis, he found someone who could take him where he wanted to go, fast. The next time he came to Nantucket, he wasn't working at the beach club. He was a member, and he was married to Lilly Francis."

"You were the first one he stepped on, Mom. You were the first rung on his ladder to the top. You should talk to George."

"I'll think about it."

"I can't believe he left you for pig nose!"

"Can't see a pig nose in the dark," she said, and smiled.

"So, what happened with you? The journal just stopped."

She shook her head. "He stopped talking to me cold. He ignored me. I was so heartbroken. I left Nantucket. I came home. He erased me, so I tried to erase him. I buried it. I told no one. There's something about that first broken heart. In some ways, it's the worst one."

A father with his two little boys sat down across from us.

"Dad hates me," I said. "What I said was terrible."

"He doesn't hate you," she said. "But you do owe him and Polly an apology. He'll cool down. He loves you, honey. He's your father. And I love you. We're your parents. No more pretending that you belong to another family, deal?"

"On one condition. You make this family better. You go out on a date with Paul Morgan."

"I don't even know who this man is."

"You will when you see him. Come on, Mom."

"I told you. I'm not ready to date," she said.

"And I'm telling you that it's time. Come on. He's handsome and nice, and he thinks you're great. And he has a cool house on Nantucket." I studied her as I sucked down the last of my neon lemonade. She wasn't budging. "Will you at least promise to stop watching *Real Life Mysteries*?"

"That's my favorite show."

"It's on Saturday nights and it's meant for people who are a hundred years old. Or at least fifty-five."

"That's not true," she said.

"Then how come all the commercials are for adult diapers and Viagra?" I sighed. "It's time to get a life, Kate."

"You make it sound easy. And you may not start calling me Kate."

"Maybe it's not as hard as you think." We threw our garbage away, walked back to the car, and got inside. We sat there for a minute staring at the water. I checked my phone. Still no word from Zack. I didn't want to go back to Nantucket. I didn't even want to go back to Providence. I wanted to stay right here, at Sue's Clam Shack. Forever.

Mom spoke first, as if she could read my mind. "I can't force you to go back. But you only have one week left. If you just quit, you'll ruin your first job reference, and who knows if that writer will write you a letter of recommendation for college? Quitting right at the end doesn't look good. And don't you think it's better to talk to Jules while it's still fresh?"

"No. The thought of going there and talking to Jules gives me a stomachache."

"Sometimes you have to do things that make you uncomfortable."

"But you don't," I said, turning to face her. "You won't even go on one date."

"That's different," she said.

"Bullshit." I unrolled the window and stuck my feet out. "This apple has landed directly under the tree."

She leaned into her seat, rubbed her temples, and closed her eyes. Then she sighed.

"Put your feet in the car." I did, and she started the engine. "Okay. If I go on a date with this Paul Morgan, will you go back to Nantucket? Will you finish out this job and talk to Jules?"

"Yes," I said, and buckled my seat belt as we headed out of the parking lot. Then I leaned over and hugged her so hard we swerved a little onto the grass.

"Quick, turn on the radio," Mom said as she steered us back onto the road. "Before I change my mind."

I put on the '80s station and turned it all the way up.

That night, I heard Mom laughing in her bedroom.

"What are you doing?" I called into the darkness.

"I'm reading my diary," she said, nearly wheezing. "This thing is hysterical."

Forty-four

"I THINK THAT GUY WAS WORKING HERE THE LAST TIME I was on the ferry," Mom said under her breath about the unfriendly white-haired guy behind the food counter. We bought hot dogs, chips, an iced tea for me, and a white wine for her, and found two seats by the railing. It was cloudy and even a little cold today. I wished I'd worn my jeans. I told Mom that she didn't have to come, but now I was glad she was here. I was scared of seeing Jules and Parker and of being rejected by Zack, but it was the thought of having another one of the moments when I couldn't breathe or move that made me want her around the most.

I'd described the moment with the red Volvo to her back

in Providence. I was sitting on her bed with my laptop as she packed. I told her it felt like someone was choking me.

"It's called an anxiety attack," Mom said. "Now, do you think we can find a picture of this Paul Morgan person?" I Googled him and found a picture on his law firm's Web site.

"Oh, yeah, I think I do remember him. He was fun." She studied the picture. "Nice hair. He remembers me?" she asked.

"I already told you, he's, like, in love with you."

Mom smiled and tucked hair behind her ear. Then she looked in her closet and pulled out . . . oh my god . . . a pair of heels. They actually had dust on them.

"Cricket, you're back!" Liz was headed upstairs with an armful of clean towels. She put them on a table and threw her arms around me. "I'm glad to see you." She pulled back and mock slapped me. "Leaving me alone with Bernadette for two whole days, the nerve." She stuck out her hand to Mom. "You must be Cricket's mum. I'm Liz."

"Nice to meet you," Mom said.

"I'm Cricket's top advisor on matters of the heart," Liz said.

"We could all use one of those," Mom said, laughing.

"Especially this one," Liz said, blowing a loose curl from her eyes. "What room are you in, Mrs. Cricket? We'll make sure you get plenty of towels. Maybe even an extra bar of soap if you play your cards right."

"I think we can put her in room fourteen. I've got to check with Gavin," I said.

"You should visit Liz in Ireland, Cricket," Mom said. "That would be fun."

"That's impossible, actually, because I'm going to be living on Nantucket full-time." Liz beamed.

"What about college?" I asked.

"Shane and I decided we're happy here and want to stay. Why mess with a good thing? If we can avoid becoming raging alcoholics, I think we have a very nice life ahead of us."

"Cool," I said. Not going to college seemed crazy to me, but Liz just did whatever she wanted.

"The rooms aren't cleaning themselves, Liz." Bernadette glared as she passed us on the steps.

"Thank you for covering for me, Bernadette."

"Yup," she said, without looking back.

Liz leaned in and whispered, "And how could I part with such island charmers as Bernadette?" She picked up the towels and headed up the stairs. I showed Mom my room with the slanted ceiling and the rose wallpaper, and the kitchen and the backyard. I knocked on the annex door, which was halfway open. George, as usual, was inside typing away.

"George, this is my mother, Kate Campbell."

"Nice to meet you," George said, rising to shake her hand. "Your daughter is just terrific. She might have a future in journalism."

"Thanks," I said. Oh, George. It was good to see him. When I'm much, much, much older, I'd like to marry someone like him. I was glad I'd come back.

"Cricket told me about your book," Mom said. "I think I might have a story that interests you." So she'd decided to talk to him!

"Great," George said. He smiled at me, mystified.

"But I'd like to remain anonymous," Mom said.

"Absolutely." He clapped once. "I'm intrigued." They agreed to meet the next morning at the Even Keel.

We were walking back inside to find Gavin when I spotted him in the rosebushes with a pair of clippers.

"Hi, Gavin, I'm back."

"Hi, Cricket." Gavin turned around. He paused. He smiled at Mom. He put down his clippers and walked toward us, wiping sweat from his brow.

"This is my mom, Kate. What room should I put her in?" I asked. "Fourteen is free, right?"

"Yes, but the ventilation isn't that great in there. How about the Admiral's Suite?"

"She doesn't need a Jacuzzi and a canopy bed," I said.

"Actually," Mom said, shooting me a look, "I could stand a little pampering."

"It's like, four hundred dollars a night," I said.

"I can get you a discount," Gavin said, waving me away. "I kind of run this place." He smiled and wiped off his face with the sleeve of his T-shirt. "Kate, I'm just about done here. Would I be able to tempt you with a fresh piece of blueberry pie and a glass of iced tea?"

"Sounds yum," Mom said with a sly smile. Pampering? Yum? Yuck! She was flirting. With Gavin. I almost preferred her in her bathrobe with her mysteries. Almost.

Forty-five

I SHOOK AS I WALKED UP TO THE DOOR AT 4 DARLING STREET. I took a deep breath and knocked. After the longest thirty seconds of my life, Jules appeared at the door. She must've checked out a window or something, because she didn't look shocked to see me.

"What do you want?" she asked, a hand on her hip. "Or, *Oh, I'm sorry, are you looking for Zack?*"

"No, I want to talk to you." I handed her the bouquet of flowers that I'd picked from the backyard at the inn, but she didn't take them. "Please."

Jules sighed, stepped outside, and plunked down on one of the little benches. I sat opposite her and put the flowers next to her on the bench.

She crossed her arms and looked at me like she didn't know me, like our history had been wiped from her memory. I wanted to remind her of how I'd practically lived at her house for the past year, or how I'd taught her to drive a stick in the Dunkin' Donuts parking lot. Or how we'd danced in her old gymnastics leotards for hours to the same Rihanna song on REPEAT, laughing until we almost wet our pants. I wanted to find the notebook with all the notes we'd ever passed, tear the pages out, and cover her with them like a quilt. I wanted to play her the three-and-a-half-minute voice mail she left me when she got her period, in which she laughed and cried as she went back and forth between being excited and sad.

I wanted to remind her of the time I'd called her, frozen with fear, when I'd found a hair growing someplace it shouldn't, worried I was a werewolf or a late-blooming hermaphrodite, and she didn't laugh or make fun of me; she made me feel better. I wanted to thank her for that. I wanted to tell her how, even though it was funny now, in that moment I'd been as scared as I'd ever been. Or the time we drove to that boarding school outside Boston for their spring weekend and pretended to be Finnish exchange students. We called sodas "fizzy fizzy pop pop" and declared everything to be "extra cool" in weird, pseudo-European accents. I wanted to read our story to her like a book. In those moments, she'd made it feel like the world was ours. Now she was looking at me like any world I inhabited was one she'd flee.

"I'm so sorry," I said, my eyes filling. "I know what I did hurt you, and I'm sorry."

"I was trying to be nice to you at the Even Keel. I thought *I'd* been the bitch all summer."

"I should've said something then," I said, tears dripping into my lap.

"I told you I needed space from you, and you slept with my little brother." She shook her head. "He's a *sophomore.* Don't you think he's a little young for you? Don't you think he's a little young for anyone?"

So, Zack had told her that we'd had sex. I wanted to say that I wasn't his first, but that wasn't my information to share. It was Zack's. "I can't help how I feel. Besides, senior guys go out with sophomore girls all the time," I added quietly. I had to point it out. "Are you mad that I lost my virginity first?"

"You didn't." She smiled. "I had sex with Fitzy in like, June."

"Oh." It made me sad for Jules. Fitzy had flirted with me when I'd run into Jay and those guys just a few days ago. Maybe it was okay that they weren't in love. But I don't know. I wanted something else for her. "That's great."

She drew a deep breath. "Is there anything else?"

"Do you think you could accept my apology?" She looked away. "I hope you at least know that I wasn't trying to hurt you. Zack and I didn't mean to fall in love."

"Maybe you're in love with him, but he's really pissed off at you."

"I know," I said.

"And so is Parker. And Jay. He said you were a tease. You led him on."

"Do you know where Zack is?" I asked. "I need to talk to him, too."

"No. Anyway, tomorrow he goes to soccer camp. He'll be at Fitzy's party tonight."

"I guess I could try to find him there," I said. "Fitz lives on Cliff Road, right?"

"I wouldn't go if I were you. Nobody wants to see you, Cricket. Not Jay, not Parker, not Zack. And not me." Jules stood up and opened the front door, leaving the flowers on the bench. "Seriously, I'm telling you this as a friend. Don't go." She went inside and shut the door. And then she did something very un-Nantucket. She locked it.

Forty-six

MOM AND I MET PAUL MORGAN AT A FRENCH RESTAURANT on Broad Street. The hostess led us inside and I spotted him right away. He was seated at a table by the window. He looked clean and handsome in searsucker pants and a crisp white shirt. He stood up to kiss Mom on both cheeks, European style. I felt proud I'd found him for Mom. "You look just the same," he said, and pulled out a chair for her. He turned to me. "Your mom was kind of like a badass Gwyneth Paltrow."

"That was a long time ago." Mom blushed and ordered a white wine spritzer. As she and Paul reminisced about their beach club days, I sipped an Arnold Palmer, watched the passersby on Broad Street, and thought about my conversation with Jules. Losing her had me hunched with sadness, weighed down by a sense that the world had unraveled.

Jay thought I'd led him on. Parker thought I was desperate for going out with a sophomore. Jules thought I was a bad friend. And worst of all, Zack thought I betrayed him. I could already hear the names: Tease. Bitch. Slut. All the words designed to make girls feel bad and small. All the words I'd worked so hard to avoid could now be stuck to me like a name tag. And I would have to bear them with quiet dignity. I'd have to put the Jenna Garbetti method back into effect: lie low, look good, and learn. In order to restore my reputation at this point I'd have to lie so low I'd be subterranean. I'd have to learn so much I could operate a NASA spacecraft. I'd have to look as good as a supermodel. I ran my hand through my half-brushed hair, which Mom had encouraged me to put into a ponytail so it was off my face. And I noticed a coffee stain on my T-shirt. I placed my napkin high on my lap to cover it as I tuned back to Paul and Mom's conversation.

"Nantucket sure has changed," she was saying. "Was it always this upscale?"

"No," Paul said. "It happened in the past fifteen years when the mega-rich discovered our little paradise."

"I was in a shop today," Mom continued as she stirred her spritzer with the little plastic straw, "and I saw a pair of sandals for seven hundred dollars. I thought, What is this?"

"Some of these shops are ridiculous, but there are also some gems." His eyes widened and his voice rose. "I should take you shopping."

"I would love that," Mom said.

"We'll get some lattes and make an afternoon of it."

"That sounds like just what I need." Mom and I exchanged a smile. How had I missed it? Paul Morgan was gay. I thought I'd found her the perfect new husband, but maybe what she needed right now was a new friend.

I looked up and saw Zack through the window, from behind, walking up Broad Street. I didn't get a good look at his face, but I knew those shorts and that red T-shirt. I sat up. My heart slammed, pushing blood faster through my veins. Here was my chance to talk to him, in person and alone.

"I have to go," I said, sitting up straight.

"Where are you going?" Mom asked. Paul looked confused.

"I see Zack," I said. "And he's alone. And I really want to talk to him before he gets to that party."

"Okay," Mom said, her brow wrinkled with concern. "Be careful."

"What's happening?" Paul asked, a hand to his chest.

"I'll explain," Mom said as I stood from the table, letting my napkin drop to the floor.

The entrance to the restaurant was crowded. There were people trying to get in and people trying to get out, and the line by the hostess podium was thick and busy with people who smelled like perfume and cologne; laughers and chatters who were slow to move out of the way. It took me a while to get clear of them. When I did, I spotted Zack at the top of the street, about to turn up Centre Street. He was on his way to Fitzy's. It was a busy August night, and the sidewalk was crowded with amblers; couples holding hands; families walking in loose, lolling groups; and kids licking dripping, precarious ice-cream cones. "Excuse me, excuse me," I said as I wove though them to get to Zack.

"Hey!" I called when I'd almost caught up to him. "Hey, it's me!" He turned around. But it wasn't Zack. It was some guy with a baby strapped to his chest.

"Sorry," I said, a little breathless. "I thought you were someone else."

"No worries," said the man, and kept walking.

The man didn't look anything like Zack. He was at least thirty or forty. My wish to see Zack was so strong I'd erased an entire baby. But now the desire to touch Zack, to hold him and kiss him and tell him that I loved him was out of its cage. It was alive and wild, set free by a man with a baby. A strong breeze pushed against my back. I caught my reflection in a store window and stared at the girl looking back at me, breathing deeply, with her hands on her hips. Her ponytail was half undone and I could see she wanted something, and wanted it bad. Why, exactly, was I going to stop her?

I was afraid to go to Fitzy's. I was afraid of what other people thought. I was afraid of what other people would say and do. I wanted to preserve some idea of me. I was practically taking a page from the book of Boaty Carmichael, caring more about my public self than my private one. Was that who I was?

The only opinion that should matter to me was that of the girl in the mirror. Edwina MacIntosh had been saying this for years in the Rosewood School for Girls annual anti-clique speeches. For the first time, it felt true. It didn't matter what other people thought of me; it mattered what I thought of me. I'm not sure why it was at that moment that it finally sank in, except that maybe this is how wisdom works sometimes. You hear it, and some extra-smart part of your brain that you don't even realize you have grabs it. It stays there, hidden away, until it's needed. I looked at my self in the window again. I bet this was what I looked like when I played lacrosse. Strong. Determined. Self-assured. I felt glad I'd gone to an all-girls' school my whole life.

I turned up Centre Street and walked toward Fitzy's house. I wasn't going to lie low. Jenna Garbetti's method wouldn't work for me. I wasn't Jenna Garbetti. I was Cricket Thompson.

Forty-seven

AT FIRST NO ONE SAW ME WHEN I WALKED INTO FITZY'S backyard. I stood by the rose trellis and scanned for Zack, but I didn't see him. Fitzy, Oliver, and a few other guys were jamming on their guitars. Jay was standing nearby, alone, pumping a keg of beer. I took a deep breath and approached him.

"Hi, Jay," I said. He looked up. I'd caught him off guard.

"Hey," he said. I braced myself for him to call me a name, but he didn't. The moment hung in the air until finally he spoke. "You know, if you didn't want to go out with me, you should've just said so."

"I know," I said. "You're so right. But here's the thing. I've liked you for a really long time. I've dreamed of going out with you since the eighth grade. You kissing me and asking me to be your girl was literally a dream come true."

"Then . . . I don't get it." He looked a little nervous as he filled his red plastic cup with beer. I never imagined that I might make Jay Logan nervous. Jules, who was sitting next to Parker on a wicker love seat, had noticed me. She was whispering to Parker. My mouth went dry.

"Well, I really don't know you. When I said that thing about your brother being a loser, I didn't know you; and when I said that I would do anything to go out with you, I didn't know you. I just knew *of* you. I kissed you because I'd thought about it so much, because it's something I've wanted for so long that I just kind of got swept up in the moment. But the thing is, I love someone else, someone I actually know."

"This is a lot of information, C.T." Jay sipped his beer. "You're complicated."

"I'm sorry if I mislead you," I said. "Maybe you could see it as a compliment?"

"Hey, it's cool." To my surprise, he grinned. "I'm sorry I couldn't make your dreams come true." He shook his head. "And I guess it turns out Zacky Clayton has some moves." He wiggled his eyebrows. I did not like where this was headed.

"Do you know where he is?" I asked.

"He's inside," Jay said. The only problem with getting inside was that I had to walk by Jules and Parker and Fitzy and Oliver and a whole gang of other kids. Some were jamming on their guitars and some smoking weed and some playing a drinking game, and others were lounging on the lawn furniture like noblemen in a palace garden. Together they radiated a force field of confidence that required physical strength to pass through.

"Hi, Jules," I said as I walked passed her, holding my breath. Just as I climbed the steps, Zack emerged from the back door. Our eyes met. He still loves me, I thought.

"Zack," I said. "I'm so sorry, but I can explain this whole thing. I really want to talk to you, alone."

"Hey, desperado!" Parker called. I was standing on the steps, under a porch light. Parker was laughing, and I felt the attention of the party shift toward me.

"If you think I'm desperate, then you must not like Zack very much," I said. Parker closed her mouth. "And that's just stupid, because Zack is the best." Jules flashed me a quick glance. She wasn't smiling, but she was looking at me like she knew me again.

"Can we talk now?" I asked Zack.

"Yeah," Zack said. "Let's go."

Forty-eight

ZACK WALKED NEXT TO ME WITH HIS ARMS FOLDED OVER his chest. I told him the whole story of how I'd liked Jay since the eighth grade, and how when you go to an all-girls' school you do a lot more imagining of boys than getting to know them. I told him that in one way I was sorry that I'd kissed Jay, but that it also helped me realize that my feelings for him were made up and the ones I had for Zack were real. In a weird way, I explained, the whole thing with Jay was what let me fully open up to Zack.

"But it wasn't just the kiss. He asked you out and you said yes," Zack said when we reached the Steps Beach rock. We kicked off our shoes and left them by the twisty wooden fence.

"It was what I had wanted for so long," I said, following

him down the steep staircase to the beach. "It was like I thought I had to. But as soon as I saw you, it was so clear how wrong I was. Does that make any sense to you? Can you understand that?"

"I don't know," he said when we reached the sand. I wanted him to take my hand, but he didn't. He kept walking.

"I wish you would've answered my calls," I said. "I wish you'd called me back. Or at least texted me." I stopped walking. I didn't want to chase after him. It took him a few paces to notice. When he did, he faced the water. "We had sex, Zack, and you didn't call me back. It was my first time and you didn't call me back. I don't even know how you felt about it. I mean, I don't even know if it was any different with me." I tried to gauge his expression, but he gave me nothing.

"I didn't know what to say," he said, and bent down to pick up a stone. "Jules showed me all those notes you'd written about Jay, and said you had this whole plan about getting some other guy to like you first so that Jay would notice you." He shook his head, skipped the stone. "That's messed up."

"I wrote that in, like, March." I walked over to him, my heels sinking into the cool, soft sand. "You could've at least given me a chance. Did you really think I was using you? Did it *feel* like I was using you?"

"No"—he looked into my eyes and sighed—"it didn't."

"So, can you accept my apology?" It felt like we were

staring at each other for hours, but it was probably less than a minute.

"Yes," he said. Finally, he wrapped his arms around me. I breathed in his T-shirt; I inhaled his Zackness.

"I'm sorry," he said. "I should've called." I stood on my tiptoes and rubbed his back, but when I looked up at him, he turned his face away.

"What's wrong?" I asked.

"I don't know, Cricket. You helped me forget about my mom. But in the past few days . . ." He shut his eyes. He held his breath. "I've started to think about everything I've lost." I pulled him closer. He was shaking. "I miss her. I miss my mom."

"Me too." I held him tighter. We stood holding each other for a long time. When his breathing seemed more even, I loosened my grip and looked up at him.

"Want to go swimming?" I asked.

"If we go swimming, I'm going to want you, and I just . . . Not right now. I know it's crazy." He pushed my hair behind my ear and stared at me.

"Do you want to just sit here?" I asked, trying not to let the rejection sting.

"Yeah," he said. We sat. He flopped back in the sand. A horn sounded.

"Last ferry of the night," I said.

"People are heading home. Summer's over."

I didn't want the summer to be over. I didn't want

Nantucket to be over. I was going to have to face my senior year without my best friend, without Nina, without the Claytons' house to run to when I couldn't deal with my own.

I was going to have to apply to college. This time next year, I'd be heading in a completely new direction.

I lay back next to Zack because, more than anything, I didn't want *this* to be over. I wanted to kiss him, but for the first time since we'd started this whole thing, I was unsure of what to say or do. His eyes were shut, and he was wincing against an invisible blow. For a moment I could feel him slipping away, into a heartbreak that was both enormous and private.

I put my hand on my chest. Was my heart breaking, too? I didn't know. I missed something, longed for something I couldn't quite name. I got up and walked into the surf up to my ankles. I stood still and quiet in the ocean mist. The water was warm, but a deep chill passed through me. Was it ghost girl making contact? Was it Nina trying to tell me something? Was it the part of me that she'd promised would stay on Nantucket leaving my body and stepping into the night air?

"It was different," he said. I turned, surprised to see Zack standing so close. I hadn't heard him approach.

"Good different?" I asked.

"Good different," he said.

"Oh," I said, smiling. "Well, that's good. Especially since, you know, the other girl was French and everything.

Historically speaking, I think the French are the best secret lovers."

"Well, she had nothing on you. With you, I was like, okay, this is it." He wrapped his arms around me and kissed my neck. There were those flutters. The sparking. The humming. This was not a broken heart. It was alive and jumping. I thought he was crying for a second, but when he pulled me closer I realized that he was actually laughing.

"What?" I asked. "What's funny?"

"I don't know," he said, facing me and brushing the hair out of my eyes. "A few minutes ago I was going to break up with you."

"Why?"

"I thought I needed to in order to, I don't know, deal with everything."

"I don't want to break up," I said. I had come this far. I had marched to Fitzy's house despite being told no one wanted me there. I had stood up to Jules. I wasn't about to hide my feelings now. "Do you?"

"No," he said. "I'm just so confused."

"What would the worry doctor say?" I asked.

He thought about it for a minute. Then he took a deep breath and said, "She'd say, *Zack, life is messy.*" He was speaking in a British accent.

"She's British?" I asked.

"Australian," he said, but continued in the British accent. "She'd say, *Life is full of conflict and complexity. The loss of your mother is going to be very painful, and I'm afraid you're going to have to go through it. And it will hurt.*"

"Of course." I nodded. A twist of pain.

"*But I'm also hearing that you're in love,*" he continued. "*And love is a rare and wonderful thing. There is nothing in the world that feels better.*" He took my hands and dropped the accent. "So maybe I'll just feel both at the same time."

"I want to be your girlfriend, not just your secret lover." I had never had a real boyfriend before.

"Me too," he said. "I want that, too."

And then we kissed. Our kissing was urgent and sweet. It was mixed with laughter. We stumbled backward until we were up to our knees in the ocean, until the bottom of my shorts were wet. When we finally stopped kissing, I looked up at the sky. There were so many stars out there. Packs of them in swirling, looping galaxies. You can't see stars like this in a city, not like you can out here on a rock in the middle of the ocean.

Feelings find each other, I thought. Let one in and the others follow. At that moment it seemed that all our feelings were shimmering above us, around us, in a new and stunning constellation.

BOOK TWO

Nantucket
RED

One

I NEVER LIKED THE LAST FEW DAYS OF SUMMER VACATION. Hot without the promise of beach days, heavy with the knowledge that a whole school year is ahead, and stuck in a muggy haze between summer and fall, they're the slowest days of the year. Today felt like the most in-between day of all. It was almost eleven o'clock and I was still in bed. The sun streaked through the blinds and made patterns on the walls. I stared at the ceiling, watching the fan go around and around. Zack was starting boarding school tomorrow and we still hadn't discussed whether we were going to stay together or break up. How was it that only a week ago we were at Steps Beach, kissing under the stars, with what felt like an ocean of time sparkling ahead of us?

A few days after we'd returned to Providence, Zack told

me he was going to Hanover Academy, an elite boarding school in northern New Hampshire. I understood why he was leaving. His mom, Nina, had died in June and his dad and sister, Jules, had completely shut down. Who could blame them?

Nina was the most alive person I'd ever met. I loved her, too. She taught me how to ice skate backward. She taught me how to make a perfect vinaigrette. She introduced me to Frida Kahlo and William Carlos Williams. She made the best paella. There was no one like her, and now she was gone. Mr. Clayton and Jules were shadows of their previous selves. Zack was living with ghosts.

Hanover would give him a chance to start fresh and be among the living. When he told me that a space had opened up at the last minute and he was taking it, I was happy for him. It didn't feel real. I still had Nantucket sand in my shoes. I was so dizzy-happy in love with him that nothing felt real, but it was starting to sink in: the boy I'd risked everything for this summer was going away. He was coming over in a few hours to spend the afternoon with me, and we had to decide what to do. Break up? I wondered as I kicked off the sheets. Stay together, I thought, and sat up.

I lifted my hair off my sweaty neck, twisted it into a bun, and turned on my laptop. When I logged onto Facebook, Zack's new profile picture was at the top of my feed. He'd taken down the photo of himself on the beach in Nantucket and replaced it with one of himself in a Hanover Academy sweatshirt. No, I thought.

Jules commented: "Don't forget your jockstrap!"

A flurry of "good lucks" and "have funs" and more specific comments followed, references to Hanover that I didn't understand. No, stay with me, I thought and felt myself contract and stiffen. My jaw tightened. My stomach clenched. I wanted to hold on to him and keep him in my world, our world. This feeling, this panicky collapse, was opposite of the sweet effervescence I felt when I was with him; it was foreign and unwelcome, and it didn't feel like love.

"Cricket, it's for you," Mom said with a girlie smile when Zack knocked on the door a few hours later. Mom had never been good with boundaries; my being in love gave her a contact blush.

Zack's eyes lit up as I walked toward him in the new white tank top Mom had bought me from the Gap after she saw the state of my clothes when I'd returned from Nantucket, and my old, worn-out cutoffs she couldn't have separated me from if she'd tried. My hair was still damp from a shower and I knew I smelled like the vanilla soap he liked. A slow grin spread across his face as he leaned in the door frame.

"Let's get lost," Zack said like someone from an old movie. He handed me an iced coffee just the way I liked it: extra ice, lots of cream, no sugar.

Mom lingered in the front hall and placed a hand over her heart, slayed by Zack's charm. "Don't forget to take an umbrella," she said. "It's supposed to rain."

"That's okay. Thanks, Mom," I said as we walked to his car. I slid my fingers through his belt loop. "I know where we can get some privacy." I'd discovered this place on an away game in Newport. It was about a half hour outside Providence, off Route 24, past Dotty's Donuts, down a shady country road. You had to drive by the farm with the self-service strawberry stand and the Catholic school with its low, humble buildings, all the way to where the road ended at the Narragansett Bay.

The air-conditioning was broken in Zack's old station wagon, so we drove with the windows down. We listened to the college station, stopped for donuts, and even spotted one of the monks from the Catholic school talking on an iPhone. We held hands and kissed at stoplights, but we didn't talk about us.

After we parked, Zack headed down to the beach. I balanced on the abandoned train tracks that hugged the shore and watched him pick up a stone, examine it, and send it skipping into the bay. He was having dinner with Jules and his dad in an hour and a half, and then they were heading to New Hampshire, where they would spend the night at an inn so they could move him into his dorm the next morning. It was time.

I hopped off the tracks, walked down the rocky hill to the beach, and wrapped my arms around his waist. There was a pale band on his neck where his hair had been cut for school.

"What are we going to do?" I asked, breathing into his back.

"I don't want to break up," he said, turning to face me. The clouds collected weight and darkness above us. He pulled me close. "What do you think?"

"I think long distance sucks." Zack pressed his fingers into my spine, confusing my chemicals. Part of me was trying to shut down so that I could deal with this, but my blood spun under his touch.

"It's only a few hours away. We can switch off weekends."

"I don't have a car."

"You can take the bus. And there are so many vacations. For as expensive as this school is, I'll hardly ever be there."

"But I don't want to be someone you text or a face on the screen," I said as his hands left swirls of heat on my back. "We'll forget each other. Or fade away. Long distance will distort everything."

"I could never forget you," Zack said as a wave washed over our ankles. My shoes got soaked. I tossed them back on the beach where they landed in ballet third position.

"When I saw you'd changed your profile picture, I felt like this." I clenched my fists and gritted my teeth. He smiled. "Zack, I'm serious." I looped my arms around his neck and leaned in. "I don't want to feel that way about you. All tight and anxious."

"Let's not do long distance, then."

"So we're breaking up?" The words were so far from

what I wanted that they didn't feel real—like I couldn't have possibly just said them. "No, no, no. I don't want that."

"I don't either."

"Maybe we can just . . . pause," I said.

"What do you mean?"

"I mean, we'll just stop here, right now, like this, and then pick up where we left off next summer." A few fat raindrops fell. "No Facebook, no Instagram, no texts, no phone."

"Okay," Zack said. "I can do that."

"But we have to stick to the rules, otherwise the pause won't work."

"I'm unfriending you right now." Zack slid one hand in my left back pocket while the other took out his phone. "Well, there's no reception out here, but I'm going to do it as soon as I get home." Then, before I knew it, Zack snapped a picture of us: me looking up as the rain started, eyebrows raised, him with his arm around my neck, smiling at me.

The rain started for real. We ran for the car and dove into the backseat. Rain splattered against the windows as if flung from a million paintbrushes.

"Paused," I said.

"Paused," Zack said. He pulled off my tank top and I slid his T-shirt over his head.

"Wait—the monk!" I said, covering myself with my hands.

"He's on his iPhone," Zack said, and we laughed, trying to guess who it was he was talking to: His mom? A nun? God?

"I love you," he said as we slid back on the seat.

"I love you, too." It was the first time we'd said those three words in that order. I shivered. I knew in my bones that the words were as true and real as the vinyl seats in that wood-paneled station wagon, the rusted rails of the train tracks, the drumroll of thunder in the distance. My foot made a print on the cool, fogged-up window.

Forty-five minutes later, flushed and unable to stop smiling, we drove off. I'd forgotten all about my shoes, which had been left on the beach, waiting, in third position, for our return.

Two

FOR THE FIRST TIME IN MY THIRTEEN YEARS OF ATTENDING the Rosewood School for Girls, I was scared to walk through the front doors. I should've been happy. As a senior, I was going to be allowed off campus for lunch. I was going to write the name of whatever colleges I was accepted into on the big piece of butcher paper hanging in the senior lounge. I was going to be captain of the field hockey and lacrosse teams, and for years I'd planned on being one of the seniors who was super nice to the freshman. As I watched girls spill out of cars in spanking-new uniforms, and gather in quartets and trios, I didn't feel nice.

"I can't go in," I said to Mom. "Jules hates me."

"She doesn't hate you. She's been through hell, but you did nothing wrong."

"What about Nina's memorial service?" I leaned against the headrest to offset the nausea.

"You thought you were doing the right thing. It was an innocent mistake."

"Zack?" *Innocent* was not the word to describe us.

"Falling in love with someone's brother is not a hanging offense," Mom said and checked herself out in the visor mirror. She applied a new shade of lipstick. Coral. It was actually kind of hip. She'd been taking antidepressants for three weeks now and I could tell they were starting to work. She readjusted the mirror. "Now, out you go, I can't be late. It's my first day, too, you know."

I shook my head. God only knows how Jules had spun the story of this summer to our friends. She could tell a story like no one else: pauses so well timed, impressions so accurate, gestures so precise that everyone in her orbit was enchanted. My stomach churned at the thought of being on the wrong side of her talent.

Mom leaned over and opened the door herself. "Cricket, go."

I was biding my time in a bathroom stall before assembly, admiring the paint job they'd done over the summer, when Jules came in. I watched her walk into the next stall. I would know those boat shoes anywhere, as well as the little white scar on the top of her left foot from when she'd dropped an ice skate in the seventh grade. The sound of her peeing seemed horribly amplified. She was humming the school song. I was going to make a run for it, but then I realized that catching her alone was exactly what I needed. I had to face her and apologize again. Better that we weren't surrounded. I opened the latch, stood by the sinks, and braced myself.

"I'm sorry," I said, when she emerged from the stall.

"Ah!" She flung a hand to her chest. "You scared me."

"I'm sorry. About the memorial service, and Zack, and everything."

"Cricket." Jules sighed my name. She looked tired, a little too tan, a little too skinny. I wanted to hug her and ask if she was okay. "I just— I can't right now." She'd said it with such naked honesty there was nothing to do but accept it.

"Okay," I said. "Okay." We washed our hands in silence. We couldn't walk out together. In a strange move, I gestured like some kind of old-fashioned gentleman for her to leave first. She gave me a confused look and left. I counted to twenty and opened the door. I saw our group of friends seamlessly envelop her as they walked toward assembly, moving in one fluid motion, like a river.

They'd repainted the auditorium, too, and even though the windows were open, the fumes were giving me a headache. I sat up front, away from Jules, and tried to focus as the principal, Edwina MacIntosh, welcomed everyone back to school. Teachers made announcements about school activities: student council, the literary magazine, yearbook, choir, community service outreach. Sign me up for everything, I thought. I may be without a best friend or a boyfriend, but this is my school.

I cast a quick glance at Jules, who was whispering to Arti Rai. My college application is going to fucking glow, I thought as I whipped out my plan book and started making notes.

I spent the midmorning break alone in the senior lounge with my school supplies. I could see Jules in the cafeteria, telling summer stories to a table of enraptured girls. They were all eating bagels the way I had invented, peeling off the hard outer shell and eating that first and saving the squishy middle in its original shape for last. That's called Cricket-style, I thought bitterly. I was eating an endlessly chewy protein bar that tasted like wood chips, labeling tabs, and trying to look busy. Miss Kang, the field hockey and lacrosse coach, noticed me as she walked by.

I smiled and held up my plan book. "Getting organized!"

"You are too much, Cricket," she said and sat down next to me on the old couch. "You know I'm in touch with Stacy, head coach over at Brown, right? She's got her eye on you. What do you say we put together some clips to send her?" She elbowed me. "What do you say we get you into Brown?"

"Really? Do you think?" I'd always imagined I'd go away for college and not stay in Providence. Where, I didn't know, but I had this picture in my head of stuffing the Honda to the gills and hitting the road. But Brown was *Ivy League*— hallowed words, a synonym for the best. I imagined what it would feel like to write *Brown* on that big piece of butcher paper. It would feel like redemption. I'd seen it happen. The senior girls accepted to Ivy Leagues basked in a haze of adoration, cleansed of all previous misdeeds. "Do you really think I could make the team?"

"They'd be lucky to have you," Miss Kang said. "And they're going to graduate their starting lineup this year." She rubbed her hands together as if devising a plan. Then, glimpsing the clock in the cafeteria, she said, "I have to prep for Algebra II. We'll talk more at practice. You should be ready to lead warm-ups with Jules."

"Yeah, sure." Cocaptains. It had been decided last year, back when we could bust into our synchronized dance moves within three seconds of hearing that Bruno Mars song, but now my stomach elevator-dropped at her name. "No problem."

Three

IT WAS ALMOST HALFTIME AND PEABODY SCHOOL WAS beating us three to zero. The field hockey season was not off to a good start. We'd won only one game out of four, and that was against Hamlin. Everyone could beat Hamlin. But this game was embarrassing. They were playing their second string in the first half. I think they were even giving some of their JV players a shot. And it was the first cold day of the year. We'd gone from summer to winter in a week with only one crisp, sweater-weather day in between. Out on Peabody's field, it was overcast and the air had teeth.

The ref blew the whistle in our favor for the first time the whole game. Jules had the ball. She tapped her elbow. That meant she'd hit the ball hard and long up the field, which was my cue to sprint, make it look like I was going to shoot, and then pass it back to Jules, who would hopefully score. But instead of wielding her stick like an ax, thwacking the ball and sending it flying, she tapped it. It rolled ten feet.

I darted for the ball, hooked it, and started dribbling. My eyes were on the goal, but my head was elsewhere. I knew there was a Halloween party that weekend at Jay Logan's and that a bunch of girls were getting ready at Jules's house. They'd talked about it right in front of me on the bus while I'd pretended to be fascinated by the highway scenery. I was tired of sitting out social events because of Jules. I'd done my time. I wanted to go out and have fun. But what was I going to do, show up alone? Invite myself over to her house to get ready?

"Cricket," Jules called, but I charged ahead, weaving through Peabody's line of defense. I was about to take a shot when a Peabody player, a freshman, I think, stole the ball right out from under me. How did I not see her? The buzzer sounded.

"That's half!" the ref called.

"Cricket and Jules, get over here," Miss Kang said. Her face was red with cold or anger or both. She gestured with a blunt-nailed index finger. "You two need to get it together. You're the captains. You need to be communicating. You're on different planets out there. What the hell is going on?"

I looked at Jules. She shrugged and stared at the ground. Her breath formed faint clouds in front of her perfect, heart-shaped lips.

"Um? You know what?" Miss Kang lowered her voice and looked over her shoulder. Our teammates looked on in curiosity. "Whatever drama you two are going through is taking down the team, and it sucks. You need to decide if you're up to this. If you're not, we need new captains. It's not fair to the other girls. You have five minutes to work this out or I'm holding an emergency election."

Miss Kang marched off. I took in a lungful of frosty air. If we quit it would look terrible on my applications. I was not going to let Jules mar my résumé.

"Well?" I said. Jules wouldn't look at me. "Ugh!" I threw down my stick. "Enough is enough! I apologized on Nantucket. I apologized the first day of school. I feel like I apologize every time I look at you. I can't apologize anymore!" The words came out hot and clear. My ears buzzed even as the tips of them froze. Jules's eyes widened. The cloud in front of her mouth vanished. There was my old friend, alive and looking right at me.

"Hey, I didn't do anything," Jules said in a fierce whisper.

"Ignoring me is not *nothing*. Excluding me is not *nothing*. I'm done walking on eggs!"

"You mean eggshells?"

"I mean what I mean," I said, because even if I'd gotten the expression wrong, eggs, with all their gooey, messy insides, seemed much worse to walk on than shells. "I can't keep feeling like I owe you something."

"*I* can't help how *you* feel," she said.

"Well, I'm done acting like I've committed the crime of

the century." I picked up my stick and kicked off the dirt.

"Okay," she said.

"Okay?"

Miss Kang jogged over. "What's the verdict?"

"We're in," Jules said, wiping her mouth guard on her kilt.

"Are you sure?" she asked.

"Definitely," I added before the wind had a chance to shift.

"Get over there and talk to your team." Miss Kang gestured to the amorphous pack of girls standing dejectedly around the giant watercooler, sucking on orange slices, shivering, stealing cautious glances in our direction. "Seriously, give them a pep talk."

We didn't score in the second half, but neither did Peabody, and by the end of the game, their coach had subbed back in at least half of their starting lineup. Miss Kang called it a dignified loss.

From that moment on, we had a truce. We could lead our team, hang out in groups, or even be paired up for the Rosewood Cares Food Drive table at the street fair, but we had to obey three simple rules. One, we didn't talk about her mom. Two, we didn't talk about Nantucket, not about her wild, partying ways, not about her mean streak, as bright as a gasoline path aflame, or about her ditching me for Parker Carmichael, the mean-girl senator's daughter. And three, we never, ever talked about Zack.

Four

ONE SATURDAY IN NOVEMBER, I WAS STUDYING FOR MID-
terms at The Coffee Exchange. Brown and RISD students
had commandeered the place, and were huddled over text-
books, laptops, and sketchbooks. I saw Jules come in with
the leather backpack Nina had bought her in Italy. She
looked around for a spot, but every seat was taken. I waved,
pushed my stuff aside, and made room for her.

"I'm so glad you're here. I'm totally lost with European
History," she said and dropped her bag, with a thud. She
found the one empty chair in the whole place and carried it
over her head across the room to our table. "'Scuse me," she
said to a bearded drama student as she lowered the chair next
to me. He gave her a dirty look and tweaked his handlebar

mustache. "What?" she asked him; then she turned around, pulled out her European History folder, and sighed.

"Which prompt did you pick?" I asked.

"The one on world markets?"

"That's the hardest one. Let me see your notes."

After almost three hours of drinking too much coffee, consuming two giant pieces of cinnamon cake each, and mapping out our essays, we decided to reward ourselves with a movie at the Avon. Since they showed only one movie at a time, we had to see whatever was playing. It was a weird Danish murder mystery set in a 1970s nudist colony, told from several naked perspectives. We were dying of laughter at all the flapping boobs and bobbing penises, even though the ten other people in the movie theater were very serious.

After, we went to CVS, even though neither one of us had anything specific to buy, and tried to figure out who the killer was.

"It had to be the guy with the man boobs," she said as she sniffed a new brand of shampoo.

"No, it was the lady with all the . . ." I said, and gestured in front of my crotch.

"That's it! She hid the weapon in her bush!" We doubled over in laughter. She handed the shampoo to me to sniff. "Is it just me or does this smell like poop?"

"Ew!" I said, pushing it away, "I don't want to sniff it." We kept bumping into each other as we meandered toward the magazines. We discussed everything from the latest teacher gossip (Miss Kang was dating Señor Rodriguez again) to the best type of jeans for our butts, to the subtle British accent one of our classmates had picked up on a recent trip to London. We sampled body lotions until our hands were sticky. They smelled like lavender and medicine and roses and grandmas. We pushed up our sleeves and sampled more on our forearms. We decided the apricot one was the best and slathered it up to our elbows. By the time we left, it was dark and we reeked of synthetic sweetness.

"So, who do you have your eye on this year?" she asked as we lingered outside CVS with mascara, some hot pink lip gloss, *Teen Vogue*, *Lucky* magazine, Red Vines, Junior Mints, and Fresca, which we'd long ago deemed the world's most underrated soda.

"No one," I said, realizing that she thought Zack and I had broken up. I opened my mouth to speak, but changed my mind. I didn't want to correct her and explain that we had "paused," because having my old best friend back, even for a day, felt like returning home, setting down a heavy suitcase, and curling up in a favorite chair. "How about you?"

"Actually," she said, sticking her hands deep in the pockets of her puffy jacket. "I kind of like Jay."

"Really?" I'd had a crush on Jay Logan from the eighth grade until last summer. It was weird to think of Jules liking him, only because of the time I'd invested in studying him, memorizing his lacrosse statistics, and daydreaming about our life together as a private school power couple. I still claimed him out of habit.

"Do you care?" she asked. Did I feel a pinch? A pang?

A twinge? Nope. Zack had turned my Jay Logan crush into ancient history.

"Not at all. Go for it." Strands of soft rock blew out of the glass doors as a group of guys carrying Brown University ice hockey equipment bags exited, dropping f-bombs and potato chip crumbs.

"Cool," she said. After our summer, it surprised me that she would care how I felt about the whole thing, but her shoulders sank with relief. Her eyelids fluttered and she smiled one of her huge, movie star smiles. It felt so good to give her something she wanted. "Good. 'Cause I think he likes me, too."

"That's great," I said.

"I'm going to call him tonight," she said, rocking on her heels.

"Do it!"

I took the shortcut home through the Brown athletic complex. Warm gusts of chlorinated air wafted from the aquatics center as I tightened the straps on my backpack. I skipped across the playing fields. The motion detector lights illuminated my path in brief, consecutive bursts.

That night I was sitting at my desk memorizing French verbs when my phone vibrated, panicking on the hard surface of my desk. I saw Zack's name, grabbed the phone, and stared at the screen as the buzzing traveled from the phone up my arm, and to my heart. He was breaking our rule. But I had to pick up. It was Zack. *Zack.*

"Hello?"

"Hey, beautiful." His voice wrapped around me like a summer breeze.

"What are you doing?" I asked, absurdly alert.

"I'm calling you," he said.

"Oh." I slid off my chair and expanded like a starfish.

"I'm coming home for Thanksgiving, and I want to see you."

"Me, too," I said, curling up, closing my eyes, and imagining him next to me.

What would I do if I saw him? I would sneak him into my room and hide him under my quilt. No, I would run away with him to Newport and we would get a room at a motel. No, at an inn with a fireplace and one of those big bathtubs. We would take wintery walks on the beach and eat clam chowder, sitting on the same side of the booth at the Black Pearl. I touched my face at the thought. My hands still smelled like the lotion Jules and I had sampled. I sat up and saw the CVS bag with the mascara and the magazines and the Junior Mints. "But Zack, I don't think it's a good idea."

"Are you kidding? It's the best idea. And I need to see you," Zack said. "I want to get back together. I want to do the whole long distance thing with texts and phone calls and Skype and bus rides."

"Um, I don't know."

"Please," he said. "This isn't working for me."

"It's not working for me either, but . . ." I held my breath.

I couldn't finish the sentence. I wanted so badly to see him. I wanted to spend the next few days tingling in anticipation.

"But what?" Zack asked.

"But, Jules," I said, on the verge of tears. If Jules and I could get through high school, we would be okay; everything changes in college anyway. But if Zack and I got back together now, Jules and I would be right back where we started. I'd be alone again.

"And what if I can't handle saying good-bye to you again?" I asked, realizing that Jules was only half of it. It'd been so hard to say good-bye once. It hurt again already, and we were still on the phone. How could I go through that over and over again for the rest of the year, wondering all the time if he was thinking of me, too; waiting for him to call; analyzing his Facebook posts? No, I didn't want that. I just wanted to be with him in person, the whole summer in front of us like that dream where the house keeps going, each step revealing better rooms, bigger windows, balconies, pools, gardens. "Just wait for the summer. The summer is our time."

"So you don't want to see me?" he asked.

"We'll be back together in June," I said, hoping it would soothe the panic in his voice.

"I can't wait," Zack said. "I can't put my life on pause."

"It's only temporary." It was easy to think that long distance would work on a cold November night a week before he was coming home, but one of us had to stay strong. "I love you, Zack. My feelings aren't going to change. I know it."

"I love you, too," he said.

I felt a "but" dangling at the end of the sentence, like a loose tooth, but I told myself I was imagining it.

Five

I WOKE UP ON CHRISTMAS MORNING AND REALIZED I'D forgotten to buy my stepmother's parents a gift. Dad had given me a speech about how Polly's parents, Rosemary and Jim, had made a big effort to include me as their grand-daughter. They'd given me a set of monogrammed towels for no apparent reason the last time I visited them. We were going to their house for Christmas dinner and he was depending on me to be a *thoughtful, responsible* person, the kind of person who didn't buy Christmas presents at CVS on the actual day, as I had done last year for Polly and Alexi. This year, I'd remembered to get Polly a special kind of pan for angel food cake and Alexi a package of glow-in-the-dark stars for his ceiling (with a book about constellations) last weekend, but I had totally spaced on Rosemary and Jim.

I had an excuse. I'd just turned in my college applications. They were so refined and sparkling they were like compressed, digital jewels. I even had a letter of reference from George Gust, the journalist I'd interned for last summer on Nantucket, that was so awesome my mom wanted to frame it. I submitted all my applications two weeks early. But I still had to get a present for Polly's parents.

Starbucks was open on Christmas and it was a step up from CVS, and two whole blocks closer, which, considering it had snowed three feet the night before, was a big plus. No one had shoveled, so I was in it up to my knees, making deep, fresh footprints, and climbing snowbanks at the curbs. Everything was cold and glinting, but with all the heaviness at home, I wasn't feeling the magic.

Mom had exclaimed at least three times that "we girls" were a "perfect team" and "fine just the two of us." No pill and no amount of chardonnay was strong enough to dull Mom's pain at being single at Christmas, and yet she was pretending that I hadn't noticed how disappointed she'd been that, without Dad, there had been so little for her under the tree. Now I was dreading my performance in the second act of the Happy Divorced Christmas play. I couldn't wait for the day to be over. This wasn't how Christmas was supposed to feel.

It had actually started snowing again when I reached Starbucks, where a neat, straight path had been shoveled from the sidewalk to the entrance, and I reached out with a mittened hand to catch a fat, glimmering flake. Bing Crosby was being piped through the outdoor speakers. A little boy made a snowman in what was usually an ugly parking lot, but now looked like the top of a frosted cake. A couple passed by on cross-country skis. I smelled chimney smoke.

I was looking at the stuff on the back wall, trying to pick out the thing that would seem the least like I had bought it that morning. A French press? A set of travel mugs? Was there *anything* without the store logo on it? Did Rosemary and Jim even drink coffee? Then I spotted a monkey mug. The handle was the monkey's arm scratching his head. The monkey had a dopey expression, but it made me laugh. I was contemplating if they would like it too when the door swung open and I felt a rush of cold air. It was Zack. He wore a black wool peacoat and a red cashmere scarf. His cheeks were pink and there was fresh snow in his hair.

I stood frozen, aglow, a monkey mug in each hand. I must've been emitting some signal, because at that moment he turned to see me among the cappuccino machines, my mouth open like I was about to burst into "O Holy Night." When his eyes met mine, he blinked twice and smiled the warmest, biggest smile. I felt a drop of happiness enter my bloodstream so potent that a second one might have sent me to the emergency room for an overdose. I was wrong not to have seen him over Thanksgiving. I was so stupid not to do long distance. How could I have denied myself *this*? I wanted to feel *this* forever.

"Come here," he said. I ran to him, wrapped my arms around his neck. He hugged me so tight my feet lifted off the ground. His cold ear pressed against my hot face. I inhaled his scent—wet wool and pine—and he spread his hand over my back and held it there. It was Christmas in three heartbeats.

"Hey, you," he said.

"Hey, you, too," I said. My cheeks burned.

"What are you doing?"

"Christmas shopping," I said, shrugging.

"Pretty lame," he said with a smile, nodding at the mugs.

"I think they're cute." I imitated the ridiculous grin of the monkeys.

Then his phone rang. "I bet this is Jules, changing her mind again. Our plane leaves in two hours and the girl is acting like we have all day." His phone persisted, but he ignored it. "She's not even packed."

"Where are you going?"

The Claytons were not a travel-on-Christmas family. They were a stockings-filled-with-clementines-chocolates-and-new socks, homemade-actual-figgy-pudding, get-dressed-up-to-go-to-midnight-mass-but-just-for-the-music family. I loved how when I used to go over on Christmas my clothes would smell like the fire that had been burning in their house all day. The one we chucked our orange peels into.

"Mexico," he said. "Cancún. Dad surprised us at the last minute."

"*Cancún?*"

His phone rang again. He silenced it without looking.

"Time for a change," he said. His phone rang again. The

caller's third attempt. He checked it. His features subtly shifted. He turned away and picked it up.

"Hey," he said quietly, too quietly, into the phone. "You, too. Of course I miss you."

I didn't have to ask if it was a girl. I just knew in my bones. As I felt air vacuumed from my lungs, I made a promise to myself not to cry. Zack stepped out of line to take the phone call. I bought the mugs, handing the cashier a twenty-dollar bill with a shaking hand. She was asking me something about a receipt—did I want it e-mailed? I couldn't even hear her. I muttered, "No, thank you," and didn't wait for my change. I ran out of the store, leaping over the snowbank, immune to the chunks of ice in my socks and the wind chafing my cheeks.

It wasn't until Jim and Rosemary opened their presents at their house that I saw that the mugs were both emblazoned with the Starbucks logo on the back. I'd even left the prices on them, showing the Christmas discount. They told me how much they loved monkeys, how much they loved Starbucks. My dad shook his head. A minute later, while Alexi was stomping around with his new toy airplane, I excused myself and fled to what Rosemary called the powder room.

Zack had moved on. I'd let Dad down, again. Mom was alone. I was in a near stranger's house on Christmas.

"You okay in there?" Rosemary said, knocking gently at the door.

"I'm fine, thanks," I said, as politely as I could. I held a Christmas-themed hand towel to my face as I silently released the tears I'd been holding in since Starbucks.

January, February, and March dragged on like one of Edwina MacIntosh's lectures about cliques. That winter there had been one blizzard, two nor'easters, and three months of dirty slush. The bitter cold had somehow helped me perfect the art of not thinking about Zack. One bright spot had been when George Gust's book came out, the one he'd been writing last summer on Nantucket. He'd put my name in the acknowledgments just like he'd promised. He'd even given me my own sentence: *A big thank-you goes to Cricket Elizabeth Thompson, my faithful intern, for providing good sense, keen insight, and a steady supply of Coke Zero.* I couldn't believe my name was in a real book for the whole world to see. It got me through waiting to hear if I was going to Brown next year.

My acceptance to Brown was a golden ticket to the future. It arrived on a Saturday. Mom and I went out for dinner and she let me sip her champagne. On Sunday, Dad took me to Nordstrom and told me to pick out anything I wanted. I didn't tell anyone else I'd been admitted until the next Monday, when I marched right into the senior lounge and wrote *Brown* on that giant piece of butcher paper, smack in the middle. My classmates congratulated me, even as, in some cases, their eyelids beat double time with jealousy.

Ed invited me to her office for lunch. We ate with real silver forks and knives. Miss Kang did a victory dance in the middle of the cafeteria. Jules even picked me a bouquet of daffodils from the school's garden. But of course, the person I wanted to tell more than anyone was Zack.

Six

I SAT ON THE GRADUATION STAGE IN MY PAST-THE-KNEE white cotton dress, my hair swept up in a chignon, sweating under the hot June sun. I could hardly believe high school was over. The microphone squeaked as our commencement speaker, Richa Singh, class of 1991 and professor emeritus of astronomy at MIT, adjusted her sari, leaned in, and said, "Today I'm going to embrace the lesson Mrs. Hart taught me many years ago: above all, be succinct." It was eleven a.m. and nearly one hundred degrees.

The crowd, perspiring in a range that stretched from light dew to full-drenched soak, laughed. A hot breeze rustled the leaves of the huge copper beech tree behind the wooden platform where my graduating class sat in two neat rows. My mom caught my eye and waved from the audience. Brad, her boyfriend of four months, was next to her, wiping sweat from his brow with a handkerchief. Dad, Polly, and Alexi sat two rows back. Alexi's head was bent in rapt concentration as he played with his iPad. Dad pointed his fancy camera in my direction. I could see his huge smile under the long lens.

"When you see stars, you are looking into the past," Richa Singh began. "You see a celestial body, such as a star or a comet, as it was when the light coming from that body began its journey to your eye. It's possible when you look into the night sky you are seeing stars that no longer exist." It was too hot to wrap my mind around this, so I tuned out and scanned the crowd. I spotted Mr. Clayton sitting alone between two empty seats. It was as if he'd saved a seat for Nina, I thought, and I felt a bright wire of pain. It surprised me how it could still hurt this much, how pain that you think has dulled can come back so sharp, so fast, just to let you know it's still there. Where was Zack? How could he miss his sister's graduation? *How could he miss mine?*

"So, I know you've all heard about Larsen's Comet," Richa continued. "It's making its rounds for the first time since 1939. It will be particularly bright in the northeastern sky for the month of August, with a tail of a hundred degrees, which is big—trust me." She turned to address my classmates and me. "You literally have a bright future, a cosmic event as spectacular as you can hope to witness in your lifetimes. But here's the trick. You must be awake to the moment. You must get out from behind your screens and handheld devices, get away from city light pollution, and take in the sky. There's no picture, no text, no YouTube video that can compare to seeing it with your own eyes. The world offers us brilliance and beauty, but it is up to us to show up. So, go get 'em, grads! Reach for the stars!"

Everyone clapped, and Edwina MacIntosh approached the podium in her powder-blue suit. I took a deep breath, preparing for my big moment. "And now, as is tradition, the student council president will read a poem. This year's president is one of the girls I can proudly say has been at Rosewood since kindergarten. I'd like to think we take partial credit for what a remarkable young woman she has turned out to be. She's headed to Brown University in the fall, and last week, here on this very lawn, she was awarded the Sarah Congdon Award for student athlete demonstrating exceptional citizenship. Cricket Thompson, will you please come and read 'A Psalm of Life' by Henry Wadsworth Longfellow?"

I slid past my classmates, stood in front of the podium, and made eye contact with the crowd. *"Tell me not—"* I began.

That's when I saw Zack take the empty seat next to his dad. He was taller, bigger, further along the road from boy to man. What had been the beginning of a transformation at Christmas was now complete. He was no longer a dorky-but-hot-to-me sophomore. In his Nantucket Reds and a white button-down, with the sleeves rolled up, he was flat-out gorgeous. My mouth went dry. I had to start again.

"Tell me not, in mournful numbers, 'Life is but an empty dream!'
For the soul is dead that slumbers," I continued, clutching my
index card. *"And things are not what they seem."*

I think something happens after you've been in love with
someone, and especially if you've had sex, because I had a
GPS on Zack as my parents asked me to pose for various
pictures near the beech tree. Even when I was facing away,
smiling at the camera, I was aware of his presence. He was
over by the lemonade. He was texting. He was laughing at
something Jules said. Where were his glasses, I wondered?
Did he get contacts?

"Okay girls," Mom said, gesturing to Jules. "Let's get the
two of you."

Jules and I put our arms around each other, though not
as tight as we once would have. We tilted our heads toward
each other. I could feel that we were both holding our
breath as my mom and Mr. Clayton snapped pictures. Then
Mr. Clayton stepped forward and handed Jules a package
wrapped in white tissue paper and a single blue ribbon.

"This is for you," Jules said, handing the package to me.

"Oh," I said, taking the gift. "Thank you."

"It's from all of us," Mr. Clayton added, smiling, throwing an arm around Zack.

I unwrapped the tissue paper and gasped. It was a picture, in a simple, wooden frame, of Nina on her graduation
day from Brown. I'd seen the picture many times. It had
sat on Nina's dresser for as long as I could remember. Nina

was in her graduation gown. Her cap was off and her hair was long and flowing. She was looking right at the camera, daring me to do something great. I held the picture to my chest. "Thank you."

"Let me see," Mom said, taking it. "Aw," she cooed, as if it were a picture of a cute puppy. I snatched it back.

"Are you sure I can have this?" I asked. It was such a part of their home I felt like I was walking away with their chimney or the stained glass window in the dining room.

"She loved you, Cricket," Mr. Clayton said. For the first time I noticed how much he'd aged this year. "And she loved Brown. She would've been so happy you were going there."

I looked at Jules. A shade of hesitation passed over her face before she smiled and said, "Hey, it's not like I was going to get in."

"Thank you," I said, hugging Jules with all of my might. I took a step toward Zack, about to hug him, too, when he held up his hand.

"Hey, Cricket. Give me five."

Honestly, it would have been better if he'd told me to fuck off.

I held up a hand, not sure if I was going to give him five or slap him. Jules took my hand and spun me around, a residual friend instinct kicking in. "There's a party tonight at Jay's house," she said as she dipped me. "Pick you up at eight."

Seven

"WOULD YOU LIKE SOME DISGUSTING CAKE, MY LADY?" ALEXI asked, his cowlick pointed north and his lip curled in repulsion. Polly had given Alexi the job of waiter to keep him busy at my graduation barbecue.

"Alexi, that's not very nice," Polly said. "Kate made that cake for Cricket."

"Sorry, Kate," Alexi said, aware he'd socially misfired, something he was working very hard not to do.

"It's okay," Mom said, tousling his hair. She stage-whispered, "Carrot cake is Cricket's favorite, but I don't really like it either. Who wants vegetables in their cake?" She made a face, and Alexi laughed like this was the funniest thing he'd heard all year.

This was a huge improvement from how this evening had

started. I didn't think I was going to make it to eight p.m., when Jules had promised to pick me up. At one point, Dad asked Mom's permission to use the "restroom," even though it had been his *bathroom* in his house for fifteen years. He not only knew where it was, he knew what kind of soap would be by the sink and where the towel hanging on the rack had been bought.

And then, later, when Polly's parents gave me a set of some top-of-the-line monogrammed sheets as a graduation present, Mom whistled and said, "Wow. Those are nicer than the ones we got for our wedding, right, Jack?" Dad coughed, Rosemary pursed her lips, and I felt like I had to apologize. And then, after that, Brad tried to teach Polly the correct stance for fly-fishing when she clearly didn't want to learn, at least not in heels in my mom's backyard. She had to firmly tell him no for him to get the picture, and he'd flushed with such embarrassment he looked like a little boy.

But now it was seven fifty p.m., the barbecue was wrapping up, and everyone had consumed enough alcohol to at least be able to simulate a normal social gathering. Except for Alexi and me. Alexi was allowed only water to keep his sugar intake down, and I was sticking to lemonade for now, though I could've used something to help me forget about Zack's high five, which was hovering in the air over my head. It was like he'd forgotten who I was.

I wasn't the girl he high-fived. I was the one he whispered secrets to in the predawn hours, the one who could make him laugh with a single raised eyebrow. The one who understood what he had lost when he lost his mother. I was the girl he loved, or at least that's what I thought. When someone stops loving you, I wondered, does that mean they never really even started?

As this thought crept across my mind, Aunt Phyllis and Uncle Rob put their arms around me and started to tell me again what it was like to go to college in Northampton, Massachusetts, in the 1980s. Lots of plaid shirts, combat boots, and crazy parties that they were hinting involved group sex. Someone needed to cut them off before they got any more concrete with their details.

Just then Mom stepped up on the big, flat rock in her garden, tapped her wineglass with a plastic fork and announced, a bit tipsily, "I'd like to toast Cricket. I have no doubt she's going to take over the world. I am so, so proud of you, baby!"

Everyone lifted glasses in my direction. Dad whistled. Alexi whooped. I took a little bow.

"That said," she continued, "I'm glad she's staying at home. Not just in Providence, but right here in this house."

Brown had offered me a great financial package, but it didn't cover everything. My parents didn't have a lot of money, and I didn't want to graduate with student loans, so we'd decided I'd live with Mom. Living in the dorms and eating in the cafeteria would have cost almost twelve thousand dollars a year. That didn't include student fees or books for classes. At the end of four years, I'd have been lucky to be only fifty thousand dollars in debt, which Dad explained would keep growing over time. Both my parents were still paying off their student loans. It seemed stupid to go into debt when we lived so close to the Brown campus that I could walk to all my classes, watch the marching band pass our porch every Saturday morning, and hear the soccer referee's whistle from my bedroom window.

"I can't deny that I feel so good knowing my daughter is right downstairs if I need her, like I did today when she helped me pick out this outfit." She curtsied, and Brad whistled. "And if she needs me for girls' chats or love advice, I'll be waiting. Who knows, we might even end up going on some double dates. We'll be double trouble, right, honey?"

"That's right," I said, downing my lemonade to mask my panic.

"I have something to say here," Dad said. I'd only heard Dad make one toast. It was at his wedding to Polly, and he hadn't mentioned me. He took a sip of his beer, staring at it for a second before beginning. "A lot of folks send their kids to public school and save for college. That was our plan, but Cricket peed her pants every day of her first three months at William McKinley Elementary."

Alexi pointed at me and cackled, checking to see who else had caught this comic gem. Polly pulled him close to her and he giggled into her skirt.

"Well, it's true," Dad said. "We hated the idea that Cricket didn't like school. So we visited Rosewood, Kate's alma mater, even though we knew we couldn't afford it." Mom smiled, nodded, and drained her glass. "And Cricket cried when it was time to come home. She said, 'I can't go home, Daddy. School's not over yet.' So, Kate and I made a decision. That weekend we sold our brand-new minivan so that she could finish kindergarten at Rosewood."

I remembered the day we sold the van. I think I was so excited that we were going to start taking the bus that it never occurred to me we were broke.

Dad continued, "We kept saying just for elementary school, just to get her on the right track. But Cricket was doing so beautifully. 'Daddy,' she'd say when I picked her up from school, 'guess what I learned today?' As teachers, it made our hearts sing.

"So then we thought, let's take out an extra mortgage and get her through those horrible middle-school years. You know, cliques and first bras and all that." I instinctively crossed my arms in front of my chest. More cackles from Alexi. The rest were quiet, listening. "And when high school came around, well, I think we all saw today how much a part of that school she was." He turned to me. "We couldn't take you out, no matter the cost. I don't think they would've let us. You were practically running the place." He shrugged, grinning, acting out his helplessness in the face of my success. "We took out another loan."

"Sorry," I said. I don't know how I had thought two teachers were paying for my expensive private-school education, but I guess I hadn't wanted to think about it, and they'd never asked me to.

"I'm not saying this to make you feel bad. Let me finish. We just hoped, year after year, that it would all pay off.

We crossed our fingers with each tuition check that we were making the right decision. We bet on you, Cricket." Here he drew a shaky breath, held it, looked at me, and glowed. "And man, did we hit the jackpot. Honey, I couldn't be prouder of you. Brown University. Member of the lacrosse team. The Ivy League! This is my daughter," Dad said, wiping his eyes, raising his voice and pointing to me like I'd just won an Oscar. "My brilliant, beautiful daughter!"

"Thank you," I said as I handed my lemonade to Aunt Phyllis and threw my arms around Dad as everyone clapped. I buried my head in his chambray-covered shoulder and smelled his Old Spice. Alexi tried to come between us, but my dad told him this was a father-daughter moment.

"We didn't realize you weren't living in the dorms," Rosemary said a few minutes later. "That's why we got you the monogrammed sheets. So you wouldn't lose them in the school laundry. They're for an extra-long twin bed."

"I love them. And I think that's what I have, anyway." It wasn't true, but I knew monogrammed things couldn't be exchanged.

"But the dorms are such a big part of the college experience," Jim added. Dad had told me that Jim came from a very poor family in Boston, and that he had worked in a hardware store to put himself through law school at night. "It was an experience I made sure Polly had, since I didn't get to."

"And I'm grateful, Dad," Polly said, patting her dad's back. "Poor Dad. He paid so much, and I was, let's say, very social."

"And it wasn't exactly Brown," Jim said.

"I know Hamilton isn't Ivy League," Polly said, putting a hand on her hip. "But it's still a good school."

"I think we'd have to ask someone who actually attended class," Jim said.

"Ouch, Dad," Polly said.

"Polly, do me a favor and get me another piece of cake, hmm?" Rosemary said, then leaned in and whispered, "Gotta break these two up sometimes."

That's when Jules pulled up, but it took a minute to recognize her. She wasn't in the Audi or the land yacht. She was in a brand-new Jeep with a bright red ribbon on its hood.

Eight

"HEY, HEY," JAY SAID AS HE WALKED TOWARD US IN HIS rooftop living room and kissed Jules. "C.T." He pulled me close for a rough hug. "What's up, girl?" Jules made a beeline for a well-known and deeply feared clique composed of three Alden girls: Chloe, Jessie, and Gemma. They greeted her with a collective shriek-giggle as she kicked off her sandals, poured herself a drink, and joined them on the sofa. As Jay's girlfriend, this was her party, too.

"What are you up to this summer, C.T.?" Jay asked.

"Working at Leo's," I said. Leo's was a sandwich shop between the Brown and RISD campuses, famous for its barrel of pickles. My first shift was in three days. For the first time, I didn't mind staying in Providence for the summer while all my classmates went off on some exotic adventure or to a second home in an elite location. I just wanted to start college.

"You're stuck in Providence?" Jay asked. "That sucks."

"I'm fine with it."

"Cool," Jay said. "I have an internship at my dad's bank in London."

"Wow," I said, as we made our way to the bar. "London." I felt a dagger of panic. Should I be going someplace like London this summer?

"And Jules, as you probably know, is—"

"Heading to Nantucket on Friday," Jules said, interrupting him.

I smiled and turned to greet the Alden Three. "Hey, Chloe; hey, Jessie; what's up, Gemma?" Gemma waved. Jessie nodded. Chloe mumbled hello.

"So here's the plan," Jay said, sitting next to Jules and squeezing her knee. "There's this secret old bowling alley in one of the old buildings at Brown."

"For real?" asked Gemma, whose heavy eyelids indicated she was already drunk.

"Yeah," Jay said. "It's from, like, the forties, and Dirt's brother knows how to break in." Rich Green, a.k.a. "Dirt," looked up through a haze of pot smoke and nodded. "So we're going bowling tonight, kids."

"It's fucking awesome," Dirt said. "They have pins and everything. And you have to go through these underground tunnels to get there." Then, noticing me for the first time, he smiled and meowed. I scooted a little farther down the couch, away from him.

"In your dreams, Dirt," Jay said. Dirt shrugged and spat.

"Dude," Jay said.

"That's brilliant," Jules said. "We have to make teams!"

"I don't know," I said.

"Don't worry," Jay said. "We're going to be quiet and cool, and no one's around. The campus is, like, dead."

A second wave of Alden kids arrived, busting through the door to the roof. "LO-GAN," Lucas Saunders shouted, pumping a fist in the air; his other arm was weighted down with a six-pack.

"I might have to sit this one out," I said.

"Oh, come on," Jules said. With the sunset behind her, she was outlined in gold. "You have to come."

"Think of it this way," Jay said, heading behind the bar and scooping ice into a plastic cup. "This is our last night of high school. Our whole life is about to change. What can I get you?"

"Just a Coke," I said.

He poured Coke into the cup, fastened a sliced lime to the rim, and handed it to me. "You only live once, right?"

"That's what they say, but I can't do it," I said.

Someone with squeaky brakes was parking on the street below. Jules tensed, stood, and peered over the edge of the rooftop, then turned around with a furrowed brow. "Ugh," she said, sinking back into her seat. "Ugh, I told them not to come."

I stood and saw the land yacht below. I held my breath as Zack stepped out of the car and judged his parking job. My heart hammered as my mind circled the pronoun *them*.

I watched as a girl climbed out of the passenger seat and combed her fingers through her dark, shiny hair. She was a little unsteady in her sky-high heels on the uneven sidewalk and Zack reached out a hand to her. As they joined hands and walked toward the front door, it sank in that Zack had a real, live girlfriend. She wasn't just a mysterious presence on the other end of a phone at Starbucks, but an actual person with fantastic hair. As I leaned farther over the railing to watch them walk, I realized I knew her. The air left my lungs as her familiar laugh drifted up from the street like a tendril of smoke.

His girlfriend was Parker Carmichael.

Nine

I FLEW BACK DOWN THE THREE FLIGHTS OF INCREASINGLY majestic stairs and out the oversize front door flanked by ceramic footmen. I just had to hope that Zack and Parker were taking the elevator. He wasn't going to have another chance to offer me a high five, not with Parker looking on. I knew they went to the same boarding school, but I never imagined they were together. I was in mid-driveway, almost clear of the bus-size Suburban, when I felt a hand on my shoulder. Jules.

"Cricket, don't go. It's our graduation night."

"What's up with Zack and your friends? First me, now Parker?" She laughed, but I wasn't joking. "Why is he with her?"

"She goes to Hanover, too," she said.

"She does? But Parker is so mean. She's the meanest girl I've ever met."

"I don't know about that." Jules held up her hands like the scales of justice. "It's not that she's mean. You don't really know her. You, like, can't be objective. She can be great when she wants to be, and she's been through a lot." Laughter spilled from the rooftop. "Come on, don't you want fun memories of tonight?"

"Why didn't you tell me about Parker?"

"I don't know. You guys were broken up."

"And what happened to his glasses?"

"He got LASIK."

For some reason, this felt like a betrayal. "I have to go. Thank you for the picture."

"I thought we could have a night like old times, but never mind. Do you want a ride?" She looked like she'd rather conjugate French verbs. In a prison cell. In Siberia.

"No thanks, I'll walk."

But as soon as I was out of sight, I ran. Instead of going home, I went to the track at Alden where my feet tried to keep pace with my heart. Had that been Parker on the phone at Christmas? That meant they'd been together for six months, at least. Six months was serious. I felt like I'd been punched. I kicked off my flats and ran on the grass. I hit my stride. What did they talk about? Did he go to her house in Connecticut on the weekends? Had they been back to Nantucket together? Had they had sex? Ugh. That was a stupid question. Of course they had. It wasn't just that he'd forgotten who I was, he'd forgotten who he was. Richa Singh had said that when you look at the stars, you're seeing what no longer exists. Was Zack like those stars, I wondered? Was he even there at all?

I'd completely sweated through my tank top when I decided to head home. I hadn't counted the laps, but I was sure I'd run at least four miles tonight. Maybe five. My flouncy skirt was clinging to my tingling quads, and though I couldn't see in the dark, I knew my feet were filthy with ground-in dirt and grass. *I have lots of parties ahead of me next year,* I told myself as I used the light on my cell phone to search the grass for my discarded shoes. *Parties full of people who don't give a shit about Nantucket.*

When I first stepped into Mom's house, I thought the TV was on. I heard kissing and moaning and wondered what channel Mom had been watching. Those *Lifetime* movies are getting pretty raunchy, I thought. It wasn't until I took a few extra steps toward the kitchen that I realized that these were live, real-time sex sounds coming from the living room sofa. It was almost like I was suffering a moment of complete disbelief so intense that it took me a regrettable extra minute to put it together. I held my breath and flung my hands over my ears.

"Cricket?" Mom asked.

I didn't answer. It would be better for her to think it was

a burglar. I tiptoed back out the door, wincing as it slammed shut behind me, and sat on the porch steps with my head between my knees.

"Cricket?" Mom asked, appearing in the doorway moments later, her bathrobe wrapped tightly around her. She sat next to me, radiating a warmth I didn't want to think about. I put my head in my hands. She ran a light hand over my back. "Honey, why are you sweating?"

"I went for a run," I said, and pulled away.

"At night?"

"Yes."

"That's odd."

"What can I say? It's been an odd night."

"Hmm. I think we should talk about this."

"No, we shouldn't," I said, shaking my head. "No need. I promise."

"Well, okay, if you say so," she said, but didn't move.

"I need to be alone right now."

She sighed and stood up, pausing in front of the door. "I almost forgot. You got a message."

"I did?" Zack, I thought in a flash of hope, calling to explain.

"It was Rosemary. She and Jim want to talk to you before they head back up to Boston tomorrow. She asked for you to meet them at Starbucks at nine."

"That's strange," I said.

"I'm going to go back inside now and Brad and I are

going to, um, retire to my bedroom. So you can feel perfectly comfortable coming back inside and—"

"Got it," I said. "I'm going to hang out here for a minute."

"You know, as roommates, we're going to have to learn to, well, communicate about these things."

"Good night, Mom," I said. I shut my eyes and held my breath until I heard the door shut behind her.

Ten

I'D ALREADY DOWNED HALF MY LATTE WHEN ROSEMARY
and Jim spotted me, waved, and joined me at the one free
table, which was really much too small for the three of us.
I hadn't slept well. I'd been so afraid of overhearing more
from Mom and Brad that it was like my ears were rebelling
and I'd become extra sensitive. I'd spent the night listening
to the walls breathe.

"We've been talking," Rosemary said.

"We're looking for a number," Jim said, rapping the table
with his knuckles.

"A number?"

"Honey, how much do you need to live in the dorms, eat
in the cafeteria, buy your books, and have some spending
money?" Rosemary asked.

"Oh. Well, I'm not sure." I gripped my latte. Were they offering what I thought they were? Did they have any idea how much money it would be? My parents and I had been over it a hundred times, and it was a lot more than any of us would've imagined. "It's a lot."

"This is no time to be shy," Jim said. He took a heavy gold pen from his shirt pocket and offered it to me along with a Starbucks napkin.

"Okay." I smoothed out the napkin. "The dorms are eight thousand." I drew an eight. "The meal plan is four." I added a four. "And anticipated student fees are two." I totaled it, writing *fourteen thousand* and turned the number to face them. "It's so much, it's really insane. I don't know how—"

"Let's add some spending money," Rosemary said. She crossed out my *fourteen thousand* and wrote *sixteen thousand*. She smiled. "A girl can't live on bread and lacrosse alone."

Jim peered down his nose through his glasses and studied the number. He rapped the table again. "Your father is a wonderful man. And he's done a world of good for Polly and the boy."

"Yes," I said.

"Now, I'm a businessman, a self-made businessman."

"His mother worked in the Necco Wafer factory," Rosemary said, patting his arm. "And his father drank her wages."

Jim raised a hand to stop her. "That doesn't mean I didn't get some help along the way. I did. And now I'd like to offer you some help and teach you a little about self-reliance."

"Okay." I was as ready to hear a plan as I'd ever been.

"If you make eight thousand dollars this summer, I'll match it," Jim said.

"Wow," I said. "That's so generous. Thank you."

"What do you think?" Rosemary asked. "Can you do it?"

"Of course," I said. "Absolutely."

"It has to be at least eight," Jim said.

"Got it," I said. "Eight."

"Then we've got a deal," Jim said. He stood up and shook my hand.

"You can use those sheets after all," Rosemary said as she kissed my cheek.

I watched in a stupor as they climbed into their Volvo and drove off, as if they went around changing lives on a daily basis. The amazement shifted to panic as I walked home. How was I going to do this? Eight thousand dollars in two months? Okay, two and almost a half, but still, it wasn't going to happen at Leo's for nine bucks an hour. Providence was hardly a summer destination. The restaurants were dead when the students were away. I mean, unless I aced an audition for the Legs & Eggs shift at the Foxy Lady. For a second I thought I could do it in secret and write a blog about it, but a second later I knew that was ridiculous. So, where was I going to get all that money?

When I got back home and saw Nina's picture propped up on my dresser, the answer came to me in a vision, the same way I imagine it does for religious people when they say they see the face of the Virgin Mary in a vegetable or a taco or whatever. Only it wasn't a holy figure that appeared before me, but a crescent-shaped island thirty miles out to sea. A place where money rolled in as thick as fog, where bills slipped through fingers like sand, where people's pockets were as deep and open as the ocean itself.

Nantucket.

Shit.

Eleven

THOUGH STARTING TOTALLY FRESH IN A NEW PLACE might've been a good thing if I had had more time, with just a little over nine weeks I needed to go where I knew the lay of the land and had a few local references. This seemed especially true once Liz, my British friend, with whom I'd been a chambermaid at the Cranberry Inn last year, offered to let me stay with her for a little bit. She was running the place now because our old boss, Gavin, was off in Bali doing yoga. She said I could crash in the manager's apartment with her, but only for a week. After that, her boyfriend Shane was moving in. "Waitressing is where the money is," she'd told me. "Mark my words."

Over the next few days, I applied for ten waitressing

jobs through *The Inquirer and Mirror* Web site, picking the ones that came with housing. I'd even had a phone interview at a restaurant called Breezes, but I had failed the wine test. It was the first thing I had ever failed in my entire life. My lowest grade to date had been a seventy-eight. Clearly, if I was going to get a waitressing job, I needed to expand my wine knowledge beyond Mom's chardonnay with the kangaroo on the label, so I bought a book called *Wine Made Simple* and studied it every day with the same dedication I had once applied to SAT vocabulary words.

At the end of the week, Mom drove me to the Steamship Authority in Hyannis where I'd catch the ferry to Nantucket.

"You got everything?" Mom asked. People were sporting their brightest clothes and monogrammed canvas bags as they filed aboard *The Eagle* with their luggage, bikes, kids, and dogs. A man directed a line of Range Rovers, Jeeps, and Volvos onto the boat. It was chilly, windy, and spitting rain.

"I guess," I said, my mouth dry with anxiety.

"Here you go," Mom said and lifted my carry-on roller bag from the trunk. It was stuffed to the gills, mostly with shorts and T-shirts, but also with my running shoes and a comfortable pair of sneakers called Easy Spirits. They were the ugliest shoes I'd ever seen, but Mom insisted that there was no way to be a good waitress without comfortable shoes. She should know. She'd waitressed all through college and teacher school. I extended the handle and tilted it on its wheels. I slid my purse over my shoulder and tucked it safely under my arm. My picture of Nina was in there, and I didn't want anything to happen to it.

"Don't forget this," Mom said, handing me the lacrosse stick I'd almost left in the backseat.

"Oh, yeah, thanks. I'm going to need that." I had to practice my stick work. Stacy, the Brown lacrosse coach, was going to be posting weekly videos with practice drills, and we were supposed to be running an average of five miles a day. I stuck my lacrosse stick through a loop in my backpack.

"Well, I have one more thing for you," Mom said. "I figured since you found mine so interesting last year, you might as well write your own."

She handed me a package. I unwrapped it. It was a journal. It was dark purple with gold along the edges of the paper. It smelled like real leather. It felt solid, substantial. I put it in my purse with the picture. "Thanks, Mom."

"Oh, and I almost forgot. Paul said to call him if you need anything. He's out there pretty much full-time through August." She handed me the business card of Paul Morgan, the lawyer I met last summer on the island and tried to fix her up with before I realized he was gay. They were now Facebook buddies who always liked each other's posts. "Stick it in your wallet so you won't lose it. You're doing the right thing," Mom said, taking my face in her hands, "but it doesn't mean I can't be a little sad for myself. I was looking forward to us being roommates."

"Oh, Mom. You and Brad are good together. You don't want me around."

"What if I do? What if I need you?"

"You're going to be fine." I hugged her, grabbed my own wrist behind her back, and squeezed her tight.

"Hey, you're going to be fine, too. Aren't you and Jules friends again?"

"Kind of," I said. I hadn't even told Jules I was going back to Nantucket. I kept making myself promise I was going to tell her by the end of the hour, the end of the morning, the end of the day, but here I was, about to get on the ferry, and she still didn't know.

"And what about Zack?"

"I can't think about that." I felt a wave of seasickness even though I was still on land.

"Remember, there's nothing more attractive than self-confidence."

"But Mom, I'm trying not to think of him at all."

"Oh, well, in that case." She fished around in her purse and pulled out a Sharpie. As a teacher, Mom had a Sharpie and a dry-erase marker on her at all times. I was about to ask her how she knew about Parker when she uncapped the Sharpie and drew a big blue number eight on my palm.

"There. So you keep your eyes on the prize. Eight thousand dollars." She glanced at her watch as I studied the inky evidence of her most un–mom-like move to date. "Honey, you have to go. Your ferry is going to leave any minute and you still need a ticket."

Twelve

"CALM DOWN MISSY, YOU'LL MAKE THE TWO O'CLOCK," THE Santa Claus look-alike at the ticket counter said as he slid me my change and added, "but you'll have to step lively. The heavens are about to open."

"Thanks." I stuffed the bills in my pocket, grabbed my roller bag, and pivoted toward the door. The rain slicked the pavement as I darted to the boat, handed my ticket over, and clambered up the metal ramp, the last one aboard. As I yanked my bag over the gap between the ramp and the deck, my lacrosse stick slipped out of the loop on my backpack.

I bent down to pick it up and my purse slammed against the cold, wet deck. My picture of Nina, I thought. I slid to my shins. My hood fell off just as the rain escalated from shower to downpour. I shoved the purse inside my raincoat, gathered my stuff as best I could, and pushed my way through the heavy door to the inside part of the ferry, where the air-conditioning, set to arctic frost, sent a chill down my back like a zipper.

The knees of my jeans were soaked through to the skin. Water dripped from my ponytail and the hem of my raincoat. I looked around for a seat, or at least a corner to shove my bags in while I tried to rescue the picture. As the steam whistle blew and we pulled away from the dock, the people who had missed the heavy rain settled in. Dry and comfortable, they removed their moisture-wicking jackets and opened hardcover books and well-respected newspapers. Kids stared into their iPads or lined up to order hot dogs while their parents typed into their phones. Chocolate Labs and golden retrievers curled on cozy fleece beds. I stood dripping in my own private puddle.

"Is someone sitting here?" I asked a guy whose guitar was taking up a seat.

He looked up, blinking, like I'd just startled him out of a dream. He was older than me, but not by much. He had messy dark blond hair with a few strands of gold and lines that went from the corners of his bright blue eyes to his cheeks. He was cute and he knew it. He smiled up at me, pulled out his earbuds, and asked, "What's that?"

"Is this seat taken? I mean, by anyone besides your guitar?"

"Oh, no," he said, laughing a little as he stood up to get his guitar. He was wearing a gray wool sweater with a hole in the elbow. There was paint on his jeans and a little in his hair. As he leaned over to place his guitar under the seat, his T-shirt lifted, exposing a tan, muscular back. Was he doing that on purpose? "Looks like you're headed to the island for a while."

"Yeah," I said, arranging my stuff in an awkward pile.

"Me, too," he said. "What are you going to be doing?"

"Working," I said, peeling my dripping jacket off. "You?"

"Working, yeah, but also just taking it all in. Surfing. Writing music. Resetting, you know? There's nothing like a summer on Nantucket to shake things up."

"That's true," I said, thinking about how last summer had completely changed my life. "Um, can you watch my stuff?"

He patted my suitcase. "I'll guard it with my life."

A little girl sucking on a Popsicle watched with interest as I held the picture over the trash can and freed it from its ruined case. I brushed it off with the soft, dry sleeve of my sweatshirt. The photo looked so small and vulnerable without the frame, but except for a tiny corner piece that had torn off with an apple-seed of glass, it had survived. I turned it over to check the back and gasped. Written in faint ballpoint pen was a list.

Nina's Life List
1. Visit Rodin Museum in Paris.
2. Learn to drive and then drive Route 1 to Big Sur.
3. Drink Campari on Amalfi Coast with Alison.
4. Be in a Woody Allen movie.
5. See St. Francis from altar.

I traced my finger over her familiar architect's handwriting. I felt Nina's presence for the first time since her death. It was like she was leaning on the counter wearing brown duck boots and a Fair Isle sweater, her hair down and her brown eyes laughing at my discovery.

I'd never heard of this list before, and I wondered where and when she'd made it. Since it was on the back of her graduation picture, it must've been right after she'd finished Brown. They all had a check mark next to them except that last one: *See St. Francis from altar.* Maybe it was the faintness of the ink, or the small, girlish hearts drawn in each corner, or the checks next to the first four items on the list, each marked by a different pen, but I had a feeling that no one else knew about it. It was her secret, and now it was mine.

I stepped outside. The air was balmy compared to the dank, clammy cabin, and the rain was now a hesitant drizzle. I stood under the overhang and studied the list again, considering the first item. *Visit Rodin Museum in Paris.* Nina had spent a year in Paris after college graduation. I Googled it on my phone. The museum itself seemed grand but human-size, with ivy-covered walls, wooden-floored galleries, and huge, arched windows that opened. There were gardens divided by neat, leafy pathways and a reflecting pool. I scrolled through the collection. There was one sculpture called *The Walking Man.* It was a headless body of a man, well, walking. The body was so exquisitely defined, so muscular, so alive. *The Walking Man* is a hottie, I thought.

Then I saw the sculpture called *The Kiss.* My breath

caught. The way the man was holding the woman's hip, how they leaned back, the tilt of her head. It reminded me of Zack. It reminded me of what it was like to want someone so badly you feel every cell in your body turn to face him like a field of sunflowers. That's what we felt, I thought. No matter whom he was going out with now or the high-five crime, he had touched me like that. He had leaned like that. I knew it and he knew it. *Don't do it, don't do it,* I told myself. *Don't think about Zack.* I shut my eyes and started counting backward from one hundred by twos until the feeling passed, a trick I'd learned sometime after Christmas.

Thirteen

"THERE YOU ARE," A VOICE SAID. "BETTER GRAB YOUR STUFF, we're almost here."

"Huh?" I said, opening my eyes to bright sunshine. Guitar Guy was standing over me. How long had I been asleep? Two hours? Twenty minutes? I looked around to get my bearings. The deck was crowded, and we were almost at Brant Point. The lighthouse greeted us in its snappy white jacket and black top hat.

"We're almost to Nantucket. And you got a sunburn."

"Where?" I asked, blinking awake. My lips were dry. I needed some water.

"There," he said and gently touched the tip of my nose.

"Oh," I said, covering my nose with my hand. "Oh."

He didn't seem to think anything of it. He tipped his

face to the sun and said, "Don't you love how the weather on Nantucket is almost always the opposite of the mainland?" When I didn't respond he turned to me, grinned, and bit his lip as if trying not to laugh.

"What?"

"You're adorable."

"Thanks for waking me up," I said, standing and straightening my sweatshirt, which had twisted during my nap. "But you really shouldn't go around touching people's faces."

"I'm sorry. It's just that you—" He was trying not to laugh.

"It's actually really rude."

"You're right," he said, giggling.

"I'm going to Brown University in the fall." I'm not sure why I said this except I wanted him to know that I was a serious person, an *Ivy League woman*. But now he was laughing harder.

"Excuse me," I said and went back inside to get my stuff.

The ferry pulled in to the harbor and I strapped on my backpack, secured my lacrosse stick, and dragged my bag out from the spot I'd wedged it into. As I stood in the line of people impatient to get off the boat, I used the camera on my phone to check my sunburn. That's when I saw that my nose wasn't just red. Oh, no. Its tip was bright blue. *Of course.* The eight my mom had drawn was smudged and running and I had rubbed it off on my face. As I tried to wipe off the perfect circle of blue on the tip of my nose, my face burned red around it. Had I really needed to brag about Brown?

"Cricket!" I heard Liz call, and I searched the crowd for her. The dock was now a beehive of sherbet-colored pants as people reunited with friends, relatives, and luggage. I was almost the last one off the boat. Even though I'd wiped every trace of blue off my nose with the help of a brown paper towel and some pink industrial soap in the bathroom, I didn't want to run into Guitar Guy again.

"Cricket, over here!" Liz's voice seemed to rise above the others and lift me an inch off the ramp, but I still didn't see her. What a difference this was from last year when no one was there to meet me.

"Liz!" I called when I finally spotted her, arms waving overhead like a drowning woman. I darted through the crowd and hugged her. She smelled exactly the same, like rose perfume and cookies, but she was dressed like a different girl. Gone were the jean shorts and neon-colored bra straps. Liz had gone business casual in a navy knee-length skirt and a white button-down blouse. At least her jewelry was still Liz-style. Big red earrings and matching plastic bracelets.

"You look so proper," I said.

"Well, I'm the manager now, aren't I? I need to look responsible. And what about you? Turn 'round."

"What? Why?"

She motioned for me to hand her some luggage. I gave her my backpack.

"Panty-line check. Go on. I want to know how my pupil has fared without my guidance." I sighed and did a little turn for her. "Well done." She put on my backpack, handling my lacrosse stick like it was a strange artifact. "And is this a weapon? Gavin left his rain stick in the cupboard. We can have a battle!"

"It's my lacrosse stick," I said, taking it back. "I need to practice, like, a lot."

"I'm kidding. You don't think I could live on Nantucket and not know what lacrosse is, do you?"

"I never know what you know or don't know." Liz could explain the rules of American baseball with absolute clarity and knew certain Nantucket billionaires on a first-name basis and three good ways to create a smoky eye, but she didn't know how to ride a bike or why, exactly, we celebrated Thanksgiving.

"Someone's got to keep you on your toes. Come on now," she said, linking her arm through mine. "We've got to get back to the inn. I have a couple coming in on a flight from New York, and I need to be there when they arrive. The Nutsaks."

"That's not their name," I said, laughing.

"N-U-T-S-A-K, from the eastern bloc, perhaps? And I've got to have the balls to look them in the eye and welcome them." We laughed as we wove through the SUVs driving off the boat and walked into town. The scent of waffle cones wafted from the Juice Bar. I drifted toward it, but Liz pulled me back.

"But there's hardly a line," I said. "And there's *always* a line."

"I have to get you stowed away before the guests arrive."

"But chocolate peanut butter cup in a waffle cone . . ."

"Soon enough," she said, steering me onward. "I haven't even heard about your love life yet."

"Nothing to tell," I said. "Zack is going out with Parker Carmichael."

"Bastard!"

"I don't want to talk about it."

"Very well."

I was grateful for her British reserve as we headed up Broad Street and the old sights came into focus. It was busy, though not nearly as busy as it was going to be in July and August. I saw the bench where I'd eaten pizza alone my first week here. I hadn't known what else to do for dinner. There was the corner where Jules had pretended not to see me, her hair flying from the passenger side of a Jeep blaring a hip-hop song I hadn't recognized.

My heart sped up when I saw the tiny, hidden-in-plain-sight park where Zack had first held my hand in public. The very late-afternoon June light was as yellow as lemon cake, and green leaves and small blooms were climbing the gazebo, creating a woody, magical frame for kissing. The memories were flying in like slanted raindrops through an open window, and I was powerless to stop them. How was I going to make it through this summer knowing Zack was here in our paradise but no longer mine? How was I going to make it to the inn? We hadn't even hit Main Street yet.

Just as we were rounding the corner of Centre Street, I caught a glimpse of Guitar Guy stepping out of a bakery with a coffee. He seemed to be smiling at nothing in particular as he removed the lid of his coffee cup to blow into it. He sat on a shady bench and tapped something into his phone.

"Turn back," I said under my breath.

Liz followed me back down Broad Street. "What's gotten into you?"

"I met that guy on the ferry," I whispered.

"The bloke with the coffee? He's quite fit."

I shushed her, but that only made her louder.

"Okay, what's the story? Did you leave your knickers on the ferry? Is that why you have no panty line? Please say yes. Then the pupil will have surpassed the master, like in the movies."

"No, no. It was nothing."

"Doesn't seem like nothing," she said, and pinched my butt. Where was her British reserve now?

"What about you, sex goddess?" I asked, changing the subject. "How's your love life?" Liz and her Irish boyfriend, Shane, had practically been living together when I left Nantucket last summer. During our mornings of scrubbing bathrooms and making beds, I'd endured endless stories of their cinematic sex, his intense understanding of great poetry, and his taste for complex whiskey. They were so into each other they'd decided to stay on Nantucket together through the winter instead of returning to the UK, so I was surprised when the briefest shadow crossed her face before she answered, "Ace."

Fourteen

"GET UP!" LIZ SAID THE NEXT DAY. SHE HANDED ME A CUP of coffee with cream and no sugar, remembering just how I liked it, and a cranberry walnut muffin. It took me a minute to register that I was on the sofa in the manager's apartment. It was still weird to me that this was where Liz lived now. Last year, this was the boss's apartment and we lived in tiny single rooms with a shared bathroom. "For a girl who needs a job you've certainly had a lazy morning," Liz said. I sipped the coffee and glanced at the clock. It was almost ten thirty.

"Oh, shit!"

"Oh, shit, is right," she said. "You have a job interview this morning at one of the island's most expensive and popular restaurants. So eat up. We can't have your energy flagging."

"What?" I almost choked on a walnut. "Where?"

"Three Ships."

"Liz!" I gasped, spilling a bit of the coffee down my new Brown Women's Lacrosse T-shirt. Three Ships was on the wharf and had amazing views of the waterfront. It was almost impossible to get a reservation.

"Waitresses make three hundred dollars a night," she said and I gasped again, "And the position comes with housing."

"You're the best. Thank you! How did you do this?" I asked as I stuffed the muffin in my mouth. A job at Three Ships was the best-case scenario.

"I just ran into Charlie, the manager, at the pharmacy. I told him to look out for an athletic blond named for an insect. He said to come by at eleven a.m."

I glanced at the clock above the TV. "Jesus. That's in, like, twenty minutes. I've got to get changed. I haven't even showered yet."

"No time for a shower. A whore's bath, maybe."

"A horse bath?"

"*Whore's* bath. The bath of a whore. You know, prostitute? Sex for money?"

"Yes, I'm familiar with the term *whore*, but . . ." I threw the covers off, hopped into the bathroom, and turned on the water. "Never mind."

"One little thing," Liz said as I stepped into the shower. "I kind of told him you worked in New York for a year."

"What?" I grabbed the shampoo.

"Oh, now, don't say it like that. He said he wanted someone with experience. What was I supposed to do?"

"Where did you tell him I worked?"

"The Russian Tea Room," Liz said. "I was really thinking on my feet."

"What's that?" I pictured furry hats and elaborate porcelain teapots as I rinsed my hair. No time for conditioner. I quickly washed my pits and shut off the water. "Can I have a towel?"

"It's legendary, a really excellent place to have worked," she said, opening the curtain and handing me a towel. "Nice tits, by the way."

"Um, thanks." I grabbed the towel and covered myself. "But, Liz? I've never even been to the Russian Tea Room. I've only been to New York once. For the day."

"Improvise! Do you want to get the job or not?" She glanced at her watch. "Oh, you'd better hurry. And a little mascara never hurts, yeah?"

I made it to Three Ships by ten fifty-nine, in my neatest-looking shirt and skirt, combed, damp hair, and a little mascara.

"You must be Cricket," said a handsome man who looked like he'd just stepped off of a sailboat.

"And you must be Charlie," I said. We shook hands and he led me to a table by a window.

"So, tell me all about the Russian Tea Room," he said.

"It's an extraordinary place," I said, doing my best not to lie. I'd Googled it on the way there and memorized a few details. "It's so centrally located. So opulent. So famous."

He smiled, tapped his pencil on the table. "What was your favorite dish?"

"The chicken Kiev," I said, maintaining cheerful eye contact.

"The Kiev, huh? How would you describe it?"

"I would describe it as delicious." I closed my eyes as if imagining the experience. "Just so, so delicious."

"How many tables were in your section?"

"Twenty?"

"You must be some waitress." He smiled, leaned forward, drummed the table. "Did you really work at the Russian Tea Room? The *opulent, famous, centrally located* Russian Tea Room?"

"I've never even been there," I said. He laughed, so I did, too.

"Do you have *any* restaurant experience?" he asked.

"No," I said. "But I'm going to Brown in the fall. So I'm a really quick study."

"Impressive."

"And I'm on the lacrosse team, so I'm quick on my feet, too."

"But that also means you'd take off before Labor Day." I shrugged. "I can't hire you. For what people spend here, I need a professional staff. We get slammed. Tonight we have almost two hundred covers and . . ."—he paused, tilted his head—"You don't even know what that means, do you? Yeah. I'm not looking for someone to train from scratch."

"Do you know anyone who might be?" I asked. "Because the thing is, I really need a job this summer."

"Have you thought about retail? A lot of girls like you do that in the summer."

"Girls like me?"

"You know, Ivy League, blond, Daddy's got a place in town."

"You've got me all wrong. Girls like me need to make real money," I said and sat up a little straighter. "I may not have a lot of waitressing experience, but I worked at the Cranberry Inn last summer six days a week. I served breakfast every morning at seven a.m. sharp and cleaned rooms all day after that. I wasn't late once, and when a guest asked me for something, I always did my best to make sure I got them what they needed. I even ended up with an internship with one of them, a famous writer. And I'm not afraid to clean a bathroom. I'd rather not. But I will." I wrote my name and number on a napkin and handed it to him. "If you hear of anything, please pass on my number."

I walked toward the door, but Charlie's voice stopped me. "Well, I feel like a first-rate asshole. You look the part, but I shouldn't have assumed." He grabbed two bottles of fancy carbonated lemonade from behind the bar, uncapped them with some unseen device, and handed one to me. "I still can't hire a waitress without fine-dining experience, but my buddy Karla is still looking for someone and she's a little more open-minded." He wrote *Breezes, Jefferson Road* on a cocktail napkin. "Tell her I sent you."

"Thanks." I was going to mention that I'd already had a phone interview with Karla and she'd rejected me, but I changed my mind. Sometimes you have to take a few shots on goal before you score.

Breezes was about a mile outside of town, right on the sand. From the outside it looked like a beach house. I could smell the ocean from the wooden-planked pathway. The restaurant name was etched in gold above a bright blue door. It was the restaurant attached to the island's most exclusive beach club, the Wampanoag Club, or the Wamp, as everyone who knew better called it. People were on the waitlist for twenty-five years or more to get in, and I could see why. With its graceful shingles, welcoming porch, combed beach, and cozy cabanas, it was the perfect picture of a classic New England summer. Even from the outside there was a casual elegance that filled you with a sense that this could be your home in some alternate universe where you were so rich you could fling fistfuls of money at the sunset as part of your evening prayers.

The inside was pure Nantucket. The opposite of the Russian Tea Room, there was nothing opulent about this place, unless you counted the ruby-pink beach roses on every table, or the sapphire-bright hydrangea blooms on the hostess stand. The wooden floors were white. Brightly painted oars hung on the pale blue-gray walls. In the middle of the room was a smooth, gleaming bar, and beyond that a giant wraparound porch, protected from the elements by sheets of canvas-trimmed plastic, secured to the frame like sails to a mast. There was a jar on the hostess's stand labeled OPERATION SMILE. PLEASE DONATE. I picked up a menu. The least expensive thing was a twenty-three-dollar artisanal grilled cheese.

"Hello?" I asked, and when no one answered, I stepped out on the porch, which faced the Nantucket sound in three directions. It couldn't be denied that it was a beautiful place, even on a foggy day like today. With the exception of perfectly spaced-out yellow and blue beach umbrellas, all slanted at the same angle, the view was identical to the one at Steps Beach, where Zack and I had spent so much time together last summer. *Don't think of Zack,* I told myself. *Don't. He doesn't deserve it.*

"A million-dollar view, right?" I turned to see a small, sinewy woman my mom's age with bright blue hair framing eyes so brown they were black. Bright blue hair is not something you see every day on Nantucket. "What can I do for you? We aren't open until noon."

"Actually, I'm looking for a job. My name is Cricket Thompson." I winced. I was hoping she wouldn't be able to place me, but people don't forget a name like mine.

"I already interviewed you, didn't I? Yeah, I remember. You bombed the wine test. Like"—she made explosion sounds with the accompanying hand gestures—"bombed."

"Charlie from Three Ships sent me," I said. "He thought I'd be a good fit."

"Is that so?" She pushed her glasses up on her head like a headband. "You didn't tell me you knew Charlie."

"And I've been studying. Ask me anything." *Please, make it easy.*

"Okay. What would you recommend with a lobster roll?"

"Pinot grigio, to cut through the richness." I was ready for that one. On Nantucket, lobster rolls were as ubiquitous as sand.

"Good." She drummed her fingers on the bar. "How about the roasted-pig confit?"

"A French pinot." According to *Wine Made Simple,* French pinot was almost always a good choice.

"Well done. You have been studying. One more." *Don't let me down, Wine Made Simple.* "Hamachi crudo, our most popular dish this summer."

What the hell was hamachi crudo? I swallowed, and remembered that the book said that when in doubt, the best wine to order was simply one you enjoyed, no matter the dish. The best drink I'd ever had was champagne, last summer, on the Fourth of July, in a little rowboat with Zack.

"Dom Perignon," I said.

Karla's face opened up in a smile. "Best answer yet."

"I know I can do this. I really think you should give me a chance. I'm an athlete, so I'm used to working under pressure."

"An athlete, huh?"

"I'm playing lacrosse at Brown in the fall."

"All right, Cricket Thompson, I'll give you a shot."

"Yay!" I actually jumped.

"Calm down. We'll give it a week. See how it goes."

"Thank you so much!"

"Staff dinner is at four. See you then."

"Tonight?"

"Is that a problem?"

"Not at all," I said, though I still needed to go for a run and practice stick drills. She ducked behind the bar and tossed me a T-shirt the same shade as the famous Nantucket Red pants. "The first shirt is on the house. After that they're twenty bucks. You got a pair of khakis?"

"I can find some," I said.

"Four o'clock," she said. Her phone rang.

"Oh, and um, I need housing, too. That's what the original ad said?"

"I'll see what I can do." She saw the number on the caller ID, muttered something under her breath, picked it up, and spoke into the phone in rapid-fire Spanish. She handed me employment forms and gestured at the door.

It's just nine weeks, I told myself as I pulled on the last of several pairs of khakis in the Nantucket Hospital Thrift Store dressing room. *And then I'll be at Brown.* I sighed at my reflection in the mirror. Nothing could make these pants look good. The waist was high, and not in a cool retro way, and they were a little too short. But they basically fit otherwise and would have to do until Mom could send me a better pair from home. I'd tried Murray's first, the store famous for Nantucket Reds. I'd found a pair that were actually almost flattering, but they were a hundred dollars.

I wandered over to the thrift store, where secondhand khakis seemed to grow like weeds. I found at least six pairs in my size, four of which didn't have stains, and two of which were from this century. "Those are half off," the elderly thrift store volunteer said when I set them on the card table with the cash box and old-fashioned adding machine, the same one I'd seen Rosemary use to balance her checkbook. "All ladies' trousers are."

"I guess I'll get them both," I said.

"You sure you don't want to check out the books? Hardcovers are a dollar today. I can put these aside for you," she said, checking the labels as she folded the pants. "Oh, Talbots. You're lucky. The good brands go quick. I'll put these out of sight so no one snags them."

"Thanks." I smiled, not having the heart to tell her that the Talbots pants would probably have been safe even if they had been displayed on their one mannequin. I ducked into the book room and spotted a display of oversize art books. Even though they varied in size and style, I could tell they'd inhabited the same space for a long period of time. I imagined they had all been donated from one person's collection, some very dedicated museum lover. One was from the Getty in Los Angeles, one from the Frick in New York, and another was from the Rodin Museum in Paris. I pulled out the Rodin book. The cover was torn, there was a coffee ring on it, and when I cracked it open, the slippery pages smelled faintly like cigarettes.

I sat on the floor and thumbed through it. It was written in French. I could only understand bits of it, but the writing wasn't the point. The pictures were. *Don't think of Zack,* I told myself as I searched frantically for *The Kiss*. I found it and snapped the book shut, biting my lip. I bought it. It was a sign of some sort. I wasn't sure what it meant exactly, but I felt Nina next to me again, whispering about something I needed to understand, a place I needed to go and see, even if I had to wear Talbots khakis to get there.

A few hours later, I was twenty-seven minutes early for my first day of training, which was somehow worse than being late. I'd left the inn with plenty of time to spare in case something came up. I don't know what I thought was going to happen, but if I wanted to train for lacrosse and make eight thousand dollars in nine weeks, I had to stick to a schedule and not screw up. Every day I was going to eat three healthy meals, run five miles, and get eight hours of sleep. The busier I was, the less time I had to think about Zack and Parker.

When I arrived at the restaurant I had a nasty blister from my flats. I'd always thought of them as comfortable shoes. I'd considered wearing the Easy Spirits Mom had forced on me. I'd taken them out of my suitcase and tried them on and everything, but I couldn't. Not with the Talbots khakis. Liz told me I looked like I'd mugged a granny and run off with her trousers and trainers. The idea of pairing my granny pants with the Easy Spirits was too awful to think about, but as I hobbled into Breezes I knew I'd been wrong to prioritize beauty.

A bartender was checking bottle levels and making notes. He was facing the Nantucket Sound, jotting something on a form. The clouds had burned off and the late afternoon light was hazy gold. The plastic sheeting that had covered the windows was rolled up. A cool breeze rustled the pages of his notebook.

"Hey," I said. "Do you have any Band-Aids?"

He turned around as if to speak, but instead of telling me where the first-aid kit was, he let the moment hang in the air, waiting long enough for the blush on my cheeks to deepen to a fevered, stinging glow. It was Guitar Guy, leaning on the bar like he owned the place.

"Nice pants," he said with a wicked grin.

Fifteen

"SO YOU'RE THE NEW WAITRESS I'VE BEEN HEARING ABOUT," Guitar Guy said as he showed me through the bustling kitchen, alive with knives chopping and Spanish chatter, to a little locker room.

"I guess so," I said, wondering if one of these lockers was going to be mine, and if so, what I was supposed to keep in it. Guitar Guy opened a drawer in a metal cabinet, pulled out a first-aid kit, and handed me the Band-Aids. I took a few, sat down on the bench, and peeled one open. He sat next to me, leaning forward, forearms on knees. He smelled like herbs and spices, in a good way. I slipped off my shoes and applied the Band-Aids, oddly self-conscious.

"Hey, Ben, glad to see you're showing Cricket around," Karla said, appearing from around the corner. "Is the inventory done?"

"*Sí, el jefe,*" he said, and turned to me. "Cricket. Cool name."

"Nice to meet you, Ben."

This would have been the appropriate place to shake hands, but for some reason neither of us made a move, until at last, he tapped my elbow with his. I tapped his back reflexively. He smiled and tapped again, and so did I. What were we doing? A deep pink punished my cheeks. Karla tossed me an apron. I caught it and held it to my hot face for a second, hiding my blush.

"Well, at least we don't have to worry about you being a *brown*-noser," he said.

"Oh, you should worry," I said, peeking out from behind the apron. "Blue-nosers are the ones you have to watch out for."

I met the rest of the employees at the staff meal—chicken curry over rice. I sat at the communal table, determined to be my most charming self. There were three busboys, Hector, Steve, and Kevin; a few line cooks whose names I didn't catch; a tattooed dishwasher who grabbed some food and returned to the kitchen before I could introduce myself; and three other servers: Nicky, who spent winters skiing in Colorado and summers hanging out in Nantucket; James, a senior at Middlebury College; and Amy, who was tiny and beautiful, like a living doll. She had a thin tattoo—a simple line that encircled her arm like a bracelet—bright red lipstick, and long, mascaraed eyelashes under which her dark eyes flickered with intelligence.

"Do you know her?" Amy asked Ben, without acknowledging that the *her* was right there, sitting next to him.

"We met on the ferry," I said. "He touched my nose, like, out of nowhere!"

"That's weird," Amy said and stabbed a bit of chicken.

"Well, look at that nose," Ben said, gesturing to me. "It's a great nose." Amy reddened, her face almost matching her lipstick. I covered my nose with my hand as Ben's knee knocked mine.

"Cricket you'll be shadowing Amy," Karla said. "Stick to her like glue."

"Okay," I said. Amy pushed her chair from the table, grabbed her plate, walked away, and kicked open the kitchen door. I looked to Ben for help, but he was texting under the table.

"Get back here, Amy," Karla called. "We're about to go over the specials, *mija*!"

It didn't take long to learn my first lesson: following someone who doesn't want to be followed sucks.

"What are you doing?" I asked Amy as she punched a number into the computer.

"Uh, clocking in," she said.

"Do I clock in?"

"Not for training," Amy said, checking her text messages.

I didn't know if I was getting paid for the training and I didn't dare ask. About a half hour later, after Amy had prepped the coffee and tea station, checked the desserts, and memorized the specials, we got our first table. Our second was ten minutes later. And then our third, fourth, and fifth were sat all at once. Before I knew it, our whole section was full. I stood behind Amy as she greeted people, offered drinks, recited specials, answered questions, and took orders, all without writing anything down. I followed her as she wove through customers and staff, hustling back and forth from the bar, the tables, the kitchen, and the computer stations, never once checking to see if she'd lost me.

By around seven thirty p.m., our first tables were finishing their desserts, three others were working their way through their entrees, and the other two were relaxing over cocktails. Amy leaned against the computer stand and I hovered. She sighed and headed toward what I thought was the kitchen, so I followed.

"I'm going to the bathroom," Amy said. "Get lost!"

"Sorry," I said and slinked back out to what I now had learned was the "floor."

Ben laughed at me from behind the bar.

"I'm supposed to follow her everywhere," I said and shrugged.

"She's in a bad mood," Ben said with a smile as he poured a glass of chardonnay, two red wines, and a gin and tonic.

"Do you have anything to do with that?" I asked, and for the first time he looked a little sad.

"Just drop these on table five for her, okay?"

"Um, which one is that?"

"The fifth one in from the door on the left."

"Hey, do you know if I get paid for tonight?" I asked, picking up the tray with both hands. I wasn't ready for a one-handed carry. Would I ever be?

"Minimum wage. Unless Amy decides to share her tips."

Minimum wage, I thought, and counted aloud to find table number five.

Right after I delivered the drinks, Karla told me I could go home for the night. "Same thing tomorrow. Wednesday you'll learn how to close."

"So I did okay?"

"You did great."

"Um, did you find out about the housing?"

"We'll put you out on Surfside Road. I'm sure we can squeeze another bed in there somehow. I think Amy has the double bed. She'll roll over for you."

"Oh, okay." Was she serious? The idea of sharing a bed with Amy sent the taste of chicken curry to the back of my throat. Amy was leaning on the bar, one foot kicking up behind her, whispering something to Ben. What sort of lipstick did she use that stayed on so perfectly like that?

"And it's a hundred and fifty each week out of your paycheck," Karla said. "For the housing."

"Sounds good," I said, though that seemed like a lot if I was going to be sharing a bed with someone who hated me.

"Cricket," Amy called. I turned. It was the first time she'd said my name even though we'd been tethered by an invisible rope for several hours. She draped a proprietary arm around Ben and pointed to my apron. "Are you taking that home for a souvenir?"

"Oh, whoops," I said. As I unknotted the coffee-stained apron and headed to the locker room I heard her say to Ben, "What kind of a name is Cricket, anyway?"

I practically crawled out of the restaurant. Several hours of waitressing had tired me out more than a whole lacrosse tournament. My blistered feet hurt even as I walked on the outside of the folded-in heels of my flats. My neck felt like it'd been stepped on, and I knew that I smelled like onion rings. I paused on Main Street, about to head into the pharmacy for an ice-cream sandwich, when I decided to go to Mitchell's Book Corner instead. Seeing my name in George Gust's book never failed to give me a little boost, and it was even better if I saw it in the actual store rather than in my own personal copy. I had one foot in the store when I spotted Zack straight ahead. *Zack!*

Don't care, I commanded myself as I silently stepped back to the sidewalk and slinked behind a tree. I steadied myself, tilted my head, breathed bark. There was the boy I knew in a baseball cap, bent over a book, turning the pages with care. He shifted his weight and turned ninety degrees, revealing the cover of the book. It was the reissued edition of her collected works, the one with the bright blue cover that my English teacher constantly praised. Emily Dickinson was what I had been reading on the beach last summer when we spent our first day alone together. Emily Dickinson was the book that held open the window he climbed into to find me. "Emily Dickinson was an American genius," I'd told him once, and we'd both burst into laughter because I'd sounded so serious. Emily Dickinson!

It was a sign. He was thinking about me. This Parker relationship was some kind of misguided illusion, some terrible strain of boarding school amnesia. I couldn't see him now, not in my Talbots khakis, not when I smelled like garlic and onions, with coffee grounds under my fingernails. I stepped out of my shoes and ran back to the inn barefoot, this new information filling me with lightness and speed.

When I got back to the manager's apartment, I took a long shower. The food smell lifted from my hair and skin after the third scrubbing. I slathered myself with lotion, put on my Brown lacrosse T-shirt, and climbed into my make-shift bed on the sofa. I heard mumbles from Liz's room. She was probably on the phone with Shane, who was out on the Cape for at least another few days.

From the window, sounds of kids laughing drifted up with the scent of honeysuckle and freshly mowed grass. I pulled out the *Musée de Rodin* book and looked at *The Kiss.* I closed my eyes and let myself slip, remembering the first time Zack and I had spent the whole night together. I gave myself the dream like a gift, like a stolen bar of chocolate.

Sixteen

"DO YOU SUPPOSE THAT'S YOUR LITTLE, UM, CORNER?" LIZ asked and pointed to a bare twin-size mattress with a tiny pillow on it on the floor. Liz said it was the kind that you got on an airplane for international flights. The mattress was one of five in a room meant for two, three of which were on actual bed frames and two of which lay on the stained carpet. The one without the sheets on it was definitely meant for me. I just knew it. "At least you won't be sharing a bed with Amy," Liz said.

It was four days later and even though I'd been prepared, I had yet to run into Zack or Jules. I certainly wasn't going to run into them out here. Liz and I were at the staff house out on Surfside Road. It was a tiny one-bedroom, one-bathroom shack that I was going to be sharing with six girls, one of whom was snoring in a thong and T-shirt, facedown on the futon in the living room in front of a TV tuned to a daytime talk show, advising as to how to "shop your own closet." The box of wine on the coffee table indicated she'd spent the previous night like this, too. I didn't recognize her, at least not from this angle, so she must have been one of the girls from the Wamp.

Inside the bedroom, only one of the beds was made. It was probably the one belonging to Nicky, the career waitress. The other beds, littered with magazines, with sheets and clothes strewn everywhere, made it look as if zombies had attacked without warning.

"And at least you're near the window?" Liz said.

"Yeah." I stepped over an empty beer bottle and an open bag of hot Cheetos and looked out the window. It was open a crack, but needed to be up all the way all the time. It smelled like a mixture of old cheese and socks in there. There was a tang to the odor that was more taste than smell. People think girls are neat and clean and boys are the messy ones, but this house was living proof that that wasn't true. I opened the screenless window and stuck my head out. Amy was in the yard reading the *New York Times*. No lipstick.

In the last few days she'd learned to tolerate having me follow her around, as long as I didn't talk too much, and I'd learned to pick up whatever I could through observation alone, since she was not about to provide instruction. If I had any questions, Nicky was the one who'd give answers. I'd also learned not to talk to Ben in front of Amy; whatever they had going on was complicated and semisecret, and she did her best to limit my time at the bar. If there were drinks to pick up, she sent me to fold napkins, wipe up the dessert station, or check on appetizers in the kitchen.

"It's not so terrible," Liz said, peering out the window to the patch of dry grass behind the house where Amy was now lighting a cigarette. "Look, there's a backyard for lacrosse practice."

"Yeah," I said, imagining practicing shots on goal over a smoking, sunbathing Amy. So far, I'd kept up with my running, but I hadn't done my stick drills at all. Amy turned around and squinted at the sound of our voices.

"Hi," I smiled too big and waved too cheerfully.

"Oh," she muttered, turned back to her newspaper, and crossed her legs. Amy had the toned legs of a dancer. She really was beautiful.

"Twat," Liz said too loudly. She pulled back from the window, and took another look around. "I'm just going to use the loo, and then I'll leave you to get settled."

I pursed my lips and nodded. I wanted to throw myself at her feet, cling to her, and beg her not to leave me there. I sat on the lumpy mattress and tried not to cry. A line of ants crawled up the wall and toward the window. If Zack and I did get back together, there was no way I wanted him climbing through this window.

I took a deep breath and searched for some empty space in a closet, but the one in the bedroom was claimed. The bar was bending under the weight of crowded, overloaded hangers. On the floor were a jumble of shoes, and two full hampers. This was one closet I did not want to shop. I shut the door as if the organisms living in the teeming piles of dirty laundry might attack.

Maybe there was another closet in the living room? Doing my best not to disturb Thonged Snoring Girl, I grasped at the first doorknob I found, but it was on the door to the bathroom. Liz was standing in front of the sink washing her hands with a vigor I'd never seen.

"It's awful," I said.

"A hovel!" Liz said. "Look." She gestured at the toilet with its nasty, rust-colored ring. Pinching together her thumb and forefinger, she opened the flimsy, ripped shower curtain to reveal a plastic stall with blackish mold blossoming in all the corners. Liz washed her hands again and then looked around for something to dry them on. She paused centimeters shy of the mildewed towels that were piled on top of one another on a single hook. Holding her breath, she dried her hands on her jeans.

"I'll scrub it myself," I said. "I'll just get some rubber gloves and some Ajax and roll up my sleeves and do it."

"Have you seen the kitchen yet?"

I shook my head.

Liz swallowed. "You can stay with me for one more night, two maximum, but you have to make yourself very scarce. It's the first night Shane is back from the Cape, and I do not want to be disturbed."

"I'll hang out in the kitchen until you text me that the coast is clear."

"It might not be until very, very late. We're sexually adventurous."

"I know. I don't care. I'll sleep outdoors in the hammock if you want."

"Let's get out of here," she said. "Quick, before we contract athlete's foot." She pointed to a stagnant puddle in the shower where a mosquito hovered lasciviously. "Or dengue fever."

We grabbed my stuff.

"Who are you?" Thonged Snoring Girl asked, groggy, wiping her crusty eyes with clumsy hands.

"Figments of your imagination," Liz said as we flew out the door. "Mere shadows."

"Hey, can you drop these on table nine?" Ben asked that night as I passed by the bar on my way to see how the customers at table sixteen were doing with their appetizers. It was my last night of training and I was pretty much a free girl. I'd managed five tables on my own, from the Lillet aperitifs to the beach plum sorbet. It killed me that Amy was going to get all the tips. Ben was chilling martini glasses, lining up highballs, and tearing off tickets all at the same time, but with such laid-back summer style, he didn't even look like he was working. "Amy's in the weeds."

"Sure," I said, noticing the appealing line of his side as he reached for a wineglass. He opened a fresh bottle of Pouilly-Fumé, ran a blade below the lower ridge to remove the wrapper, twisted the corkscrew with a confident wrist, and poured two cool, pale, straw-colored glasses with the kind of relaxed competence that made watching him so easy. "And I know exactly where table nine is."

"I'm starting to see why you got into Brown," he said, and, without breaking eye contact, placed the drinks on a tray. "You should come by the brewery tomorrow, I'm playing some new songs. I've been meaning to ask you for a few days, but it's hard to get you alone."

"Oh," I said. *Was he asking me out?*

"Everyone's invited," he said.

"Fuck," Amy said under her breath as she punched an order into a nearby computer and messed up. "Fuck me." She canceled the order, blinked her long, luxurious lashes, and started again. "Hey, are you moving into the Surfside house, or what?"

"Tomorrow," I said.

"Just so you know, I get the first shower in the morning."

"Okay," I said, too cheerful, as always. I was probably always going to be too cheerful for grumpy alternative girls. I sighed. She marched off.

Ben waited until Amy was in the kitchen, and then he leaned a little closer. He smelled like a man. Herbs and spices. Gin and lime. Summer and salt. "Before the show I'm going surfing. Want to come?"

"I don't surf," I said. Not only was I certain that Amy would suffocate me with my own pillow in my sleep if I went surfing with Ben, I was so focused on seeing Zack I didn't think I'd be able to concentrate on another activity.

It had been almost a week since I'd seen him at Mitchell's Book Corner, and even though I'd been hanging out in town on my mornings off, always ready, always in cute outfits, I had yet to run into him again.

"I can teach you," he said.

"I think I have plans," I said.

"Okay," Ben said, biting his lip. "You sure about that?"

I nodded, turning away. Again with the blushing! I was going to have to start wearing ski masks to work so I could hide, even as my cheeks betrayed me. It was like my face had its own relationship with him.

"Okay, no pressure." He seemed to mean it, like he wasn't disappointed at all, and I was considering changing my mind as he handed me the tray of drinks. It was heavier than I'd expected. "If you look at them, you'll spill. Don't look."

"I got it," I said. I steadied my gaze on my destination: table nine. I knew Ben was watching, and I was determined to deliver the drinks without spilling a drop. But when I stepped out on the porch and their faces came into view, I almost lost the drinks, my footing, my breath, and my mind.

It was the Claytons.

Seventeen

"CRICKET!" JULES SAID AS I ARRIVED AT THE TABLE SHAKING so hard that I had to put the tray down in front of her. It was Jules, Mr. Clayton, Zack, and one empty chair. Mom had been right about the Easy Spirits. Work had been a lot more comfortable once I'd surrendered, but seeing Zack in nursing home shoes made me want to crawl under the table, out of the restaurant, and down the beach, and swim home to Providence. I swallowed, not sure I had enough saliva to speak. I'd wanted to see him. I'd dreamed about it, but not like this.

"Surprise," I said and laughed weakly. "Again?"

"Hi." Zack said. He held me with his eyes. For a second, it was just us. This was no high five. For a moment, I thought he was going to stand up and kiss me in front of Amy and Ben and Jules and everyone.

"Hi," I said. His cheeks patched with red.

"Cricket Elizabeth Thompson," Jules said. "*Sérieusement?* What are you doing here? What happened to Leo's?"

"It's kind of a long story." I handed a Coke to Jules. "And I've been meaning to call you, but I just kept, I don't know, not doing it." I was about to give Zack his Coke, but my hand was trembling so much that I had to put the glass down.

"I got it," Zack said, leaning over and taking it. His pinkie brushed the back of my hand. I willed my blood to slow its pace.

"Hi, Mr. Clayton," I said.

"It's great to see you," Mr. Clayton said. "I'm glad you're working here. This means we'll be seeing a lot of you this summer."

"We joined the Wamp!" Jules said. "We finally got in off the waiting list!"

"After fifteen years," Mr. Clayton said, laughing and pushing his Prada glasses up the bridge of his nose.

"Yes," Jules said, making pointed eye contact with Mr. Clayton. "Because of Mom. It's what Mom wanted."

"Jules, can we just enjoy the night?" Mr. Clayton asked. Zack stared into his Coke and stirred it with the cocktail straw.

"Well, I think it's great. Here's your wine." I handed Mr. Clayton his Pouilly-Fumé, which left me with one more glass. I looked at the empty seat. Who was it for? Oh, god, I thought, did seventeen-year-old Parker have the gall to order wine? I watched Jules frown as a pretty woman in a hot-pink minidress sat in the remaining seat. I placed the wine in front of her.

"This is my friend, Jennifer," Mr. Clayton said. I heard the quotation marks snap into place around the word *friend*. "Jennifer, this is Cricket."

"Cricket, what a cute name!" Jennifer said. "I'm so very pleased to meet you."

"You, too," I said. I felt a hand on my back. A strong, tiny hand. It was Amy. She cleared her throat and gestured for me to step aside.

"I'm Amy, and I'll be your server tonight. Any questions about the menu?"

"We need a few minutes, right, guys?" Mr. Clayton said.

"Are the moules-frites good?" Zack asked.

"The best. Our chef brought the recipe back from Paris," Amy said.

"That's what I'm having," Zack said and shut his menu.

"Aw, because of Parker?" Jennifer mewled. "How cute is that, y'all? His girl is in Paris, so he's ordering French food!"

His girl?

"Is that right?" asked Amy in her fake waitress voice. "That *is* romantic."

Paris? The Paris I'd been reading about in my *Musée de Rodin* book?

"Not really," Zack said. "My girlfriend is in Paris, but I just feel like mussels."

Girlfriend. The way he tossed off the word felt like a rock through my window.

"What's she doing there?" I asked, too loud, too serious.

Amy glared at me from under her mascaraed eyelashes. "Uh, don't mind Cricket, she's training. We're not sure she's going to last."

"We know her." Jules eyed Amy, ready to throw a punch.

"She's like family," Mr. Clayton added. I wanted to send him a thank-you note.

"Parker's studying in Paris," Zack said to me.

"Right!" Jules rolled her eyes. "She's 'studying.' Puh-leez."

"Jules," Zack began, but I couldn't hang around for another word.

I backed away from the table and wove through the restaurant to the ladies' room, still carrying that stupid tray. I looked in the mirror and splashed cold water on my face. *Don't cry,* I told my reflection. *Don't you dare cry!* I patted my face dry with one of the cloth-quality paper towels and opened the door, where I found myself inches from Zack, who was headed to the men's room.

"I don't understand," I blurted out before I could stop myself, knowing even as the words were leaving my mouth that I would regret them later. "Why are you with her?"

"I called you," he said, looking almost scared. "Remember? And you told me it was over."

"What?" Anger, quick as lightning, flashed through me. "*THAT's* how you interpreted that phone call?" I uncurled my fists, took a deep breath. "I didn't think . . . Zack, I had no friends at school. I was trying to get my life back. I told you to wait! If you interpreted it like that it's because you wanted to!"

"I needed you. And you weren't there."

"What? No." I reached out to take his hand.

He squeezed it quickly and let go. "Yes, Cricket."

It was like the high five, part two. "But Parker? *Parker?* Are you fucking kidding me?"

"Hey," he said, giving me a stop-sign hand. "Hey."

"You're going to stay with her?" I asked. I was on a roll.

"You don't know her or—"

"Oh, I know enough," I said. Amy was walking toward me, looking super pissed off, but I couldn't deal with her right now. "What I don't know is why you read Emily Dickinson in your spare time."

"What are you talking about?" He flushed, bright as one of the buoys bobbing in the harbor.

Amy grabbed me by the apron and pulled me into the hot kitchen. I'd learned on the lacrosse field that some of those tiny girls sure are strong.

"What the hell was that? If I get a shitty tip, I swear, you are going down."

"This isn't about your tip, Amy," I said as I retied my apron. One of the cooks licked his lips as he watched us. I turned my back to the kitchen and lowered my voice. "And it's not like you've been giving me any actual training."

"You want training? Okay. You spent way too long at that table, even if you do know them. Table six doesn't even have menus yet. Your shirt is untucked in the back. Two days ago you ate a pastry within sight of the floor. That's enough for some of these dickheads to refuse to pay their bill. And you should never, never put a tray on the table like you just did. If Karla sees you do that, she'll fire you like this." She snapped her fingers.

"Thanks for the help," I said, not sure myself if I was being serious or sarcastic. Then I kicked open the door and walked straight to the bar.

Ben took one look at me, poured me a Coke, and pushed it toward me. It was sweet and soothing. Maybe I was done with high school boys. Maybe all this blushing in front of Ben was because my nervous system knew what was up. "How do you get to the brewery?"

"It's on the way to Cisco," he said, grinning. "Why, you're gonna come?"

I wrote my number on a napkin. "Text me the address."

"What about surfing?" he asked.

"I'll think about it," I said.

"Oh, you're going to come surfing with me," he said as he entered my number into his phone. "And you're going to love it."

"Hey, Cricket," Amy snapped as she walked by. "Table six?"

Eighteen

I SHOULD HAVE KNOWN BETTER, I TOLD MYSELF AS I HEADED home that night. I was like a lobster that had willingly jumped into the pot. What was I thinking? After the high five, it had been clear that Zack and I were through. How could he have misunderstood me on the phone before Thanksgiving? I'd told him I loved him. But that's what happened when people did long distance, right? Love got lost in translation, scrambled at the cell-phone towers, twisted in the wireless wind. I'd tried so hard to avoid it, but it'd happened anyway.

Who knows why he was reading Emily Dickinson? Maybe it was for school. Maybe it was pure, unemotional, intellectual curiosity. Maybe I had dreamed up the moment, because I wanted it to exist. A Jeep full of college dudes blasted by, blaring ghetto rap and emitting such high levels of testosterone it was a wonder I didn't sprout a pair of balls from proximity. As Amy would say, they were FAAs (pronounced *fahs*), Future Assholes of America. Amy probably thought Zack was a FAA, which of course, he wasn't.

Or was he? I mean, he was dating Parker. *Parker.* I shook my head. It didn't make sense. I walked past the Nantucket Yacht Club, where sounds of a wedding band playing "I Heard It Through the Grapevine" blew in on a harbor breeze. I wished someone would tell me through the grapevine what he saw in her. Though it made me snarl, I tried to list her good qualities just so I could understand.

Okay, so Parker had awesome hair. That much could not be denied. She was bold, in her way. She had a number of horse-related achievements. She was a senator's daughter, rich, exposed to music and art, well traveled, well dressed. I stood still for a moment, wondering if this made her better than me in Zack's eyes. Did all those first-class tickets to the wonders of the world, all those two-hundred-dollar jeans and skillful descents of double black diamond trails distinguish her from me in a way I couldn't even see?

I turned up Main Street. My pace quickened. Was she, like, really elegant or something and I didn't even realize it? Impossible, I thought. No one was more elegant than Nina, and Parker was nothing like Nina. But was I like Nina? It's not like I could do the things on Nina's life list the way Parker could. I couldn't go to Paris, not until it was time for my junior year abroad, anyway. As I climbed the stairs to the manager's apartment, I felt that dagger of panic. How was I supposed to do everything, be everything? I'd done the best I could in high school, run myself ragged, but suddenly that wasn't enough. The rules had changed and I didn't even know what they were.

That was when I noticed that the shades weren't drawn in the manager's apartment. Liz was supposed to be having her wild sex marathon with Shane, and I was under strict instructions to insert cotton balls in my ears and head straight to the sofa. But all the lights were on. I could see directly into the bedroom. It was empty. Liz was in the kitchen, pacing with a bottle of wine. Not a glass, a bottle.

"Liz, are you okay?" I asked, barging in. She burst into tears.

"What happened?" I'd never seen Liz cry. I'd never even imagined it, but she was shaking and sobbing. I put my arms around her.

"He dumped me," she said, gasping for breath. "He was seeing someone else this whole time!"

"Oh, Liz," I said, guiding her to the sofa and handing her a box of tissues. "Are you sure?"

"Am I sure?" she slurred. She flung an arm in what I guessed was the general direction of Shane. "I saw the bastard with my own eyes."

"How? Where?" I ran to the sink and poured her a glass of water, but she reached for the wine again.

"He called to cancel our date, said he needed one more day on the Cape."

"That doesn't necessarily mean anything." I handed her the water again.

"I just had this weird feeling that he wasn't actually on the Cape. Like, it was weird. Paranormal. A sixth sense. I drove by his house."

"Uh-oh."

"He was out on the porch, kissing another girl." Her face screwed up. "Svetlana. Skinny, horrible Svetlana. Svetlana the cow!"

"No!"

"Normally, I'm like, stiff upper lip, but, Cricket?" She waved her hand as another rush of tears came on. "I thought we were going to get married. I didn't go to university." She gripped my shoulders, eyes round with fear. "I didn't go to university."

"You still can."

"Where?"

"I don't know, but you can."

"I've got to start my applications." She tripped as she reached toward her laptop. "University!"

"Why don't we tackle that tomorrow?" I guided her toward the bedroom and turned down her perfectly made bed, which was scattered with rose petals and surrounded by unlit candles. I swept my arm across the coverlet, sending the rose petals to the floor. "What do you say we get you to bed?"

"I can't," Liz said as she crawled under the covers. She looked like a little kid, the sheets pulled up to her nose, her curls fanned out on the pillow. "Then I'll have to get up. And if I get up, it will all be real."

"You just sleep. I'll set up tomorrow," I said, as I sat on the edge of the bed.

"The muffins and everything?"

"The muffins and everything." I got up and backed away and turned off the light.

"Don't go," Liz said. "Don't leave me alone tonight."

"Okay," I lay down next to her. I spotted a tube of some kind of sex oil and gingerly knocked it under the bed and out of sight.

"Tell me a story," she said, flipping the pillow over.

"Once upon a time, there was a frog."

"Was he actually a prince?" she asked.

"Nope, just a frog," I said, making it up as I went along. "A girl frog. And she had many, many adventures."

The frog had moved to a lovely new pond, gained employment with an alligator, learned to play the banjo, and entertained a flock of fairies before Liz finally started snoring.

Nineteen

"YOU JUST LET ME HANDLE GETTING US THE DRINKS," LIZ said the next afternoon. We were at the brewery, which was in the middle of the island, near Bartlett's Farm. It was made up of a cluster of small buildings, each one with a little bar inside it. One served beer, one served wine, and the third served vodka drinks. In the middle was a courtyard with picnic tables, crowded with people in sundresses and flip-flops. Someone was grilling hamburgers in the parking lot and selling them for a mere five bucks, which was way below the going Nantucket rate of eighteen.

"I'm not drinking, because I have to practice, remember?" I said, even though I knew Liz wouldn't listen. She hadn't surfaced until almost noon. I'd made the coffee and muffins at five a.m., handled the checkouts, and canceled my date with Ben in order to greet any early new arrivals. I'd been planning on working out that afternoon, but I made the mistake of telling Liz that Ben, the bartender I'd met on the ferry, was playing at the brewery, and she'd said the only cure for her horribly broken heart was cranberry vodka, a good crowd, and the company of a loyal friend. "Please," she'd said, her curls tossed and messy. "Please come with me." So there I was, putting off my lacrosse practice yet again.

"Besides," I added, scoping out the small stage where Ben would soon be playing, "we don't have ID."

"I know everyone who works here," Liz said. "Get us a couple of hamburgers and find us a seat up front."

I had just paid for the burgers and found a picnic bench in the shade when I saw Karla. It was pretty much impossible to miss her blue hair. She had her arm around a petite woman with coffee-colored skin and dangly earrings. She waved just as Liz returned with two cranberry drinks.

"It's Karla," I said, watching my boss approach, a cold, alcoholic drink in my hand. "She knows I'm not twenty-one."

"When are you going to realize that you don't have to be such a very good girl?" Liz said. I thought this was a little harsh after I'd improvised a thirty-minute frog story for her the night before.

"Hi, Karla," I said, hiding the drink behind my back as she introduced me to her girlfriend, Marie.

"Heard about Shane," Karla said to Liz. "What a jerk. Did he really think he could get away with it on this island?"

"I'd rather not discuss it," Liz said and gulped her drink, shaking the ice at the bottom.

"Marie, this is Cricket, my newest waitress," Karla said, introducing me to her girlfriend. "Amy trained her all week and she's ready to bust out on her own."

"Hey, there," Marie said, and then laughed a little. "How did your niece feel about training a cute blond?"

"Your niece?" I asked.

"Oh, Karla, look, it's Lisa. I've got to talk to her about the garden tour before Annabelle Burke does," Marie said.

"Gotta run," Karla said. "And hey, when are you moving into the Surfside house?"

"She's not," Liz said before I could answer. "She's living with me."

"Okay, see ya," Karla said. She pointed to my cup and added, "Don't get caught with that drink."

"Liz, are you sure?" I asked, handing the rest of my drink to her. She handed it back.

"'Course I'm sure. I'm not one of those girls who likes to be alone."

"Thank you!" I said. "That's so awesome of you. Seriously."

"Is that your bartender?" Liz asked, not letting me fuss. I turned to see Ben step onstage with his guitar. "This better not be a love song. I'm not drunk enough."

Ben began to strum. It was a love song. His voice was low and kind of country. It was a little rough, so that even though he was singing quietly about the moon, it had grit.

I was just starting to melt into his voice when I saw Amy swaying to the music, front and center, gazing at him like he was a rock star.

"I can't tell if they're dating," I said to Liz, motioning to Amy. "But she's definitely—"

"Fucking him," Liz said with a full mouth.

"I was going to say 'in love.' Check out the way she's looking at him." Amy's head was tilted. Her eyes were focused and soft with emotion. For the first time, she looked sweet.

"She may be looking at him," Liz said, "but he can't take his eyes off of you."

Twenty

I WAS IN THE WALK-IN FRIDGE AT BREEZES, STANDING ON my tiptoes and reaching for a fresh container of nonfat milk so I could stock the coffee station (nonfat milk is a lot easier to foam than whole), when I felt a sharp, searing pain in my neck. I gasped and clutched the place where my shoulder met my neck on the right side and which was now tight and throbbing. *Ouch.* My whole body contracted and curled. I was bent over, eyes squeezed shut, seeing yellow spots, when I felt a sure, calm hand on my back.

"Breathe."

It was Ben.

"My neck," I said, sucking refrigerator air in through my teeth.

"It's probably just a muscle spasm," Ben said, guiding me to a milk crate.

"It really hurts," I said, sitting down on the crate.

"It's tension. You need to relax."

It was true. I was exhausted from seven consecutive days of waitressing, early mornings covering for Liz, and squeezing in lacrosse practice whenever I could, which had only been twice. My plan was working. I'd only been waitressing for a week, and I'd already made a thousand dollars—but as another flash of pain struck, I knew it was time for a break.

"I got ya," Ben said, pulling up another milk crate and sitting behind me. "Let go of your shoulder."

"I can't." I was afraid if I let go, the pain would spread.

"Breathe with me."

I took a deep breath in and he rested his callused guitar hands on my shoulders, pressing his thumbs into my neck. We breathed together a few times.

"Oh," I said. "Oh." The pain changed color, broke apart. I risked turning my head. "Ouch!"

"Just focus on what's right in front of you."

"Mayonnaise," I said, looking up at a wall of industrial-size jars of condiments. Ben laughed, and I could feel it in his hands as he continued to knead my shoulders.

"How's it now?"

"Still pretty bad," I said. Even though the pain had dissipated, I didn't want him to stop.

"I know what you need. You need some time on the ocean. You want to go surfing tomorrow?"

"Yes," I said, glad he couldn't see me smiling. Neither of us had talked about our surfing date since the morning I'd canceled. I kept waiting for him to bring it up, but he hadn't. Maybe he was waiting for me to bring it up. We were in some kind of standoff, and my interest in the date had risen an additional ten percent every day it went unmentioned. I had reserved tomorrow afternoon for running and going over lacrosse drills, but surfing was a form of exercise, wasn't it?

"You're so tense you're like a shrinky dink," he said just as the door was flung open.

"What the hell is going on in here?" Karla asked.

Ben lifted his hands. I instantly missed them. They were experts, those hands.

"I had a muscle spasm," I said. "Ben was helping me."

"I'm sure he was," Karla said. Her glare scared me. Authority figures rarely looked at me with anything other than affection or relief. Her eyes were full of accusation. "You guys know my policy about staff relationships, right? You get into one, you're outta here."

"Um, I actually didn't know that policy," I said, standing up, no problem. My neck was miraculously healed.

"Karla," Ben said, cool as a gimlet. He pulled a carton of milk from the high shelf and handed it to me. "I walked in here and she was doubled over in pain."

"Well, just don't make me call you into my office, okay? Ben, you of all people should know better, and that bar's not going to prep itself. Cricket, you have a visitor."

"I do?" I took my milk and headed to the floor. My heart pirouetted. For a second, I thought it might be Zack.

It was Jules, in her black bikini and paisley cover-up, all long legs, highlights, and freckles. I felt a kick of disappointment. Would I ever learn? She helped herself to a couple of olives from the bar and asked, "What happened to you?"

"What do you mean?" I nodded toward a table where a stack of napkins awaited folding.

"You're all flushed and flustered and shit."

I shook my head and waved my hand, like, *Oh, nothing*, but I must've glanced at Ben without realizing it, because Jules took him in, his magic hands full of lemons, and cocked an eyebrow. I shrugged. She grinned.

"Well," she said, folding her slender hands on the table as we sat down. "I'm here for a few reasons. There's something about Parker—"

"Jules, I can't even . . ." I trailed off as Jules knocked some sand off her foot onto the floor. Karla had warned us that club members acted like they owned this place. *And that's good*, she'd said. *That's how they're supposed to feel.* Still, I had to bite my cheek to stop myself from making a face. I'd swept that floor twenty minutes ago. I peeled a napkin from the stack and started folding. "I don't want to hear about them."

"It's just that, well, it's complicated," Jules said.

"Yeah, you've both told me."

"And, like, so stereotypical."

"I don't want to know," I said. The last thing I wanted was a whiff of hope. I'd volunteered to take the indoor section every night, the one nearest the entrance. It was the least desirable. The big spenders all wanted to sit on the porch or the patio, but I was willing to take the less lucrative section if it meant I didn't have to risk seeing Zack and Parker frolicking on the beach.

"Okay," Jules sighed. "If you say so. Do you want to go to the beach tomorrow?"

"I'm going surfing," I said, and I nodded in Ben's direction.

"How old is he?" she mouthed.

Twenty-two, I mouthed back.

"Then the next day," she said, standing and tossing her bag over her shoulder. "We'll have lots to talk about. Meet me at the club at noon."

"Will they let me in?"

"Of course." Her laugh was as sunny as her freckled face. Never had she looked so pretty. Never had she sounded more grown-up. "Just tell them you're with me."

Twenty-one

FROM FAR AWAY, SURFING LOOKED LIKE A GRACEFUL activity, but now that I'd lugged the long, unwieldy board over the sand and was paddling ineffectively, Ben pushing me from behind, it didn't feel elegant or smooth. Cisco was a different beach from Jetties or Steps. It was on the ocean side, and I realized that what I'd sometimes been calling the ocean at Steps wasn't the ocean at all. It was the Nantucket Sound, protected and sheltered. Out here, on the southern side of the island, the waves were big. You could feel them rolling in with power and force, pushed from a wild place.

I was lying on the surfboard just like Ben had showed me when he'd given me a little lesson on the sand. We were headed out to beyond where the waves broke. We weren't even surfing yet, but it was already hard. A big wave, one that

I wouldn't have attempted to body surf, was coming right at us. "Point the nose straight ahead," he said, swimming right behind. Water crashed over me and filled my nose and mouth. I held on tight to the board, even as my body lifted and slammed back down again. I'd always thought of myself as so courageous, but I felt small. Tiny even. I coughed saltwater.

"You okay?" he asked when we finally got to the place where the water rolled, soft and lilting. Ben held onto the board and shook his hair from his face.

"I'm fine," I said, even though I wanted to turn around.

"That was kind of big," he said, "but don't worry. Once you get up, you're going to love it. It's all about trusting the unknown."

I nodded as if I totally got it, wishing we could just stay right there, drifting and floating in the sun.

"So, what's going on with you and Amy?"

He sighed. "Nothing." I raised my eyebrows. "Not anymore. We were together, but it didn't work out. She's looking for something I just can't give." He shifted so that his torso rested on the board.

"I have this weird feeling she's really smart. Besides, I think she really likes you. You sound a little insensitive, you know." I splashed him. He didn't splash back.

"I came to Nantucket to get away from a complicated situation, not to get back into one."

"What do you mean?" The afternoon sun was strong. It pressed on my back. "What was your situation?"

"I was engaged," he said, looking away.

"Really?" *I was old enough to know someone who could be engaged?* "Like, to be married?"

"Yes," he said with a sad laugh. "We broke up in April."

His face shifted into an expression that seemed ancient. Even though I barely knew him, I imagined that his father and grandfather and great-grandfather had also looked like this at certain moments in their lives.

I scooted up on the surfboard. "What happened?"

"She cheated on me."

"Oh, I'm sorry."

He squinted, looking out in the distance. "Okay, a set is coming, are you ready?"

"I guess. Listen, I'm sorry if I brought up—"

"No worries. So, it's going to be just like I showed you on the beach." He turned the board around, pointing it toward the shore. "You're going to paddle, paddle, paddle, and when I say 'pop,' you hop up on your feet. Super fast."

"How will I know if it's the right time to pop?"

"I'll tell you," he said, and I was off. He was pushing me and I was paddling, paddling, paddling. "Pop!"

I tried to stand but hesitated, and when my body froze up, I fell off. I hit the surface and the wave swallowed me. Salt stung my throat as I tumbled, inhaling water. I spat it out as my head popped up, gasping. The leash that tethered me to the board tugged on my ankle, yanking me forward, and I was back under, feeling sand and pebbles and water spinning, churning over me. When I tried to break through the surface again, the board swung back and hit me in the ribs. A second wave rolled in and dragged me backward by the waist.

Stay calm, I told myself, *relax.* And calling up ancient information from some long-ago swimming class at the Providence YMCA, I allowed my body to move with the water instead of against it. Finally I felt the sand under my feet. I stood up and took big swallows of air. I held on to the board and let a smaller wave push me toward the beach.

By the time I was in the surf, Ben had caught up. "Hey, you okay?"

"I think I'm done," I said. I reached down and pulled the Velcro leash off, stumbling as another wave frothed around my legs. Ben carried the board to the beach.

"The good news is you look okay," he said, gazing into my eyes with a soft smile. "A little scared, but okay. We can try some smaller, gentler waves if you want."

I didn't want smaller waves. I didn't want gentler waves. I didn't want any waves. My inner forearms were raw and chafed from holding on to the board so tightly. I was out of breath. I was on the brink of tears. My ribs hurt.

"I'm going to rest," I said and peeled off the girls' wet suit lent to him by some surfer friend of his. I didn't even care what my bathing suit looked like or that I could feel the bottoms riding up my butt. I shook out the towel I'd bought from the thrift store and sat down on the warm, solid sand.

"You sure you're okay?" He crouched next to me.

"Yes," I said, digging my heels into the sand. I didn't want to let on how shaken up I was. I wasn't used to being physically scared or intimidated. I laid a cold hand over my left rib, where I felt the beginnings of a bruise. "You go ahead. I'll watch. Really, I'm fine." His eyes met mine. I wanted a few minutes alone. I put some confidence behind my shaky voice and a reassuring smile on my face. "I swear. I've just had a long week."

He went. A few minutes later, after I'd shaken the water from my ears, I watched him surf. He paddled and popped and rode. I stood up to get a better look. Usually Ben had his watchful spot from behind the bar and I was in his view as I waitressed. But now I was the watcher. I placed one hand on my forehead like a visor and the other on my aching side. Ben wasn't in a wet suit, so I could see the strength of his legs, the power of his core, and the beauty in his balance. His body was both familiar and foreign. He was a living Rodin. *The Walking Man. The Thinker. Saint John the Baptist.* He was all of them, but not made of marble, stuck in a museum in Paris. He was in motion. He was alive in the Atlantic.

I thought about Nina's list, and a great idea came to me, the kind that feels like opening a window. I didn't need Parker's money or connections. Screw that. I could live Nina's list, here on Nantucket. I could follow it and see where it led me. *Rodin is at Cisco,* I thought. *I don't need to go anywhere. I just need to open my eyes.*

A few good waves were Ben's medicine, because an hour later, when he emerged from the water with his board under his arm, he had that wicked grin on his face. And as the late afternoon sun caught the drops of water that slipped down his skin, he was actually sparkling.

Ben's car was an army green Land Rover from the 1970s with a canvas top that rolled up in the back. It belonged to his grandmother Sadie, whom he described as Joni Mitchell meets Rosie the Riveter. He was staying with her for the summer. I changed in the back, under the tent of my towel. I checked my side and saw that a bruise was forming where the board had hit me. It was sore, but it was going to be okay. We drove out to Madaket, the westernmost part of the island, and ate fish tacos at a place called Millie's, where Ben knew the bartenders.

Later, we sat on the beach and watched an orange sun drop into the sea. I'd never seen a sky so red. It was as if the sun had left a memory of flames that was brighter than actual flames. The lowest sky glowed like coals. Above it, hot pink clouds skidded into a purple night. As the sky darkened, the ocean carried the colors in ripples and shocks.

I thought of those salmon-colored pants called Nantucket Reds. They were a copy of a copy of a copy of the most tepid version of this sky, the real Nantucket Red. I thought of Zack, acting like nothing had happened between us, treating me as if I were any old girl, despite the fact that we had been in love. *In love.* And it just seemed so lame to me, lame like those stupid fucking pants.

Ben put an arm around me, resting his hand on my hip. He was here. His arm had weight and warmth. He was real.

His heart was alive enough to have been broken. He leaned into me. "Can I kiss you?"

"Yes."

He pulled me close, tilted my head back, and pressed his lips to mine.

We kissed on the beach until a dad approached us, several toddlers in tow, and told us this was a "family setting." We burst out laughing. He grabbed my hand as we walked to the car and we barely let go on the drive back to Fair Street. Then we kissed in the Land Rover in front of the inn as we shared the most basic details of our lives, the kind of stuff I'd known about Zack forever. Ben told me he was twenty-two. *Kiss.* He grew up in Maine. *Kiss.* He graduated from Sarah Lawrence College last year. *Kiss.* He was helping Sadie fix up her house. *Kiss.* He'd lived in Brooklyn until May, when he came to Nantucket. *Kiss.* He didn't think he was going back.

"Because of . . . what's her name?"

"Amelia." He disappeared for a second.

"What about you?" He touched my neck. "Where are you from?"

"Providence."

"Go on." His hand traced my collarbone.

"I'm eighteen."

"Thank god." His finger dropped to my breastbone, outside the T-shirt.

"Nineteen soon. I'm going to Brown."

"We've been over that." We both laughed.

He ran his hand through my hair, tugging on it a little

as he went for another kiss, and I had the feeling that guys his age either kissed or had sex but didn't do anything in between. But before I even had a chance to tell him to slow it down, he surprised me by transitioning into a hug, telling me he had to go check on Sadie, and planting a chaste kiss on my burning forehead.

Liz was drinking wine out of a jam jar, making her way through a sleeve of Oreos, and watching *Big Brother*.

"Holy hair extensions," I said, as the girl on the TV twirled her mane and addressed the camera. I sat next to Liz on the sofa.

"Yeah, but Shayla's really cool," Liz said. "She's going to win this whole thing. What's going on? Did you do it with Mr. Bartender?"

"No. I'm just getting to know him."

"Watch out. He's probably a right ass." Liz refilled her jam jar with wine and reached for another cookie. "They all are. Men are not to be trusted."

I didn't have the heart to remind her that she was the one who had told me I didn't need to be such a very, very good girl. And I wasn't going to ask her if "right asses" spend their summers fixing up their grandmothers' houses.

"You're probably right," I said. I snuggled under the covers with her and laid my head on her shoulder. She passed me the Oreos and I took one. "Liz, are you okay? I heard you crying last night."

She paused the TV. "I keep going over it in my head,

trying to locate the moment."

"What moment?"

"The moment I lost him. But I can't find it. Where did I go wrong?"

"You didn't do anything wrong," I said, as fat tears rolled down her pink cheeks. "He lied. He's a right ass, remember?"

"But why doesn't he want to be with me?" she asked, hiccuping. "What's wrong with me?"

"Nothing's wrong with you." I handed her a tissue. She blew her nose loudly.

"I sound like a stupid, stupid girl. I sound like a bloody Phil Collins song."

"You aren't stupid. Shane's stupid. You're badass!"

"Do I look badass?" she asked, gesturing to her oversize Cranberry Inn T-shirt and pajama bottoms with kittens on them.

"You look . . . casual. Hey, remember when you bought me that thong last year? And made me unwrap it in front of Gavin?" She laughed, snorting a bit. "Or how everyone on this island, including the rich and famous—*especially* the rich and famous—know and love you? Or the fact that you stayed out on Nantucket instead of doing what everyone expected?

"I suppose that was adventurous."

"It was badass! You're only twenty years old and you're running an inn."

"A stupid person might have more trouble, it's true."

"See? Exactly." I turned back to the TV and grabbed an Oreo. "Now, tell me why Shayla's going to win."

Twenty-two

THE WAMP'S LOBBY DELIVERED THE CLASSIC NEW ENGLAND elegance that its shingled exterior promised: wooden floors, white wicker furniture, a fireplace, vases of blue-purple hydrangeas, lush potted plants, and a coffee setup that with silver spoons, sugar cubes, and china cups, was at least 30 percent fancier than the one we had at the Cranberry Inn.

"I'm a guest of the Claytons," I said to the front desk girl.

"Cricket, right?" When I heard her husky, party-girl voice, I realized she was Thonged Snoring Girl. "Jules is waiting for you on the beach." From the way she was looking at me, it was clear she was trying to place me. I couldn't wait to tell Liz.

"I'm a waitress at Breezes," I said. "It's my day off."

"No wonder you look so familiar." She lowered her voice. "Weren't you gonna move into the Surfside house with us?"

"I found something else."

"That's too bad. It's like a constant party. We didn't go to bed until like five this morning."

"Sounds fun," I said.

"So, if you want to change into your suit, the Claytons' cabana is number sixteen." She pointed down a hallway. "Just go all the way to the end and make a right. It's the last one."

The cabana was actually a simple wooden changing room built right over the sand. The door to number sixteen was open. Inside were some little closetlike rooms for changing, a shower, and several hooks for bathing suits and towels. I knew that if Nina were alive she would've loved to decorate this little space. She would've hung the perfect photo or an antique mirror above the white dresser.

I could see how each of the family members had claimed some small corner for their own. Here was Jules's nook, with her boyfriend jeans, shampoo, and razor lined up on a bench. There was Mr. Clayton's corner, with his large flip-flops, sunglasses, and a vat of sunblock, SPF 75. There were Zack's things, hanging on hooks: his blue bathing suit, still wet; the towel with the Tropicana logo that he'd used all last summer; his Whale's Tale T-shirt, inside out.

I had been hoping Ben's kiss would cure me of Zack. But I grabbed Zack's shirt, brought it to my face, and inhaled until I was light-headed and flooded with memories of last summer. *Sunscreen, sand, salt water, him.* I flipped it over and smelled the back, coaxing every last bit of Zackness from its fibers.

Ben's kiss was expert, just like his hands. He knew when to move in, when to pull away. He knew when to press and when to release. And it worked: my body responded without waiting for my thoughts. It had been different with Zack. We belonged to each other when we had kissed. I buried my face in the shirt one last time before reminding myself that he didn't belong to me anymore. I was about to hang the shirt up on its hook when I decided to stuff it in the bottom of my beach bag instead. I folded my clothes and placed them over it and made my way down the pathway to the beach.

When I stepped onto the hot sand, one of the Wamp employees sprang to his feet and offered me a cup of ice water and a towel. I didn't know if I was supposed to tip him. Since I was wearing only my bathing suit it was pretty obvious that I didn't have any cash on me.

"It's okay," he said. "Are you looking for Jules?"

"Yeah." Who was this clairvoyant beach boy?

He laughed. "She told me you were coming. She's right there."

He pointed and I saw Nina wearing one of her signature black bikinis, her hair in a messy bun and her sunglasses on her forehead. She was reclining in a beach chair under a yellow umbrella, reading a magazine. I couldn't wait to tell her about Rodin at Cisco. I couldn't wait to make her laugh.

"Why are you looking at me like that?" Jules asked, startling me out of my mistake. I adjusted the beach chair next to hers. "Do I have kale in my teeth? I just had a salad."

"No," I said. "It's nothing."

"Whatever you say. Since when did everyone decide kale tasted good, anyway?" She handed me a magazine. It was *Vogue Paris*. "For you. It's not like I can read it, but you probably can."

"Cool," I said, and opened it up, testing out my French.

"Parker brought it from Paris."

I dropped the magazine on the sand, not even bothering to close it. I was about to ask Jules what she was trying to do in bringing up Parker, but then I noticed the page the magazine had opened to. It was a piece about Rodin. I couldn't believe it.

"My mom loved this guy." Jules picked up the magazine and dusted off the sand. Her eyes narrowed as she studied the glossy spread.

"I know." I propped myself up on my elbow and debated telling her about the list. I'd already come up with a plan for the second item: *Learn to drive and then drive Route 1 to Big Sur.* Nina didn't know how to drive, because she had grown up in Manhattan. I knew how to drive, but I didn't know how to drive stick. I was going to ask Ben to teach me in the Land Rover.

Jules pressed her hands against the page, flattening it for the best view. "She doesn't like art."

"Who?"

"Jennifer. I'm not sure what she's into besides my dad."

"He's probably just having a fling."

"He'd better be." She flipped the page and inhaled a perfume sample. "Do you hate Polly?"

"No," I said, thinking. "It's just, she's not my family, and my dad wants me to pretend like she is, and I have to do it all the time."

"That sucks," Jules said, flipping through the pages. "But she is family, right?"

"She's *his* family," I said.

"But he's *your* dad."

"I don't want to think about it." I stared out at the water. "Let's go for a swim."

She got up and I followed her, but turned back when I realized I was still wearing my sunglasses. I could see the Breezes staff setting up for dinner. I could see Amy looking out at me from the porch, a hand on her hip, her bright red lipstick visible from here. I wondered if Ben had told her that we'd hooked up. I wondered if I was her Parker. I was not going to be anyone's Parker. "Hey," I called. I smiled and waved.

"Is that girl giving you the finger?" Jules asked.

"Yup," I said, continuing to wave. "She sure is."

Twenty-three

"NO, NO," BEN SAID, AS THE LAND ROVER STALLED YET again. "You need to lift your foot off the clutch while you put your foot on the gas."

"I did."

"You have to do it *at the same time*. Like I've been telling you. For an hour."

"That's what I was doing," I said, tapping the steering wheel with my palms.

It was the first time I'd seen Ben tense. Even on Saturday nights when the bar was slammed, he moved as if knowing that the world was going to wait for his easy smile, sun-lightened hair, and faded shirts. Now, on these sandy back roads, a little furrow disturbed his smooth brow.

"I was lifting my foot gently off the clutch just like you said," I insisted. He pointed at my foot, which was still depressing the clutch. I jerked it away. "I mean that's what I *did*. Seriously, when it was happening, that's what I was doing. I swear."

He tilted his head and raised his eyebrows as if he didn't believe me. I sighed, trying desperately to appear even-tempered and in control. I was going to drive this Land Rover if it killed me.

"Here's the thing. If you don't lift your foot off the clutch, the gear can't catch," Ben said, sounding like someone's dad. "Want me to draw you a picture?" I glared at him. "Whoa. Okay. You want to take a break?" He put a hand on my knee. "Sadie is expecting us for dinner soon."

"No," I said, pushing his hand away. "I can get this."

His cell phone rang. He paled as he glanced at the number and silenced it. Was it Amelia?

"I'm ready when you are," he said.

I took a deep breath and turned the key. It wouldn't start. "Shit."

"You're foot isn't on the—"

"I know!" I took another breath and pulled an old lacrosse trick: visualizing. In lacrosse, it was the ball landing in the net I saw in my mind's eye. Now, it was the car traveling effortlessly down the road. I started the car again, releasing the clutch as I applied my foot to the gas—*at the same time*—and we started to move.

"Yay!" I said. "Yay, yay, yay!"

"All right, nice job." He rubbed his hands together. "Now we're cooking with gas."

"Oh, shit, oh, shit, oh, shit," I said as I saw another car approaching. These back roads had been ours alone for an hour now. Why did other people have to show up now? "There's another car on the road."

"That'll happen from time to time, but you got it," he said, tilting the steering wheel toward him to give the other car, which was full of kids headed to the beach, enough room to pass.

"Good work. Now you're going to shift into second gear. This is easy, since you're already moving."

"Okay." I pressed on the clutch and shifted. Ben whistled.

"I like second gear," I said, unable to suppress a huge smile. "Second gear is, like, my favorite."

"You want to drive all the way to Sadie's?"

"I'll try," I said, exhilarated by my triumph. He directed me down a few roads and casually turned on the radio. Fleetwood Mac was singing "Gypsy" on the classic rock station from the Cape. Mom loved this song. I knew every word. I was so focused on the task at hand, so deep in my concentration, that I started to sing along quietly without even realizing it.

"You have a pretty voice," Ben said. "I didn't know you could sing."

"Thanks, but I can't. My mom's the singer."

"You sound good to me," he said, tossing off one of his gorgeous smiles.

"I don't have perfect pitch," I said. Mom had checked my pitch a few times and even though she tried to hide it, I knew it disappointed her that I hadn't inherited her gift. Somewhere along the line, I'd decided that if I couldn't sing perfectly, I wouldn't do it at all.

"It's not about perfect," Ben said as the road changed from dirt to paved. "It's about expression."

Two trucks peeled out from a big driveway and trailed us. Ahead, a stop sign loomed. My grip on the wheel tightened.

"Oh, god," I said, eying my rearview mirror. One was a gigantic Suburban and the other a Ford Expedition.

"One foot on the clutch, one foot on the brake," Ben said as we approached the stop sign.

I did what he said, and miraculously, the Land Rover came to a halt.

"I did it! I did it!" We high-fived. Once the road was clear, I stepped on the gas, forgetting all the little steps I was supposed to do between. Something screeched. I tried to get us going again, choosing two different pedals. The car lurched.

"My transmission!" Ben said. My back was sweating. My thighs were sticking to the seat. I couldn't remember which pedal was which and I didn't want to touch any of them. Behind me, the driver of the Ford Expedition leaned on his horn.

"What the hell?" the driver called out the window.

"Calm down, dude," Ben said under his breath.

"Can we switch?" I asked Ben as the guy pressed on his horn again, this time sticking his middle finger out his window. He kept jabbing it higher and higher. "Uh, we have to switch."

"Okay. Turn the car off."

I did and we both climbed out of the car. But then the car started to roll onto whatever main road I'd been trying to turn onto. It was moving on its own! An oncoming car slammed on its brakes, forcing the car behind it to do the same.

"Jesus," Ben said, as we ran alongside the car, opened the doors, and climbed inside. It wasn't rolling fast, but it was the first time I'd ever jumped inside a moving car. Ben did whatever it was people who drive stick know to do, and we pulled over to the side of the road. The Expedition guy shouted something as he turned in the opposite direction.

"I, um, forgot the emergency brake," I said.

"I know," he said. And we burst into laughter as he started the car. I was laughing so hard that I almost didn't notice that it was Parker's car that had slammed on the brakes and was now passing us. Her dark hair streamed out the window like a raven taking flight. Zack was in the passenger seat, craning his neck to get a better look at me. I knew in my gut that he'd seen the whole thing. The Rolling Stones came on the radio. I turned up the volume, put my feet on the dash, and sang my heart out.

Twenty-four

"AND THESE WERE MY PARENTS, HARRIET AND BERNARD, Broadway actors. They were part of the 'Sconset Actors Colony back in the Roaring Twenties," Sadie said, pointing to a photo of a dramatic woman with a draped Grecian dress and a wreath of flowers in her hair, striking a pose next to a man who was lounging on a porch looking both guilty and delighted with himself. "My parents built this cottage themselves."

"That's this cottage?" I asked, taking a closer look at the picture. "Where we are right now?" Ben sat next to me with a fresh beer, and I tried not to squeal as he slipped a cold hand between my lower back and the sofa. Sadie's house was tiny, with one bedroom, one bathroom, a little kitchen, and a living room that doubled as Ben's bedroom at night. We were both couch surfing this summer.

Sadie was older than I'd thought. From the way Ben had spoken about her, swimming in the ocean every day and peppering her speech with her favorite four-letter words, I'd imagined her to be the same age as Polly's parents, Rosemary and Jim, and neither of them had gray hair. But Sadie was old-lady old, with white hair and watery eyes, even though she'd lit up like a teenager when she'd seen Ben waving to her as we headed into the driveway.

"You don't recognize it because so much has been built up around it," she said. "You used to be able to see the ocean from the porch."

"And there was an actors' colony on Nantucket?"

"There certainly was. And what free spirits they were," she said, turning the page to reveal a sepia-toned group hanging out on a porch. Some were smoking pipes, some were wearing crazy hats. Some were in costumes and others in bathing suits, but they all looked like they were having the time of their lives. "They came out here to write and act and make music and, let's face it, get laid."

"I warned you about her," Ben said, smiling, sipping his beer, and sliding that hand farther down my back.

"I had no idea. I'd always thought of Nantucket as a vacation spot, not a place where artists go."

"Nantucket has always been a place for oddballs and wanderers; that's the nature of an island." She turned another page, to a picture in which a busty girl in a bikini posed in the sand. "Oh, that's me, the summer I met Ben's grand-father. We made love for the very first time on that beach."

"Wow," was all I could think of to say.

"We had fun in the old days," Sadie continued. "Now I don't know what young people want."

"We want the same stuff," Ben said.

"But these kids driving seventy-thousand-dollar cars? It's like they're already middle-aged. I didn't want fancy cars when I was young. I wanted adventure. Sex. Romance. The open road."

"Cricket almost got us killed on the open road today," Ben said, and I pinched his leg.

"But it takes money to travel and be free," I said, thinking of Parker and her new Parisian wardrobe, Jules's graduation car, Nina on the Amalfi Coast.

"No, it doesn't. During these summers, I didn't have a dime," Sadie said. "No one did. Didn't bother us. Look." She pointed to a picture of a bunch of people standing around a fire on the beach. Some were drinking beer. Some were laughing. Some peered pensively at the fire. A handsome guy with one of those rockabilly hairstyles was playing the guitar. She tapped the face of a girl who was dancing. "That's me, in a dress I made from Mother's curtains. Fun is free, as they say, and adventure is there for those who look for it. Especially on a warm July night in Nantucket." She placed a cool, soft hand on my cheek.

Sadie loved Nantucket as much as Nina did, but in such a different way. Nina had worn designer clothes and wanted to join the most exclusive club. Sadie was a waitress, dancing on the beach in a dress made of curtains.

"Okay, kiddos, I'm going to turn in. Up she goes," Sadie said, hoisting herself off the sofa. "I didn't have my nap today, and I'm tired. Benjamin, take Amelia to the beach and show her the stars. Somehow, on Nantucket, the stars are closer."

"This isn't Amelia," Ben said. His voice lowered. "She's gone, remember?"

"Sorry." Sadie shook her head. "Of course. Force of habit."

Did I look like Amelia? Had she come here with Ben? How many times? I wanted to ask Ben, but his mood had downshifted. His eyes had darkened and were far away.

"There's a comet that's supposed to be visible soon," I said, grasping for the lightness that had been present just moments ago.

"Larsen's Comet. It's visible now," Sadie said. "Great idea! Go have a look."

"I think she's kicking us out," Ben said as Sadie headed into her room with a glass of water and a book under her arm.

"Can we go to that beach and build a bonfire?" I asked, pointing to the picture of Sadie and her friends.

"We're not supposed to," Ben said, sounding like himself again. "But we can."

Ben led me down a path through a grove of trees to a fire pit in the sand. The breeze off the water was chilly. I sat down in the sand and pulled my Brown sweatshirt over my knees. I stared up to see if I could spot the comet, but it was cloudy. I could only see the moon and a couple of very bright stars.

Ben unloaded some wood and newspaper from a canvas bag and built a mini-tepee with wood. As he lit the newspaper, he explained that fires weren't allowed on the beach without a permit, but that it was almost impossible to see the bonfire from the road.

"What would happen if we got caught?" The flame caught the paper and jumped to life. Ben's face was focused and glowing in the firelight. There was something about watching him build a fire that was making me aware of my breath, my heartbeat, and the way they worked together.

"We might get arrested."

"What?"

"Yeah, they're cracking down," he said, enjoying my discomfort. "And it all goes in the newspaper."

"Really?"

"Karla does not like to see her staff in the *Inky*." Ben stood up, admired his work, and dusted off his hands. Normally, information like this would have made me want to snuff out the fire and head back home, but I fought the impulse. Ben said no one could see us from the road. And besides, he had picked up his guitar, and the fire was dancing. The air was swirling with cool, salty breezes and heat from the flames, and the surf was whispering, *Stay, shh, stay, shh, stay, shh, stay.*

I realized Ben was strumming "Gypsy." He started to sing and I joined in, thinking that the words reminded me of Nina. But no. They didn't. They reminded me of Sadie. No. They reminded me of my own mom, singing in the kitchen and in the car. They reminded me of myself, dancing around the living room when I was a little kid. I was remembering a part of me that I'd forgotten about, or maybe I was seeing a glimmer of the person I might become. A girl who was free. A girl on the open road. A girl singing on the beach. I felt connected to something. Something in the moon and the fire and the ocean. I felt a light stream of electricity in my limbs. A sense of belonging to this moment, this place on earth—an ancient kind of happiness.

"What are you thinking about?" Ben asked. "Scoring lacrosse goals at Brown?"

"No. Not at all."

"When do you start practice?"

"I don't know." The idea of lacrosse startled me out of my open-road reverie. I hid my face in my palms, feeling guilty. Lacrosse. I'd put off practice for weeks now. I dug my heels into the sand and inhaled the beach air. The dagger of panic was sharper than ever. It was pointed right at my throat.

"What?" Ben asked.

"Nothing," I said, burying my head in my arms. The future was vast and open, so why was I headed back to Providence, to do exactly what I'd done all through high school, in the same small city I'd lived my whole life?

"What is it?" he asked.

I couldn't bring myself to say it aloud. I shut my eyes as that feeling of connection, of inexplicable security and feather-light joy, vanished like a wisp of smoke into the night.

Twenty-five

LATER, I COULDN'T SLEEP. AS I WATCHED THE SKY LIGHTEN from black to purple, I debated as to whether I was making a big mistake by staying in Rhode Island for college. I pulled the sheet over my eyes and wondered if I even cared about lacrosse anymore. It was not like I'd even read the last two e-mails from Coach Stacy. I hadn't gone running in over a week. *What did that mean?* I asked myself as I breathed under my cotton tent.

At three thirty I got out of bed, pulled out my acceptance letter to Brown, and turned on the kitchen light. I smoothed out the letter on the kitchen table, reread it, and remembered what it had felt like to get in. How Mom had screamed as the mailman called, "Congrats!" over his shoulder. How I'd slipped the letter to my dad at Jake's Diner, telling him very casually that I had something interesting for him to read. He hooted, then popped a quarter in the jukebox and jitterbugged me around the restaurant. I remembered the new looks of respect I received from everyone I told. Mrs. Hart, the ancient English teacher, kissed me on the forehead. Jim and Rosemary were offering me eight thousand dollars so that I could have the full Ivy League experience. I remembered the speech Dad gave in my mom's driveway at my graduation party, saying that he "couldn't be prouder."

How could going to Brown University, *the* Brown University, ever be a mistake? That was impossible any way you looked at it. And of course, I cared about lacrosse. Of course, I loved it. I poured myself a glass of cold water and drank it all. I closed my eyes and remembered the rush of scoring a goal, the smell of warm grass on a spring afternoon, the pasta dinners with the team the night before a big game. I laid my head on the cool, indifferent kitchen table and repeated the words *I'm doing the right thing. I'm doing the right thing. I'm doing the right thing.* I crawled back to my bed, the sofa, and fell asleep as the first birds were starting to sing.

"He's going to propose!" Jules said as she flew through the door of the inn's laundry room.

I was so in my own world, so exhausted, nursing a coffee as I folded yet another load of the inn's signature cranberry-colored towels, and Jules was so out of context that it took a minute to register her as real and not a figment of my imagination. My arrangement of covering for Liz two mornings a week was great for my bank account, because I wasn't paying rent, and I was still very grateful to her, but it was almost impossible for me to catch up on rest.

"Cricket, hello; did you hear me?" Jules asked, her fingers rigid and fully extended. She was dressed for work at the Needle and Thread in a white miniskirt, Tory Burch flats, and a scarf tied artfully around the handle of her purse. Her hair was blown out in perfect waves. But there was chaos in the details of her face: the wrinkled forehead, the frantic eyes, lip gloss that went just beyond the boundary of her lower lip.

"I'm sorry. Propose what?" I was so tired, so taken by surprise, that her words didn't quite make sense.

"Marriage!" She huffed at my slowness.

"Who's getting married?" Was she talking about Zack and Parker? Would that even be legal? My heart rate dragged, despite three cups of coffee. I leaned on the hot, rumbling dryer.

"Dad!" Jules said, the cords of her lean, pale throat tightening like strained wires. "Who else?"

"To that girl? Are you sure?"

"Yes. My dad is going to propose to Jennifer, a woman he met three months ago on Friendly Adults dot-com."

"Oh, no," I said. *Friendly Adults dot-com?* I wasn't sure, but I thought that was a kinky Web site. Like, XXX. "You think, but how do you know?"

"I saw the ring." She started to pace as much as the small laundry room would allow. "I was looking for this picture of

Mom in her vintage von Furstenberg dress; you know, the one where she's actually talking to Diane von Furstenberg at a party?"

"Yes," I said. I knew the picture. Nina was wearing one of her signature wrap dresses and a dramatic necklace, holding a martini. I remembered looking at that photo and thinking, *This is what I want to look like when I grow up.*

"I wanted to show it to Maggie, my boss. And for as long as I can remember, Dad kept it in a drawer by their bed. So I went looking for it. But I didn't find it. Instead, I found a ring." Jules began breathing rapidly, fanning herself. For a second I wondered if she was going to faint. I pushed a little stepladder toward her. "A big, fat, cheesy engagement ring."

"Hold the phone," I said, using one of my mom's phrases as Jules lowered herself onto the stepladder. "You don't know he's going to propose to her. That ring could've been your mom's."

"It wasn't my mom's. It was a new ring. It was tacky as fuck. I know it's for her. It was just the kind of thing she thinks is beautiful. Mom would never wear it." She shook her head and looked at her watch. "And now I'm going to be late for work." She placed a trembling hand at her temple, grabbed one of the freshly folded Cranberry Inn towels, and held it to her face, shoulders shaking.

"It's okay," I said, rubbing her back as she let out a sob and blew her nose into the towel. "Go ahead. Make yourself at home." We both laughed.

"I have to go," she sighed.

"Call me later, okay? We'll figure it out," I said, although I wasn't sure how. These were adult problems. I'd learned from my parents what could be controlled and what couldn't. If Jules was right, this was one of those things that couldn't, and she was just starting to get a taste of how much it was going to suck.

"Okay," she said, holding her breath in an attempt to stop crying. She was looking at me as if I might actually be able to make this all right.

"So I've started the list," Liz said as she walked in, a notebook under her arm. I had promised Liz that when she woke up we would make a list going over the pros and cons of her moving back to England or staying in America. She, too, was dressed for work, but hadn't quite managed to pull herself together. What with the circles under my eyes, Jules's runny nose, and Liz's ill-buttoned shirt, we were a sad crew. "Oh, hello," Liz said to Jules. "We can have fresh towels delivered to you. What room are you in?"

"I'm not staying here," Jules said, dabbing her eyes with the towel.

"How did you know where to find me?" I asked Jules.

"I just looked around. I opened doors until you were standing behind one." I laughed. It was so Jules, so blazingly confident.

"Pardon, but who are you, exactly?" Liz asked.

"Jules."

"I've heard about you," Liz said and crossed her arms.

"Good things, I hope?"

Liz shook her head no.

"We had a rough time last year," I said and shrugged.

"Yeah," Jules said, as if last summer had been a very, very long time ago. "We did."

"Hey," I said. "What did Zack have to say about all this?"

"I didn't tell him." She watched sudsy sheets going around in the washer and said quietly, "I only wanted to talk to you. Hey, you know what I want, like, more than anything? One of our adventures."

In the old days, our adventures involved sneaking into dances at the boarding schools within driving distance and playing "exchange student," or putting balloons under our shirts and walking around the mall like regretful pregnant teens, or taking the bus to Boston and getting hot chocolates at the Four Seasons Hotel. During those excursions we created our own world. We moved in sync, spoke in code, and laughed so hard that hot chocolate came out of our noses.

An adventure with Jules would be the perfect escape. Between waitressing and covering for Liz, I hadn't had a single day off since I'd landed on Nantucket. I had almost four thousand dollars, but I was tired. Tired of taking drink orders and carrying plates of calamari and never being able to catch up on sleep. And last year, Liz had been my wild yet sensible British ally, buying me lingerie and texting me sex tips. But ever since her breakup, she was in bed by eight thirty. She'd stopped wearing mascara. Her walk had lost its swagger. I'd seen my mom go through heartbreak.

I'd watched her retreat into a mental castle and pull up the drawbridge, and something similar was happening to Liz. Once again, I was on the other side of the moat, unable to reach the lonely lady. Yes, an adventure was in order.

"I have the best idea," I said. Our eyes met in mischief.

"Yay!" Jules gave me a quick, hard hug. "Text me."

Watching her leave, I felt like I'd just heard an old favorite song on the radio.

Liz squinted in concern. "Be careful, insect."

Twenty-six

"NASTY!" I SAID AS I SPIT THE CAMPARI OUT IN THE Claytons' kitchen sink and guzzled water directly from the tap to wash away the bitter, medicinal taste. Jules was laughing her really laughing laugh. The one that was mixed with snorts and gasps, and that I hadn't heard in almost a year.

"Why did you get this stuff?" Jules asked, wiping a tear away.

"It looks so pretty," I said, admiring the ruby liquor with the stylish, European label. I couldn't tell her that it was because it was number three on Nina's life list: *Drink Campari on the Amalfi Coast with Alison.* Even after her laundry room breakdown, even though I'd felt comfortable enough to spit in her sink, I was still scared she'd tell me that Nina was her mom and I had no right—*no right at all!*—to follow that list, copy it, inhabit it, make it mine.

"You're not supposed to drink it straight. It's one of those things you mix."

"Why didn't you tell me as I was pouring myself a whole glass?" I asked, holding up the juice glass I'd filled three-quarters full without even an ice cube. "I mean, it looks like fruit punch."

"I wanted to see what happened," she said, and laughed again. "Besides, you never drink. I wasn't about to stop you. You missed that night at the secret bowling alley. And tonight is all about fun!"

We'd been texting for a few days, trying to plan our adventure. Since Liz seemed to have secret connections everywhere, I had asked her to get me a bottle of Campari. And then tonight, when it was slow enough to send one of the waitresses home early, I'd volunteered and texted Jules immediately.

Me: Are you up for some Campari and a midnight dip?

Jules: Hells yeah! Come over. Dad in NYC.

Mr. Clayton had said he was on a business trip. Although Jules's theory that he was going to propose hadn't been con-firmed, it seemed pretty likely that it was true and was going to go down soon, maybe even this weekend. Jennifer was with him and the ring was missing.

I headed to the fridge to find a mixer for the Campari. Jules turned on her iPod and played an old Katy Perry song we used to dance around to. I noticed a picture of Zack and Parker on the fridge. Their arms were around each other and they were in front of some ivy-covered building at their boarding school. He's probably with her right now, I thought. I flipped it over and stuck the magnet back on it. I opened the fridge, grabbed a can of Sprite, and drank it down. The Campari flavor mixed with the sweet soda.

"Sprite and Campari is a different story," I said. Jules was dancing around the kitchen. I poured the Sprite into a glass, added Campari, and took a long swallow. "Yum."

"Make me one," Jules said. I poured her a taste.

"Nice," she said, taking a sip and considering. "Tart and fizzy. I know. I'll fill up thermoses. We'll take our drinks with us."

"Sassy and classy!"

"Goofy and glamorous!" She hit *repeat* on the Katy Perry song.

"Bitter and sweet, like love!" I added dramatically, and I spun out of the kitchen, right into Zack. Our eyes met and locked.

"You're not supposed to be here," Jules said to Zack. "Did you have a fight with Parker?"

"None of your business," Zack said.

"Whatever. We're leaving." Jules grabbed a monogrammed canvas bag that she'd had as long as I'd known her and put the thermoses in it.

"Where are you headed?" Zack asked.

"None of your business," Jules said, mimicking his tone.

"We're going on an adventure," I said. "We're going to Steps." I wanted him to know that if he could traipse all over our magical island, well, so could I.

"Oh, yeah?" Zack said, leaning against the door frame. "What are you going to do there?"

"We're going for a swim," I said, raising my eyebrows, a hand on my hip. Teaming up with Jules had given me a dose of my old confidence. "A midnight dip."

"Towels! Can't forget the towels." Jules took off for the laundry room.

"Hey, have you seen my Whale's Tale shirt?" he called after her.

"No!"

"Steps, huh?" He asked me. The night we'd gone skinny-dipping there was the moment I knew I was in love with him. It had been a perfect night. Bright moon. Summer air. Dark water. When we moved, the water glowed with phosphorescence.

"Yes. Steps," I said, watching a slow smile spread over his face.

"I saw you the other day. Like maybe a week ago. Out on Milestone Road. You were, like, jumping into a Jeep with some guy?"

"Ben." I nodded. Tucked my hair behind my ear. "He's teaching me how to drive stick."

"Ha! I bet he is," Jules called from the other room. "Woo-hoo!"

"That guy works at Breezes, right? At the bar?"

I nodded again. Zack crossed his arms and shook his head. "I've seen that dude around." He lowered his voice to a whisper. "You're not falling for that shit, are you?"

"You just don't know him," I said, throwing what he'd said to me about Parker back at him. "You haven't given him a chance."

Jules returned, the canvas bag now stuffed with towels, and tripped over the threshold. "Whoops!"

"Are you sure this is a good idea?" Zack asked. "You guys seem kind of drunk."

"I'm not drunk," I said, though I could feel the Campari warming my joints. Tipsy, I thought, as Jules linked an arm in mine and I leaned on her; I'm tipsy.

"Besides, it's late," Zack said.

"We'll sleep when we're dead," Jules said, and we marched out the door, soldiers of silliness.

"So, what's going on with this Ben guy?" Jules asked as we kicked off our shoes and descended the stairs to the beach. "Is he your boyfriend?"

"Yeah," I said, though I wondered if I would I have answered the question like that if he had been standing next to me. "Are you and Jay going to stay together next year?"

"Absolutely," she said. "That's why we're going to school in Boston." As soon as we hit the sand, we stripped to our suits, took sips from our thermoses for courage, and made a run for it into the water. We screamed with delight as we dove under the surface. We shut our eyes against the salt and kicked up into handstands and floated on our backs.

"I could just forget everything out here," Jules said, breaking the silence. "Maybe when we're both in college next year we can come here for a weekend. Like when it's snowing."

"We'll go for a polar bear swim," I said, and dove back under, sliding through the water like a fish. I grinned at the thought of being grown-up enough to have a weekend away with just my friend. I grinned because we were talking about our future as friends, and I knew that we had surmounted the hurt that had fallen like a massive tree between us last summer. I grinned because I felt free for the first time since I had arrived on the ferry. Held by the Nantucket Sound, I unhooked myself from my worries. Water filled my ears, closing out the world. Lacrosse didn't exist here. Brown was far away. I felt cleansed. *Sadie was right*, I thought, and came up for a breath, *fun is free.*

"I'm getting cold," Jules said when I resurfaced.

"Okay. Let's head in." My bottom lip was trembling, too. Also, I was starved. I hadn't eaten since the staff meal at four. I noticed we were farther from the shore than I'd realized. "Whoa. We drifted."

"Yeah, let's go," Jules said, her face serious. We were both good swimmers, and made silent and effortful progress to the beach. I could feel myself working against the tide, and the Campari, and was relieved when we finally reached the shallow water.

"Holy shit," Jules said, "There's a man on the beach and he's looking right at us. Cricket, we're going to die!"

"That's no man," I said, laughing. "It's Zack."

"What are you doing here?" Jules called to Zack as we climbed out of the water, teeth chattering.

"Every summer there's a story about someone who drowns," he said, and handed us each a towel. "I didn't want it to be you guys."

"Thanks," I said, shivering and wrapping the towel around me. For a minute, I saw the old Zack: unguarded and kind.

Jules looked at him sideways as she roughly dried off her legs. "Since when did you get so concerned with my safety?"

"I've always been concerned with your safety," he said.

"Turn around. I'm going to change," Jules said. "Don't want a yeast infection."

"Why do you have to be so nasty?" Zack said, turning around and shielding his eyes with his hands like we were going to play hide-and-seek.

"Well, Zack, it's what happens to girls when they walk around in wet bathing suits. And we all know you're no stranger to fungus," she said. She turned around, ripped off her bathing suit, and put on her underwear and bra. I wrapped the towel under my arms, tucking it in on itself so it wouldn't fall off, and slid my wet bathing suit off under it.

"You're never going to let me forget about that, are you?" Zack asked.

"Nope," Jules said, laughing as she hopped into her jeans.

"You know, that was over a year ago, and the doctor said it was perfectly—" he said, turning around. "Normal." We made eye contact. Jules was facing away. I watched his gaze travel from my discarded bathing suit to my bare shoulders. When our eyes met again, his were soft, pleading. A blue flame burned in my chest, but I signaled for him to turn around. He did. I let my towel fall, stepped into my shorts, and grabbed my T-shirt.

"There's something else you should know," Jules said, pulling her shirt over her head, "since we're on the subject of ugly truths and you've decided to care. Dad is proposing to Jennifer."

I froze. I really had been the only one she'd told. Zack turned around.

"What? Are you serious?"

"I found an engagement ring," Jules said. "It wasn't Mom's."

Twenty-seven

THE THREE OF US WALKED BACK TOWARD TOWN ON CLIFF Road. It was empty and quiet. The houses were still with sleep, and the darkness was weightless and unthreatening. The cool air held the smells of the daytime: beach roses, sandy towels, and sun-warmed pavement. I couldn't hear the ocean, but I could sense it, close by, lulling the island. It was the nighttime of dreaming children. The only sounds were our footsteps as we walked in the middle of the street. Jules and I drank from our thermoses. Zack took swigs from a bottle of vodka that Jules had brought as backup.

"I thought he was just 'getting back out there,'" Zack said.

"Me, too," Jules said.

"She's too young," Zack said.

"She's too stupid," Jules said.

"She has cats," Zack said.

"She's never been out of the country," Jules said.

"She's Republican," Zack said.

"She's not even funny," Jules said.

"She doesn't even like us," Zack said.

"What will happen to Mom's stuff?" Jules asked.

"Will she want to have kids?" Zack asked.

"It hasn't happened yet," I said, stopping this runaway train of thought. "He might not do it. Your dad is a good man. A smart man. He married your mom."

Over the next stretch of road, we walked again in silence. Jules walked ahead. She had gallantly offered to carry our wet towels and suits, and the damp canvas bag bumped against her hip. Zack hung back near me. A car sped by, and he changed places with me so that he was walking closer to the road. Our pinkie fingers brushed and my pulse jumped. Two steps later, our shoulders touched. My cheeks burned so that the air felt cold. His palm crossed mine, and the shock of it nearly transformed me into an electrical impulse, one that could travel on telephone wires. When Zack held my hand, I gasped with pleasure.

I brought the thermos to my mouth and drank until I was dizzy with Campari and confusion as Zack and I ran our thumbs over each other's knuckles. We swayed as we walked. I knew I needed to let go of him, and that he couldn't just show up and hold my hand after the distance he'd put between us, but instead I held his hand tighter. I told myself I would allow myself ten more seconds of touching him. I counted slowly, savoring each second. *One one thousand, two one thousand, three one thousand. . . .* I was at seven when Jules called, "Do you guys smell that?" Zack and I dropped our hands.

The delicious smell was coming from Something Natural sandwich shop. The ghost of homemade bread hovered in the air and beckoned us into its driveway. My mouth was actually watering.

"Wait, they're not open. What're we doing?" I asked as we walked closer, realizing that my words weren't coming out right. I couldn't quite catch up to my thoughts. "Uh, I think I'm drunk." I giggled, plucked a hydrangea blossom from a bush, and tucked it behind my ear.

"Yes," Jules said, laughing as we locked arms and tripped closer to the building. "You are!"

"I need a picture of this," Zack said, turning on his camera phone, but not before dropping it on the ground; he picked it up and fumbled with the buttons. He was even drunker than I was. "I need a video."

"Why?" I asked, leaning toward him.

"So when we're old we can remember we were kids once," he said.

I tilted my head back and breathed in the night. "Look at the sky," I said, arms extended, walking in an uneven circle. I just knew at that moment that Nina was with us. She was watching us and wanting us to be together. Jules and me as best friends. Zack and me as a couple. Together, our own kind of family.

"This is us," Zack said, holding the camera away so that it was facing us, and we were in the frame together. He put an arm around me, and I tilted my head so that it was resting on his shoulder. He turned to face me. Our lips brushed in an almost-kiss. Then he tilted the camera to the sky. "And this is the middle of the night." He turned the camera back on us. "This is us in the middle of the night."

"Give me the camera," Jules said. Zack handed it to her. "And put your arms around each other." We did. "You guys look so happy it's not even funny." She handed the camera back to Zack. "And I'm so hungry! I'm so hungry I could faint!" She sat on the ground.

"Poor Jules," I said to the camera. "She's so hungry."

"And drunk," she said. "I'm very, very drunk."

"Me, too!" I said. "I, Cricket Thompson, am so very drunk."

"You know what I need?" Jules said.

"What do you need?" I answered. "I'll get you anything you need!"

"I need a sandwich!" she said, rolling onto her stomach. "I need a sandwich like I've never needed anything before in my whole life. Turkey and avocado. Oh, and cheddar. On Portuguese bread."

"Then a sandwich you shall have!" I said.

"But they're not open," Jules said, waving a finger. "I checked."

"But there's an open window," I said. "If I stand on your back, I bet I could climb inside."

"Look what happens to the angel with some Campari in her," Zack said, staggering behind me with the camera.

"I've got the devil in me, too," I said.

"Oh, yeah, Miss Brown Lacrosse Player?" Zack asked.

"Don't remind me about lacrosse. I haven't practiced lacrosse in, like, weeks," I said. "Now, do you want a sandwich, too? Give me your order. I'm an expert!"

"Roast beef!" Zack proclaimed. "With mustard and lettuce and tomato."

"That sounds good. We want roast-beef sandwiches," Jules said, stumbling to a standing position and then squatting by the open window. "Climb aboard, birthday girl."

"Sandwich party!" I said.

"Don't forget the Portuguese bread!"

Was I really going to do this? To climb on Jules's back, through an open window, and make sandwiches? Yes, I was. I'd missed out on my senior-year fun. This was one of the best things about Nantucket. It can make you feel so separate, so out to sea. Untouchable. For the first time ever, I felt like one of the people who belonged here. That was how the Claytons had made me feel before Nina died, that I had a place in the world. It was right next to them.

We were all laughing as I hoisted my body through the

window. "I'm in!" I called as I landed on a countertop. I lowered myself into the kitchen sink. I tried to orient myself as my feet found the floor. I knocked into a dishwasher and felt around until I located a light switch and turned it on. Digging out my tip money from my pocket, I pulled two twenty-dollar bills and put them on the counter. That would more than cover the cost of three sandwiches. I smiled, imagining the staff wondering about where that money had come from. Then I took a few extra bucks and stuck them in the tip jar, because we food-service workers needed to help each other out. There was a knock on the door, and I made my way out of the back room and into the front, expecting to see Zack and Jules waiting for me.

"Coming!" I called. I saw an apron hanging up with the Something Natural insignia on it and thought it would be a nice touch to answer the door with it on. Then I saw a box of latex gloves and giggled to myself, thinking how this would really complete the outfit. But when I opened the door, it wasn't Jules and Zack standing on the other side. It was the cops.

Twenty-eight

"OH," I SAID TO THE TWO YOUNG, GOOD-LOOKING OFFICERS. "I was just going to make a sandwich." They looked like people I'd grown up with, just a little older, like someone's big brother and maybe a cousin from New Hampshire. So in the first few seconds after I opened the door, I wasn't that nervous, just surprised. They knew I was a good person, the kind of person who obeyed the rules 99.9 percent of the time, right? Everyone knew that.

I mean, I knew I wasn't *supposed* to be inside of Something Natural, but it didn't feel like I was doing something wrong, either. I had left forty dollars on the counter and a tip in the jar, even though I was my own server. In fact, there was something that felt right about being in Something Natural in the middle of the night. I loved this place. I knew my way around a kitchen. I was planning on cleaning up afterward.

And all that Campari didn't feel like a bad thing, either. It had given me energy and off-kilter bravery. It had pushed glitter through my bloodstream, and, like a liquid magnet, it had brought Jules and Zack and me together again. For the past few hours, the world was a party to which I'd finally been invited.

But the stern eyes and straight mouths of the officers clarified the situation. I took in their heavy shoes and their big, bright flashlights and my good feeling went away. So I tried to explain again, but my tongue felt slow and sticky. I couldn't get my words to come out right no matter how hard I concentrated.

When the blond officer asked me to step outside and began to read me my rights, while the other went into Something Natural to "check for damages," I was so surprised, so scared, so turned upside down that I vomited right into one of the hydrangea bushes from which just a half hour earlier I had plucked a blossom.

Jules and I were arrested and taken to the police station, where we were fingerprinted and had our pictures taken. We were both charged with underage drinking, but I was also charged with the more serious offense of breaking and entering. It was a misdemeanor, the officer said. *A misdemeanor.* I didn't know what the word meant, but it scared me past the point of crying. I was going to throw up again.

The officer must've seen my color change, because he asked if I needed the bathroom. I nodded, clamping my hands over my mouth, certain now I was going to vomit. He let Jules accompany me while I ran down the hallway, barged into a stall, and hung my head over the toilet as the Campari rose again in a burning, acidic wave. Afterward, I sat on the closed toilet seat, shaking. Jules dampened a paper towel and held it to my head.

"It's going to be okay," she said.

"What happened to Zack?" I asked, wiping away a tear.

Jules whispered that she'd given Zack the thermoses and the bottle of vodka and told him to run. She didn't want to get charged with possession of alcohol or open-container violations. He was drunker than both of us combined. "There was no need for the three of us to go down. He's either at home or passed out in the bushes somewhere." She pressed the paper towel to my clammy forehead.

When we returned from the bathroom, the bail commissioner was there, and because I had my tips in my pocket, I was able to pay our bail amounts, which were forty dollars each. He told us that we needed to appear in court a week later and we signed forms promising that we would.

"If I were you," the bail commissioner said, a meaty finger pointed right at my heart, "I'd get a lawyer."

"Why didn't you run away when Zack did?" I asked later that night in Jules's bedroom. It was my first time in her Nantucket bedroom, which was a lot smaller than her Providence one, with one single bed, a small desk, and one window. There was evidence of Nina in the rug, the mosaic of family Polaroids arranged like a quilt, and the high-quality sheets. Neither Jules nor I wanted to sleep alone, so she lent me a T-shirt and pajama bottoms and we arranged ourselves head to toe in her single, iron-framed bed. We still didn't know where Zack was, but at least he hadn't been arrested.

"I couldn't leave you alone," she said as she handed me one of the pillows from behind her head. "I got you drunk."

"You didn't exactly force it down my throat. You didn't make me drink." I thought of the heat and excitement of Zack's hand passing over mine, how it had almost been too much happiness, how I'd swallowed the Campari in gulps.

"This is going to sound kind of crazy," Jules said, lying back and staring at the ceiling. Her feet, in socks with little Santa Clauses on them, were next to my face.

"What?"

"I could feel Mom there." She was whispering, even though we were the only two people in the house. "It was like I just knew she wanted me to . . ."

"What?" I felt her breathing next to me.

"Stay with you." She exhaled. Silence enclosed us like a canopy of trees. We stepped into its cool, leafy darkness.

After a few minutes I said, "You know that picture you gave me? Of your mom when she graduated from Brown?"

"Yeah?"

"On the back it has a list, a life list, of things she wanted to do."

"It does?"

"I think she must've written it right after she graduated.

She lists five things. And one of them is about drinking Campari with Alison in Italy."

"So that's why you brought Campari," Jules said, lifting herself onto her elbows.

"Yes."

"What else is on this list?" Jules asked, sitting up and drawing her knees into her chest. She looked like she was about seven years old as she tilted her head and bit her lower lip. I knew it had been wrong to keep the list from her.

"Let's see," I said, sitting up. "Well, the first one is *Visit the Rodin Museum in Paris.*"

"She definitely did that, like, ten times. What else?"

"The second one is *Learn to drive and then drive Route 1 to Big Sur.*"

"She did that when she was pregnant with me."

"And then there's *Drink Campari on the Amalfi Coast with Alison.*"

"What else?" Jules asked.

"She wanted to be in a Woody Allen movie," I said.

"I wonder if she ever was."

"It's checked off," I said and shrugged. "So she must've been."

"Wait a second." Jules drummed on the coverlet. "She told me about this. I'd forgotten. She was cast as an extra, but she wasn't in the movie."

"Which movie was it?"

Jules covered her mouth with both hands. "Oh, Cricket, you don't want to know."

"I do." I kicked her under the covers. "I really, really do."

"I'm sorry, I can't tell you. Not right now." She was trying not to laugh.

"Jules, what was it?" I asked, grabbing her feet, holding her toes hostage.

"It was—" Jules began, but she couldn't finish, because she was laughing too hard, snorting and crying, the works.

"What?" I asked, as serious as she was ridiculous.

"It was . . . *Crimes and Misdemeanors.*"

"No," I said, shaking my head. "This can't be what she meant."

"Cricket!" Jules was laughing so hard she was wheezing. "We got arrested."

"They put us in the patrol car and we got fingerprinted," I said, and I started laughing, too.

"We had mug shots taken," she said. "We're outlaws."

"We've committed crimes and misdemeanors," I said. We were crying and laughing and laughing and crying.

"I'm crimes and you're misdemeanors," Jules said as we clutched our stomachs. We fell off the bed we were laughing so hard. We rolled around on the rug, tears streaming down our faces. We crawled to the bathroom so we wouldn't wet our pants. We were releasing the tension of the day, of the night, of the whole year. We laughed until we were so exhausted that we were communicating exclusively in grunts and giggles and sighs, until we finally fell asleep, her Santa Claus feet in my face. I never did get to tell her about the last thing on Nina's list.

Twenty-nine

I WASN'T LAUGHING WHEN I WOKE UP AFTER ONLY A FEW hours of sleep. For a moment, I thought maybe it had all been a dream, or a nightmare, but when I realized I was wearing Jules's Rosewood Basketball T-shirt, when I felt my head pounding and saw the ink on my fingertip, I knew it had actually happened. I had been arrested for breaking and entering and underage drinking. Jules was still asleep. I tiptoed through the rest of the house, looking for Zack. When I opened the door to what had to be his room, he wasn't there. I checked my phone to see if I had any texts from him. There was the one he'd sent last night. The picture of the two of us. The moment came back to me. I typed out a text: I love us in the middle of the night. My finger hovered over the send button for a moment before I hit it, and listened to it whoosh away from me.

"What happened to you?" Liz asked when I showed up back at the inn. She made us a pot of coffee and I told her the story. I told her everything, the details coming back to me in startling, crisp detail as I recounted the night: the skinny-dipping, climbing through the window, vomiting on the hydrangeas.

"Jules is horrible!"

"It wasn't her fault," I said. "I got drunk all on my own. It was my idea to make the sandwiches." When I described the officers, she knew exactly whom I was talking about. She said that the blond one in particular was on a personal mission to crack down on the summer kids. All traces of Liz's depression seemed to vanish as she went into crisis mode. She made me an omelet and wrote a list of what I needed to do. It was Liz's idea to call Paul Morgan, the lawyer who was my mom's friend. I still had his card in my wallet.

"It's very early for a social call," he said when he answered my call at eight a.m.

"It's an emergency," I said.

"A legal one?"

"Yes," I said, choking back tears. "Yes."

"Come over in an hour."

It was also Liz's idea that I write a letter of apology to the owners of Something Natural. She knew them from spending the winter on Nantucket and would personally deliver the letter to them. "Stuart and Jill are reasonable people," she said. "And they'll appreciate a note." She also said that I needed to talk to Karla as soon as possible. If I could get to her before my name showed up in the police blotter, I might have a chance of keeping my job.

"My job," I said, shutting my eyes and shaking my head, realizing that if I got fired, I'd lose my opportunity to live in the dorms next year. I was several thousand dollars short of my goal. Jim had been very clear that I needed to have all eight thousand for him to match my earnings. I felt a sharp, shooting pain in my side. I'd have to explain to Jim and Rosemary what had happened. I'd have to explain to everyone. I started crying all over again.

Liz led me from the inn's kitchen to the manager's apartment. She started a hot shower for me and laid out a fluffy clean towel, my best skirt, and a blouse that she herself had ironed within a starched inch of its life. She blew out my hair and applied a tasteful amount of makeup. She helped me compose a letter to the owners of Something Natural, and by that I mean she dictated it to me.

"I sincerely regret having crawled through the window of my most favorite sandwich shop, thereby violating not only you, but also the sacred trust that exists among neighbors on Nantucket," she began. I was incapable of forming my own sentences, so I copied her words, hoping that her charming British inflection would somehow seep into the ink. When I'd finished the letter and she'd checked it for mistakes, we delivered it to their mailbox.

We drove to Paul Morgan's house on Orange Street. I was shaking as we approached his door. "I'm so scared," I said.

"Come on now," Liz said. She rapped with the shell-shaped knocker with confidence and placed an arm around my waist. "Just stand up straight and tell him exactly what happened."

Paul answered the door, looking freshly showered and grave. He led me into his living room and gestured to the sofa. Liz sat next to me and took my hand as I explained what happened. Paul took notes on a yellow legal pad. I sweated through my blouse in several places.

"I screwed up," I said, my voice shaking. "But I swear I didn't mean it. I paid for the sandwiches. I even left a tip in the jar. Not that that excuses anything, but . . ." I dissolved into tears.

"Calm down," he said. "Take a breath and walk me through the whole thing." He crossed his long legs and listened as I told the story.

"Breaking and entering is no joke," he said, when I finished the sordid tale. "And neither is underage drinking."

"I know," I said, wiping my tears. "It was the first time in my life that I've been drunk. I'm so ashamed."

"Take it easy. I'll defend you," he said. "When do we go in front of the judge?'

"Tomorrow," I sobbed. "I have almost four thousand dollars. Will that be enough for your fees?"

"Honey, I'm not going to charge you. And hey, do you

have any idea how many kids this happens to every summer?" He handed me an actual cloth handkerchief.

"How many?" I asked. "Tell me."

"Many," he said. "I'm not saying that what you did wasn't very serious. I'm not saying that it's in any way excusable. But we're going to do the best we can. There have been presidents of the United States who've done far worse than climb through the window of a sandwich shop."

"Thank you," I said, throwing my arms around him. "Thank you so much."

"Okay, kiddo. Take a deep breath."

"Are you going to tell my mother?" I asked, ending the one-sided hug and taking a short, sharp breath.

"I'm *your* lawyer," Paul said, pushing his Prada glasses up his straight, patrician nose. "This is between us."

I don't know that I'd ever loved anyone more than I did Paul at that moment.

"Karla? I've had an incident," I said thirty minutes later after Liz had marched me over to Breezes, insisting that I get this over with as soon as possible. Liz waited for me outside in the car. Karla was sitting at her desk, filling out purchase orders. I sat down in the cold, metal folding chair opposite her.

"What kind of incident?" she asked

"The kind you're going to read about in the police blotter," I said.

She dropped her pen and sighed. "Oh, Thompson." She shook her head. "Oh, boy. What happened?"

I recounted the story for the third time that day. The repetition was giving me a chance to find the narrative and tell it faster. I focused only on the salient details: a girl who'd never been drunk before does something really, really stupid and gets caught.

For the first time, I avoided tears, but Karla was not charmed. "What kind of an idiot breaks into Something Natural?"

I proceeded to beg and plead as I had never done before. I told her I was sorry. I told her I'd never even been drunk before and I didn't intend to be again anytime soon. I told her I'd written a letter of apology to the owners of Something Natural.

She rubbed her eyes. "I have to think about this."

I told her all that was at stake for me. I told her about Rosemary and Jim. I told her about having to live at home if I couldn't earn the money I'd promised. I told her how good I'd been at saving everything I'd earned. I pulled a crumpled bank deposit receipt from inside my wallet, smoothed it out, and passed it to her.

"I don't need to see that," she said.

"I'm different from the other summer kids. I work hard."

"We're all hard workers," she said, flicking the receipt back at me. "That doesn't make you special. It only means you meet the minimum qualification for the job."

I nodded, shoving the bank receipt in my pocket and my humiliation down deep. I stared intently at the wood grain of her desk, darkened by a new shade of shame. "I'll clean the cappuccino machine every night until . . . it shines like the top of the Chrysler Building." It wasn't until after I said that that I realized I was quoting *Annie*.

Karla sighed from some very tired place. "I said I'd think about it."

"When will you let me know?" I asked, licking my dehydrated lips.

"When I'm ready," she said, waving toward the door and giving me a look that said *get out of here.*

"I'll be ready when you are," I said with as much confidence as I could muster.

"How'd it go?" Liz asked when I walked back outside. It was a mercilessly beautiful summer day. The sky was royal blue. The birds sounded like they'd flown straight out of an animated movie and into my nightmare. "Did she fire you?"

"No," I said as I shut the car door and secured my seat belt. "But she didn't *not* fire me, either."

I glanced at my phone. Still no word from Zack. I texted him again: R U ok? Then I texted Jules: Is Zack ok?

"What are you going to do?" Liz asked. "What's the plan?"

"Show up anyway."

Thirty

I ARRIVED EARLY, IN A CLEAN SHIRT, PRESSED KHAKIS, AND full makeup to try to hide my hangover, which had not gone away by three o'clock as Liz had promised it would.

"Rough night?" Ben asked, as I went behind the bar to grab a Coke.

"You have no idea." Had I cheated on him last night when Zack and I held hands and almost kissed? I wasn't sure. Were Ben and I even going out?

"That's some serious concealer you've got going on." He tugged on my T-shirt. "You want to tell me about it in the fridge?"

"No!"

"Whoa." Ben lifted his hand and stepped back three paces.

"I'm sorry. It's just . . ." I stepped toward him and whispered, "I'm not even supposed to be here. I was arrested."

"What?" He furrowed his brow in concern. He leaned on the bar, listening, as I told him the short version. "I didn't know you had it in you."

"What's that supposed to mean?"

"Nothing bad. What were you drinking?"

"Campari and Sprite."

"Campari and Sprite? *Sprite?* Have I taught you nothing?" He reached for my hand.

"I can't." I sidestepped him without a smile as I saw Karla emerge from the kitchen.

Karla paused when she saw me, but seemed to accept my presence. The restaurant filled up fast, and she didn't send me home. It was the busiest night of the summer, and she wouldn't have made it through the shift short a waitress. I was a machine, working strong right up until closing, even on only a few hours of sleep. I was shaking with hunger and fatigue at the end of the shift. I was stained with coffee and wine and sweating through my T-shirt, but I stayed late and cleaned the cappuccino beast until it gleamed. Then I counted my tips and put them in the jar Karla kept on the bar for her charity, Operation Smile, all two hundred fifty dollars. It was a penance. I put my arms on the bar, laid my head down, and had a small moment of reprieve.

I didn't know Karla was watching until she gave my shoulder a rough squeeze and said, "Hope you have a backup shirt for tomorrow night's shift. The one you've got on is a mess."

"Thank you," I called as she walked back to the office, wiping tears of pure exhaustion from my cheeks. "Thank you so much."

It was then that I noticed a text from Jules. He's fine. He spent the night in Lily Park. Showed up around 11 today.

So he just wasn't going to text me back? After all that we had been through? After me getting arrested? I would've thrown my phone across the room, except I couldn't afford a new one.

The court date arrived quickly. Paul defended me, explained that this was a first-time offense, that I had a stellar academic record and numerous character references, and that it was the first time I'd ever been drunk in my life. He emphasized the fact that no windows had been broken and that I hadn't actually made any sandwiches. The police confirmed that not only had nothing gone missing or been broken, but also that I'd left forty dollars on the counter and a tip in the tip jar. I guessed that this and my letter had made an impression on the owners of Something Natural, because they decided not to press charges. I was required to stay out of trouble for six months and to write a composition about the dangers of alcohol abuse.

The judge dismissed both Jules's case and mine. I thanked Paul. I leapt into his arms and planted a lip-glossed kiss on his smooth, moisturized cheek. Jules and I walked out of the courtroom arm and arm, a pair of free women. Instead of the whole, heavy world, it was only the midday sun that rested on our shoulders.

Jules, Liz, and I went out for a celebratory lunch at the Brotherhood of Thieves. Liz felt this was the only appropriate place for a burger and fries. Whatever problems she had with Jules she had decided to put aside for the moment. Jules was in the middle of telling us the story of Zack's night spent sleeping in Lily Park and later being awakened by a group exploring Nanucket's natural flora when I interrupted.

"I texted him," I said. "Twice. He never texted me back."

"He's in deep shit right now," Jules said, shaking her head.

"We're the ones who got arrested," I reminded her.

"I saw what was going on between you two that night, by the way," Jules said.

"What do you mean?" I asked. She didn't look mad about it. She was smiling.

"Oh, come on, the hand-holding, the whispering, the kissing."

"The kissing?" Liz asked.

"We didn't kiss," I said. Jules cocked an eyebrow. "We brushed lips."

They burst out laughing. Jules slurped her Coke. Liz slapped the table.

I blushed. "What?"

"Brushed lips," Liz repeated and wiped her eyes. "That's

rich! Listen, I have a big surprise for your birthday. You must make sure you get the evening off."

"Oh, yeah! My birthday is next week. I'm going to be nineteen." After such a stressful few days, it was a relief to think of something as normal as a birthday.

"In a year you'll be 'in your twenties,'" Jules added with an ominous air as she squeezed one stripe of mustard and one stripe of ketchup down the length of one of my french fries.

"Don't act like we're that different. You're only three months younger than I am."

"Shut up, the pair of you," Liz said. "I'm twenty." She lowered her voice and nodded toward the bartender. "But don't tell Jack over there. He thinks I'm twenty-two."

"I can't believe you've already planned something for me, Liz," I said and rested my head on her shoulder.

"Course!" Liz said. "That's what friends do."

"Obviously I have your morning planned," Jules said, stealing another one of my fries. She'd ordered a salad instead of fries with her burger, but she clearly had no intention of touching it. "Because of our usual ritual. The one we've done for years now." Every year since we'd known each other, Jules and I had had waffles on our birthdays and brought out the stuffed pig, Lulu, whom we had co-adopted from FAO Schwarz on my one and only trip to New York with Jules and Nina in the eighth grade. Last year, Jules had tried to carry out the ritual, but she'd walked in on Zack in my bed. I was worried our birthday ritual had been ruined forever, so I felt a happy relief that she'd mentioned it. "But what do you want to do after that?" she asked.

"I think, after this whole mess, I just want to go the beach and have fun," I said with a sigh. "Good, clean, summer fun."

"Perfect. You two can come to the club!" Jules said. I noticed with surprise that she was including Liz, who had left her out of the evening invitation.

"You know I love those cabana boys in their polo shirts, but I have a business to run," Liz said. Her phone vibrated. "That's the inn phone now." Jules rolled her eyes, but luckily Liz didn't notice; she was back to her efficient, inn-running self, even if she did still get teary-eyed at the Samsung commercial with the guy who looked like Shane in it. She finished replying to a text and looked up. "My only request is that you're back at the inn by five for the surprise."

"I can do that, and I'd love to come to the beach club, Jules," I said. "Can I bring Ben?"

"Hells yeah. I wouldn't mind seeing him in his bathing suit," Jules said. She raised her Coke. "To good, clean, summer fun."

"I prefer a bit of dirt with my fun, but okay," Liz added, lifting her wineglass.

"To escaping the long arm of the law," I said, joining with my lemonade. And we all drank to that.

Thirty-one

ON MY BIRTHDAY, I WOKE UP EARLY TO THE CHIMING OF the bells from the gold-domed tower of the nearby church. Liz brought me, on a tray with a pitcher of cream, a piping hot cup of coffee, which I sipped on the hammock in the garden. The morning was balmy and sweet with the scent of freshly mowed grass and blooming gardens. The air hummed an August tune. Mom called to tell me the story of the day I was born. Dad called a few minutes later and sang "Happy Birthday" into the phone and promised a back-to-school shopping trip when I came home.

When each of them asked me how the summer was going, I felt a pinch of guilt replying, "Fine." I didn't tell either of them about getting arrested or about my day in court. It's not like they read the *Inquirer and Mirror*, and

Paul Morgan had sworn secrecy, so they were unlikely ever to find out. Everything had ended up just fine, so why not wait to tell them until I was much older and we could laugh about the whole thing? Right now it would only have needlessly worried and disappointed them.

Jules picked me up in her graduation Jeep with Lulu the stuffed pig in the backseat. We drove to the island airport, where Jules had promised they served the best breakfast on the island. We both ordered waffles, of course, and big bowls of cappuccino with extra foam, and guessed about the lives of the travelers coming and going with their rolling luggage and Vera Bradley bags. Jules covered Lulu's ears when she asked for a side of bacon. When our cappuccinos arrived, I luxuriated in the knowledge that I wouldn't have to clean the machine that produced them.

On our way back into town, my phone dinged with a text. It was Ben, wishing me a friendly "happy birthday!" and I texted back a friendly "thanks!" I was happy to hear from Ben, but at the same time, it reminded me that I hadn't heard from Zack and probably wouldn't. He hadn't texted me after I'd been arrested, so why would he contact me on my birthday?

"Hey, cheer up," Jules said as she parked in front of Needle and Thread, the fancy Main Street boutique where she worked. "We're going to go shopping. I'm going to let you use my employee discount."

"But I thought you'd get fired if you let your friends use your discount," I said.

"The boss is in New York," Jules said. "I'll just say I bought it for myself."

As soon as we stepped into the store, Jules started chatting up her coworker, Jennie. I spied a red bikini.

"What do you think?" I asked when I stepped out of the dressing room.

"Hot," Jules said.

"Red hot," Jennie echoed.

"It's actually kind of conservative," I said, turning around in front of the three-way mirror, noting its full coverage of boobs and butt and the innocent bows at the hips.

"But that's what makes it hot," Jules said. "It leaves something to the imagination. It's asking the world, *Good girl or bad girl?*" She stood behind me, took out my ponytail, and shook my hair over my shoulders.

"Girls can be both," I said.

"Of course. We women are very complex."

"Guys are, too," I said, thinking of Zack, so sweet one day and so harsh the next.

"Yes, humankind is full of contradictions. We could write a thesis, but I'd rather go to the beach," Jules said. "So I'm buying you this red bikini."

"Jules, are you sure?" I asked.

But she had already clipped the tags and was whispering with Jennie at the cash register.

"You girls want to sit next to Zack and Parker, right?" the cabana boy asked when Jules and I made our way down the boardwalk, she in Nina's black bathing suit and I in my brand-new red bikini. He picked up two blue recliners and nodded to the left. "They're right there."

I shook my head.

"Actually, I think we'll sit over there," Jules said, pointing to the opposite end of the beach. "As far away as possible."

"You invited Parker?" I asked Jules. The sand was soft and deep and still morning-cool as we walked down the beach, the cabana boy trailing a few feet behind us with our chairs. "On my birthday?"

"She belongs here," Jules said under her breath. "I can't tell her not to come here. Her family practically owns this place. Even on your birthday."

"Oh." She had a point. I looked over my shoulder. Parker was stretched on a recliner in an aquamarine cover-up that looked expensive even from here; one leg dangled as she read a magazine. Zack was sitting next to her in the sand on his Tropicana towel, reading a book. What was he reading? What was he thinking? Did he remember it was my birthday? Did he know we were coming?

Jules thanked the cabana boy as he set up our chairs, then turned to me. "Besides, what do you care that she's here? You look amazing." She flapped her hand at me. "Text your bartender. Tell him to join us."

"Okay." I sent Ben a text. I looked back up at Jules and felt a wave of affection. She was back. My best friend was really back. Ben replied immediately. "He'll be here in an hour," I said.

As usual, Jules and I couldn't sit still for long. After about ten minutes of sunbathing, we started tossing the Frisbee. When that became boring, we challenged ourselves to take a step back with every successful connection. Then we had to incorporate a funny dance into either the catch or the release. We switched it up to see how deep we could go in the water and still complete the pass. This was one of the things I loved best about Jules. She was always in motion. Wearing Nina's black bikini, she looked like her mother, but only in repose. She moved like her own girl.

I caught Zack staring in our direction a few times, but every time I returned his glances, he looked away. Ben arrived. "Look at you!" he said when he saw me in my new suit. He joined in our Frisbee game, and Zack started openly staring. And then, when we were playing Monkey in the Middle and Ben tackled me, Zack actually came over. Parker followed, arms crossed as her aquamarine cover-up billowed out behind her in the breeze.

"Are you guys going to play?" Jules asked.

"I am," Zack said, taking off his T-shirt. His body. So familiar. Mine, I thought.

"I'm just going to watch," Parker said in her husky, party-girl voice. Now that she was in front of me, I noticed she didn't look so good. Her Grecian-style cover-up made her elegant from a distance, but up close, something was off. There was a hollowness in her eyes, a sallowness to her skin. It looked like she needed protein, a cheeseburger, maybe. Or at least some blush. But who needed blush on a perfect summer day?

"So what are we playing?" Zack asked.

"Frisbee football," Jules said. "You see where that seaweed is? That's one end zone. And the other one is over here." She jogged down the beach away from kids, babies, and fancy people under umbrellas, and drew a line in the sand by dragging her heel, placing a piece of driftwood at one end and a bunch of seaweed at the other. "It's me and Zack versus Cricket and Ben."

"This is like Ultimate," Ben said.

"Basically," Jules said, "but tackling is allowed."

"Hee-haw!" Ben said.

"We're on the same team," I reminded him.

"Oh, yeah," Ben said.

"Are we going to let the birthday girl win?" Zack asked. So he did remember.

"No way," I said. "Play your heart out."

"So you can pivot but not run with the disk," Jules said. "If it gets intercepted or you don't complete the pass, it goes to the other team. The first team to get three points wins. Cricket, since it is your birthday, you get the first pass. Zack, if you let me down, your ass is grass."

"Shut up, Jules," Zack said, and tossed the disk to me, fast, hard, and direct, and I caught it with one hand.

"Damn," Ben muttered under his breath. "Girl can catch."

"Girl can also throw," I said with a smile as we backtracked to our end zone. "Go long." I released the disk in a perfect, sailing arc. Ben leapt into the air and caught it. Jules tried to guard him, but Ben was agile, and with one sharp pivot, he tossed it back to me. Zack was all over me, but wasn't taking advantage of the tackle rule.

"Go, Zack," Parker called from the sidelines.

I saw Ben was in the zone, so I tried a skip shot, and sure enough, it briefly touched the ground and bounced. Ben caught it, raised it over his head, and whopped.

"One–zip," I called.

Jules and Zack conferenced before they mounted their counterattack.

"Come on Zacky," Parker called as she clapped.

My stomach flipped. Zacky. Bleccch!

Jules and Zack advanced toward us in a series of short passes, but I intercepted one and tossed it to Ben, who pivoted and tossed it back to me, and we scored again. It was almost too easy.

"It's not looking good, guys," I said, a little breathless as I passed the disk to Jules.

"But you are," Ben said, bumping hips with me. Zack looked like he was going to be sick.

"Time out," Jules said. "Zack, get your ass over here." That was the other thing I loved about Jules. She was seriously competitive. Ben and I drifted toward the water for our own little huddle.

"You're good," Ben said, and took a quick dunk. As he stood up again, the water slid down his body.

"I've been trying to tell you," I said, wading into the water with him.

"Tell me what?" he asked, pulling me toward him for a kiss.

"I'm a lot better at sports than I am at waitressing." We kissed, lightly, tastefully.

"Let's do this," Zack said, clapping his hands.

"I want to play now," Parker said, stepping out of her gossamer cover-up. Her horse-jumping legs didn't seem as rock-strong as usual. She was thinner than I remembered.

"We can't have three against two," Jules said.

"We can handle it," Ben said.

"Yeah, bring it on," I said.

"Okay, then," Jules called. "You cocky bastards."

"The literary term is *hubris*," Zack added.

"Call it whatever you want. We just say 'kicking ass,'" Ben said.

Zack whispered something to Jules and she nodded. Then she flung the disk way out into the Nantucket Sound. I could barely see it.

"What the hell?" Parker asked as Zack started swimming for it, a little leisurely, I thought.

"What are you waiting for?" Jules asked me. "That bikini is made to move."

I dove into the sound and swam hard. Zack was now doing the backstroke, so it wasn't hard to gain on him. Besides, the current was pushing the disk in my direction. I was actually going to beat him to it if he didn't pick up the pace. He was practically treading water.

"Cricket," he said, as we grabbed the disk at the same time. I was completely out of breath. "Put your feet down. We're at the sandbar."

I touched the soft sand with my feet. I knew my face was bright red with exertion. I coughed up some water and gave myself a chance to catch my breath. I was about to jerk that disk from his hand and turn back to shore when he yanked it from my hand instead. He pushed it underwater and stood on it.

"What are you doing?"

"I wanted to talk to you. Alone." He looked back at the shore, where Parker, Jules, and Ben were watching us.

"How are you?" he asked quietly.

"I'm okay," I said in disbelief. "I mean, besides the fact that I was arrested and had to go to court."

"You must've been so scared," Zack said, touching my arm underwater.

"What are you doing out there?" Parker called from the shore.

"We're looking for it!" Zack called back.

"I'll help you," Parker said.

"I was so scared," I searched his green eyes. "I texted you."

"I know," he said, taking my hand. Parker was swimming toward us, fast. "I couldn't text you back, but I wanted to tell you how much that night meant to me. I know we were drunk and you got arrested, but other than that, I loved it."

"Other than that," I said, laughing. His eyes softened. *He'd said "love."*

"Happy birthday, Cricket," he said, squeezing my hand. "I'm trying to be a good person right now. I'm trying to do the right thing. You have to trust me."

"What are you talking about?" I asked.

"Do you love that guy?" he asked.

"I don't know. Do you love her?" I hated that we were tossing *that word* around like the Frisbee he was currently standing on. We'd only used *that word* when we truly meant it.

"I'm protecting her," he said. "I owe it to her."

"But you don't owe anything to me?"

Parker popped up. "What's taking you guys so long?"

Zack and I held each other's gaze for another breath. There would be no high five, part three. Ever. I dove under, freed the disk, and held it up high. "Found it," I said, loud enough so they could all hear me.

"Frisbees don't sink," Parker was saying as I started back. The salt water disguised my tears as I swam back to where I could throw it to Ben. I was ready to win this game and get out of here.

Thirty-two

AFTER OUR 3–0 FRISBEE FOOTBALL VICTORY, AFTER I'D thanked Jules with a big hug and politely said good-bye to Zack and Parker in the name of sportsmanship, Ben and I left the club holding hands. He said he wanted to take me somewhere. He had to be back at Sadie's in time to change and get to work, but when he glanced at his watch, he said, "That gives us plenty of time." I was in my wet bathing suit, a towel around my waist, when Ben told me to take the driver's seat. I followed his directions out of town to a remote part of the island, down a quiet road. Ben told me that we only had access because Sadie had a special permit as a trustee of the Wildlife Refuge. I drove the whole way, only stalling once. Ben took over when it came to driving on the actual beach. There was hardly anyone out here except for a few fishermen thigh-deep in the gentle, foaming surf.

We parked near a dune, and Ben pulled out a blanket and a cooler from the back of the Land Rover. Then he took my hand and led me over the hill of sand to the perfect hiding spot. We were surrounded by dunes on all sides. He smiled up at me as he spread the blanket out, and I realized he'd brought me there to have sex.

So far, we'd had all of these external obstacles that made sex logistically difficult. I wasn't about to take him back to the apartment with heartbroken Liz, and he wasn't going to invite me to spend the night on his grandmother's sofa. We couldn't even exchange longing glances at work without risking our jobs. The Land Rover had been our make-out mobile, but even that had its limitations. The seats didn't recline, and the backseat was boxy and too short in both directions. But that had been okay with me. I liked how if we tried to recline all the way, we'd bump our heads or jam our knees. I liked the obstacles.

But here, in this warm white valley of sand, with the sun burning above us and the lulling waves so close, there were no obstacles, unless you counted the eelgrass, the wild beach roses fretting in the breeze, or the solitary cloud that lay haphazardly at the bottom of the sky. As I joined him on the cool cotton blanket and he gallantly removed my TOMS one by one, I felt myself shaking. I needed to tell him up front how I was feeling.

"I'm not ready to have sex," I blurted out.

"That's okay," he said. "That's not why I brought you here."

"Oh, come on," I said, joke hitting him. "The blanket?"

He laughed a little. "Can't blame a guy for trying, can you?" He pulled a flask from the little cooler.

"What's that?" I asked.

"A Bicyclette. Every girl should have a drink. And a Bicyclette is yours, I think. It's refreshing, spunky, and a little surprising. It's Italian white wine and your favorite, Campari."

"Don't say the C-word!" I said, my mouth cottoning at the thought. He threw back his head in a laugh, and I noticed the place where the top of his chest met the hollow of his throat. I wondered what it would be like to have sex with him. I had only ever had sex with Zack. I had only loved Zack.

Maybe I still did love him, I thought, remembering what it had been like to hold his hand the night we'd gotten in trouble, and how as soon as our fingers interlaced the world had clicked into place. I thought of what it had been like to be face to face with him on the sandbar earlier, how I could've sworn I still saw love in his green, LASIKed eyes. But no. I remembered what it had felt like when he didn't text me back after the scariest moment of my life. That had felt like a punch. Love wasn't supposed to feel like that.

"Are you sure I can't tempt you?" Ben asked and uncapped the frosty metal container. "The Campari and wine work together to create a new flavor, and it whets your appetite. Come on, it's *your* drink."

"I'm on probation."

"One sip," he said, inching closer.

"I guess if it's my drink, I should at least try it. One sip." I brought the cold flask to my lips and drank. Ben was right. It was refreshing, bright, almost startling, but it also had that familiar Campari aftertaste and my stomach clenched.

"Too soon?" he asked.

"How can something so pretty be so bitter?"

"I brought iced tea, too," he said, and handed me a Nantucket Nectars.

"Yum," I said, guzzling the sweet drink. He took a long swallow from his drink. Then he touched the cold flask to my shoulder. "You're burning up. Take this." He unbuttoned his white shirt, took it off, and handed it to me.

"Now you'll burn."

"No, I won't." Ben was one of those people with skin that caramelized in the sun.

I put on his shirt. It was soft and worn.

"So what's the story with that kid?" Ben asked, leaning on an elbow.

"What kid?"

"You know who," he said, smiling, one hand spidering my kneecap.

"Oh. Zack. We used to . . ."—I paused, held my breath, and considered—"go out."

"I could tell," Ben said, but he didn't sound jealous. He tilted his head, his eyes asking for more information. I had to look away.

"It's over now." I lay back, folded my arms behind my head, closed my eyes. "Just so you know."

"It's okay, you know. I don't expect you not to have ex-boyfriends." I knew this was meant in a nice way, but I couldn't help feeling that it was really unromantic.

"What about you? What about Amelia?"

"What do you want to know?" I heard the metal cap hit the flask. I shaded my eyes and peered up. He tilted his head back for a quick drink.

"Just normal, basic stuff. Like, how old is she?"

"Twenty-seven."

"Twenty-seven?" I sat up on my elbows.

"Twenty-seven."

"That's old! I'm nineteen! Today!"

"I know. But twenty-seven is only eight years away."

"Well, eight years ago I was eleven," I pointed out. "So it's old."

"Not really." He laughed. "Anyway, she's a lawyer."

"A *lawyer*?" I turned onto my stomach and ran through a quick catalogue in my mind of all the lawyers I knew. Arti's dad was a lawyer. He had a big Mercedes, a comb-over, and bad breath. My aunt Phyllis was a lawyer for criminals. She was always working. Her hair had turned gray early and Mom said it was because her job stressed her out so much. I thought of the lawyers on TV, dazzling judges and juries with their quick tongues. "Like in a courtroom with a judge? Or in an office with a desk?"

"She doesn't actually have a job yet, but she passed the

bar. Anyway, it's over now. Just so you know." He ran a hand down the back of my leg and back up again. I shivered with pleasure. His touch was so light I wasn't entirely sure he was making contact. I stayed really still, hoping he would press a little harder. "The past is the past, you know? That's why I'm glad to make a fresh start."

"So, are you really not moving back to Brooklyn?"

"That's right," he said, and his hand moved to the other leg. "Do you want to go for a swim?"

"Not really." Although I would've said it was impossible, his touch became even lighter as his hand drifted farther up, to the very tops of my thighs, and then, just when I was getting used to it, to the backs of my knees. I dug my toes into the sand.

"Do you want to practice driving again?" he asked.

"Maybe later," I said. His hand was approaching and pulling away and approaching and pulling away. He was tracing, retreating. I wanted to keep the conversation going so he wouldn't stop. "So, if you aren't going back to Brooklyn, where are you going to go?"

"Maybe I'll stay here," he said.

"I think that would be really lonely. Anyplace else?" I rested my cheek on my forearm and breathed in the smell of herbs and spices. The sun warmed my back. My heart beat against the blanket. There was some sort of magnet in his fingertips, because all of my protons, neutrons, and electrons had sparked awake and were following his lead.

"Maybe I'll go to California," he said. "For the surfing. Can you tell what I'm writing?" he asked.

"No."

"I'm writing a message on your leg." I heard the flask open, and the next time his finger touched me, it was cold. "Concentrate." He started on my inner ankle and traveled up to the back of my knee.

Please make this be a long message, I thought, as he continued up my thigh.

"Did you get it?"

"Nope. Try again."

"Okay, I'm going to go bigger and more slowly and in cursive."

"Good idea."

He traced his message again, and my entire body buzzed as he reached the bottom of my bathing suit in what I think was an exclamation point.

"Oh my god," I said, looking up at him, clutching the blanket.

"What? You got it."

"Touch me! Right now!"

He slid his hand inside my bikini and moments later the whole world fractured into color and light, like a kaleidoscope, like all wishes granted at the same time. I rested my head on the sand and heard the heartbeat of the whole world. Or maybe it was just mine. I sighed, laughed, and blinked into the lowering sun.

Thirty-three

"LIZ!" I BURST THROUGH THE DOOR OF THE INN. "LIZ Baxter, where are you?"

"Hiya. Just the girl I'm looking for," Liz said, peeking out from her little reservations closet. "Your surprise is in the kitchen."

"Wait, I need to tell you something." I motioned for her to follow me into the laundry room. "Something's happened to me!"

"It's not another arrest, I hope," Liz said. I shook my head. She wrinkled her nose and leaned closer. "You need a shower, darling. You're a hot mess."

"Yes," I said, taking her hands. "I am a hot mess. Something's happened to me. Something big."

"You did it with the bartender?"

"No," I said. "But it's, um, along those lines. We drove out to some dunes, and. . . ." I fanned myself with my hand and giggled.

"Darling." Her face brightened as she balanced the laundry basket on her hip. "Did he blow your whistle?"

I wasn't exactly sure what she meant. "I think, maybe."

"If he had, you'd know," she said, patting my arm.

"Wait! Then I think he did." I bit my lip.

"So he spun your top, did he? He sounded the alarm? Flipped the switch?"

"Um . . ."

"Did you see the light, darling?"

"Yes!" I jumped. "Yes, I did!"

"Wonderful!"

"It's so wonderful." I leaned against the wall.

"Now, I must warn you." She took hold of my shoulders. "Your body is currently emitting bonding hormones. You mustn't pay too much attention to them. It's just biology. He is not God's gift, no matter what your hormones are telling you. You must promise me that you understand this."

"I can't promise anything." I giggled, sliding down the wall.

"Shall we go tell George?"

"What? George is here?"

"That's my big surprise," she said. "George Gust is in the kitchen."

"George!" I hadn't seen him since last summer, since his book had been published (with my name in it).

"And we have a reservation at Black-Eyed Susan's. Come on, let's tell him."

"Liz, don't you dare."

"But it's such delightful news," she said, laughing her loudest laugh. "I'm sure he'll be very happy for you."

"Liz," I said, showing my most serious face as she hoisted me up. "No."

"George!" Liz said, dragging me into the kitchen. "Here she is!"

"Hi!" I said. In his black T-shirt, faded jeans, and sneakers, George Gust looked almost identical to the way he had the first time I'd met him in this very kitchen and discovered him eating my sandwich, even though he was now a *New York Times* best-selling author.

"Cricket Thompson, faithful intern and birthday girl! I was starting to worry you weren't going to come!"

"Oh, she came!" Liz said, beaming. "She came, George!" My cheeks burned from my hairline to the tips of my ears down to my throat. I shot Liz a look and turned back to George.

"I'm here for a book signing at Mitchell's," he said. "Can you believe it, Cricket? After all that work last summer?"

"I know! And it's great to see you, George, but I've been told I'm a hot mess. So I'm going to go take a shower before dinner. I can't wait to catch up." I turned to go.

"Hurry up," George said. "Our reservation is in fifteen minutes."

George told us about his big news over dinner in the back garden at Black-Eyed Susan's. As we feasted on cold corn soup with chunks of crabmeat and avocado, pan-seared diver scallops, local lettuces with fried green tomatoes, and linguine and quahogs, George told us he had a new book deal, this one about the life of Hillary Clinton. "So many women connect with her," George said. "And there's good reason for it. I'm interested in the psychology of Hillary, her many contradictions and how she's changed the idea of the American woman."

"Is it weird that you're writing this and you're not a woman?" Liz asked, as she helped herself to another glass of the wine. I was sticking to water.

"Not at all," George said. "You wouldn't say that if it were a woman writing about a man, would you?"

Liz considered as she sipped. "No, I suppose not."

"But trust me: my editor and I thought of that. And I have to get this exactly right, because my last book has been so successful. And this advance they gave me? It's no joke. So, I'm under a lot of pressure."

"Are you rich now, George?" Liz asked, eyes popping.

"Let's just say my wife and I were able to make a down payment on an apartment in Park Slope." Liz and I looked at him blankly. "For a journalist, that's basically a miracle. So

I really have to deliver. My career depends on it." He furrowed his brow and he looked a bit pale.

"You just need a female perspective," I said, spearing a scallop. "You know, as you write. And you can interview a lot of women, get a lot of perspectives."

"Exactly," George said, smiling and twirling up a big spoonful of the linguine and quahogs with his fork. "Too bad you'll be busy at Brown, Cricket. I could use you in New York."

I felt a little rush of adrenaline at the idea of myself in a smart-looking dress, walking down a New York street with a notepad under my arm. I thought about Nina and all her New York stories. Maybe I could have my own.

"Brown is a great school," George said. He shook his head, laughing. "What an opportunity. You know, the admissions people at Brown would've laughed their asses off if I'd applied there."

"You don't think you would've gotten in?"

"Not in a million years. Make it a trillion."

"But you're a famous author. I always assumed you went to Yale or Harvard or something." My phone rang. It was a Rhode Island number I didn't recognize, so I ignored the call. It was probably a wrong number. I silenced the phone and placed it on the table.

"In high school I was lot more interested in girls than grades. My SAT scores were a joke. I barely got into CUNY."

"Really?" My whole life had been about getting into

the right college, but here was George, with a shiny new book deal, a best seller on his hands, and a Park Slope apartment, and he hadn't gone anywhere fancy. He was one of the smartest, best people I'd ever met. Did college not actually matter that much?

George twirled up the last of the linguine and threw his napkin on the table. "What do you say: Juice Bar for dessert?"

"Yay! I love the Juice Bar, and Liz will never wait in line with me."

"Some things are worth waiting for, Liz."

"Not tonight. I need to get back for a late check-in. But you two go. I'll see you back at the inn. Thank you for dinner, George. And I'm so happy to finally have a rich friend in New York."

"Don't get carried away," George said as he counted out bills to pay the check. "Come on, Cricket. Let's blow this pop stand." We were halfway out the door when I realized I'd left my phone on the table. I glanced at the screen. The Rhode Island caller had left a voice mail. I'd listen to it later, I thought. Whoever it was, they could wait until after we'd gone to the Juice Bar.

"Maybe I could work for you from Brown," I said to George as we stood in line at the Juice Bar. The late ferry had just come in, and the new arrivals streamed past with their bags over their shoulders, faces lit up with visions of what their time on the island held for them. "I could come to New York on the weekends. I bet I could even find a way to get credit for it."

"There's nothing I'd like more," he said. "You did a great job for me last summer. You have a great attitude. You're smart, fast, and fun to be around. You kept me organized, provided insight, and kept things running smoothly." I beamed at the praise. "But I'm going to need someone full-time. Not just weekends."

"Promise me you'll think about it? I'm going to New York soon anyway," I said as the line moved up and we stepped inside the screen door. "I need to audition for Woody Allen." I hadn't made any concrete plans to do this, but it was on the list and I was going to make it happen somehow.

"Woody Allen? You're an actress now?"

"No, not at all. It's for this, um, project I'm doing."

"What kind of project? For school?"

"No, it's research," I said, studying the menu even though I knew exactly what I was going to order. "Personal research."

George clapped his hand on my shoulder. "That's what I like about you, Thompson. You're always working something out. You're always thinking, always questioning. It's the mark of a good person. And a good journalist."

I made a mental note to stay in touch with George, always.

"So, what's it going to be?" George asked when it was finally our turn to order.

"Chocolate peanut butter, in a waffle cone."

"Make that two," George told the pimply ice-cream scooper as he stuffed a ten-dollar bill in the tip jar.

It wasn't until the next day, when I was getting ready for work, that I listened to the mysterious Rhode Island voice-mail message. I was sitting on the sofa, lacing up my Easy Spirits, when I played it on speaker.

"Hi, Cricket. This is Claudia Gonzales from Brown University admissions. I'm calling with some important information regarding your status. You were admitted with the understanding that you would maintain the exemplary behavior you demonstrated in high school. Our office received some disturbing news regarding an incident on Nantucket. It's crucial that you return my call as soon as possible."

Thirty-four

I HAD A HALF HOUR UNTIL I HAD TO BE AT WORK. I STUFFED my feet into my sneakers and called Claudia Gonzales at the Brown University Admissions Office. I tried her three times, but she didn't answer her phone. I could only leave her a voice mail. I called back and dialed zero to try to reach a human.

"I got a very important message from Ms. Gonzales," I told the girl who picked up. "I need to talk to her."

"It's only me in the office right now," she said. "And I'm just on work study."

"Can I have her cell-phone number? I need to talk to her, like, now."

"Um, I'm not supposed to, um, give out any numbers."

I wanted to reach through the phone and throttle her. "Um, I think I need to go," she said, and hung up.

I flew into the inn's kitchen, where Liz was preparing a salad.

"What's happened now?" she asked.

"I might not get into Brown," I said, my voice rising in panic. "They know that I got shitfaced and broke into Something Natural. They know everything."

"What?"

I played her the voice mail. I was short of breath, studying her face as she listened, hoping that she might have a brilliant British insight or some take on the situation that would mean this was no big deal. But she just shook her head and said, "This is bad, really, really bad."

"I know," I whispered. The panic was climbing back down my throat, clogging my air passages. I sat down and put my head between my knees.

"It was Jules who told them," Liz said.

"We don't know that." I couldn't believe it, but it was the first time the question of who had contacted Brown had entered my mind. Until now, it had just seemed like the all-seeing god of college admissions, the one I'd lived in fear of, to whom I'd prayed with all of my extracurricular activities and made sweet offerings of bright, shiny report cards, was now striking me down out of displeasure.

"Then who was it?" Liz asked. "Do they read the Nantucket police blotter?"

I closed my eyes and placed a hand on my churning stomach. I didn't want to think about it. I tucked in my Breezes T-shirt. "I have to get to work. I need to taste the specials so that I can accurately describe them." As if this were my biggest problem. How was I supposed to recite a speech about wild salmon when my future was in ruins?

Liz put her half-made salad in the fridge and grabbed her keys. "You must talk to this Brown University woman right now. I'll drive. You dial."

"I tried calling Brown," I said, following her out the door. "Claudia Gonzales has gone home for the night."

"Call her at home," Liz said as we climbed into the Jeep. "She must understand what's at stake."

"I don't have her home number. They don't just give home numbers out."

Liz made a show of removing her cell phone from her purse and dialing a number as she started the engine. "Hello, operator? I'm looking for a number in Providence, Rhode Island. A Claudia Gonzales." I handed her the piece of paper on which I'd written her name. "G-O-N-Z-A-L-E-S, as in Sam," Liz raised her eyebrows and nodded. She scribbled on a piece of Cranberry Inn stationery, trying to get the pen to work. "I'll take all three." She spat on the end of her pen and wrote down three numbers.

I called all three Claudia Gonzaleses while Liz drove. The first one didn't speak English, the second sounded like she was a hundred years old; but on the third try I found the Claudia I was looking for.

"How did you get this number?" she asked, sounding too young to be in charge of my life.

"You're listed in information," I said. Liz nodded, as if to confirm that this was totally valid. "I didn't know what to do and I had to talk to you."

"At least you recognize that this is an emergency," she said. I put my hand back on my stomach as it flipped once again, and Claudia Gonzales went on to explain that she'd been sent a video in which I'd identified myself and exhibited behavior that was in no way in line with Brown's code of conduct. Liz watched as I nodded and made notes.

Ms. Gonzales explained that in the next few days I was going to get a certified letter that stated that I had a hearing in a week in front of the Brown Student Conduct Committee. She would be there along with an academic dean, and, because of my place on the team, so would the lacrosse coach. I had one week to prepare an explanation and defend my place at Brown. I jotted down: "video," "one week," "place at Brown," "defend myself."

"We want to know why you did this," she said, "and what your thoughts are upon reflection. We take this kind of thing very seriously."

I wrote "why?" and underlined it twice. After I hung up, I closed my eyes.

"Well?" Liz asked. We were parked in a shaded spot near the restaurant.

"Someone sent them a video of that night at Something Natural."

"Jules! I told you!"

"That doesn't make sense," I said, shaking my head. "We've been so good lately."

"Well, are you still accepted to the university?"

"I have to defend myself," I said. "In some kind of hearing."

"But you're not kicked out?" Liz asked.

"No," I said. "Not yet anyway, but I'm in deep shit."

"Maybe your bartender has some ideas," she said, noticing Ben walking through the back door of the restaurant. She squeezed my khaki knee. I was wearing my ugly thrift-store pants. "In the meantime, we'll both think about how to get you out of this, yeah?"

"So, you have to go on trial? Again?" Ben took my hand in the little alley behind the restaurant. We were hiding out for a few minutes before opening.

"Something like that," I said.

"I don't get it. Who sent the video?"

"I don't know," I said.

"Well, who took it?"

"Jules," I said.

"But she wouldn't send it. It doesn't make sense."

"Have you told your parents?" Ben asked, placing a steadying hand on my lower back.

I shook my head no. I wanted to stay here, in the shelter of his arms, in the alley between Breezes and the Wamp, for as long as possible.

"Honey, I'm so sorry." I never thought I'd like being called "honey" or "sweetie" or any of those names old guys sometimes casually tossed off at the restaurant, but right now, it felt comforting. I leaned against him. For the first time, he felt like my boyfriend. I closed my eyes as those bonding chemicals Liz had warned me about flooded my bloodstream.

"So, what's your plan?" asked Ben.

"I'm going to do what I always do," I said.

"What's that?"

"Fight like hell." Behind Ben, a nighthawk looped through the sky, searching for dinner. Dad used to point out their long, pointed wings on our bike rides on summer evenings in Providence.

"You're one tough girl," he said.

"I'm an attack wing," I said. "In lacrosse."

"And in life," Ben said, as he kissed the top of my head. "Sadie's going off island for a few days tomorrow. You can stay with me if you want."

"I'd like that," I said. His arms felt strong and protective. Older.

"We'd better get back in there. Tonight's going to be a nightmare. We're booked solid."

Ben was right. That night we didn't have one rush or two rushes. The whole shift was a rush. What everyone said was true. August was the busiest, craziest time of all. I made more mistakes than usual. A lady who'd ordered the lobster roll with butter got it with mayonnaise. A fat-fingered man who'd wanted the bluefish wound up with the snapper. But their complaining looks and sharp words barely registered, and thankfully, even Karla was too busy acting as both hostess and busboy, and even hopping behind the bar at one point, to notice. I kept thinking about Claudia Gonzales's words and that video. I barely remembered it, but I could picture Jules filming Zack and me and telling us to put our arms around each other.

As I bused a table, gathering dirty glasses and dessert dishes onto a tray, another memory came back to me: of Jules flinching when I told her about Nina's life list. I dumped the glasses and plates at the dish-washing station, realizing that Jules's sending the video to Brown was another version of what had happened last year, when I'd spoken at her mother's memorial service. Jules had been very angry, but instead of telling me like a normal person, she had lashed out.

I headed back to the dining room and saw that Karla had seated my whole section again. Six new tables at once. I barely had time to breathe.

At the end of the night, after I'd counted out over three hundred dollars in tips, and just as I was about to clean the cappuccino machine, which was particularly milk-encrusted and sticky, I got a text from Jules: Hey, Misdemeanors. It's me, Crimes. Come over tomorrow? We can watch those Woody Allen movies. It's supposed to rain.

Was this what she was going to do? I thought as I wiped down the metal grate on the stupid cappuccino machine. She'll just let me go down in flames and think that I would never suspect her?

I turned on the milk steamer, not realizing the nozzle was aimed right at my hand. The steam seared my skin in a hissing blast. I ran to the sink and let cold water run over the distinct band of red, which was swelling and blistering, marking my hand like lashes of a whip.

Thirty-five

"LOOK WHAT I HAVE," JULES SAID, OPENING THE FRONT door of the Claytons' house the next morning. I didn't step inside, even though it was cold and wet where I stood. According to my iPhone, it was already raining, but I stood in the misting air, arms crossed, careful not to touch the place on my hand that had burned. Even though I'd let the icy cold water run over it for several minutes last night, it was still too tender to touch.

Minutes before, I had been on the phone with Coach Stacy, who told me, among other things, that she was extremely disappointed that I'd mentioned on the video that I hadn't been keeping up with my training. Not only was she sitting on the committee at the hearing, but also, her decision would be based on how I performed at a scrimmage at the training camp she was running at St. Timothy's. I would be expected to be there the day before the hearing for the camp's closing scrimmage, to demonstrate that I was up to the task of playing at the college level.

Jules was holding the door open with her foot, not picking up on my vibes. She displayed three Woody Allen DVDs, running a hand over them as if I'd just won them on a game show. "I have *Manhattan*, *Annie Hall*, and *Hannah and Her Sisters*. I also have *Crimes and Misdemeanors*, but then I thought, nah, too soon." She laughed, but her face fell when she registered my stony expression and crossed arms. She wrinkled her nose and said, "Are you going to come in or what?"

"Just tell me why."

"Why what?" Jules stepped outside, tucking the DVDs under her arm.

"This is because I didn't tell you about the list I found on the back of your mom's picture, isn't it? Or is this about last year? You still haven't forgiven me. You're never going to forgive me, are you?"

"What the fuck are you talking about?" When she lied, she pursed her lips and didn't make eye contact. Her mouth was hanging open, and she wasn't even blinking. "I'm not mad about the list. I stayed up last night digging through boxes to find these." She held up the DVDs. "I wanted to watch them with you. Maybe it's you who hasn't forgiven me. Ever thought of that?"

"Then who sent the video?"

"What video?"

"Of us getting drunk and breaking into Something Natural? Someone sent it to Brown, and now I might not get in. I have a hearing in a week with an academic dean, the head of admissions, and the lacrosse coach. And not only that, but the lacrosse coach saw me saying I hadn't been keeping up with my training. I have to prove myself in a scrimmage. If I don't do well, I don't get her vote."

"Are you serious? Jesus, Cricket," Jules said. "ZACK, GET OUT HERE!" Despite the obvious fact that he'd been there too, I hadn't even considered the idea that he might have sent it. He couldn't have. He was my first love. First loves don't do that.

"Don't give me that look," Jules said to me. "He took the video, not me." She was right. Jules had only held the camera for a moment. It was Zack's phone. It was his idea.

"Why do you have to yell?" Zack asked as he emerged from the house holding a bowl of cereal. He was wearing just his Hanover soccer shorts. I studied his perfect torso, his sweet features, and his hair, rumpled from sleeping. "Hey, Cricket," he said with a soft smile.

"You know that video you took of us?" Jules asked.

"What video?" Zack asked, eating his Cheerios.

"You took a video that night," Jules said. "At Something Natural."

"Oh, yeah," he said, remembering. "I did."

"Did you send it to Brown?" Jules asked.

"Why the hell would I do that?"

"Someone sent that video to Brown and now I might not get in," I said.

"What?" Zack paused in midbite. "I would never do that."

I wanted to believe him so badly.

"You were passed out all night," Jules said. "Maybe you did it when you were passed out."

"I couldn't even find my way home; you think I could locate the e-mail address of someone in the admissions office at Brown?"

"Someone sent that video," I said.

"Take us through what happened that night," Jules said to Zack.

"I took the thermoses from Jules," Zack said, "and I started walking, and I remember getting really disoriented and lying down in the park and telling myself I was camping."

"That has nothing to do with anything. When did you wake up?" Jules asked.

"I woke up because my phone was ringing," Zack said. "It was light out by then."

"Who was it?" I asked.

"Parker," Zack said. "She came and got me."

"We're so dumb," Jules said. "Get me your phone."

"Screw you."

"Go!"

Zack went inside and came back with his phone. Jules snatched it from him and opened his sent mail folder. She scrolled until she found what she was looking for: an e-mail to the Brown University Admissions Office, with a video attachment. It had been sent on my birthday.

"I swear I didn't send it."

"No shit," I said. "Your girlfriend did."

He closed his eyes. "I'm so sorry." I held my breath, waiting for something else, but he just shook his head.

"Sorry? Sorry is not good enough," I said. "It's not even close."

He covered his face with his hands.

I felt a shard of glass lodge in my heart. "You're not even going to break up with her, are you?"

"Shit," he said.

"You really have changed. You know that?"

"Um, do you guys want me to leave?" Jules asked.

"Yes," Zack said.

"No," I said.

She froze.

"This is all going to work out," Zack said. "It has to."

"What are you talking about, it has to work out? No, it doesn't. I'm not a senator's daughter. I can't just snap my fingers and have my troubles go away. This is my life, Zack. My life! Everything I've ever worked for!"

"Cricket," Zack said. "I'm so, so sorry."

"Stop saying that. Sorry doesn't help me."

"I'll help you," he said, breathless. "I'll fix it."

"How?" I asked. He said nothing. "Guess what, Zack? While you were busy protecting Parker, she ruined my life."

"Cricket, please."

"I never want to talk to you again," I said and took off.

"Wait," Jules said, catching up to me. It had really started to rain now. Jules wasn't wearing shoes. Her toes were red against the pavement. "We're going to make sure you get back in."

"Can you admit Parker is a mean girl now? I just want to hear you admit it. I want you to say it. I want to know that you're on my side."

"I'm on your side," she said. "But Parker is severely troubled—"

"No, no, no. Fuck 'troubled,'" I said and ran away, fast enough so that even someone wearing shoes couldn't have caught me.

Thirty-six

I RODE MY BIKE TO SADIE'S COTTAGE IN THE RAIN. WITH the exception of some hard-core bicyclists decked out in spandex, I was the only one on the path. The rain had quieted the island, filling the air with the scent of wet grass and cooling pavement, urging people indoors to board games and sweaters. But I was racing my own thoughts on the way to 'Sconset. *I choose Ben over Zack,* I told myself as I whirred past Polpis Road. *I will write over the story of Zack with the story of Ben. I will take my heart in my own hands.*

By the time I arrived, the muscles in my legs were tingling, my hands were cold, and I was soaked to the bone. When Ben opened the screen door, he looked like the perfect picture of a hot summer boy. He stood framed in the warm light of the cottage, barefoot in an old Sarah Lawrence

T-shirt and jeans. He smiled and I stepped inside the house, rain dripping from my hair onto the hooked rug with the Sankaty lighthouse on it. He was playing an old-fashioned record on an actual record player. His guitar was out of its case, leaning against the fireplace.

"You look like a drowned rat," he said. I frowned. "A cute rat," he added. He handed me a T-shirt and sweatpants from his makeshift dresser next to the sofa. "Go change. I'll make you an Irish coffee."

"That sounds perfect," I said. After my fight with Zack and Jules and the rainy ride to 'Sconset, an Irish coffee felt like the most civilized, exquisite thing known to human-kind. I took the clothes from him and headed into the bathroom. Though, what was the point? I wondered as I shut the door behind me. I wasn't planning on staying dressed for long.

I took off my wet clothes and hung them on the towel rack. I looked in the mirror and shook out my damp hair. I was about to pull on the sweatpants, but I paused and left them folded by the sink. My cheeks were pink from the ride over. I searched my eyes for evidence of tears, splashed a little water on my face, and dabbed on some lip gloss.

"Well, hello, there, pantless one," Ben said, as I stepped out of the bathroom.

"They were way too big." I shrugged, took the Irish coffee and sat on the sofa, stretching my legs out.

"So," he said, sitting next to me. "Did you talk to Jules?" I nodded. "And?"

"And Zack." The name had an electric charge. It shocked my mouth.

"I meant, AND what did she say? Did she send the video?"

"No. That other girl did. Parker."

"Ah," Ben said. He nodded. "Zack's girlfriend, right?" I didn't like the sound of his name on Ben's tongue, and I'd never, ever get use to the phrase *Zack's girlfriend*.

"I don't want to talk about them," I said, sipping my Irish coffee. It was strong and a little bitter. "I'm going to add a little more sugar to this. Not quite sweet enough."

"Don't be long," Ben said as I headed toward the kitchen. "You look good in my T-shirt, but I think you'd look even better without it."

"Where's the sugar?" I asked, searching the cupboards.

"In the cupcake," he said.

"Oh, okay." I spied the ceramic cupcake and set about looking for a spoon.

"Maybe we should go surfing later. I bet the waves are awesome right now," Ben said. As I searched for a spoon, he went on talking, about surfing before a storm. I opened a drawer and found what Mom would have called the "catch-all"—the place where one kept keys, gum, coupons, and take-out menus. Staring up at me was a picture of Ben kissing a girl with dark hair sitting under a CONGRATS! banner on the front porch. Amelia, I thought. I picked it up and studied it. I had always pictured her fair, like Ben and me, but I'd been wrong. She had dark hair and olive skin. I caught my breath as I realized who she was. Her hair was longer in this picture, and her body was a little more ample than it was now, but there was no mistaking the thin band of a tattoo around her arm, or her high, distinctive cheekbones.

"Ben?" I said, stepping out into the living room with the picture in my hand, interrupting his monologue on currents and storms. "Were you engaged to Amy? Is Amy Amelia?"

A full five seconds passed before he spoke. "I didn't know how to tell you." He reddened. He bit his lip.

"I feel like such an idiot," I said. "Why didn't you tell me? Why did you lie?"

"Everything I told you was true. I was engaged. She cheated on me. I came to Nantucket to start over."

"You left out a pretty important detail."

"I told her it was over, but I couldn't stop her from coming out here and getting a job. Karla's her aunt."

"Why didn't you get a job somewhere else?"

"Bartending jobs are hard to find on Nantucket."

"That hard? So hard you have to work with your ex-fiancée?"

"Actually, yes. And it's not like you told me everything about your past."

"Me?" I put a hand on my chest. "What did I hide?"

"That you're still in love with Zack?"

"I am not!" I said, hoping that if I said the words, they'd be true.

"Cricket, you should see your face when you say his name." Ben's eyes were liquid with compassion. "It takes one to know one."

"You're still in love with Amelia? I mean Amy, whatever her real name is."

He covered his face with his hands and sighed. "I don't know. But she did break my heart. And I don't think I'm going to get over it for a long time."

"Then what are we doing together?" I swallowed, trying to make sense of the situation. "What have we been doing all summer?"

"Having fun? Helping each other move on?"

I inhaled sharply. "You were using me."

"Hey, that's not true," Ben said. "Not any more than you were using me."

I stared at the wooden floor, speechless. Was he right? Had I been using him, too? I headed to the bathroom to change. He followed me, but I closed the door on him.

"You don't have to go, Cricket. I like you and I think you like me," he said through the door as I took off his shirt. "Not everything fits in a neat little box. Not every relationship needs a label. Let's just surrender and enjoy each other."

"That sounds like a pile of crap." My skin goose-pimpled as I put on my cold, rain-soaked clothes.

"Sometimes you just have to let go," he said.

"I have to get out of here," I said. I handed him his clothes and jammed my feet into my wet sneakers.

"At least let me drive you?" Ben said, but I was already out the door.

I pedaled back toward town. I thought about that picture of Sadie dancing on the beach and wondered why I couldn't be more like her. Sadie herself said that at my age she'd just wanted to have fun and get laid, and it had seemed cool when she said it. So why did I have to care so much about what things meant? Why couldn't I just enjoy this hot older surfer guy who turned me on like crazy? And I wasn't like Nina, either. I wasn't a rich Park Avenue girl with a penchant for art and high culture. I was just a middle-class kid who had blown her chance at an Ivy League education.

As the sun ripped through the cloud layer, a deep anger swelled inside me. I was angry with Ben and Amy and even Karla, for keeping me in the dark. I was angry with myself. I had allowed myself to take my eye off the ball. I knew better. I was angry at Jules for letting me get that drunk when she knew I had no experience with alcohol. I was angry at Zack for protecting Parker. And I was enraged at Parker for being so cavalier with my life. But none of this surprised me.

What surprised me was that I was angry at Nina. I was angry at her for loving me when she was alive in a way that made me feel like I was one of her own. I was pissed that she had lived long enough to let me believe that I could be like her, but hadn't hung around long enough to show me how. Instead, she had left me with a list of rich-girl fantasies that I could only pretend to actualize. She'd filled my head with dreams of places I couldn't really go. I wouldn't be able to go to Paris or Italy until I was grown-up, with a job of my own. And then I wouldn't be able to do it with the style and insouciance that she had had. That wasn't something you could earn through hard work and scholarships. It was something you were born with. She was the reason I had come out to this stupid island, and I hated her for it. My mom had been right last year. I *had* worshiped Nina, and it *was* silly and useless, and, worst of all, it was probably even tacky.

When I got back to the manager's apartment, I took the picture of Nina off the wall. I was going to rip it up. My hands were poised and ready to tear when I saw a pile of Woody Allen DVDs, tied up with a ribbon, sitting on my sofa bed with a note from Jules.

Hey, Miss Demeanors!

You forgot your DVDs. I found them for you. We're going to fight this. We're going to get you back into Brown. I promise. AND I love you forever! Love, Miss Crimes.

P.S.: Got to get you in shape for the coach. Your lacrosse training starts tomorrow at 9 a.m. sharp! See you then.

P.P.S.: Start with Manhattan. *It was Mom's favorite, since she went to the same school as the girl in the movie.*

Jules had sealed it with a lipstick kiss. She'd even drawn a bunch of funny pictures of us. There was one of us playing lacrosse. There was one of me standing on her back crawling through the window of Something Natural. There was one of us swimming at night, our boobs floating to the surface under a full moon. As angry as I was, I had to laugh. What if Jules had been right when she said that I was the one who had been unable to forgive her for last summer? What if I was the one holding on to anger? What if Ben was right about my needing to let go?

I released the photo of Nina from my closed fist. I took three deep breaths, smoothed it out, and hid it in a secret pocket on the inside of my suitcase. Then I picked up the phone and did what I'd been dreading doing.

"Hello?" Mom's voice was chipper, happy to hear from me out of the blue. I imagined her in her Cape Cod T-shirt and running shorts, her heavy, golden hair falling in front of her face as she reached for the phone.

"It's me," I said. I took a deep breath and gathered my courage. "There's something I need to tell you."

Thirty-seven

THE CONVERSATION LASTED ALMOST AN HOUR. SHE TOOK the phone into her bedroom so that Brad wouldn't overhear. He had officially moved in. I talked her through what happened scene by scene. For the first time in my life, her voice offered me no comfort. Each "What?" was hard as concrete, and each silence was as cold as March rain.

"You're going to get back in, right?" Mom asked when I'd finished by telling her about my conversation with Claudia Gonzales. "I mean, she said you were going to get back into Brown, didn't she?"

"I don't know, Mom. That's the whole thing. I don't know. That's why I have a hearing next Monday. Weren't you listening?" It had been painful enough to go over the details with her once. I filled a glass with tap water and drank it down.

"Well, you'll just have to get a waitressing job here. It will have to be someplace you can walk to, because you won't have a car. You'll have to take classes at the community college. Maybe pick up some babysitting work."

"Stop it, Mom," I said. The picture she was painting had me on the verge of tears. I had known she was going to be pissed off, but I hadn't expected this.

"This is going to be your reality, Cricket. And mine, too. This is not what I imagined for myself, either, you know. I had started to get used to the idea of starting over, just Brad and me. But it's too late to do anything else, isn't it? How could you do this to yourself?"

"I don't know, Mom, okay? Haven't you ever made a mistake?"

"Oh, I've made plenty. But this isn't about me. This is about you. And this story you've told me about getting wasted and breaking into a café? Jesus, it doesn't even sound like you, Cricket. Is this who you are now?"

"I don't know, Mom," I said. "I don't know who I am right now." These might have been the truest words I'd ever spoken, and there was at least some calm in that.

"Have you told your father yet?"

"Tomorrow," I said. I was dreading telling Dad. Snippets of the speech he had given at my graduation party kept coming back to me. The stuff about how he couldn't be prouder of me, and the part about how they'd placed a bet on me, putting all of their money into my education, and hit the jackpot when I got into Brown. I thought of how they'd sold the minivan; I thought of the extra mortgages, the bank loans, and the vacations they hadn't taken. Their sacrifices stared me down.

"So, you don't want to upset him, but you'll upset me?" Mom asked.

"Well, you're . . . my mom," I said.

"Yes, I am." She sighed. "I have to work in the morning and I don't know how I'm going to fall asleep tonight. I'm going to have to take a pill."

I knew those pills. They were small and blue, and she'd taken them every night in the year after the divorce.

"Mama?"

"What?"

"I'm sorry." I curled myself around a pillow. "I'm really, really sorry."

"I know you are, baby." She sighed again. "I know."

I debated calling Dad, but I couldn't. I would do it tomorrow. I took a hot shower, then I watched *Manhattan* on the old TV in the manager's apartment. I pulled the blankets up under my chin as the images of a big city flickered across the screen: a crowded deli; a bakery; that museum with the wide, swirling staircase; the awning of a fancy hotel; an enormous bridge over a black river; a candlelit bistro. It seemed so enchanting and foreign and far away.

Thirty-eight

"WAKE UP, SPORTY!"

I blinked awake to see Liz smiling down at me in what looked like her version of workout clothes: a tank top with hot pink bra straps peeking out; cutoffs; and a pair of slip-on sneakers that were meant for skateboarding.

"What?" I glanced at the clock. It was eight a.m. I'd only had a few hours of sleep.

"The muffins are made, the girls have the inn under control, and we need to work out. Need to get you back in shape, don't we? Come on," she said, pulling me up to a sitting position. "Get moving."

"You're going to work out with me?"

"I'm going to damned well try. It's about time I lost some weight. Wine and cookies add up." She grabbed the flesh around her middle and jiggled it. I laughed. "Oh, you laugh, but by the time we get you back into Brown, I'm going to look like Pippa Middleton." She sucked in her stomach and struck a pose.

"Liz, I only have a week. Six days now."

"Then we'd better get working, hadn't we? Up you go. Get on your trainers. We're going to go for a run. Look, I even brought you breakfast." One of her famous cranberry-orange muffins sat on a napkin on the coffee table next to a steaming cup of coffee. "You're going to need fuel. We should run at least a mile. Maybe two."

"Okay," I said, not having the heart to tell her that a mile wasn't very far at all.

There was a knock at the door. I turned to see Jules's face pressed up against the window.

"Her!" Liz said, narrowing her eyes and grabbing Gavin's rain stick from the closet. She shook it menacingly as she opened the door. "You're not welcome here!"

"Jules didn't send it," I said, jumping in front of Jules. "Liz! She wants to help me. It wasn't her. I promise."

"Were you going to hit me with that?" Jules asked, holding her lacrosse stick in front of her face in self-defense.

"Yes," Liz said, raising the rain stick up like a baseball bat, "and I still might."

"Liz, she has nothing to do with it." I seized the rain stick.

"Do you have proof?" Liz's eyes were wild behind her thickly mascaraed lashes.

"Yes," I said. "We found the video attached to an e-mail sent from her brother's account."

"Zack sent the movie? Bastard! They're all bastards, the lot of 'em."

"It was my brother's girlfriend, Parker," Jules said. The word *girlfriend* landed like a brick. Jules met my eyes. "His *mean, nasty* girlfriend."

"Is this true?" Liz asked me. "Parker sent it? The Carmichael girl?"

"A hundred percent," I said.

"Shady family, they are," Liz said.

"Now that we've narrowly avoided an assault," Jules said, "are you ready to work out, Cricket?"

"Actually, we were just about to go for a run," Liz said.

"I was going to . . ." Jules started, but I cut her off.

"We're all going running together," I said.

"I say we go to Altar Rock," Jules said as she stretched her hamstrings.

"But that's miles away," Liz said.

"That's kind of the point," Jules said. "Cricket needs to get her endurance up."

I put a hand on Liz's shoulder. "Head home whenever you feel like it."

We were barely out of town when Liz, red-faced and panting, said, "Tell you what, mates. I think I've exerted myself enough for today. I'll go home, get some refreshments, and meet you at the rock. In the car."

"You did well for your first run, Liz," I said, jogging in place. "You'll go a little farther each day." It was a Miss Kangism.

Liz headed back toward the inn. Jules and I picked up the pace. Even though I was a faster sprinter, we were pretty evenly matched when it came to distance.

"What's up with Ben?" Jules asked.

"We broke up yesterday. I don't really want to talk about it." Could I even call it breaking up if we'd never actually been together?

"Rough day," she said. "I'm sorry."

"It's okay. How's Jay?"

"Awesome," she said. Out of my peripheral vision, I could see her beaming. I had a weird premonition that they might get married one day, even though it had been Jay's and my wedding that we'd joked about back before everything happened with Zack. "I'm going to see him in Boston on Friday, and I'm staying for a few nights. I can't wait, if you know what I mean." She meant sex.

"And what's going on with your dad?" I asked, changing the subject.

"Still officially single," she said, and we high-fived.

Several miles later, after Liz had passed us in her car, with the radio blaring, Jules pointed down a dirt road, and we followed it toward what looked like a water tower. We'd been running for another five minutes or so when she said, "Race you to the top of the rock!"

Ahead of us, Liz waved. She was shouting something at us, but I couldn't understand her. The wind was swirling in my ears as I put all of my frustration and anger into the last one hundred yards, leaving Jules in my actual dust.

"Jesus, you're fast," Jules said when she reached the top seconds after I did and we collapsed in a heaving, sweaty pile. I pulled out my iPhone and checked the pedometer. Five miles. My face was burning up. I was happy to see Liz and her gallon of fresh lemonade.

"Well done," Liz said, pouring us each a cupful.

I drank it all in three swallows. "Thank you," I said, savoring the sweet, tart liquid. "Liz, you are the best."

"This is awesome," Jules said, as she tossed back her second cup and went for a third.

The top of this rock was the highest point I'd ever been to on Nantucket. I could see a scalloped harbor. A stretch of low, rugged land. In the distance were scattered several shingled houses, and beyond them lay a faint stroke of ocean. My phone rang. "It's my dad."

"Get it," Jules said.

"I can't. I can't tell him."

"You have to," Liz said. And when I didn't make a move, she leveled a stern look at me. "Cricket, now."

I answered the phone. "Hi, Dad." I said, and held my breath. I put the phone to my ear and walked several paces away from the girls.

"Your mom called me this morning," Dad said. "She told me what happened. Sweetheart, what are you going to do?" His sympathetic tone surprised me.

"Just tell me that you're mad," I said, gazing out at that small harbor, so perfect it looked like a painting, with three sailboats gliding across it. "Tell me how disappointed you are."

"Yes, I'm disappointed. But I'm more worried," he said. "This could be one of those big mistakes."

"Sometimes it feels like everyone's allowed to make mistakes but me."

He laughed.

"What?"

"I'm laughing because it's true. If there's ever been a model student, a model kid, it's you. But as far as mistakes go, you picked a big one."

"Did you ever make a big mistake?" I asked. My chin was trembling.

"Did I tell you about the time I failed my only daughter?"

My throat tightened. I closed my eyes. "No."

"There were so many times I should have been there for you and I wasn't. You were always so on top of things that I didn't think you needed me. But every girl needs her dad. I didn't ask you to be in my wedding. I devoted all of my time to my new marriage. Not getting into college? That seems like small potatoes when I think about my mistakes."

"You didn't fail me, Dad," I said, as I mangled the branch of an innocent shrub. "I failed myself."

"But when you came to me last summer, and you were

so angry, I should've talked to you then. I shouldn't have let you leave that house."

I wiped away tears. Last summer, he had pretty much ignored my eighteenth birthday but thrown a hoedown for his stepchild, Alexi, who was turning six.

"I don't think I was a very good party guest," I said.

"I should've wrapped my arms around you," Dad said. "I should've told you that I loved you, sweetie. You needed me, and I wasn't there. And I'm sorry."

"I need you now," I said quietly.

"I'm here."

"I have this hearing and I have no idea what I'm going to say. I'm going to have to write a speech and explain to the coach. I can't say that I was just being stupid. But that's what it was. I was being stupid. At the wrong time and in the wrong place."

"Well, why did you do it?" he asked. "Why did you get drunk and break into a sandwich shop?"

"I was working so hard," I said. "I hadn't had a real day off since I got here."

"You haven't really had a day off since you started high school," Dad said. "But you've never done anything like this before. So, I ask you again, why?"

Why *had* I done this? I'd had a perfect opportunity to get drunk and be rebellious with Jules before the summer began, at Jay's house, when everyone was going to break into the secret Brown bowling alley. But I hadn't wanted it then. So what had changed?

"I found this list," I said. I hadn't been able to tell Mom about Nina's list. She resented Nina. I knew it would've made her sympathize with me less, not more.

"What list?"

I told Dad about Nina's picture, about Rodin and Paris, about driving a stick shift. I told him about Sadie and the photos of people dancing on the beach. I told him about Campari and the Amalfi Coast with Alison Huang. Dad listened on the other line, saying, *"Uh-huh,"* and *"Hmm."*

"Nina went to Brown, didn't she?" he asked.

"Yes," I said.

"You know, it's not every student who gets a list like that and does that kind of research. It took creativity and passion and some original thinking. Sounds like Brown material to me."

I felt space open up inside me. The light of possibility. The glow of hope.

"You're right," I said. I would use the list to defend myself. I would tell the story of how I'd followed it as an example of why I was exactly Brown material. "Are you going to tell Rosemary and Jim?"

"Do you want me to?"

"No," I said. "Not unless we have to."

"Then I won't tell," he said.

"You won't tell Polly?" I asked. I held my breath.

"I won't tell a soul," he said. "And let me know if you need help. I am an English professor, you know."

"Thanks, Dad."

I climbed back up the rock where Jules and Liz were sunning themselves like lizards.

"I'm going to use the list to defend myself," I told them, as I poured myself another big cup of lemonade. "I'm going to go through it and explain how I followed each step and how it led me to the moment at Something Natural."

"That's perfect," Jules said, propping herself up on her elbow.

"Actually, that's brilliant," Liz said. "You can talk about how you wish to take art classes about Rodin."

"And a class about the history of the car?" Jules said.

"You think they offer 'the history of the car' at Brown?" I asked.

"Why not?" Jules shrugged.

"Anyway, it's all true," I said. "It's not bullshit."

"This means you have to go to New York now," Jules said, "to learn about Woody Allen."

"I can just watch the DVDs," I said. "I can watch them until I draw some meaning from them."

Liz squinted into the sun. "But that's a place you can actually go."

"Besides," Jules said. "I don't know what you're going to learn from watching *Manhattan*. It's really creepy how he dates that young girl."

"What about the last thing on the list?" I asked.

"There was another thing?" Jules asked, sitting up straight.

"Oh, yeah, I didn't tell you," I said. "It was 'See Saint Francis from altar.' I figure it was something she wanted to see on her wedding day."

"Cricket. We're at Altar. Right now. This is Altar Rock."

"Is Saint Francis a church?" I asked. "Is it a church you can see from here?"

"I have no idea," Jules said. "I'll ask Dad."

I took another look around. I felt so close to the sky. I could see for miles. I could see that glistening, pristine harbor; fields of low, green shrubs forked by winding, sandy paths; a pale stripe of ocean. But no churches, no crosses, no saints.

Thirty-nine

"WHAT'S HAPPENED NOW, THOMPSON?" KARLA ASKED WHEN I knocked on the door of her office. She was looking over purchase orders and working out some numbers on an old-fashioned adding machine. "Did you rob a bank?"

"Not funny," I said. "I'm here to get my paycheck."

"It's in here somewhere." She handed me the stack of envelopes with staff names written on them. I paused when I saw Amy's full name—Amelia Garcia—then continued on to find mine.

"How come no one told me Ben and Amy used to be engaged?"

"Why would that be a topic of conversation?" Karla said, looking up. "Especially since there's nothing going on

537

between you two?" She raised an eyebrow. I shrugged. "Love and business do not mix. Trust me."

"But you hired her after you hired Ben?"

"She happens to be my favorite niece. I've never been able to say no to that girl. Anyway, I don't see how this is your business. Is there something else you need? I'm kinda busy." She gestured to her piles of paperwork.

"Yeah. I'm just confirming that I have Saturday, Sunday, and Monday off." I needed to be back in Rhode Island on Saturday in order to be well rested and ready for the scrimmage at nine a.m. on Sunday, and Monday was my hearing at Brown. "Because of my mistake? I mentioned it last week?"

Karla spun around on her office chair to check the schedule hanging on the wall. "I've got you covered for the weekend, but you have to figure out Monday."

"But I told you—"

"Ask Amy. She's off, although she'll have had a really tough weekend. Being down a waitress in August is no joke."

It occurred to me I could just quit at the end of the week. If I was lucky enough to still be attending college, I had seven thousand in the bank, and I could probably make another grand in my next four or five shifts. But I'd promised Karla that I would work through the end of August, and she'd been so nice to not fire me after my arrest that I didn't want to break that promise.

"Amy's the only one?"

"Better say pretty please," Karla said as I left her office. "With sugar on top."

Amy was sitting at the bar refilling salt shakers. All of her behavior now made sense. Trying to get rid of me. Her high fever of emotions. Her lipstick and mascara.

"Amy, I have a favor to ask."

"What is it?" She didn't look up as she poured a steady stream of salt into the delicate, silver-topped shaker, then tapped it to shake off the excess.

"I'm wondering if there's any chance you can cover for me on Monday?"

"After that weekend of double shifts? No frickin' way. I'm going to the beach."

"Please." I sat on the barstool next to her and faced her. "It's really important. I need that time if I want to get back into college. It's my one chance to correct the mistake I made. Imagine making one mistake that had the potential to ruin your life."

"I don't need to imagine," she said, screwing on the top of one saltshaker and reaching for another. Maybe it was because of her small stature, but until Ben told me that she was also Amelia, I had thought Amy was my age. Now that I really looked at her, I could see some fine lines around her eyes. I could see long nights in the library and the broken engagement. I could see that she was twenty-seven.

"Because you cheated on Ben?"

She turned to me with fanned fingers and anxious eyes. "He told you?"

"I found a picture."

"He has a picture? What picture? Where is it?"

"I found it at Sadie's house. I think it's from your engagement party."

"He took you to Sadie's?" Her chest caved. Her eyes webbed with red.

"We're not together anymore," I said.

"Oh!" She gasped with relief. The lines around her eyes softened. "What happened?"

"He's not over you."

"Did he say that?"

"Basically."

"I love him so much," she said, hiding her face. "I just got freaked out, you know? It was one stupid night. I turned down an internship to come here and try to get him back, but he met you."

"He doesn't love me," I said, reaching over the bar to grab a cocktail napkin. I handed it to her and she dabbed her eyes. It was true. No matter which way I'd dissected it, I'd come to the same conclusion. He liked me. He liked teaching me how to surf and how to drive stick. He liked playing the guitar for me and building fires by the ocean while I watched, soft with awe. And I'm pretty sure he enjoyed making me feel like a firecracker on the Fourth of July in the dunes of the nature preserve. I guess if you've had an older girlfriend for a while, it would feel good to be the one who knows something for a change, but it didn't make his heart any more available, and there's just no substitute for someone's heart.

"He's here," I said, watching Ben walk through the door with his earbuds in. As he took in the two of us huddled by the bar, his pace slowed. He looked genuinely nervous.

"Don't tell him I cried," she whispered as she hopped off the stool.

"I won't. Are you going to cover for me on Monday?"

"Yeah, fine." She pushed the tray of saltshakers toward me. "Finish these while I go fix my makeup."

"What was that about?" Ben asked as he stepped behind the bar. "Or should I even ask?"

"Amy's going to cover for me on Monday," I said.

"That's it?" Ben asked, setting up his cutting board and knife.

"I told her I knew," I said, taking over the salt duties. "She really loves you, you know." Ben seemed unmoved as he rinsed off lemons and limes. I wiped the extra salt from the rim of the small container with my finger.

"She cheated on me after I proposed to her. That's one of those actions that crosses a line. I just don't think there's any going back after that. Not for me, anyway." Amy emerged from the ladies' room with a fresh layer of bright red lipstick, and my heart broke for her. She was going to wear herself out trying to get him back. "I'm sorry she's sad, but I was straight up with her. She followed me here anyway."

"You're tough," I said.

"Says the attack wing. Hey," he said, touching my hand. "Are we friends?"

"Sure," I said. "I don't have any guy friends."

"You do now. So, do you want to know how to make a perfect martini? It's a skill that comes in surprisingly handy."

For the next five days I was on a strict schedule. Every night I worked at Breezes. Things were always a little awkward with Ben and Amy for the first half hour, but we were too slammed for them to stay weird. Amy was a lot nicer to me now that Ben and I weren't together. She whispered funny remarks to me about the customers, delivered drinks for me when I was in the weeds, and even took over a table of jerks for me. The busy nights, I went home with at least two hundred and fifty dollars. It all went straight into my bank account. When I reached eight thousand, on Thursday night, I sent an e-mail to Rosemary and Jim.

Every morning, Jules and I worked out. We ran to Altar Rock. We ran to Surfside. We ran to Cisco. We practiced ground balls and shots on goal in the fields of Nantucket High School.

"You know what I want more than anything?" I asked, collapsing in the sand after a workout that had ended with a game of catch at Children's Beach. "A sandwich from Something Natural."

"I don't think we're welcome there," Jules said, laughing.

"They probably have our pictures in the back." I laughed. "Nantucket's Most Wanted."

"Let's go to the Juice Bar, where they don't know about our criminal history."

"Hey," I said as she grabbed my hands and pulled me up. "Did Zack break up with Parker?"

"Not yet. But don't give up on him, Cricket."

"It's too late." It was like Ben said. There were some things that you couldn't go back from.

"When it comes to love, it's never too late. Come on," she said, dusting the sand off her butt. "Let's think of what you'll say in this letter to Woody Allen."

"Do you think he'll actually let me audition if he knows the whole story?"

"You never know," Jules said. "Hey, have you ever had a watermelon cream from the Juice Bar? You have to try one. They were my mom's favorite."

Later, when I was writing my letter to Woody Allen, explaining Nina's life list and my mission to reenact it, Zack called. I didn't pick up. If he chose to stay with someone who would do what she had done to me, he didn't love me. He called twice more, but I didn't answer. I deleted the voice mails without listening to them. Liz found the address of Woody Allen's agent. I mailed the letter on my way to work.

Every day, I worked on my presentation. I pored over the Brown Web site and wrote down what they were looking for in a student: inspired, talented, motivated, creative, resourceful, committed, independent. I focused on those qualities in my speech. I found the picture of Nina, now permanently bent from the night I'd thought about ripping it up, and Liz made copies for me to give to the committee as part of my presentation.

Jules had asked her dad what he thought "See St. Francis from altar" meant, and he said that he had no idea. Nina had never said anything about St. Francis to him. So, after hashing it out, Liz and Jules and I decided that I would use this fifth item in my speech to discuss the mystery of what was ahead of me at Brown. I wrote about how embracing mystery was the hallmark of a great education, because mystery is what leads us to seek out knowledge.

Every day, Liz or Jules or both of them listened as I practiced my presentation. They applauded, gave me feedback, or gave me thumbs down if something seemed over the top. I put the whole speech on index cards. The afternoon before I left, Liz told me that I needed to memorize it. The index cards were distracting.

"She's right," Jules said. "It's going to be, like, perfect if you don't have to look at your cards."

I nodded in agreement. "Should I sing the song, or is that too much?"

"I say, sing it," Liz said with passion. "Sing it with all your heart!"

"Sing just a verse," Jules said, considering. "You sound really good. But I could also see it, like, getting awkward?"

"Perhaps she's right," Liz said. "Perhaps Crown Jules actually has a point."

"All right, it's settled," I said. "I'll sing the first verse only.

And I'll memorize these"—I waved my index cards in the air—"by tomorrow."

"You have the ferry ride," Liz said.

"And the bus ride," Jules added.

"You're going to do well," Liz said.

"You're going to kick ass," Jules said.

"They're going to love it," Liz said.

"They're going to, like, readmit you so fast you'll already be a sophomore," Jules said.

"That makes no sense," Liz said.

"She knows what I mean," Jules said with a shrug.

"Yeah, I do," I said, pausing for a moment to observe the scene before me: Jules sprawled on my sofa bed, rubbing the silky part of the blanket, and Liz with her legs crossed, one foot bouncing, one hand twirling a curl. They were my two best friends, and they would be for a long time.

"Thank you so much for everything," I said.

"Don't get sentimental on us till you're back in," Liz said.

"Well, in that case . . ." I said, as I threw my index cards in the air, took a running start, jumped on the sofa, and tackled them both.

"You're heavier than you look, mate!" Liz said.

Forty

I HEARD DAD'S TAXICAB WHISTLE FROM THE SIDELINES AS I sprinted to catch a pass from a midfielder named Bitsy, who was anything but. She had to be over six feet tall and her legs looked so strong that they seemed like they could only belong to a professional athlete. Or a man. I caught the pass, which was so powerful it nearly pinned me to the field. But I found my balance, rolled past a defender who looked like she had issued from the same Norse god as Bitsy, and passed to Fiona, a left attack wing so fast I swear her cleats were smoking.

Even though my lungs ached and a cramp pinched my side and it looked like Fiona was going to score all on her own, I sprinted wide for a pass. My legs were shaking and my heart was beating so fast it was in danger of exploding, but I was afraid if I stopped moving I just might drop dead on the field of St. Timothy's at the final scrimmage for the Women's Lacrosse Ivy League Training Camp.

I'd played lacrosse since the fifth grade, but the girls at this camp were of a different breed. Usually, I was the fastest girl on the field. I knew a couple of players in our high school league as fast as I was: Patricia Cassell, Katie Rothwell, and maybe, *maybe* Izzy what's-her-face from Middletown Academy. But this was a whole field of Patricias, Katies, and Izzys.

And not only were they all fast, they were also driven, well-spoken, and smart. They were in such good shape they could practically fly. They were focused, agile, alert; perfect pictures of health; excellence made physical. There wasn't a mediocre or even second-best among them. And all together, despite different hair color, skin color, and body shapes, in a weird way, they looked exactly alike. They looked like the finest examples of everyone I had grown up with. They looked like what I had always imagined I would become if I tried my hardest.

"Lacrosse is our life," Fiona said when we were stretching out before the scrimmage. She was a junior at Brown, originally from Virginia. "Three hours a day. Every day. And every weekend, too. It's awesome." As I stretched out my calves, my mouth went dry.

"Are you okay?" she asked.

"Yeah, I'm fine." I smiled. I didn't know how much these girls knew about my situation.

"You look like you just saw a ghost."

"Just nervous," I said.

"Don't be," she said, and smiled. "You're going to be great. Besides, you're already on the team."

When Fiona saw that I was open, she called out a play we'd gone over at halftime. I had never moved so fast or been so aggressive. I sprang free from the defensive wing who was guarding me, taking full advantage of a pick set by Bitsy, leapt up to catch the ball, and slammed it straight into the goal. The whistle blew. My team cheered. Two minutes later, I did it again.

It wasn't my stickwork, which was actually weak compared to the other girls', or my conditioning, which was below par and had me bent over and heaving after I'd scored. And it sure wasn't that I was more innately talented than the other girls. It was determination, that superpower that can be willed into existence by those with something on the line. It made me better than I should have been. It made me shine. Or maybe it was just that the other girls were playing a game, and I was fighting for everything I'd lost.

Whatever it was, it worked. I saw Coach Stacy smiling on the sidelines. She wrote something on her clipboard. At the end of the scrimmage, when the Brown kids were huddled up, drinking water and trading stories about the summer, she squeezed my shoulder and said, "Great job, Cricket." The assistant coach winked at me. Fiona gave me her number and told me I could call her if I had any questions or just wanted to hang out with the team in the next few days.

"Oh, thanks," I said. "But I'm going to be on Nantucket."

"You go to Nantucket? I love Nantucket! Do you belong to the Wampanoag?"

"I work there," I said. "I'm a waitress at Breezes."

"Cool," she said. "Call me when you're back in town."

"Holy crap," Dad said, when we got in the car. "You were like a fish leaping out of the ocean. You were like some kind of flying squirrel. Let me see those cleats. Are there springs in there?"

"I was fighting for my life," I said as I eased off my cleats and peeled away my socks. My feet were bright red and throbbing. A ruptured blister on my heel was oozing.

"You know what? You weren't a fish or a squirrel. You were a warrior!" He couldn't wipe the grin off his face. His forehead wrinkled with amazement. "I'm the father of a warrior. 'That's my girl,' I said when you scored that goal. 'That's *my* girl!'"

"Yeah. I did all right."

"You did better than all right. I'm proud of you, sweetie," Dad said; he kissed my sweaty hand. "I couldn't be prouder."

"That's what you said at my graduation party."

"I'm prouder now," he said, as we passed the white clapboard dorms of St. Timothy's and the idyllic, pristine Newport coastline came into view. "No matter what happens tomorrow. I'm as proud of you right now as I have ever been."

Dad and I went to the Newport Creamery. Dad drank a decaf coffee and watched in amazement as I ate a grilled-cheese sandwich and drank a whole vanilla Awful Awful, the Newport Creamery's signature milk shake, in about three minutes. I kept telling myself to slow down, but the shake was so cold and so sweet. If forgiveness had a taste, I thought as I wiped my mouth with my grass-stained hand, it would be this.

Forty-one

"YOU ASKED ME TO COME HERE AND EXPLAIN MYSELF, AND I thank you for the opportunity," I said; and I took a deep breath and made eye contact with each member of the committee in the small, formal room in the Brown Admissions Office. Claudia Gonzales looked even younger than she'd sounded on the phone. Coach Stacy was barely recognizable in a suit. Dr. Fantini, a tall, bow-tied dean from the science department, was the third member.

My hands were shaking, so I clasped them behind my back. I was wearing an outfit that Mom had ironed: a khaki skirt, a white blouse, and navy flats. Mom had blown out my hair and pulled it back with a silver barrette, just as she had done for picture day at Rosewood every year since I could remember.

Whatever anger and frustration she'd demonstrated when I first told her what had happened had morphed into mothering.

After she picked me up from the bus station, she'd made me my favorite dinner—spaghetti with clam sauce—put clean sheets on my bed, and even stocked the fridge with my favorite kind of yogurt. And that night, when I couldn't sleep despite being exhausted, she came into my room with her guitar.

"*Oh, the summertime has come and the leaves are sweetly blooming,*" Mom sang softly. "*And the wild mountain thyme grows around the purple heather.*"

"*Will you go?*" we whisper-sang together. "*Lassie, will you go?*"

"Remember when I used to sing that to you?" she asked. "Every night, you wanted to hear that song."

"Keep singing," I said. "And then sing it again."

And she did—we did, until I fell asleep.

The air-conditioning in the admissions office wasn't working. The four of us were perspiring. I took a sip of water from a bottle they had handed me when I walked in. As I fumbled to replace the cap on the bottle, it fell to the floor. Despite the fact that their eyes followed it to the edge of the carpet where it landed, I didn't dare pick it up for fear I'd spill the whole bottle, knock over the table, send a lamp crashing down, and set the building on fire. I placed the water bottle carefully down and continued.

"I want to start by saying that I know what I did was wrong. I know that I abused alcohol. I take full responsibility for my behavior, which was immature, cavalier, and potentially dangerous. It was the first time in my life getting drunk, and because of the repercussions, I take alcohol use very seriously." I took a breath and another sip of water. "It says in the Brown Code of Conduct that the university expects that members of the Brown community be truthful and forthright, so I've prepared as forthright and truthful an explanation as possible."

Coach Stacy leaned in. Dean Fantini recrossed his long legs. Claudia Gonzales sighed and made some notes. I pulled out the copies of the picture of Nina and the list and handed one to each of them. "This is Nina Clayton; she was in the class of 1989."

I went on to explain that she had been my best friend's mother and a role model to me. I told them that she had passed away the year before. I told them the story of the broken frame and my discovery of the list. Coach Stacy smiled as she read the list. "This is so eighties!" she said.

I held up the Rodin book. "Rodin said, 'Nothing is a waste of time if you use the experience wisely.' It was in the spirit of these words that I set about living this list on Nantucket. I wanted to do something with my summer besides serve lobster rolls to people in pink pants and seersucker jackets."

Dr. Fantini nodded.

"When I found this book in the thrift store, it felt like a sign so I began with number one: *Visit Rodin Museum in Paris.* I studied these pictures every night. I couldn't believe how alive they felt, even in a book that's thirty years old. The sculptures have the spark of life. When I watched a surfer out at Cisco Beach, I saw *Saint John the Baptist* and *The Walking Man.* I saw *The Thinker* and *The Kiss.* Because of Rodin, I saw something more than a surfer. I saw art in motion. So, in this first endeavor, I was successful. I had experienced Rodin without leaving Nantucket."

Dr. Fantini adjusted his glasses and made some notes.

"I moved on to number two: *Learn to drive and then drive Route 1 to Big Sur.*" I took a sip of water and continued. "I already know how to drive, so I decided to learn to drive stick. I learned in a 1976 Land Rover on the back roads of Nantucket." I smiled, remembering the day with Ben and how the car had taken off without us. "And this led me down a surprising path, both literal and figurative. I saw parts of the island I wouldn't have seen, but also I think learning a new skill can open up a new road. While I was focusing on driving, I allowed myself to sing without self-consciousness, and it reminded me how much I like to sing, even if I don't have perfect pitch. In pushing ourselves to try new things, we find other parts of ourselves, the back roads of our souls." I scanned the faces of the committee members. Coach Stacy and Dr. Fantini looked pleased, but Claudia Gonzales remained expressionless. Maybe I'd pushed it too far with "back roads of our souls." In a last-minute decision, I decided not to sing. Jules had been right. It was too awkward.

"When you look at number three, you might see the connection between the list and why I'm standing here today. *Drink Campari on the Amalfi Coast with Alison.* Alison was Nina's best friend. Nina's daughter, Jules, was my best friend. Until Nina died. The tragedy of her death separated us, and I missed her so much. Losing a best friend is like losing a piece of yourself, and I wanted so much to connect with her again. I wanted the ease we used to have in our friendship, an ease that seemed epitomized by the idea of drinking Campari in Italy.

"I was so inexperienced with alcohol. Like I said, I'd never been drunk before. That night, I was totally caught up with a feeling of freedom. At some point, I let that freedom get the better of me. I lost control. It was so scary." My voice shook a little. "I never want to lose control like that again. If anything good came out of this, it's that I have a deeper commitment to my own health and safety and that of those around me."

I mentioned that Jules had revealed to me that the Woody Allen movie Nina had been in was *Crimes and Misdemeanors*, and this made all of them laugh, even Claudia Gonzales. I told them that I had written a letter to Woody Allen to see if he would let me audition for him.

"How did that go?" Ms. Gonzales asked, blinking in amazement.

"Let's put it this way," I said, "I'm not exactly a working actress." They laughed again.

"I'm not auditioning for Woody Allen," I said, "I'm auditioning for the role of Brown student, and I am ready to throw myself into the part. See, I don't just want to read about Rodin in a book. I want to take a class with an expert. And I don't just want to look at pictures from the 1950s. I want to study midcentury America. Instead of drinking Campari from a liquor store on Nantucket, I want to take Italian classes. And while I'm pretty sure I don't want to audition for a movie, I want to know why people are so crazy about Woody Allen, maybe through a film-theory class.

"I know I made a mistake," I continued. "A big mistake. But I am exactly the kind of student you want. With this list, I've demonstrated that I live my curiosity. I pursue learning with a passion. I take meaningful risks. And I want to take more of them, here, at Brown."

"What about the last item on the list?" Ms. Gonzales asked, holding up her copy.

"Oh, yeah." I'd gotten so swept up in my grand finale that I'd forgotten about Nina's last wish: *See St. Francis from altar.* "That one's a mystery to me," I said, trying to remember what I'd planned to say. "It represents what I don't know, and maybe what none of us knows, what eludes us but keeps us looking."

"Wow," Coach Stacy said, beaming. "Good answer. "

"That was quite a presentation," Dr. Fantini said.

"We'll talk and get back to you in twenty-four hours," Claudia Gonzales said. Coach Stacy smiled and gave me a secret thumbs-up.

I nodded. "I look forward to hearing from you." Why, I wondered, did I feel a knot in the back of my throat? I thanked them all again and gathered my things. *This is what I want,* I told myself.

"You know, Cricket," Dr. Fantini said as I was leaving, "I think that last thing on the list is about Larsen's Comet."

"What do you mean?" I asked. "Why?"

"A group of French monks near the Italian border viewed this comet during the feast of Saint Francis and thought it was a sign from the heavens. There was a sickness in their village, and after the comet appeared, many were healed. They thought it was Saint Francis himself. Scientists have always credited the discovery of the comet to the Danish astronomer Anders Larsen. But some folks from a certain part of France have always believed it was Saint Francis. Was Nina French?"

"Her grandmother was," I said.

Dr. Fantini beamed. "The last time the comet was visible was in 1939, so her grandmother probably saw it herself, and perhaps she wanted her granddaughter to see Saint Francis in the sky. It's one theory, anyway. I can't explain the 'altar' part, though."

"I can," I said. "It's a place on Nantucket."

"Would it be a good place to see the stars?"

"It would be perfect," I said, realizing that if I could see the comet from Altar Rock, it would be the only thing on the list I could actually complete, for now, anyway. It was the one thing that Nina hadn't actually been able to do.

"This is the last week that the comet is going to be visible, and the forecast calls for rain for the rest of the week, so I suggest you get out there. It's not coming this way for another seventy-five years," Dean Fantini said. "I can't wait to tell my wife. She will love this story. It's very romantic."

"Wow, thanks," I said. "You solved the mystery."

"There's still plenty of mystery out there. For all of us," he said.

I thanked him, and as soon as I was out of the office, I pulled up the ferry schedule on my phone.

Forty-two

"JULES, I FIGURED IT OUT," I SAID, STANDING OUTSIDE THE Brown admissions office. "You're not going to believe this. But you know that last thing on the list? Your mom was talking about Larsen's Comet. I guess a lot of French people think that it was Saint Francis, appearing in a miracle. And your great-grandmother is French, right?"

"Yes. She's French, all right. Why do you think I suffered through so many years of Madame Smith? That's so crazy. And you know what? Mom always said that Altar Rock was the best place to see the stars."

"This is one thing on her life list that she didn't get to do, Jules! We need to get out to Altar Rock tonight, because it's supposed to rain the rest of the week and then it's not coming again for another seventy-five years. Seventy-five years! Oh my god, there's a fast ferry that leaves at six p.m. Can you get to Hyannis? Can you pick me up on the way?"

"Cricket, this is so cool, but I'm not going back to Nantucket. I'm with Jay."

Oh, I thought. Oh, yeah. She was in love, and when a person is in love, there is no one else as important as *that person*. I knew what that felt like. Once, I had felt that way. Once, Zack had been *that person* and I had been *that person* to Zack. I squinted against the pain of knowing that that wasn't true anymore.

"I just got here," Jules said. "Besides, I've already seen the comet. This list? It's your thing. Your thing with my mom. You go ahead."

"Are you sure?"

"Yeah," she said. "He did it last night, by the way. Dad's engaged."

"Really? I'm sorry."

"I'll get over it," she said. "We'll talk about it later, okay? Jay and I are at a restaurant. He's waiting for me. I kind of have to go."

"Okay," I said, starting my walk back home.

"But wait," she said. "How'd it go with Brown?"

"It went well," I said, heading toward Thayer Street. "I think I did it. I mean, fingers crossed."

"How was the scrimmage?"

"I scored. Twice."

"That's awesome! I knew it! Okay, Jay is waving to me.

He got us a table. Igottagoloveyoubye." I felt her growing up, arcing away from high school. I didn't want her to grow up any faster than I did. Now that we were best friends again, I wanted us to be in lockstep with each other, but she was getting out of Providence, even if only to Boston, and I had just fought with all of my might to stay.

As I walked down Thayer Street toward my mom's house, my heart was heavy. I was in the center of the Brown campus. And I knew every café. I knew every store. I knew every crack in the sidewalk. There was the Avon, the single-screen movie theater where I'd seen foreign films with Jules. There was the Thai place that Mom ordered from twice a week the year of the divorce. There was the hot-dog stand I'd been going to since I was six. I knew these streets so well I could've walked home blindfolded.

A girl in a Brown Women's Lacrosse T-shirt came out of the 7-Eleven and started walking in my direction. I saw Fiona and Bitsy a few steps behind her, chatting and laughing. I darted into the vintage clothing store where Jules and I had bought our Halloween costumes two years ago. I held my breath and watched them pass by from the window. Fiona's words haunted me. *Lacrosse is our life. Three hours a day. Every day. And every weekend, too.*

My phone rang. It was a Brown number.

"Hello?" I said. The bell above the door rang faintly as I left the store. I leaned against the glass of the storefront and pressed the phone to my ear.

"Hi, Cricket. It's Claudia Gonzales. I'm so delighted to welcome you back into the class of 2018. We were right about you the first time."

"Thank you," I said. "Thank you so much."

She went on to tell me about registration and orientation, but I could barely hear her. I was light-headed. My ears were buzzing. I felt faint. I sat on the curb. As soon as I hung up, I burst into tears.

Forty-three

I FELT ZACK BEFORE I SAW HIM. I APPROACHED ALTAR ROCK and shivered, even though the evening air was soft and warm and beckoning. I'd taken the bus and the fast ferry and then ridden one of the inn's bikes to Altar Road. I ditched it when I realized it'd be easier to walk on the wide dirt path. I felt Zack here, but when I climbed to the top of Altar Rock and saw him waiting for me, I lost my breath with surprise.

"No," I said. "You need to go. Because I'm not leaving until I see this comet, and we can't both be here."

"There's room for two," he said, fanning out his arms.

"Zack, come on."

"I needed to see you." He shifted his weight. "Jules called me. She told me that you'd be here. Because of Mom."

"You could've warned me. Is Parker here? Is your *girl-friend* here?" I covered my face and shook my head. "I came all the way from Providence. Please, Zack. Don't ruin this for me. Just go away."

"She's not here. And she's not my girlfriend. Look, if I told you I was going to be here, you would've run away." He stepped toward me. I stepped back. "Jules told me that you got back in?"

"Yeah," I said, "after fighting like a warrior." Zack smiled, and I felt a flash of embarrassment at my word choice. "But what Parker did? It's not okay. It will never be okay. And the fact that you didn't break up with her, that will never be okay with me, either. Ever."

"I did break up with her. This morning. There's a lot you don't know about her."

"Don't ask me to have sympathy for her, Zack. Jesus Christ. Don't do that."

"She tried to kill herself this year."

"Oh." I covered my mouth.

"You can't just break up with a girl like that. You have to make sure she's stable. I mean, can you imagine what it would be like if she tried it again, right after I broke up with her? If she'd actually done it? I'd have to carry that my whole life."

"I'm sorry," I said quietly. "I had no idea."

"She's got a real problem," Zack said. "I tried to tell you without telling you. Jules did, too."

"Why didn't you just tell me?"

"When a United States senator asks you to keep your mouth shut"—he shook his head—"you keep your mouth shut."

"But I still don't understand why. Why does she care about me?"

"She saw the video I took of you," he said, "and it was so clear."

"What was?" I wanted more than suggestion from him. I wanted him to spell out his thoughts for me in plain, brave English. No more high fives. No more drunken almost-kisses. No more meaningful underwater touches. I crossed my arms. "What was clear?"

"That I'm still in love with you!" He sounded almost pissed off about it.

"Oh." The words I'd dreamed about and hungered for didn't come out the way I would have expected. I stood there, stunned, trying to absorb them.

"She shouldn't have tried to sabotage you," he said. "It was really messed-up. She's really messed-up. But it's not so simple. She was there for me last year. I was all alone. My mom died. I was at a new school. I was lost."

The idea of Zack alone, in pain, felt like a pill stuck in my throat or a splinter on the verge of infection, too tender to touch. "Why didn't you tell me?" I asked. "I was lost, too. I was alone."

"I tried to tell you," he said. "That call before Thanksgiving?"

"You interpreted that all wrong. I told you."

"Parker actually showed up, in person." My blood pressure dropped below sea level. "Everything changed. I had friends. I had fun. And one night it just kind of happened. I didn't know what I was getting into. I didn't know how screwed up she was. I don't think she did, either. The doctor said depression can come on suddenly at this age."

"This is a lot to deal with. Do you have any idea what the past few weeks have been like for me?"

"I'm sorry. I'm so, so sorry," he said. He wrapped his hand around mine. I closed my eyes. It was *his* hand. Zack's hand. *That person's* hand. "I understand if you don't feel the same."

"I do, though. I do feel the same."

He took my other hand and leaned in so that our heads touched. "I've missed you. That night. I wanted to be with you. I wanted to kiss you so badly." He stepped closer so that our cheeks were touching, so that he was whispering in my ear. "I wanted to do more. I wanted to do everything."

He turned to kiss me. I kissed him back, but pulled away when I felt tears rising. "This whole thing really hurt, Zack. I think we need to just be friends for a little while." I said this even as my whole body was sending me another message. He met my gaze and nodded. "I'm so confused. About so many things."

"Tell me," he said. We sat on the rock and he put his arms around me. I looked up. The sky was getting darker now, but it was also getting cloudier. "Tell me what you're confused about."

"I don't want to go to Brown." I leaned into him.

"What?"

"I've lived in Providence my whole life. I want to live somewhere else." It felt so good to release the truth, to surrender to it. "I don't want to go. And I love lacrosse. But I also feel, I don't know, done with it."

"When did this happen?" he asked, weaving his fingers with mine.

"It's been happening," I said, wiping away tears with the heel of my hand. "All summer." I tried to pinpoint the moment when I had started to want something else; to go somewhere else; to be myself, but different.

"Because of that guy?"

"No, not really." Was it that night singing on the beach? "I don't know." Was it when I first cracked open the Rodin book? Or was it that moment on the ferry, when I'd seen Nina's list and felt her with me?

"You don't have to go to Brown," Zack said, pulling me close.

"People will think I'm crazy. I mean, after all this." I pulled my knees to my chest and lowered my head. "It's not like I have a plan. It's not like I know what I'd even do."

"You'll figure it out. You're the smartest person I know."

"Me?"

"You."

"Oh." I smiled into my arm. "Do you think we're going to see this comet?" I looked up, wishing the clouds would part. I thought of something that Ben had said that day we met on the ferry, about how the weather on Nantucket is often the opposite of what it is on the mainland. I probably would've been able to see the comet if I'd stayed in Providence. "I can't believe the one thing your mom didn't get to do on her list has been in front of me the whole time."

"Above you," Zack said. We lay back on the rock in silence for a while, waiting for the sky to clear up. Every minute, we inched closer until we were curled up together. When we were officially spooning, he pulled his arm away and sat up.

"What are you doing?" I asked.

"Trying to be friends."

"Don't try *that* hard." We laughed as he lay back down and I rested my head on his chest, an ear to his thumping heart. "I need some time, okay?"

Maybe Ben had actually been on to something. Maybe there are times when labels like *boyfriend* and *girlfriend* and *friend* just don't apply. Maybe what couldn't be named was just as real as what could be. Maybe sometimes love existed in the spaces in between. Maybe, I thought staring up at the clouds, I just need to let what wants to be revealed appear.

Forty-four

I DIDN'T SEE LARSEN'S COMET UNTIL A WEEK LATER.

This was after I'd called Brown and asked to defer my acceptance for a year, after I'd broken the news to my family that I needed what Liz called a gap year. It was after Liz and I decided that we would move to New York together and get an apartment, maybe on the Upper West Side, or maybe in Brooklyn. It was after Jules and Jay had started at BU together and Zack had returned to Hanover, and the only people left on Nantucket were the late-season tourists and the people who worked there.

I called George Gust and explained why I would make the perfect assistant. I was organized, passionate, and perspicacious (SAT word). He hired me on the spot. Liz was going to find work in a hotel, maybe go to school for social work. We both agreed she was good in a crisis. She and I decided to stay on Nantucket through early September. She had to wait for Gavin to get back from Bali, and I could make as much money as possible before we moved. I was close to having ten thousand dollars in the bank, which was enough to get me on my feet in New York. Rosemary and Jim were still going to match what I made, but instead of giving it to me right away, they would put it in a bank account for a year where it couldn't be touched and would gather interest.

I saw Larsen's Comet when I was walking home from Breezes. I looked up and saw a smudge of light in the moonless sky. It was carelessly bright, naturally captivating, effortlessly stunning. Just like Nina. I had no idea how I'd missed it all summer.

I texted Jules and Zack: Look up!

Jules texted back: St. Francis in the sky!

Zack joined in: Awesome.

I wrote: True beauty!

A second later, as I was standing with my head tilted all the way back, Zack texted me privately. It was a picture of me the night at Something Natural, looking at the camera, looking at Zack, my eyes wide open, awake with wonder, my smile a little mysterious. Beneath it he wrote: True beauty.

Later, back at the inn, I opened the journal Mom gave me. I finally knew what to do with it. I picked up a pen, wrote *Cricket's Life List*, and started to dream.

Epilogue

LIZ AND I MOVED TO NEW YORK IN THE MIDDLE OF
September. We found a little apartment in Park Slope, right
near George Gust's. It's a fourth-floor walk-up with one
tiny bedroom, but the windows are big, the water pressure
is great, and as former chambermaids, we keep it extremely
clean. My dad drove us down in the minivan. We bought
a pair of twin beds from 1-800-Get-A-Bed and a kitchen
table and chairs that we carried twelve blocks all by ourselves from someone on Craigslist. When we smelled bread
baking on our way home, we had to stop for a snack. We
bought warm, fresh brioche rolls with butter and jam. We
couldn't wait, so we ate them seated at our new table, right
on the sidewalk.

Liz is taking a social work class at NYU and working at

the front desk of the Soho Grand Hotel, where people go crazy for her accent. "They think I'm so posh and proper!" she says with giddy delight. "If only they knew I'm a humble Yorkshire lass, with knickers from Target and a ravenous appetite for love."

I started working for George right away. I organize his office, keep track of his research, run errands, maintain his calendar, and talk things out with him when he gets stuck or wants a fresh perspective. No two days are ever alike, and I love that. I've talked to Hillary Clinton's personal assistant twice on the phone, which is cool any way you look at it. George always has a cup of coffee waiting for me when I show up, and I make sure he has a salad for lunch at least twice a week.

George really only needs a part-time assistant, so I picked up a couple of waitressing shifts at a neighborhood bistro around the corner from our apartment. It's called Vanessa Jane's. The walls are painted red and covered with black-and-white photographs of Paris. The onion soup is perfect on a crisp fall day, the coq au vin melts on the tongue, and the crème brûlée is heaven in a ramekin. The owner, the actual Vanessa Jane, is more like a friend than a boss. I don't make as much as I did at Breezes, but it's a lot less stressful, and I can always cover for someone if I need a little extra cash to buy a sweater or a dress that I have to have.

Sometimes, when I see pictures of Jules hanging out in her dorm with a whole group of new friends, I wonder if I made the right decision, but then I remind myself that

I still have my spot at Brown waiting for me. George told me that Columbia has an excellent journalism program, so I'm applying there as well. "There's nothing wrong with options," George said, and I think he's right.

I ran into Amy/Amelia on the N train last week. I almost didn't recognize her in her suit and loafers, but when I called her name, she came right over and sat next to me. She'd moved back to New York when she was hired at a high-profile law firm in midtown. She said Ben stayed on Nantucket, which I figured he would. "But I had to move on," she said. "I'm a city girl." I gave her my number and told her to call me sometime, but I have a feeling that's not going to happen.

Zack and I are doing what we swore we never would: long distance. Only, we're doing it the old-fashioned way, with letters. We write to each other at least once a week. It gives me the space and time to get to know him all over again after our year apart. When I see the white envelopes with my name and address scrawled in his boyish hand-writing in our dented mailbox, I rush up all four flights of stairs in seconds flat. The letters inside, written on paper torn from a notebook, are long and full of funny details. He writes exactly like he talks. I write back right away with my tales of Brooklyn, George, the customers at the restaurant, and the people I see on the subway. I'm collecting his letters in a yellow and blue Cuban cigar box I found at an antique store. We're writing a story together. Our story. When he asked me in his last letter to spend Thanksgiving with him on Nantucket, I wasn't about to make the same mistake I did last year. I sent a postcard right away from the Brooklyn Botanic Garden that said simply, "Yes."

I can't stop smiling as the ferry slows, approaching the now familiar shore. It's a different season now, and the sun washes the island in amber light. Instead of lush green, the tree-tops are red, yellow, orange, and brown. The late November breeze is cold off the choppy water, but I'm too excited to feel a chill. I throw my duffel bag over my shoulder and search the dock for Zack. I see him and hold my breath. He's wearing his black peacoat and a red scarf. I can't wait to show him my new haircut. I can't wait to be with him in winter, to snuggle next to him under a blanket on the porch and trade stories and kisses. I can't wait to hold him. He sees me and his face fills with light. As I walk down the ramp, my heart heats to life. It's a spark, a flame. A fire.

Acknowledgments

I AM ETERNALLY GRATEFUL TO EMILY MEEHAN, EDITOR extraordinaire and visionary, for believing in these books. I thank my lucky stars every day that it was you who launched my writing career.

Sara Crowe is my incomparable agent and dear, wise, and funny friend. Working with you is a dream come true. Thank you for standing by my side all these many years. I'm looking forward to all the good times ahead.

Hyperion is up to its mouse ears with amazing and talented people, including, but not limited to, the super-smart Kieran Viola, whom I'm thrilled to be working with; the lovely and savvy Jamie Baker; and the crazy gifted Marci Senders. Laura Schreiber and Elizabeth Holcomb were incredibly helpful in bringing these books to fruition.

A warm and heartfelt thanks to the people of Nantucket for their hospitality and insight, especially Eileen McGrath and Bob Crowe. Wendy Hudson and the staff at Nantucket Bookworks and Mitchell's Book Corner who, in addition to creating two of the best independent bookstores in the country, have been great supporters. A visit to Nantucket is not complete without a visit to both of these places!

And thank you to my family and friends. Mom, Dad, Gifford, and Maryhope, you are my heroes. Kayla and Vanessa, you are the best readers and friends I could ever hope for. Thanks most of all to my sweet boy, Henry, who is my heart and soul.

TURN THE PAGE FOR A SNEAK PEEK AT

Hello, Sunshine

PROLOGUE

"OH MY GOD, we're almost there!"

Alex smirks at my enthusiasm as we see a sign for the exit we've been headed toward for two weeks. We've driven all the way from Boston in this rickety old Volvo, and the passenger seat has kind of started to feel like home. I can't believe our trip is almost over. My breath gets shallow and my heart accelerates. The dream that's been in the future since April—since I was a little kid, actually—is about to be the present.

I'm totally psyched, but as a clammy sweat breaks out on my forehead, I also feel queasy. It doesn't help that it's a hundred and twelve degrees outside, and this car's old air-conditioning system only gets the temperature down to the low nineties. I switch to a more upbeat playlist on the iPhone, unroll the passenger side window of Alex's car, and let the hot, dry wind wash over me.

"Look out, LA! Here I come!" I shout out the window.

A guy in an old BMW makes a nasty gesture with his tongue.

"Ew!" I say, and I duck back inside the car and roll up the window. "Ew! Alex, that guy just went like this." I show him the tongue move and Alex laughs, waving it off.

"Forget about him, Becca," Alex says. "Stay focused. What's your number one goal again?"

"Get an agent. I will not rest until I have one. If Brooke can do it, so can I."

"Bet your ass," Alex says, and switches lanes.

Brooke was my main acting competition in high school, and she got into Tisch, NYU's theater school. When I didn't get accepted anywhere she was such a dick about it. Everyone felt bad for me—Carter Academy has a 99.9 percent matriculation rate, after all—but Brooke took her pity to a new level. I almost barfed on the spot when I learned that she'd found an agent literally the day after she moved to New York for a summer Shakespeare seminar. She'd been discovered at a café near Washington Square Park, wherever that is. Within a week, she'd booked an in-flight safety video for Delta.

"Oh, I love this song." I turn up the volume to get Brooke and her perfect skin out of my mind. The latest girl-power song from my favorite pop princess blasts from the speakers. "I know you hate this jam, but I really need to sing it right now. Okay?"

"Go for it," Alex says, and turns up the volume even higher. He grins at me as I belt out the song off-key. When he smiles, lines from his eyes frame his cheeks—the result of a relentlessly happy childhood. He's had everything that money can buy and everything it can't, too. It was really no surprise when he got in to Stanford early.

The car does that shaky thing it's been doing since Utah whenever we get up to seventy miles an hour. "Come on, Ruby, don't fail us now," Alex says.

I thought of the name Ruby when he bought the car from his next-door neighbor last year.

"What do you think, is Ruby actually going to make it all the way to Palo Alto?" Alex asked. After he drops me at my cousin's place, he'll be taking the scenic route up the coast.

"Oh yeah," I say. "She's a trouper."

"Easy, baby," Alex says to Ruby, who is rattling more than usual. Alex's jaw flexes as he signals and heads toward the exit. Even after two years of dating he can still make me melt. He has a strong jaw and the nose of a future leader. His eyes are the color of a lake on an overcast day, and his blond hair smells woodsy close to his neck. And don't even get me started on his body. He's a champion skier and has the legs and ass to show for it. Last night we had the most amazing time at a motel in Palm Springs. We couldn't get enough of each other. We barely slept. The people in the next room actually complained to the front desk, which we laughed about for the next hour, as quietly as possible, of course.

Alex turns on his indicator and takes the exit for Orange

Grove Boulevard. Vivian's exit. We're almost there. Oh my God. *We're almost there.*

"How hard can getting an agent actually be?" I ask. Alex opens his mouth to answer, but I stop him. "Famous last words, I know. I should probably learn how to wear eye makeup for on camera auditions. I'm going to need some new looking-for-agent clothes, because everything I have feels a little too . . . I don't know . . . Boston." Alex seems nervous as the car slows, and we turn onto a wide boulevard lined with tall, evenly spaced palm trees. I know how he feels. I'm so nervous I can't seem to stop talking. "Can you believe how perfect last night was? That was the best night ever. We have to go back to Palm Springs!"

"Becca," Alex says. He bites his lip as he makes a left on to Bradford Street, Vivian's street.

"I don't want to say good-bye. I really, really don't want to," I say. I feel carsick actually, and a little untethered. We slow down in front of Vivian's complex.

Alex looks pale as he parallel parks, and yet, even with his pallid complexion, the sight of him nearly takes my breath away. I snap a picture, the last of the roll of film. Before we left, my mom gave me her old camera so that I could take pictures with actual film. It's nothing fancy, just a vintage-y point-and-shoot from when she was my age. I've spaced the twenty-four shots out over the course of our road trip.

"Why'd you do that?" he asks.

"You just look so cute when you parallel park, and I'm not going to get to see you do it again for a while," I say, and inhale sharply. I have a cramp, like I get when we do the mile run for gym class. I clutch my side.

"You okay?" he asks.

"I'm just freaking out a little. I can do this, right?"

"Of course you can," he says. He turns the engine off and faces me. I put my hand on his leg. "But . . . we need to say good-bye now."

"I know. Your orientation is tomorrow. At least we have the Jones concert in six weeks. How many days? I think it'll be easier if I think in terms of days—"

"Actually," he says, his face rearranging in an unfamiliar way, "I think we should take a beat."

"A what?" At first his words don't register. But then he tilts his head, looks me in the eye, and squeezes my hand. My heart drops straight through the floor of the car and lands with a sizzle on the hot tar. "Wait. You're breaking up with me?"

He inhales a definitive breath.

"Why?" I ask. My stomach turns over. For a second I think I might throw up.

"Everyone knows long distance doesn't work," he says.

"But we won't be *that* far apart. It's only an hour by plane. There are airfare deals all the time!"

"It's not just that. I want to make a fresh start, you know? It's a new chapter of my life, and I want to be able to throw myself into it. And so should you."

"Are you telling me this is for my own good or something?" I ask.

"We're going to be doing such different things. I think it'll be hard for us to relate. We're in different phases of our lives."

"I wouldn't call it a different *life phase*. Didn't we just graduate from the same high school?"

"Look," Alex says as he wipes sweat from his upper lip. "A part of me wishes that I could stay with you and cheer you on. . . ."

"You can!"

"But I'm going to be so involved in my own life at Stanford. And I deserve to be able to enjoy myself."

"You *deserve* it?" It sounds like a sentence he's been practicing. I feel a sharp stab in my chest as I wonder how long he's known he's going to do this. "How long have you been planning this? The whole trip?"

"I guess I've been thinking about it for a while. Hey, you deserve your freedom, too."

"I don't want any more freedom," I say. "I'm scared of all the freedom I have."

"You're going to be fine," he says.

"You don't really think I'm going to make it, do you?" I ask. I'm in so much pain that I'm on the verge of hyperventilating. My ears are buzzing.

"That's not true," he says without looking me in the eye. He pops the trunk and gets out of the car.

Vivian emerges from her condo wearing a preppy tunic, white jeans, and a huge grin. She waves from her door. I try to signal for her to go back inside until Alex and I can talk more—this is all happening so suddenly, can it even be real?—but she doesn't get it. I step out of the car, heart pounding even as my blood seems to slow. Alex hands me my suitcase and purse as Vivian walks toward us across an impossibly green lawn.

"Hey, girl!" Vivian calls.

"Hi," I say through a broken smile, and then I turn back to Alex and ask quietly, "What about last night?"

"It was great," he says as though this has nothing to do with anything.

I open my mouth to speak, but I can't think of what to say to this boy who I've loved for two years, who I thought loved me.

"Take care," he says.

Take care? What does that even mean?

Seconds before Vivian reaches us, he gives me a stiff hug and hops in the still-running car. I wait for Ruby to be out of sight, and then I turn to Vivian and burst into tears.

ONE

"REFRIGERATOR, what are you trying to tell me?" I ask. It's five days later. It's also 4 a.m. I've been listening to the refrigerator's cycle of whines and moans for hours now. Since other methods of quieting it have failed, I talk to it. My hand grazes the white door. "I can't help you unless you tell me what's wrong." It sputters. "Fine, be that way." I turn over, curling into a question mark on my sleeping bag. I'm lying on the kitchen floor in my Carter Academy T-shirt and granny panties I've had since eighth grade. I thought they'd be comforting, but they aren't.

I've been trying to fall asleep for five hours. I've breathed according to a pocket-size book about meditation, read the *People* magazine I bought near the bus stop in Pasadena, memorized half of a Shakespearian sonnet, and flipped the pillow to the cool side, but nothing has worked. I'd hoped that tonight's sleep would be long and deep and give me a new perspective in the morning, because right now the challenges ahead seem to await me like the pack of wolves that I imagine are prowling outside the door of this Hollywood apartment building. The building is named the Chateau Bronson. The only castle-y things about it are the majestic font on the building's sign and the odd drawbridge-inspired door.

At 4:17, I decide to get up and finish cleaning my new apartment. Maybe scrubbing this place until it gleams will get my spirits up. A single bird chirps somewhere outside. I kick myself out of the sleeping bag that still smells vaguely like a camping trip I took as part of the junior year science program, the one where Alex and I first kissed. Why does everything have to remind me of him? And why does it take five whole business days for 1-800-Get-A-Bed to deliver a twin bed to a major US city?

I turn on the halogen lamp that I found on the sidewalk yesterday. It leans a little to the left, but it works. I almost took the mattress that was next to it—it looked brand-new, but in a flash I could see my mom's face grimacing in disgust, and I didn't touch it. I blink for a second against the light and look around at my new place. I'd shut the curtains, but I don't have any. I pull on my pajama bottoms, tie up my hair in a ponytail, and get to work.

The apartment is one room, about the size of my bedroom back home, with a wooden floor that's covered in a thick layer of brown paint. The kitchenette is off to the right. There's my friend the fridge, whining and pitched slightly forward, a mustard-yellow 1970s oven, and a small sink. It could be depressing, but the nook by the window has potential. I narrow my eyes and picture curtains, a bunch of wildflowers in a mason jar, a steaming cup of tea. I can fix this up, I think, instagramming it in my mind.

I open a kitchen cabinet that has a strange metal interior. I don't know what it's for, but I feel like Alex would because he just knows stuff—like that the raised stones on the cobblestone streets in Beacon Hill were used by ladies to step into their horse-drawn carriages. Or that when people say something is "neither here nor there" they're quoting Shakespeare without knowing it.

My heart lurches at the thought of him up at Stanford, where he's probably started his classes. Did we really break up? How is it possible that just a week ago we were in Texas, dancing in a country bar, laughing and getting stepped on because we were the only ones who didn't know the moves? How have we not spoken since he dropped me at Vivian's? I feel a sharp pain in my gut, like a thumbtack is being stuck into a vital organ. What the hell happened?

I've gone over our conversation a hundred times at least, trying to remember every detail in order to make sense of it, and it doesn't add up. How does a person just cut another person off like that with no warning? Was he just having a pre-college freakout? That's got to be it. He had a similar freakout the summer after junior year before he headed to Maine. He broke up with me saying that he wanted space, but called me the next day practically in tears and invited me up for the fourth of July. This is probably just a more exaggerated version of that.

And anyway, he didn't actually say he wanted to break up. He said he wanted to "take a beat," which is a totally different thing. I was the one who said the words *break up*. He's obviously in denial. It's not possible that I can just be erased. Right? I'm not calling him first, though; there's no way. He's the one who messed up. I have to let him figure that out on his own.

Be present, I think, fishing up a bit of wisdom from the mini-meditation book. Be where you are. I grab the cleaning spray and paper towels from the weird metal cabinet and open up all the windows. I lean out of one and inhale the predawn air, looking for the bird with the continuous, high-pitched chirp. The streetlights illuminate the treetops, telephone wires, other apartment buildings, and the sidewalk below. A subtle breeze washes over me. There is the faint smell of jasmine, which I only recognize because of the tea my mom drinks by the gallon back home.

A few streets over there's some kind of palace. The grand, gold-tipped turrets stand high above the dingy rooftops crawling with satellite dishes. What is that place? A temple? An embassy? A movie star's home?

I hold the windowsill and feel the grime like soft sand on my fingertips. I pull my hand away—it's gray. This place is so dirty. I'd better tackle the bathroom before I lose all my courage. It's like Mom always said: do the hardest homework first while you have the energy. I take in one more lungful of morning air and get down to business.

The bathroom looks like it hasn't been updated . . . ever. There's black mold in the corners of the shower, mysterious yellowy-brown spots on the ceiling, and an all-over film of filth. I admit it: for a moment I think about going back to Boston, but there's no chance in hell. I'm not going back east until I prove that everyone is wrong to feel sorry for me for not getting accepted into college. It was all so unfair. I was suspended for skipping school to go to a secret daytime concert at Cambridge Comics. A bunch of us did it, but I was the only one who got caught, and I wouldn't name names. It turns out that one black mark on my school record was enough for college admissions people to put me in the reject pile. It makes me so mad to think about it. I'm not leaving this place without a victory.

I can do this, I tell myself as I spray the bathroom mirror and wipe it down. I already am doing this. I smile at my reflection. Even though Mom didn't want me to go, even though she wants me to do something practical and résumé building, or as she puts it "creative *and* practical," I can't help but think that on some level, if she could see me right now with this adventurous spirit flickering behind my tired eyes, she'd be proud.

"So can I ask your advice about something?" I ask Mom a few minutes later on FaceTime. I'm still in the bathroom cleaning, but I hold the phone close to my face so that she can't get a good look at my surroundings until I've had some time to explain. She's going to be pissed. I was thinking I would wait until the just-right moment to tell her, but the state of this bathroom is an emergency. I've doused the tub with several blasts of All-Natural Multipurpose Cleaner but can't make any headway with the stains.

"Sure, honey. What is it?" Mom blinks back at me from our kitchen, where I watch her pour hot water into a mug. "Wait, what time is it there?"

"Four thirty, I think."

She almost chokes on her tea. "What are you doing up?"

"I never went to sleep."

"Why?" Mom asks. I drop the soaked paper towel in the grocery bag, which I'm using as the trash, and head into the main room. The faintest light is seeping into the sky. If I had a comfy sofa, I'd flop on it. Instead, I sit back down on my sleeping bag and lean against the wall. Noticing the background for the first time, Mom asks, "Where are you?"

"Before you freak out, I want you to know that I'm safe," I say.

"Jesus. Where's Vivian?" Mom asks, trying to see behind me.

"Probably at her place in Pasadena?" I say, and I brace myself.

I was supposed to stay with Vivian until I got a job to support my acting dreams in LA. Mom was hoping for some sort of 9-to-5 office-job-with-potential, even though I explained I needed something more flexible for auditions, like waitressing. But Pasadena felt almost worse than Boston, where my failure followed me like a stinky fart. Vivian's condo complex was full of what she calls "young professionals," but what I call "middle-aged squares." There were literally no sidewalks within a two-mile radius, so I couldn't go anywhere except the condo complex gym, and she made her point of view on my situation abundantly clear. ("Acting is a total waste of time. Hardly anyone makes it. You're just going to wake up when you're my age and realize that you're five years behind everyone else! Quit now and focus on getting your shit together.")

"You've lost me, Becca," Mom says, her brow pinched with concern.

"I'm not exactly at Vivian's anymore," I say, gritting my teeth.

"What?" Mom yells. "Becca Harrington, where are you?"

"I couldn't stay there. Vivian's energy was really getting me down. She's not a feminist, Mom. She told me I needed to get married on 'the right side of twenty-five.' Can you believe it?"

"I want answers," Mom says in her sternest voice.

"I found a place in Hollywood. It's a studio in a vintage building. It's cute. See?" I pull the phone back to give her a narrow view of my place.

"No, no, no. This was not our deal. Our deal was that you were supposed to find a job before you left Vivian's—if you left Vivian's at all."

"I'll find some sort of way to pay my rent. Bartending or babysitting or something."

"Babysitting?" The vein in Mom's right temple pops out.

"How is that going to look on your college applications? Don't you know how important this year is?"

"I'm going to put my *acting* work on my applications," I say, regretting this phone call with my entire being. "That's the whole point of being here!"

"We agreed that you'd find something résumé-building to do out there *while* you auditioned. You can do two things at once, you know. We had a plan—"

"I never agreed to that part of the plan, remember? The only thing I officially agreed to was reapplying to college, and that I'd come home after a year if I didn't get in anywhere. That's what we shook on." She sighs. "It's just one year, Mom. If I'm going to do this, I have to really do it, you know? I can't hide out in a condo in Pasadena."

Mom closes her eyes and takes a deep breath.

"Where is this apartment?" she asks. She looks as tired as I feel. Mom had me when she was only twenty. I was the result of a one-night stand she had on Martha's Vineyard. My dad, some guy who could speak French fluently and who had awesome cheekbones, was never in the picture. This was right after her sophomore year of college, so she's much younger than my friends' moms. Her dream was to be a marine biologist. She'd just declared her major when she learned I was on the way. She promises me that she doesn't regret a single moment of my existence, but I know being a pharmaceutical sales rep was not what she had in mind for herself. I swear, sometimes she could pass for a teenager herself, especially when she does stuff like sit on the floor in bookstores. But right now, she looks older than her age, and I don't like it.

"I'm near the Hollywood Hills. That's where the movie stars live." I say. "See?" I hold the phone so that she can see the Hollywood sign in the distance. I have to hang out the window a bit and twist my body to the left to get a view of the whole thing, but it's worth it for the inspiration.

"That *is* kind of cool," Mom says, her voice a little softer now. I turn the phone back to face me and see in her eyes that light I've been waiting for. "But is this neighborhood safe?"

"Would movie stars live somewhere unsafe?" I ask, glancing at the sidewalk below. A skinny guy talks to himself as he searches through garbage cans. I smile back at Mom, and she raises an eyebrow. She's not exactly buying this pitch. "It's really cute, Mom. There are cafés and a used bookstore and a supermarket all within walking distance. You'd love it."

"You know you can always come home, right?"

"I know."

We stare at each other for a second. She's sensing something's off. I can tell by the way she's searching my eyes. I study the floor.

"What does Alex think of all this?" she asks.

Damn! She's good.

"Actually, we're . . . taking a beat," I say, and hold my breath.

"A what? A *beep*?"

"A *beat*. Like a rest. As in . . . not permanent," I say.

"That doesn't sound good, Becca," Mom says. "Are you

okay?" I nod, still holding my breath. "I want to talk to you about this, but I'm already running late. Why didn't you call me earlier?"

"Because I'm fine and he's just having a panic attack. Please, trust me, okay?"

"I'm trying," she says, lines gathering in the corners of her eyes as she squints. "I'm trying. Bye, sweetie. And remember you can always come home."

"Wait, wait, Mom! What about the advice?"

"Oh yeah. What is it?"

"The bathroom is a little . . . nasty. I need to know how to get rid of mold and rust." Her eyes widen in horror. "Mom, deep breath. It's fine, really. It just needs some freshening up. Please."

"What have you been using?" she asks.

I hold up the All-Natural Multipurpose Cleaner.

"You need bleach," she says, shaking her head. "And Lime Out for the rust." Then she tells me how to put a rag on the end of the broom to get the corners of the shower. "And please wear gloves."

"Should I really use stuff that toxic?" I ask.

"You know what's toxic? Mold. Call me tonight. I love you, Becca."

"Love you, too," I say. "Mom?" I'm waiting for her to tell me that she loves me to the sky, to which I always reply "and back." It's our thing. But it's too late. She's already hung up.

TWO

ONCE THE SUN RISES, I throw on some clean clothes, deciding there's nothing more civilized than fresh, well-fitting underwear, and head to the supermarket to get my toxic cleaning supplies and some food. A cool breeze rustles the palm fronds high above me, though I can feel heat coiled in the air. Bright, tropical-looking flowers peek at me from slightly dilapidated front yards. I reach Franklin Avenue and am surprised by the number of cars rushing by. It's not even 6 a.m. yet. Where is everyone going?

I stop by a supermarket called the Mayfair Market and pick up yogurt, a bagel, soap, Lime Out, and bleach, and then search for shower curtains. They don't sell them here, so I'm going to have to make my own. I'll get a real one later, but the need for a shower *now* is intense. I feel a little kick of pride at my ingenuity as I throw duct tape and extra-large, heavy-duty garbage bags into the cart.

I spot a copy of *Backstage*, the trade magazine for actors, in the checkout lane. For a moment my hunger and discomfort disappear. The lead to my first job might be inside this magazine. Slightly breathless, I open to the casting section. The first notice calls for four "adorable actresses" who must be "comfortable with love scenes." After noting where aspiring ingénues should send their headshots it says in bold: "Nudity required. No pay."

Ugh.

"Miss, are you okay?" the cashier asks.

"Yes," I say, debating whether to buy the magazine. It's just one ad, I tell myself. I toss the *Backstage* on the conveyor belt. "I'm fine."

When I get back to the Chateau Bronson, I put my cleaning supplies and groceries away and then head all the way up the stairs with my untoasted, unadorned bagel. The landlord said something about a rooftop terrace. I push the door open and almost laugh. This is hardly a "terrace." It's just a regular roof, the uneven surface covered in a gray, sandpaper-like material. There are a couple of scattered, rusty beach chairs. Still, the light is a cool blue-yellow and there's a nice breeze. I see a bunch of tall buildings in the distance, and I'm trying to figure out what it is—Santa Monica? Downtown?—when a voice startles me.

"Sometimes you can see the ocean."

"Huh?" I relax when I see the guy who's sitting in a beach chair with a computer on his lap. He looks about my age, maybe a little older. He has a soft smile and bright eyes. His hair is cropped close and neat. An open collar displays his long neck and a peek of clavicle. Even though he's sitting down, I can tell he's not too tall, which I like. I already feel too short most of the time.

"Sorry," he says. "I didn't mean to scare you. I came up here to see if I could find some writing inspiration. I'm Raj Singh."

"I'm Becca Harrington," I say.

"Did you just move in?" he asks, and stands up.

"Yesterday," I say. I was right. He isn't too tall. In fact, he might be one of those rare guys short enough for me to kiss without having to stand on my tiptoes. I hope that thought travels to Alex. I hope it zips up the 5 Freeway all the way to Palo Alto and bites him like a horsefly.

"Welcome to the Chateau." He makes a goofy gesture, bowing like he's lord of a great castle, and I have to laugh. He's suddenly serious again, and I worry that I've embarrassed him. "It's kind of smoggy today. But on a clear day after it rains, you really can see all the way to the ocean." I squint, but a stripe of brownish haze rests along the horizon, blocking the view. "Raymond Chandler used to live across the street." I'm not totally sure who Raymond Chandler is, but from the way Raj said his name I know I'm supposed to. "But who knows. They say he lived everywhere. Pretty much any historical building you go to, Raymond Chandler lived there."

"The guy got around, I guess. Hey, what's that place?" I ask, pointing to the golden turrets.

"Oh, that's the Scientology Centre. Stay away. You don't want to mess with them," Raj says. "Did you move here by yourself?"

"Yeah," I say. And even though seconds ago I wished my thoughts would sting Alex, I miss him in a punched-in-the-gut way.

"That's really brave," he says.

"Thanks." But I don't feel brave, just alone. Alex literally left me on the curb, Vivian thinks I'm a nut, and if I'm honest with Mom about how I feel, she might actually convince me to go home. Don't cry, I tell myself. Hold it in.

"You okay?" Raj asks.

"I'm just really tired. I didn't sleep much last night."

"Maybe you could sleep now?" Raj asks.

"I think I'll try," I say.

"Hey, I'm in number seven if you need anything."

"Thanks," I say, and I head back down to my apartment, more exhausted than I've ever been in my whole life.

Despite my grand plans and new supplies, I can't imagine cleaning the shower right now. I put on flip-flops, make my duct-tape-and-garbage-bag shower curtain, and take a hot shower without touching anything but the faucet handles. Then I climb back into my sleeping bag, throw a T-shirt over my eyes to keep out the light, and after twenty-four hours of being painfully awake, I finally fall asleep.